WITCH IN DISGUISE

A CRYSTAL BEACH PARANORMAL COZY MYSTERY COLLECTION

CRYSTAL BEACH MAGIC MYSTERY SERIES (BOOKS 6-10)

KAREN MCSPADE

NEWCASTLE
 MEDIA

Edited by Darci Heikkinen

Cover art by The Cover Coven

This is a work of fiction. Names, characters, places, and incidents either are products of the author's imagination or are used fictitiously. Any similarity to actual events or locales or persons, living or dead, is entirely coincidental.

Printed in the United States of America
LCCN: 2024906945
ISBN (paperback): 9781960896087

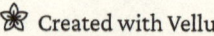 Created with Vellum

~

This book is dedicated to all those who believe in the things they can't see, who know that there is the real possibility for miracles and magic, and to those who delight in conversing out loud with their pets.
You are my tribe.

~

DESCRIPTION

Welcome to Crystal Beach, an enchanting town with a dangerous magical secret.

When psychic witch Sidney Grace discovers a crime wave in Crystal Beach, she's determined to use her magic to unveil the culprit. But her plans take a dramatic turn when her witchy grandmother enrolls her into a school of magic.

"What? Enrolled me? Into a school for witches? But I'm too old to be in school!" Her telepathic cat, Mojo, agrees...until he finds himself in his own predicament, leaving Sidney to navigate her newfound powers and solve a perilous mystery, one that leads to murder.

Guided by her grandmother's wisdom, Sidney evokes the spirits to ask for guidance. But a surprise spectral figure joins the séance, and Sidney must convince this unlikely helper to aid them in solving the murder.

With time ticking away, Sidney grapples with a malevolent force that threatens to devastate the town and the people she cares for deeply. Can she convince the authorities that magic is real, unravel the mystery surrounding a strange death, and decode a ghost's ominous prophecy in time to save Crystal Beach from impending disaster?

Books included in this series collection:
Witch Under Pressure
Witch In The Middle
A Grave Mistake
Tangled in Magic
Charmed and Dangerous

FREE GIFT

Receive your FREE copy of **Dog Gone Troubles**, the Crystal Beach Magic Mystery series prequel, and get notified via email of new releases, giveaways, contests, cover reveals, and insider fun when you sign up for my Mystery Book Club mailing list!

Scan the QR Code To Sign Up and Claim Your FREE Exclusive Book

NOTE: If you're already a member of my VIP Mystery Book Club, your email will not be added again.

KAREN MCSPADE

WITCH UNDER PRESSURE

A Crystal Beach Paranormal Cozy Mystery
Book Six

Edited by Darci Heikkinen

Cover art by The Cover Coven

This is a work of fiction. Names, characters, places, and incidents either are products of the author's imagination or are used fictitiously. Any similarity to actual events or locales or persons, living or dead, is entirely coincidental.

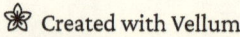 Created with Vellum

CHAPTER

ONE

I wanted her... Bastet, the Egyptian cat goddess. She was a beautiful black statue, around sixteen inches in height. Thin and feline in the noble Egyptian style, she had a black scarab pendant against her chest and stood on a short pedestal with hieroglyphs around her base.

She was an object I greatly desired. I picked her up and pretended not to notice Ada-Mae as she raised an eyebrow.

We—my grandmother, her best friend from the retirement center, Ernie, and I—were perusing the stalls at the antique market that had settled itself in the middle of Crystal Beach for the week. The market had closed one-half of Citrus Way to traffic, extending away from the sea at the crossroads with Mangrove Street in the heart of town. In another city, this might be inconvenient, but in Crystal Beach, the traffic was light, and the residents could find another way around to accommodate the market.

"How much for this?" I asked, holding the statue up toward the stall owner. He was a rather dapper gentleman with a dashing mop of what looked like natural light brown hair, green eyes, and thin lips above a prominent jaw. In his fifties, he rocked the open-at-the-neck pink shirt he wore. Despite the thick heat and a blazer worn over his shirt, there was not a single bead of sweat on him.

"Ah, Bastet," he said, "daughter of Ra and Isis."

"If this is an original from Egypt, I may not be able to afford it."

He smiled. "I believe in matching all my objects with the right owner; we can work something out. And while this is indeed an antique, it is around one hundred years old. Not four thousand."

I swallowed. One hundred years old still sounded expensive to me. "Hm... I'm not sure...?"

"For you, charming young lady, one hundred and fifty dollars."

I casually turned the statue in my hand, inwardly cringing at the price. I only wanted it because it was a cat. And it wasn't even an actual cat, just a statue. Who knew where I would put it in my van, Maude, anyway. Being the crazy cat lady of Crystal Beach was becoming expensive.

I didn't have the money to waste. *Living It Large in Boston* magazine had paid well for the last article, but I had to make the money last as it was almost my only income. I made a little from helping the seniors at Shifting Sands Retirement Center contact their dead relatives, yet I always felt weird about taking any money for those kinds of services. Either way, it wasn't much. The hope that helping Eileen with the Kelp Seafood Grill's food truck at the mini-golf tournament might lead to something more had not panned out.

I looked around for Ada-Mae, sure that she would talk me out of my foolishness, but she had already moved on to the next stall, which was run by a hippie-looking woman with long gray hair that looked like she was the recipient of an electric shock.

I rolled Bastet back and forth in my hands and pondered the offer when a youngish guy with wavy blonde hair and a surfer-dude attitude wandered up to the stall. His vibe didn't give off "antique collector," yet I still clutched the cat statue a little tighter.

"One forty, for you," the stall owner said, mistaking my silent dithering for bartering. Though I could see he was keeping an eye on the young surfer dude, perhaps worried he might be a thief. The statue was a thing of elegant beauty, and I had owned nothing older than I was before. Well, apart from Maude. Still...

"I think I'll pass, after all. I should be good." I said, placing Bastet, the cat goddess, back on the table.

"Be good tomorrow," the stall owner said, flashing me a charming grin and taking a step forward so that only the width of the table lay between us. Those green eyes were like enormous pools that must have charmed plenty of people before, and not just into buying antique statues. He was about the same age as my dad. So... you know, eww. But if I was twenty years older. "Living a little is how to keep yourself young," he added.

I smiled at him, then had an idea and stared back into his eyes, focusing all my will and intention on them. Then reaching out, I laid a hand on the head of the statue. "You will do as I say and give me this for seventy dollars," I told him in a low, undulating voice that sounded like I was a hokey medium calling out to a spirit at a 1930s séance table. "And maybe throw in that nice brooch."

The man's eyes seemed locked onto mine for a long moment, then he relaxed his shoulders, his lips quivering to hold back a laugh. "Was that supposed to be haggling?"

"Um..."

"Tell you what, you can have it for one-hundred-and-thirty dollars and a promise that you will work on your haggling skills."

"Sold!" I said, trying to cover my embarrassment, although I could feel my cheeks burning red.

Ada-Mae was waiting for me at the next stall when I arrived with my bagged-up cat statue. She held an object of her own, something that looked ugly compared to my prize. "Did you just try to cast a spell on that man?" Ada-Mae hissed, leaning forward so no one else in the busy market could hear.

"I can't haggle," I explained.

"That's no excuse for... what, attempting mind-control magic? Do you know how unethical that is? Not to mention dangerous?"

"I wasn't trying to get it for free. Just for... less." That wasn't the point, and I knew it. I had gotten carried away and done something I shouldn't have. "Sorry," I added. "It didn't work, anyway."

We walked away from the market. Ernie, a tall, broad, and dark-skinned man with a thick fuzz of gray hair, was waiting a few paces behind Ada-Mae as if he had sensed that my admonishment was coming. He joined us, and we headed to the crossroads with Mangrove Street, taking a left onto it.

After a few moments, Ada-Mae shook her head. "My fault, I guess. I've not been giving you enough guidance, dear."

This irked me a little. It seemed as if Ada-Mae was treating me like a little girl. Okay, I shouldn't have tried to use magic to haggle, but I was also a thirty-year-old woman and not her responsibility. I bit my tongue, though, and changed the subject.

"So, what did you get there?" I asked, pointing to the odd

lump of pottery or stone... maybe it was bronze. Whatever it was, it was rough, and some of the base had turned green. It made me feel better about my expensive cat statue. The figure looked like a cross between a fish and a frog crouched down a little as if creeping along or about to spring. Something that was either a fin or a mane ran down its back.

"A Dargi, I think," she answered.

I looked at the thing again; it was enough to give someone nightmares. "Didn't pay too much for it, did we?"

"Ten dollars and a steal at that."

"And what's a Dargi?"

"If I'm right, it's a ritual statue, representing a god of where the land meets the sea. I mean, it's not *actually* from ancient tribal times, or I'm quite sure I would have paid over ten dollars for it."

"Cool," I said, humoring her. "Is there a reason you wanted it? I can't see where it would go in your apartment."

Ada-Mae looked almost longingly as she turned it over in her hands. "It's not for display," she answered. "No, I think I might use it as a focus for a spell."

"Were you planning to terrify all the fish out of the sea?"

Ada-Mae laughed. "I want to know who Sam Barlow is working with and what he is doing. This statue is a good focus because the Dargi bridges the area between the land and the sea. Whatever Sam is up to revolves around Mystic Dunes."

"Which sits at the edge of the sea," Ernie said. He had been quiet up to that point.

"Exactly," Ada-Mae said. "In fact, it will probably sink into the sea before long, so the statue makes a great focus for a spell about the place."

"Makes sense," I said as we reached the Crystal Beach police station. Deputy Jessie was at the front of the building, switching out details on a noticeboard close to the entrance. She smiled as she saw us, her pretty face lighting up, her dark brown ponytail swishing as she turned.

"Hey," she said. "Have you been to the antique market? I was going to check it out when I get off."

I held up my purchase. "Cat goddess."

Jessie's smile was almost wistful. "Yes. Yes, you are, Sidney. I mean... you are lucky you found something."

I hadn't been expecting that and felt myself blushing.

Ernie pointed toward the noticeboard, where the poster that Jessie had just tacked up had a big, bold title at the top: BEWARE!

"Beware of what?" he asked.

"I'm glad you asked," Jessie replied and handed a couple of copies of the poster to Ada-Mae. "There have been several thefts and break-ins in Crystal Beach. John is out making inquiries right now."

There was a brief twinge in my stomach at the mention of Officer John Reece, formerly the senior police officer in Crystal Beach. For reasons I wasn't sure of—which might be mere coincidence—I had barely seen him since he had made me his temporary deputy and used me as bait in an eventful sting operation that ultimately led to the capture of the mini-golf invitational killer.

Two weeks after the arrest, the Mayor and town officials promoted John to "Chief of Police" because of the solved murders in Crystal Beach. So I assumed his new position kept him quite busy.

"Might be the work of the same person or group," Jessie went on and looked at Ada-Mae. "Would you put those up at the retirement center, please? We need people to be vigilant."

Ada-Mae held up the posters. "We will spread the word, Jessie."

Leaving the police station, we crossed the street and

approached the right turn that led toward the Shifting Sands Retirement Center and the ocean.

"That girl really likes you," Ada-Mae said once we were across the street from the police station.

I sighed, awkward with the mere idea of a beauty like Jessie being attracted to plain old, slightly dumpy me. "I think there's not a lot of choice for her in a small town like Crystal Beach."

Ada-Mae huffed her displeasure at my self-deprecation. "And do you have your eye on the other half of the Crystal Beach Police Department?" Ernie grinned hawkishly at me when Ada-Mae said that. The two of them were an interfering old pair.

"Hard to have my eye on him when I've hardly seen him in weeks. If it's that hard, maybe the world is trying to tell me something."

"Like, 'try harder,'" Ernie said.

"Even if there was a chance of anything... I'd feel bad for Jessie. It's silly, I know, but...." I paused, considering for a moment whether to tell Ada-Mae what I had been thinking, especially considering the reprimand I had just received from her about trying to use my magic to haggle. "I... um... I was wondering about trying a spell to help Jessie meet someone. For practice with my magic, you know?"

Here we go, I thought. *Love spells are dangerous, blah, blah, blah. Be more responsible, Sidney.*

Ada-Mae clapped her hands together like an excitable child. "Oh, what a wonderful idea, Sid."

"You think I'm up to it?" I was surprised at her enthusiasm.

"I think, with my help, it could be an excellent project for you. Not a love spell, too powerful, but an attraction spell. Yes! Something to help Jesse find the right person for her."

I felt great about that. Having Ada-Mae on board would help, and Jessie deserved to find someone special. She had a whole bundle of cuteness and sweetness to give, plus she made the police uniform work for her.

We carried on walking down the road toward the retirement center. Ada-Mae was going to be eighty soon, and Ernie was only a little younger, but they both walked a lot and were fit for their age. Ada-Mae took out her recent purchase for a moment and appeared to be admiring it. I held out a hand and took it, looking doubtfully at the thing. *Yeesh.* It gave me the creeps. I handed it back to Ada-Mae, who stashed it in her bag again.

About thirty seconds later, out of the corner of my eye, I noticed something wispy, like smoke. I realized it was coming from Ada-Mae's bag. There wasn't much, not like anything was seriously on fire. More like the dirty green-colored smoke drifting up from an incense stick.

I pointed. "Ada-Mae… your bag."

Ada-Mae peered into the large shoulder bag she carried and pulled out the ugly Dargi statue. The smoke or mist, or whatever it was, was coming from its base, although, as we watched, it stopped.

"Well," Ada-Mae said, "that's odd."

TWO

"I can't figure out what happened," Ada-Mae said, turning the Dargi around in her hands. "There are no cracks or holes in the base that I can see."

"Mist," I said.

"Huh?"

"The more I think about it, the more it seemed like mist than smoke."

"Mist, smoke, what's the difference, dear?"

I don't know why, but something in my stomach felt differently. Like it might matter.

"Either way," she went on, "there is more to this statue than meets the eye. So before I attempt a ritual with it, I need to look at it more closely."

We were in the living area of Ada-Mae's apartment at Shifting Sands Retirement Center. I was making both of us a cup of tea as she sat at the table. She had found a large magnifying glass and was peering through it at the statue under the lamp light above her table. "I thought this was just a piece of art," she said. From the other side of the table, her right eye appeared enormous to me behind the magnifying glass. "An eclectic decoration. Might be it's more than that."

The doorbell rang, and I went to answer the door. "Hey, Ernie," I said. "Hey, Judd." Judd, the former astronaut, was in a cream-colored robe and flip-flops. The bottom of his legs, visible below the bathrobe, was damp, with wiry white hairs sticking against his legs. Ernie, who had gone back to his apartment to drop off his shopping, must have run into Judd where he was almost always to be found—by the pool. "There's hot water if you guys want tea?"

"Have you got coffee?" Judd asked. "I've only had one coffee today, and cups of coffee are like rocket boosters."

I took the bait. It looked like he wanted me to take the bait, like he had been thinking this one up all day. "How so?"

"Well, no cups of coffee, and I can't even get off the ground. Just one cup of coffee and I'm all wonky," he swerved a flattened hand off to one side, "*way* off course."

"And that second cup of coffee makes you all spacey?" I suggested.

Judd looked a little crestfallen. "I was just going to say that it gets me all the way there."

I felt a little bad about ruining his coffee analogy, but as we walked into the living room, Ernie saved me. "Talking of spacey, did you hear that Howie Rockford got caught growing his own cannabis?"

I did not know that. In fact, I had only met Howie Rockford once, the previous week, when I spied him performing a tribal dance on the beach in just a loincloth. I wasn't the only one who did a double take at the sight of it.

"Poor Wendy," Ada-Mae said, not taking her eye away from her magnifying glass. Wendy was Howie's wife. After the loincloth incident, Ada-Mae informed me that Howie had been a straight-down-the-middle type his whole life. A postal employee. Never drank and rarely missed a day of work. Then he retired and decided to catch up on all those experiences he felt he had missed. Howie's term for it was "finding his inner child." It looked a lot like going off the rails if you asked me.

Wendy, on the other hand, liked to play bridge and lawn bowling and was considering taking up quilting. They were quite the odd couple together.

"I thought I might suggest to him about enrolling in the academy," Ada-Mae said.

"What, Howie?" Ernie asked.

"And Wendy. I thought it could be a shared interest between their, well... two extremes."

Unusual for the gentle giant, Ernie looked a little put out. I had no idea what they were talking about and headed into the kitchen to finish making the drinks.

"Do either of them have any magical talent?" Ernie asked.

Ada-Mae stopped staring through the magnifying glass and looked up at Ernie. "As you well know, the witches' academy is not just about talent."

"Witches'... what?" I asked, sticking my head back out of the kitchen.

"Academy," Ada-Mae said with an off-hand flick of her wrist,

"I've enrolled you, too, dear. I told you that, didn't I? I'll be eighty soon, and although I hate to admit it, the odd thing here and there slips my mind if I don't remember to write it down."

Many things slipped my mind, and I was almost fifty years younger than Ada-Mae. This, however, I would like to have known about. I stepped into the living room, the drinks forgotten. "You enrolled me into an academy?"

"Into *the* academy... for witches," Ada-Mae said with a self-satisfied grin.

"I can't go to school. I'm thirty years old, for one thing. And I've got to work."

The other three, who were all aware of my employment troubles, gave me various doubtful looks.

"Or find work, same difference. I can't do that at witch school. And I'm not wearing a uniform with stripy tights and a pointed hat, either."

Ada-Mae rolled her eyes, but I could tell she was not going to let it go. I decided it was best to change the subject.

"Why don't you just break the Dargi statue at the base to see if there's a smoke—or mist—machine in it?"

Ada-Mae looked at me like I was an alien. "Break it? When we don't even know what it is, for sure? That could be dangerous. At the very least, it could render it useless for whatever purpose it was made for."

As my grandmother turned it around in her hands, I couldn't help but feel that might not be such a bad idea. "Haven't you ever heard of Gorilla Glue?"

Ada-Mae's brow creased, and her eyes narrowed a little. It was all the reply she needed to make.

"I'm just saying," I said, "I would be careful with anything that leaks gas."

"Like Ernie," Judd said, then chuckled at his own joke.

"It's true," Ernie said with an expression that couldn't have looked guiltier.

Ada-Mae and I both rolled our eyes. *Men.*

AROUND THIRTY MINUTES and a good cup of tea later, I was walking along the beach, my now signature flip-flops in one hand, my prized cat statue in the other. I was excited to show it to Mojo. Although knowing my acerbic older cat, it was fifty-fifty whether he would just turn his nose up at the thing.

I wasn't happy about the idea of witch school, or whatever Ada-Mae was calling it. The whole thing sounded far too much like a television program for teenagers for my liking. And anyway, I had yet to pay off the student loans that had seen me through my journalism degree, so I didn't need more debt looming in my future.

Why couldn't Ada-Mae just keep teaching me the way she had been doing? I didn't like the idea of some stranger teaching me instead because learning magic felt personal. Every time I learned something new, it felt a little like opening myself up. There was a... vulnerability about it. Now I imagined all those pairs of eyes watching me as I tried and failed to cast a spell. How embarrassing.

What is that? said a familiar voice in my head before I had even opened Maude's side door.

"Do you like her?" I asked Mojo, trying to keep the irony out of my voice. "She is Bastet, an Egyptian cat goddess."

Then why isn't she in Egypt, where she belongs?

I was determined to remain chipper. "Because I bought her for a very reasonable price at the antique market."

They saw you coming from a mile away.

"You don't even know how much I paid for it."

If they didn't pay you, then you were robbed.

I huffed and decided just to ignore Mojo and stepped past him into the camper van, placing the Bastet statue down on the side table.

It's not going to stay there, is it?

"I haven't thought about where the statue is going to go yet. I just got home with it."

I mean, it's not staying in Maude... with us?

"What did you think I was going to do with it?"

I don't know. Use it for firewood. Or I can bury it in the sand for you.

I glowered at him. "You were a lot easier to deal with when I couldn't hear your voice in my head."

You were a lot easier to deal with when I didn't have to see you all day. Remember that? When you had a real job?

"Remember who feeds you?"

Remember who helped save your life at the space center?

"You can't keep using that one. It can only be valid so many times."

Mojo had followed us to the space center as we pursued the culprits for the murders of Ben Chalmers and Eduardo Fitch. Ada-Mae and I had combined to cast an illusion spell that had distracted the killers as they hunted us, a spell that had only been possible with Mojo there as the source of the illusion. He hadn't let me forget it since.

I started to look through Maude's cupboards, trying to decide what I could have for dinner. "Ada-Mae has enrolled me in some sort of witches' academy," I grumbled. "It starts tomorrow morning."

Oh, dear.

"I know, right?"

Does she think you are a teenager?

"Exactly!" Mojo might be a sarcastic pain in my behind at times, yet it was also uncanny how often we thought the same way. "And get this. It's called 'Quipley's School of Magic.' Have you ever heard of anything like it?

Well, it does bring a famous book series to mind. It's like you're starring in your own installment: Sidney Splotter and the Evil, Ugly Cat Statue.

"Well, I guess that makes you my familiar."

I would have gone with superior.

"Oh... I like that!"

Superior?

"No, the other thing. You can be my familiar. Come with me, so I don't have to face stupid witch school alone."

Now, hang on...

"Yup, that's settled then," I said, grinning at my cat. "You are coming with me tomorrow."

CHAPTER

THREE

Considering that I did not want to go to this witches' academy thing, it sure took me a long time to decide on an outfit before leaving Maude the following morning. I had joked about striped tights and pointed hats, yet I rejected my first two outfit choices because they weren't "witchy enough."

The next ensemble included some rather Goth-like pieces I didn't realize I still owned, so I rejected it on the basis of "trying too hard." Instead, I settled on something a bit more quirky. The mustard-colored tights with turquoise and pink seahorses were my favorite part, although I had been waiting for a special occasion to wear the aqua, vintage-style blouse. The finishing touch was a see-through hot pink scarf tied around my neck that matched a pink and black pointy hat. Of course, in Maude's tight quarters, I couldn't get a full look at myself in a mirror, so this would have to do.

Due to my outfit conundrum, I was late to meet Ada-Mae, who had asked me to join her at nine am sharp in the main building's recreation room at Shifting Sands, where retirees gathered to play games and work on jigsaw puzzles. I now wished I had asked a few more details, as I didn't even know where the academy was being held or who my teacher would be.

At almost ten past nine, I burst into the room marked with a "Game of Thrones Room" sign, Mojo hot on my heels, to find a small roomful of people already there. All of them looked up at me. If it weren't for the large banner hanging at the front that read "Quipley's School of Magic," I would have sworn I had barged into the wrong room.

They appeared, almost exclusively, to be residents of Shifting Sands—or, at least, old enough to be. Only one among them was under fifty, a raven-haired young woman in her early to mid-twenties. Several familiar faces were sitting among the students —Ernie and Judd included. Yet the most familiar face was at the front of the class, giving instructions next to a whiteboard with a marker in her hand.

"Sidney," Ada-Mae said, "good of you to finally join us."

My mouth fell open, and my gaze moved back and forth between my grandmother at the front of the class and the gathered students, of which there were about twenty.

You're... um... about to dribble, Mojo informed me.

"*You're* the teacher?" I gasped incredulously.

I had imagined the witches' academy as something more...

official. In something that looked like a nineteenth-century mansion, with a severe-looking schoolmarm in charge. Not my very own grandmother. Although I had to admit, Ada-Mae looked like a professional instructor of wizardry right then.

"Seeing as you are already standing up," she said, "you might as well be our first volunteer."

"Volun...?"

"You just got voluntold."

"Thanks, Mojo."

"Hey, you're the one who insisted I come."

"For moral support, not heckling," I glared at my cat. He flicked his tail in response and stared right back.

Ada-Mae put down the marker and beckoned me to stand with her at the front of the class. "It's okay, dear," she said. "We'll start with something simple."

I watched as she reached into a bag on the desk behind her and brought out something unexpected. "A cucumber?" I said.

"Yes, what appears to be an ordinary object to the untrained eye, is a lever of magic under the right conditions." Ada-Mae accentuated her statement with a wave of her wand. She appeared to notice Mojo for the first time as the tortoiseshell tabby cat wound his way between her legs. Teacher's pet. "Oh, hello there," she said to Mojo, then looked at me again. "You've brought your familiar to class?"

I must have looked uncertain as she held up a placating hand. "No, no, that's fine. We draw our strength from many places."

I wasn't sure how much strength I drew from Mojo, but if I needed a little sarcasm...

"Come, come," Ada-Mae beckoned me. I joined her next to the whiteboard, staring out at the interested faces of the rest of the class. I focused my gaze on Ernie and Judd, hoping to find some courage in familiar faces, but both of them looked worried. Wow, thanks, guys.

I looked down at the cucumber on the table and said the first thing that came to mind. "Are we going to make a magical salad?"

There was a snicker among the students that squeezed a surprised chuckle from me. Ada-Mae frowned before turning and addressing the rest of the class. "What was the first thing I told you this morning about magic?"

Several hands shot up into the air, which, in a group of mainly seniors, made the whole thing seem like some hilarious parody of high school. Finally, Ada-Mae pointed to a Caucasian woman in her fifties with a neat bob that was such a bright red it was verging on orange. "Yes, Wendy?"

"Change!" Wendy answered with so much excitement that she was almost shouting.

"That's right. The first thing we can say about magic is that it is about change."

"But that doesn't make it special. Change is happening everywhere all the time," Wendy said as if parroting back something she had already been told.

"Yes," Ada-Mae said patiently. "As I said before, change is the most constant force in the universe. Everything, everywhere, all the time, is in a state of change. Ask any scientist about that fact, and they will tell you it is true. And much of magic—arguably, *everything* about magic—is about helping that change along."

Ada-Mae picked up the cucumber and waved it back and forth in front of the gathering. "If we let time and nature take their course, what would happen to this cucumber if we just left it there on the table?"

"I reckon Administrator Jessop would start charging it boarding fees," called out a rowdy-sounding male voice from the back of the room. I shifted to the side and tilted my head over until I could see where the voice was coming from. Sitting next to Wendy—who was, from what I could see of her, a well-presented, middle-aged woman in a shimmering white blouse with pearls at her neckline and gold earrings of a discreet size—there was a man in what appeared to be a bathrobe. He had several string bead necklaces dangling across his exposed chest, which was thick with wiry white hair. He had a scraggly white-and-gray beard, although the top of his head was smooth and shiny. I recognized him from a recent and mentally scarring incident where I had seen him dancing in nothing but a loincloth.

"Thank you, Howie," Ada-Mae said with what sounded like good humor. Although knowing my grandmother as well as I did, I could hear the slightest touch of irritation in there somewhere. "Probably true. But if the cucumber paid its boarding fees, it would eventually...."

"Shrivel up and die." The voice that spoke those five words sounded younger than the others in the room, and I zeroed in on the raven-haired woman in her twenties, who made that Goth look I had briefly flirted with earlier in the morning work much better for her than it ever did for me. As I looked at her, she turned and held my gaze for a moment, smiling a lazy, confident smile through purple lips. I smiled weakly back. There was something at once a little sinister and also intriguing about her.

"That's correct, Zoe, "Ada Mae said to the girl. "Not quite how I would have put it, but the cucumber, even in the coolness of our Florida air conditioning, would desiccate and eventually rot. Now, it's the desiccating part that we are interested in. The cucumber would lose moisture to the surrounding air. Which is what we will do in an accelerated and controlled manner in a moment."

"Would that be water magic?" Ernie asked. I noticed he was sitting with an open book, taking notes.

"It would be," Ada Mae agreed. "Elemental water magic. It

was once thought the elemental forces governed all magic. The elements of earth, air, fire, and water—and, in certain magical practices, spirit. Modern science has shown us that things are a little more complicated than that, yet the idea of elemental magic as a framework to work within is useful." She turned to me. "So this is what Sidney and I will do for the first demonstration this morning. Observe."

Ada-Mae took out a long rectangular glass roasting dish. For a moment, I thought I might have hurried into a cooking class by mistake.

"Obviously, we need something to catch the water in," Ada-Mae said, "although a more advanced spell would move the water before depositing it."

Many of those gathered in the seats shuffled forward, eager to get a good view of what was about to happen.

"Successful magic," Ada-Mae continued, is about focus. "And although not strictly necessary, we use incantations, props, ingredients, and rituals to provide the environment and focus essential for success. And for potency. We want our spells to work as well as possible.

"Now, this is a little off the top of my head, but anything that helps frame my intention will do...."

Ada-Mae held her hands over the bowl, and there was a long moment of silence. I realized I was even holding my breath. My grandmother's brow creased with concentration.

She doesn't need the bathroom, does she?

I giggled; I couldn't help it. My stupid cat's sarcastic words had caught me unprepared. Ada-Mae sighed and fixed me with a glare. "Sidney!"

"I... It was Mojo. He made a joke."

Ada-Mae didn't look like she believed me, and I opened my mouth to apologize when...

I think they have pills that help with that...

"Shut up!"

I felt the disapproving eyes of the entire class now staring at me after that outburst. "Sorry, not you," I said to Ada-Mae. "Mojo."

Ada-Mae looked at me a moment longer, shaking her head back and forth. "Now, if you and your cat will permit me...." She held her hands above the roasting dish and the cucumber again, frowning in deep concentration. She then began her improvised incantation and moved her hands back and forth over it.

"Oh, spirits of water and spirits of air, let's get the moisture... um, out of there."

My cat rolled onto his back and started pawing at the air while his laughter erupted in my head. I was beginning to think that bringing him might have been a mistake. The cucumber wobbled in the glass roasting dish, then broke into two pieces. There were several long, silent moments as Ada-Mae stared down at it, and the gathered students appeared to wait with bated breath—presumably for something else to happen.

The silence was broken when the double entrance doors on the far side of the room swung open. Eileen McCann, the owner of the Kelp Seafood Grill, walked in. She was wearing an olive-green cleaner's uniform and towing a vacuum cleaner. Eileen took several paces into the room before noticing anyone was already there. Characteristically for the sharp-faced, sharp-tongued restaurant owner, it took about a third of a second for her expression to change from a look of confusion to a scowl. She appeared to silently challenge every single person in the room as she took us in, at the same time reaching into the breast pocket of her uniform and pulling out a folded piece of paper.

She opened it. "Says here this room should be empty."

"Late booking," Ada-Mae explained. "They set the cleaning

rotation at the start of the week, so we must have slipped by. We'll be in here every week at this time for the next few months."

Eileen huffed like this was a personal affront to her. She looked down at the vacuum cleaner as if considering whether to just use it anyway. Instead, she reached a hand into one of her uniform's deep side pockets and produced a cloth, then reached out and gently rubbed it on the side of a billiards table that lay just within reach. As the silence continued, there was an air of a Wild West standoff about the whole thing. Mojo rolled across the carpet between us, his paws reaching into thin air. He seemed like the proverbial piece of tumbleweed.

"We're... um, running a witches' academy," Ada-Mae tried, attempting to fill the awkward silence.

Eileen looked at the cucumber, then back at Ada-Mae. "Whatever," she said.

"If you were free, you could...."

"Do I look like I have time for cucumber worship?" Eileen snapped, then turned and stalked out, dragging her vacuum cleaner behind her.

Everyone watched the swinging doors settle back into place after Eileen's exit, then Ada-Mae spoke. "Alrighty then. Where were we?"

"You were about to take the water from the cucumber," said a woman in the front row.

"Oh no," Ada-Mae corrected, "I intentionally didn't do that. We only have one cucumber, I realized. So..." She held a hand toward me, showing it was my turn. My eyes narrowed. I had my suspicions that Ada-Mae's spell had just, well, failed. Still, the class was now looking at me, so I guessed I would have to give it a try.

"I've opened it up in the center for you, Sidney," Ada-Mae said as I stepped up and held my hands above the cucumber. "Should make it a little easier."

Feeling ridiculous, I closed my eyes and tried to block out everyone and everything around me. This wasn't the sort of magic spell I had ever imagined myself doing. My magic had helped catch murderers and had connected some residents of Shifting Sands with their deceased loved ones. Victimizing salad veggies felt a little below me.

And yet, I was Ada-Mae's granddaughter. I knew that my reputation would precede me, and there was family honor to uphold. I was going to do this well and show the entire class what a great witch I could be. I was going to desiccate the heck out of that cuc—

PHUT!!!

I felt something wet splatter across my face, down my front. Several gasps came from those seated in front of me. I opened one eye, trying to figure out what had happened. The first couple of rows appeared to be covered in specks of a slimy green substance. As was I. As was Ada-Mae. In the middle of the carpet, Mojo was staring at me, wide-eyed. Finally, I looked down at the glass roasting dish. A small amount of the green slime was all that was left in it.

"Woah," came the voice of Howie Rockford from several rows back. "Exploding cucumber. Righteous, dude."

CHAPTER

FOUR

"I do think you're going to need to take this a little more seriously, Sidney." Ada-Mae had been grumbling away at me since the inaugural class of Quipley's School of Magic had wrapped up early on account of cucumber-related complications. "There's a serious purpose to this academy. We need to train and prepare as many witches as possible to face the danger lurking in this town. And, more than that, we have a tradition to uphold."

I started to laugh, which turned into a cough. "Tradition?"

"Quipley's isn't just something I made up, dear."

Keep your face straight, Sidney.

"There is an unofficial tradition of teaching that goes halfway back through the twentieth century. We are not a typical Hogwarts school, mind you, if that's what you were expecting. No, we are not a brick-and-mortar school because we have something that transcends any single place. Although this is the first instance of Quipley's outside of New England, I'll admit. But then that makes us pioneers, too, with double the responsibility of getting things right."

With Judd's and Ernie's help, we were putting the last of the chairs away into the corner of the room, wiping off the cucumber sludge from the ones closest to the "magical event" as we did so. "Well, you could have told me you were going to be the one teaching the academy," I shot back. "I had no idea what I was walking into."

"What difference does that make?" Ada-Mae said.

"Well, you picked on me, for starters. Put me on the spot."

"You were late."

"I couldn't decide what to wear."

Ada-Mae raised an eyebrow.

"That's beside the point. I'm a grown woman, and you humiliated me in front of everyone." I took a breath and thought twice before almost saying what was on my mind. *Your stupid spell didn't even work. At least my magic did something.*

As if Ada-Mae had read my mind, she blinked, her jaw tight with shock. Then the jaw softened, and her expression became pained. Suddenly, placing the last of the chairs to the side, I didn't want to be in the room anymore, especially with Ernie and Judd both not knowing where to look.

It wasn't my nature to speak harshly with my grandmother, and the fact that she read my hurtful thoughts almost made me tear up. My heart felt torn between feelings of being singled out and picked on and feeling horrible for how I spoke to Ada-Mae. I needed to get out of there before I burst into tears.

"I'm heading out," I said. "I've got things to do." Not true. I had a misfortunate lack of things to do. My latest magazine article would keep me going for a while, but if I was going to have to help solve a murder every time I needed money.... Well, Crystal Beach was going to have to become the murder capital of Florida.

Rushing out of the Game of Thrones Room, my cat hot on my heels, I almost ran into Eileen. She was using a cloth to polish the framed pictures in a gallery of the Shifting Sands senior staff members, cleaning them with a fast, insistent rubbing as though she might be trying to polish them out of existence.

"Eileen," I said. Then, before thinking about what I was saying, I added, "Is everything okay?"

"Bet we're pleased as punch now, aren't we, Sidney? Seeing me reduced to part-time cleaning shifts at the retirement center."

"I didn't know," I said, genuinely confused. "What about the restaurant?"

"Rent's up, customers are down. Especially since people keep dying in the town." She cocked an eyebrow at me. "Something which I've noticed you always seem to be in the vicinity of."

"But wasn't the food truck at the mini-golf tournament a success?"

"Only reason I've still got a restaurant, but it's not enough. So now I've got to clean in the morning, so I can afford to open my restaurant in the afternoon." She sighed. "Need to take up something more profitable, like crime."

I coughed out an awkward laugh. Tough cookie though she might be, I could not quite see Eileen McCann holding up a bank with a sawed-off shotgun. My laugh only earned me a pair of narrowed eyes and a huff before Eileen moved away, grumbling, "Don't know what she thinks is so funny."

KAREN MCSPADE

As I watched her go, I couldn't help but feel sorry about her predicament, even if I couldn't quite decide whether Eileen liked me or hated me. I had only been in Crystal Beach for a short while, but I already understood that if the Kelp Seafood Grill ended up closing, a part of the town's soul would go with it.

Moving on, I hurried down a carpeted corridor that led back toward the main foyer. Ahead of me, a familiar figure came out of a door to the left. It was that unscrupulous realtor, Sam Barlow, or Savvy Sam, as he advertised himself. He had also, briefly, been my mother's, well... boy toy. I was going to need therapy to recover from it.

He glanced around and walked toward the main foyer—the same direction I was heading—but stopped after a few steps, his shoulders sagging. As he turned, I could see his expression appeared put out, but by the time he was facing me, Sam was wearing the sort of smile that no doubt sold flea-infested fixer-uppers with subsidence to decent, hard-working people.

"Oh, my my," he said, putting as much southern drawl into his accent as possible, "save our souls if it isn't Sidney Grace, Crystal Beach's favorite vagrant. How is that hot property mother of yours?"

I was about to unleash a smart and witty retort of my own when I caught the sign on the door of the room he had just exited out of the corner of my eye. I turned back to him, all business. "What are you doing coming out of a supplies closet in a retirement community?" I demanded.

If my question made Sam uncomfortable, the most he showed of it was a twitch of his left eye. "I'm a realtor," he said. "Shifting Sands Retirement Center has a regular supply of properties that need selling, and in the current climate, they need my expertise to help with moving them." He looked me up and down with something verging on a sneer. "Not that it is any of your business.

Although, please remember me when your grandmother's apartment becomes available."

I bristled. "Is that a threat?"

Sam Barlow sighed, all false patience. "No, Sidney, it's called marketing. If you had any ability to market yourself, maybe you would find yourself a proper job and not have to live in that unsightly van of yours."

I had to give it to him. He was in fine form today. But no, wait, I didn't have to give it to him at all. Sam Barlow was a scoundrel and a criminal, albeit one freely walking the streets of Crystal Beach and roaming the hallways of Shifting Sands. The very fact made me sick to my stomach.

For the first time, Sam appeared to notice Mojo behind me. "Look, you brought your cat with you. That's not weird at all." He should have left it at that, but Sam made the mistake of leaning forward and reaching out toward Mojo. "Here, kitty. Aargh!"

His painful exclamation came just after Mojo's paw had whipped out lightning fast, claws raking the back of Sam's hand. He snatched his hand back and took half a step away from us, looking up to glare at me. "You should keep that animal of yours under control," he said. "Or it might need to be put down."

"Sorry," I said—my turn to be false. "He has an allergy to pieces of—"

Before I could finish my unladylike sentence, my cell phone rang and interrupted me. Sam glared at me one more time and turned to stalk down the corridor while I eyed the supplies closet again, remembering the ability of the CAD-Astra employees using the portal at Sam's Mystic Dunes properties to move significant distances in an instant. Why else would he be emerging out of a closet?

My hand reached out toward the handle, but the phone continued to ring, interrupting my train of thought. I swiped to answer it without even looking at who it was. "What do you want?" I snapped.

"Sidney?" came a hesitant but familiar voice on the other end of the line. *Officer Reece*, I thought at the same time I felt a tight clenching sensation in my chest. *Wait, no. It's Chief Reece now.* Congratulations were in order. Maybe a get-together to celebrate his promotion.

"Yes. This is she." *This is she?* Why the heck did I say that?

"It's John. Offi... uh, Chief Reece."

"Oh, yes, of course," I said as if remembering some random person I had talked to at a conference or wedding the previous year. I wasn't sure why I was being so difficult about just saying "hi." Perhaps it was because he had caught me off guard.

There was a long, silent beat before he spoke again. "I... um, just thought I would call as I haven't had much chance to talk to you since the events surrounding the Ben... CAD-Astra investigation."

He had almost said Ben Chalmers but then thought better of it. Ben, my childhood sweetheart, had met an untimely demise at the Crystal Beach Mini-Golf Invitational. After a sudden and unexplained separation followed by over a decade since I'd seen him, I had only spoken to Ben briefly before he was killed. Yes, it was a sore subject, and I was still a little intrigued about why John had strayed away from talking to me about it.

I am, I will admit, too much of a slave to my emotions at times. If he hadn't accidentally touched a nerve, I would have been a little gentler. "Yes, I remember that. The operation where you used me, a civilian, as bait. Got a promotion out of it but then didn't call me in all the time since. Yes, I think I remember that."

To his credit, John didn't miss a beat. It was like he was getting to know me. "And that's why I called," he said evenly. "I at least owe you a drink, and it would be nice to catch up, wouldn't it?"

Sometimes, the way John held a normal conversation, like asking a girl out for a drink, sounded a lot like how he asked a suspect to join him down at the station for an interrogation. Was it weird that I kind of liked that? "Sure," I said. "Do you want to meet later, maybe at The Kelp? We can make a dinner of it. I think Eileen could use the business."

"That would be good, but I'm on a later shift today that starts at four. I'm free—"

"Now?" I interjected a little too quickly.

"Now would be good."

THERE WAS a bar right at the northern end of Crystal Beach. I had seen it before once when I had passed by but had not yet visited. Cody's Cocktails was a proper beach bar, all wood and bamboo, situated entirely on the golden sands of the beach. Since The Kelp wasn't yet open, we had settled on this place. When I arrived, John was waiting for me at the side of the building facing the sea.

The day was unusually cool, and a fresh breeze brought the smell of salt from the sea, with the occasional hint of spray carried with it. Hazy, wispy clouds hid the sun but didn't darken the day, and I felt safe from the possibility of a fierce Florida downpour.

"Hey," I said. John was in jeans and, quite suitable for the venue, a Hawaiian shirt. I had rushed back to Maude to change into a white dress with red flowers that, coincidentally, also had a Hawaiian vibe.

"Look at us," he said with a laugh as I sat down, "don't we look the part together?"

Apparently, I was the only one of the two of us who noticed

how forward that sounded. Shame. "I've wanted to visit Cody's for some time, but it's so out of the way at this end of town. A wonder it stays in business."

"It gets good business from the next town to the north, Tanyard Bay. Plus, Cody's one of those people who can live off dimes when he needs to."

I glanced over at the guy behind the bar, remembering that I had seen him at the antique market in town the previous day, hanging around the stall where I had bought my Bastet statue. He was also looking the part, wearing a Hawaiian shirt—red with a yellow pattern on it. Unlike John's, it was open on a chest that was thin but wiry and solid... and darkly tanned. A surfer's body. Blond hair fell wavy and uneven to just above his shoulders, the hair bleached even blonder by the same sun that had darkened his hairless chest.

Everything about his face was youthful, except for the slight crow's feet around both eyes, which meant he could have been anywhere between twenty-five and forty but still looking great for his age. It was almost impossible to tell. Cody had the air of a surf bum, for sure, and there were several boards around, propped up against the building or the secondary bar that ringed the establishment on three sides. He beamed at me as he caught my eye, and I noticed a collection of idols and statues on a shelf behind the bar, close to the various bottles of spirits. Apparently, he was a bit of a collector, after all.

I leaned in a little, lowering my voice, although Cody wouldn't have a chance of hearing me over the sounds of the wind and the sea. I didn't want to stereotype, but Cody looked like he lived by his own rules. "You don't worry that there are other reasons he makes ends meet out here, so far from the center of town?"

John let out a whistling breath between his teeth. "Look at you, Sidney Grace. Getting quite the taste for being a cop, I'd say."

I didn't reply but favored him with the hint of a smile.

He glanced back to where the bar owner was now rolling himself a homemade cigarette on the bar. I assumed it was *just* a cigarette. "Well, I'm not saying a law never gets broken out here, but I make a point of coming out at least once a week. Usually as a civilian. I think Cody knows the boundaries.

"Anyway..." He pushed a tall glass toward me that was topped with ice, fruit, and leaves. A peach and pink-colored drink filled the rest of it, the colors swirling together like some magical potion."

"Is this...?"

"Alcoholic? Oh yeah."

I giggled like a schoolgirl, one who had stolen her older sister's ID. "Feels naughty. It's barely past noon."

John raised his eyebrows. "Just the one. I'm still several hours away from my shift." His drink had more of a "something on the rocks" vibe about it. I took a long drink of mine through the straw after moving aside the pink umbrella. It was sweet and fragrant. Cody knew his business. The cool breeze tickled my bare upper arms; I hadn't felt so present, so perfectly where I was supposed to be, since coming to Crystal Beach. Angry thoughts of the morning's humiliation and that snake Sam Barlow melted away until they were a distant memory.

Then my phone rang.

"Dad?" I answered questioningly after checking the screen this time before accepting the call. I hadn't spoken to my father, who was divorced from my mother, since right after I moved to Crystal Beach. That wasn't a big deal, of course. We had the sort of relationship that could always be picked up again at a moment's notice, whether it had been five minutes or five months.

Across the bar, I saw John's interest piqued.

"Sidney. How's it going, sweetheart? Down there in Florida?"

I looked at the dark, tall, and handsome policeman sitting opposite me. "Yes... interesting. Sorry I haven't called. More going on in this small Florida town than you might think."

"Well, that's good news then. Because I thought I might come to visit."

First, my mom, and now, my dad. I guess that was the perk of living in the state where everyone goes on vacation. "Great. When are you coming?"

"Well, I'm kinda packing right now. Got a plane booked for tomorrow morning... if that's okay?"

Geez, Dad. Can't you give a girl a little notice? "Well, luckily, my schedule is pretty flexible, so I'm sure I can fit you in."

John grinned at that. Equal parts cute and annoying.

"I know, I know. Short notice. Look, Sid, I'm taking an early retirement because I feel like I'm ready. I just don't want to put it off any longer."

"You've not been watching those medical insurance ads again, have you? Not everyone gets cancer as soon as they turn fifty-five." I paused a moment, irrational fear flooding through me. "God, you haven't got cancer, have you?"

"No, no. Nothing like that. I just, you know... want to see my daughter and do those things I've never done. Meet Mickey Mouse, maybe visit the Space Center."

"You'll find some keen tour guides for that one around here. Look, you realize I live in a camper van with four cats? There's not a lot of room in there. I'm sure you'll be welcome to stay at Ada-Mae's, though, or you can find a place in town if you prefer."

"To be honest, I want to see your grandmother, too. I haven't seen her since your grandpa's funeral."

"I'm sure we can figure out something for you."

"Thanks, sweetheart."

After a brief conversation about his schedule, I hung up after promising to pick up my dad from the airport the following day. Hearing from him had been a surprise, and the more I thought about it, the more I felt like I needed my dad. He had always been a calm, reasonable influence that offset the whirlwind that was my mother. Also, he wasn't carrying the baggage of magic or murder investigations. Some normality from outside of Crystal Beach might be good.

I realized John was grinning at me. "Your dad's coming, huh? Can't wait to meet him, especially after your mother was so interesting."

"Oh," I said with a wave of my hand. "Don't worry about him. My dad doesn't do interesting, not in that sense. I mean, he works in finance. Well, *worked* in finance. Apparently, he's decided to retire."

We finished our drinks and headed back into town separately. On the way, I made the very adult decision to head to Shifting Sands so I could patch things up with Ada-Mae. I also needed to tell her that Dad was coming and check that it would be okay for him to stay with her. If my grandmother and I weren't on good terms, then my dad's visit wouldn't be as fun for anyone. Hopefully, the news of his visit would provide some sort of reconciliation by osmosis.

When I reached Ada-Mae's apartment, the door was already open, which was odd. Worried, I rushed inside and found Ernie standing in the living room as Ada-Mae moved around, pulling cushions up from the sofa, then moving to look behind the sideboard. Ada-Mae stopped when she saw me and shrieked out my name. "Sidney," she cried, her voice shrill. "I've been robbed!"

CHAPTER
FIVE

The following morning, I awoke early with lots to do. Nothing major had come of the break-in at Ada-Mae's apartment at Shifting Sands, and to be honest, I didn't know what to think.

The only item supposedly stolen from Ada-Mae's apartment was that ugly Dargi statue, which she had been planning to use for her ritual. Now, I had to admit; there was something mysterious about the statue, what with the way it leaked misty-smoky stuff. But it hadn't appeared valuable—especially considering that Ada-Mae had bought it for such a low price at the antique market.

Other than that, nothing else had gone missing from Ada-Mae's apartment. Indeed, there were no signs of forced entry or so much as a single thing out of place. It just didn't seem likely that someone would go to all the trouble of stealing a statue that, personally, I wouldn't bother displaying in my downstairs powder room—if I had a downstairs powder room, of course.

And yet, Ada-Mae had been insistent, so I had called the police station only to find that the only thing picking up was their voicemail. Ada-Mae had been so fretful that I then texted John. And when he hadn't responded, I messaged his deputy, Jessie, as well. Still, no answer. Which was weird.

Eventually, late in the afternoon, Jessie had responded with an apology. They were dealing with a wave of robberies and could not get to us until the following day.

Ada-Mae, of course, had taken this as proof that she had also been robbed. I was on the verge of reluctantly agreeing with her when she realized that the linen bag she often took shopping was missing too.

"Oh, my," she had said, placing a hand on her chest. "Maybe I left it at The Invisible Cloak. I went shopping for ingredients there after class. They have a very reasonable price on Black Sand. And did you know that it's the only place a witch can find monkey toenail clippings in the entire county?"

I wasn't *that* surprised.

The Invisible Cloak was a magic shop in town on Citrus Way, where the antique market was also being held. I had not been inside yet, but I had seen that it had a literal "cloak" across the entrance. "Do you think the Dargi statue could have been in that bag?" I had asked.

Ada Mae looked confused. "Why would I do that?"

I shrugged. "You said yourself that sometimes you're a little forgetful."

"Forgetful, yes, "Ada Mae shot back, "but I'm not downright dotty!"

Ada-Mae flushed, and again, I regretted not learning to engage my brain before opening my mouth. Ever since our cucumber fiasco at the witch's academy, there was conflict simmering beneath the surface. Even with the news of my father's imminent visit, there remained tension in the air between us, and it was gnawing a pit in my stomach.

Either way, it was too late to check out The Invisible Cloak, as it would already be closed by the time we got there. I suggested we try the following day and then headed back to Maude before there was a chance for any more awkwardness between us.

So now, before an early visit to recover Ada-Mae's shopping bag and, hopefully, the Dargi statue, I also had to pick up my father from the airport. But before I did that, I was planning to cast a spell. I was determined to help Deputy Jessie find a suitable romantic interest in the little town of Crystal Beach and hoped that a gentle spell of like-minded attraction would help her do that.

It had been my plan to work with Ada-Mae, but considering how things were between us and the fact that she was distracted with her missing statue and the spell she wanted to cast to discover what was happening at Mystic Dunes, I figured I could try it myself. What happened with the cucumber yesterday had been unfortunate, but it had proven that I had all the power I needed to make things happen.

What are you doing with that creepy statue? Mojo asked. He came over to where I sat cross-legged on my bed and rubbed himself along my arm.

"It's not creepy," I said. "If you want to see creepy, you should see the statue that Ada-Mae has... well, *had*. Possibly lost. Maybe it got stolen." I glanced back to where the other three cats were still asleep toward the rear of the van. I didn't want them waking up and running around like crazy, as they often did in the evenings. Concentration was required.

"I'm casting a spell. An attraction spell. The statue of Bastet is my focus." I held up the "BEWARE of Thieves" poster that Jessie had given me two days before when we were returning from the antique market. "And I have something that, at least briefly, belonged to the person I am, um... trying to find love for."

A love spell? Mojo asked, alarm finding its way into his usually relaxed, feline inner voice. *Love spells are never a good idea.*

"It's not a love spell," I insisted. "Gentle attraction at most."

I could feel Mojo's skepticism inside my head, although he said nothing further. As I settled down to cast my spell, I wondered whether an incantation was needed or whether my intention—my strong desire to see Jessie happy—would be enough. In the end, my mind almost subconsciously formed words that I guessed wouldn't hurt to chant. A short mantra while I built up the energy and intention I would send out into Crystal Beach.

I focused on the lithe, feline form of the statue in front of me and placed a hand on the poster that Jessie had handled. For a moment, my attention wandered. It would have been nice to get hold of something more personal, like a strand of her hair or even her work badge. Then again, maybe the picture of sweet, smiling Deputy Jessie in my head would be enough.

"Spirits of passion; spirits of desire. Find something true for Jessie; I implore you, ignite love's fire."

With those last words, the piece of paper under my hand burst into a bright flame. I shrieked and took hold of the only corner of it that wasn't already burning before my bed caught fire as well. Panicking as flaming embers dropped from it, my free hand fiddled with the catch on Maude's side door until it unlocked. I slid the door open and threw the poster out onto the sand at the back of the beach, where the fire consumed the last of it.

Mojo padded up to my side. *Was that supposed to happen?*

I stared at the ashes, now being picked up by the breeze, which was blowing from the south. "I don't think so. I had barely even started the spell."

"Yeah, love can be messy. Not saying I told you so... but I told you so."

~

BY THE TIME I got to the airport the next morning, there were distant rumbles of thunder, and the sky was a dark, angry sort of gray that suggested we were in for a fierce downpour. Maybe even a protracted one.

"Welcome to the Sunshine State," I said with a grin as I hugged my father. Then behind me, almost as if the sky had heard and wanted to spite me, the rain started to fall.

Jacob Grace was a little like a cross between an aging Matthew McConaughey and Clark Kent. Just a lot more nerdy looking and, well... my dad. He wore thick, round, black-rimmed glasses all the time and had curly, mousy-colored hair swept back from a high hairline, which became unruly if he went more than three weeks between haircuts. The relaxed set of his jaw and a smile always playing about his lips gave a mischievous look to his baby blue eyes. In his fifties, he was still a handsome man.

He took my shoulders in his hands and leaned back a little, taking me in. "You look good, Sidney. I think this climate agrees with you."

"I'm getting used to it," I said. "The sweat patches are getting smaller. Although... one way or another, you're going to get a little wet here in Florida," I swept a hand back to indicate the day and its weather. It was finally raining, but the humidity was still high, even after the sun had disappeared behind the clouds.

Dad pulled at his linen shirt—it was white with thick tan-colored lines down it. He was also wearing khaki cotton trousers, sock-less brown-leather loafers, and a Panama-style straw hat I had never seen before. He was doing his best to fit right in with the Florida vacationers. Bless him. "Tell me about it. I was fine in the air-conditioning, but I can already feel my clothes sticking to me."

"Don't worry," I said, grabbing one of his bags and pointing him toward Maude. "This rain will clear things out. Give you an easier first day, at least."

With that, a flash of lightning went off overhead, followed by a simultaneous ear-shattering "bang"' and a yelp from the woman loading her bags into a taxi. My dad jumped, too, failing to keep the worried look off his face.

"And if you're here for much time at all, you'll probably get used to that too." The thunderclap had signaled the start of the downpour, soaking us to the skin before we could even get inside Maude.

Not realizing the intensity of the storm that had been building, I had let the cats out onto the beach to roam. I couldn't leave them trying to shelter from it now, though, so I told my dad that we would need to swing by the beach and gather them up before heading over to Ada-Mae's.

For the first time since coming to Crystal Beach—and for one of the very few times in my whole life—I was nervous about seeing Ada-Mae. In part because I had said things to upset her, sure. But also because a part of me was still upset with her for putting me on the spot in front of the class.

And I realized that was just as uncomfortable a feeling. Maybe more so. I felt stuck on this emotional rollercoaster that was excited to become what she believed I could be, a powerful witch who would do great things, and the fear that I might disappoint her if I failed. Somehow that fear was twisting itself into a streak of anger that I didn't quite understand or like.

"So, early retirement?" I finally asked as we approached the outskirts of Crystal Beach.

My dad seemed deep in thought. He had been staring out the window for much of the journey, although I guessed that maybe he was just interested in the landscape. Or hoping to see gators. More than a month in Florida, and I hadn't seen a gator yet. I did not consider this to be a bad thing.

"Uh-huh," he answered eventually without expounding any further.

"Why not, eh?" I pushed on. "I mean, the business has always done well. You can afford to, I guess?"

"Yup." This time, he managed a little more of a smile. Not exactly verbose, however. "How's Ada-Mae been without Gramps around?"

That was a loaded question that I wasn't prepared to answer. "*Well, I've seen quite a bit of Gramps*" probably wasn't the way to begin. "She's okay," I said. "She's got some good friends. Keeps herself busy. She started up a kinda club. Had the first meeting yesterday."

"Oh...that's good to hear. And you? How are you doing, Sid?"

Okay, a different subject. Fine. The thing was, I wasn't sure how to answer the question about myself either. For some reason, I couldn't bring myself to talk about magic, which was odd. Dad had always been the one who was okay with magic. I don't think he actually *believed* in it until the one time he had seen genuine proof of it himself. Of course, it's hard to ignore a group of cloaked figures drawing symbols on a kitchen floor to find a kidnapped pooch—stemming from another one of my "butterfingers" moments. Regardless, though, he had always respected that Ada-Mae, Gramps, and I did believe. Unlike Mom.

We pulled up at the spot next to the back of the beach that had been my home since arriving in town. Rain was still falling so heavily that it sat in vast puddles on the road, and the heavy clouds were blocking out so much light that it almost felt like twilight.

Pulling a jacket over my head, I ran around to open the side door and called out the names of my cats. "Mojo! Jinx? Abra-Cadabra!" I almost always said the names of the two Siamese cats quickly together. How could I not?

"Are you casting a spell?" my dad joked from the front.

"Ugh, I don't think they can hear me," I said. "Maybe they've gone further away to find shelter. I'll just check farther up the beach a little way."

Before I could tell my dad to stay put, he jumped from the passenger seat and joined me.

"You don't—" I began, but he went straight past me, pushing into the southerly wind that was occasionally blowing so hard the rain kept coming at us sideways. We walked about fifty yards along the back of the beach and found the cats sheltering beneath an upturned boat.

You left us to drown! A familiar inner voice accused me.

Sorry. I didn't know it was going to storm. I thought back.

We were almost back at Maude when I noticed that something was wrong. I turned to my dad. "I shut that, right?" I was talking about Maude's side door. I was sure I had shut it as I wouldn't want the inside of my home half-flooded. Yet, it was open.

"Think so," he said, then tried to grab my arm to stop me as I broke into a trot. "Sidney!"

My wet arm slipped out of his grip, and Mojo rushed after me as I ran to see what was going on. I stuck my head inside the camper van, and my jaw dropped at what I saw. Sitting inside the back of Maude, holding my Bastet statue, was Sam Barlow. If it surprised him to see me, he recovered quite well. "What's this?" he asked, holding out the cat statue.

"Get out of my van!" I screamed at him.

He did so with a smug smile, and I snatched the cat statue from him as he stepped outside the van. Standing in his suit, he was already wet and got wetter as he joined me outside, where my dad had now caught up with us. Sam raised an eyebrow at him but spoke on a different subject when he turned back to me. "How long can you park a van in the same spot on the back of the same beach and not pay any rent, Sidney?"

"As long as I want," I bristled.

He straightened his dripping-wet suit and walked away. "We'll see, Sidney. We'll see."

Looking down at the cat statue, I frowned to myself and glanced back up to watch Sam disappear through the falling rain.

"I'M TELLING YOU, *Chief Reece*, it is a powerful magical item, and someone has stolen it from me. Do you know the sort of problems a thing like that could cause in the wrong hands?"

Ada-Mae and John were standing in the doorway to her apartment when my dad and I arrived. Ada-Mae sounded like she had resorted to her haughty "this town pays your wages" best, something I rarely ever saw her do.

"Look, Ada-Mae," he said. He sounded tired, like being diplomatic was a little taxing right now. "We have had several burglaries recently, it's true. There was even one here at Shifting Sands." Ada-Mae's crossed arms relaxed a little like she thought she was about to be vindicated and didn't see the "but" coming. "Buuut... they all sort of fit an M.O. At least, they stole multiple items at each burglary. Things like jewelry and cash. Not... a da... ggi—"

"Dargi."

"Okay, A Dargi statue bought at the market." They both noticed us approaching. "Ah, you must be Mr. Grace," John said, holding out a hand. "Sidney said you were coming."

"Yes, and you are...?" my dad asked.

"Chief John Reece. I'm here on official business today, I'm afraid. But I'm sure I'll see you around Crystal Beach during your visit. I've gotten to know—"

"Ada-Mae, why don't you get Dad settled? I'm sure he could use a change of clothes after we got caught in the storm." I wasn't sure I wanted my dad to learn how we'd gotten to know John better—all that murder and mayhem.

Ada-Mae took Dad inside, all smiles and good graces for the ex-son-in-law she still adored. I lingered, my encounter with Sam Barlow still fresh in my mind and casting a different light on things. "You okay?" I said when John smiled weakly at me as the moments since Ada-Mae and my dad's disappearance into the apartment threatened to grow long and quiet.

"Yeah," he said with a sigh. "The Crystal Beach Police Department is not equipped for crime sprees, and that's what these burglaries are turning into."

"Look, I know that this statue thing doesn't seem like a big deal compared to the other burglaries that have been happening-"

"If this even is a burglary."

I nodded, all diplomacy. "I thought the same. But...." I paused.

"Go on."

"Well, I just caught Sam Barlow snooping around Maude." I saw John's eyes glaze over a little. He knew that Sam and I had a history of conflict. "I mean, *in* my van when I had left her closed."

"And locked?"

"Well, no. That's beside the point."

"If he did that, then I'll have a word with him," John said. "But I'm pretty sure the town's most successful realtor isn't our guy."

"But," I said, "when I found him, he had my cat statue in his hand."

"Your... cat statue?"

"I bought it at the antique market. Don't you think that's weird?"

"Buying a cat statue? I mean, maybe."

"Not buying a cat statue! Sam. Sitting inside my van holding my cat statue. He was here yesterday too. Not long before Ada-Mae's Dargi went missing."

"He was here, in Ada-Mae's apartment?"

"No, not in her apartment. He... um, came out of a closet."

John looked at me, his eyes narrowed in clear confusion, and backed away a few steps. "I'm going now, Sidney. I genuinely don't have time for this."

"No, wait..."

But John waved me away irritably. "Just hang onto your statue and stop trying to pick a fight with Sam Barlow. Spend some quality time with your dad."

CHAPTER

SIX

"I think it was the real deal."

All three of us were in the living room of Ada-Mae's apartment. Dad had used Ada-Mae's bathroom to get changed out of his wet clothes, although I was still damp and feeling the chill of the air conditioning. Ada-Mae made tea, and we were now sitting down, drinking it and snacking on some little fairy cakes she had baked the previous evening. Drizzled with icing and covered in sprinkles, this was my breakfast. Naughty Sidney.

Ada-Mae had been speaking about her missing statue. "Real deal, as in from ancient times?" I asked.

She nodded. "Yes, dear, old and valuable." The awkwardness between us seemed to have evaporated for the moment, perhaps only because of Dad's presence. Since finding Sam with my statue in his hands, I was seeing things a little differently, too. Yet John's reaction had still given me pause.

"And genuinely magical too. Remember the mist that came out of the base?"

"How could anyone forget that?"

My dad beamed. "I've missed you ladies, and I don't know... the world that you live in. So exotic compared with long-term IRAs."

We both grinned back, and I assumed that Ada-Mae was, like me, taking his comment as a compliment.

"But you bought it for what? Ten dollars?" I said.

"The shop owner obviously didn't realize what she had. I mean, I didn't know it was the real thing at first, either." She shook her head. "Such a shame. With such a powerful item for focus, I probably could have performed the ritual myself. Maybe without having to go to Mystic Dunes to do it. Now we don't even have a fake Dargi statue as a focus. I'll see what else I can find, but we're going to need all the help we can get."

I drew in a breath, hoping not to cause any further upset with my grandmother. "We should still check out the shop," I said. "Find your bag. You never know."

I saw Ada-Mae's shoulders tighten, her jaw set, but she didn't answer. "Or shall I call them?" I pushed on. "That way, we don't need to go down there." I looked up the number on my cell and dialed it, but it just rang and rang without going to voicemail. "Geez. Doesn't anyone pick up their phone in this town anymore?"

Ada-Mae stood up. "It's okay. We'll go down there. Just to prove to you once and for all that your grandmother is not losing her marbles."

~

"Oh, look," I said as we drove in Maude toward the center of town, the sun now peeking through the clouds after the downpour subsided. Ada-Mae was next to me in the passenger seat, and my dad was in the back with the cats. They seemed to like him. "The Kelp Seafood Grill is open."

Ada-Mae picked up my meaning straight away. "Eileen should still be cleaning at the retirement center."

"Is it a good restaurant?" my dad asked from the rear.

"Best seafood in Crystal Beach," I said. "You've just got to put up with Eileen, who's like an angry, sarcastic cloud on a sunshiny day."

"She's not so bad," Ada-Mae said.

As we got closer, Eileen appeared, carrying a tray of food for eager customers who had already claimed an outdoor table after drying the bench with a towel that now lay sopping wet beside them. We pulled over, and Ada-Mae rolled down the window. Eileen noticed us and came over after delivering the food. She smiled, and I noted how surprisingly warm it was for the day that Hell froze over. "Morning," she said. "Going to stop in for some brunch? I've got smoked salmon and dill waffles."

My stomach, already well past the two fairy cakes I had wolfed down at Ada-Mae's, rumbled at the mention of food.

"Sorry," Ada-Mae said, "we're on a mission. Didn't realize you were opening for breakfast again. Have you quit at the retirement center?"

Eileen's smile widened, and her expression became coy. It

made her look a decade younger. "Quit yesterday, in fact, right after my shift. I came into some unexpected money... and well, I liked working at the retirement center 'bout as much as I like an impromptu health inspection." She chuckled, glancing back toward the restaurant. "Opening back up for breakfast is great for business, and it's cut down on the complaints I was getting. If you'll excuse me now, I gotta get back to work."

Eileen headed back inside as Ada-Mae rolled up the window, a flash of curiosity twinkling in her eye. "Who is she, and what has she done with Eileen?" I said, curious myself now.

Ada-Mae tsked at me. "She's been under a lot of financial pressure for some time now. It's been hard for her to keep the restaurant going; that's why she's been... until now anyway, a bit abrasive and rough around the edges."

"But today, she was almost pleasant. Do you think it's strange that she came into some unexpected money, huh?" I mused out loud.

Ada-Mae did a double-take across the passenger seat. "You can't be serious. Not Eileen. She would never...." I kept a poker face. "Anyway, she's hardly the type to mastermind a crime spree."

I shrugged. "Maybe there is more than one burglar at work in Crystal Beach. But John said there was another break-in at Shifting Sands recently. Then, a day after your maybe two-thou-sand-year-old statue goes missing, she quits her job there. She has the motive to save the restaurant, and the job at Shifting Sands gives her an opportunity."

Ada-Mae huffed her displeasure. "So, *now* you believe that it was stolen, eh? Really, Sidney. That woman gave you a job."

It hadn't taken long, even with my dad there, for me and Ada-Mae to find cause for disagreement. It seemed that I couldn't win, whether or not I believed in this supposed robbery. "I'm just saying," I whined, feeling like a chastised child. "Let's just get to the magic store and get your bag back."

Ada-Mae and I finished the drive to The Invisible Cloak in silence. As I pulled up in the middle of the market and parked the car, I felt sorry for my dad. I could almost sense his awkwardness coming from the back of the camper van. He had no clue what was going on between my beloved grandmother and me, but I was sure he could sense something uncomfortable was wedged between us.

The antique market was still in full swing and would run for three more days. Plenty of people were milling around the stalls, haggling and bargaining for their next must-have prize. I had asked Ada-Mae before we made our separate purchases the other day how the vendors could make any money in such a small town like Crystal Beach. She told me that many of the neighboring communities came to attend the annual market, which brought a lot of traffic—and money—into the beachside town.

Looking at the various booths now, I saw the woman who Ada-Mae had bought the statue from, along with the suave antique dealer who had sold me the Bastet statue. I wondered if it might be worth browsing for a replacement should we not find the Dargi statue with Ada-Mae's bag.

As we approached the magic shop, which had a semi-transparent cloak like a net curtain hanging across the entrance, a familiar figure burst through it. At least Howie was wearing more clothing than the previous times I had seen him—no loincloth or exposed hairless chest in sight. Today, he wore stonewashed, striped harem pants and a patchwork poncho in darker, faded shades of blue, green, and purple. The clothes granted him a middle-class hippie vibe that he was proudly owning.

Behind Howie, standing in the doorway, was the young woman I had seen at Quipley's School of Magic during our first meeting of the witches' academy at Shifting Sands. Just like before, she had almost luminously pale skin that seemed like a direct challenge to the intense Florida sunshine that was now beginning to reappear. Her hair, dyed an inky, slightly glossy black, was cut in a close-cropped style, and she wore a long black dress over purple Dr. Martens boots. She folded her arms and glared at Howie.

"You're banned, Mr. Rockford," she said. "You're lucky I don't call the police."

I turned to look at Howie Rockford, who seemed a little unsteady on his feet and was having a few problems focusing his eyes. "I just need some white sage," he whined.

"Then do the paying-for-it thing like everyone else," the young woman snapped, then turned to smile at us, lifting the cloak to one side so we could enter. "Welcome, Ada-Mae." She looked at me. "Sidney." And to my dad. "And..."

"Jacob," my dad said. "I'm Sidney's father."

I felt embarrassed that I could not remember the young woman's name, even though I was sure I had heard it at the academy session the previous morning. Ada-Mae stepped in and saved me with this one. "Morning, Zoe," she said.

"Zoe," I nodded as I stepped into the store, saying her name with the confidence of someone who had always known it. The Invisible Cloak was a magical wonderland, the sort of store that I had loved as a child—straddling the line between being a kitschy, hocus-pocus tourist trap and a genuine, serious store for magic users and those with alternative practices and beliefs.

Alongside books on Wicca and Druidism, there was a sort of "pick & mix" section of ingredients like St John's Wort, rosemary, fairy wings—whatever those were—moth chrysalises, and more. My eyes scanned across one dark wooden shelf that held cast-metal statues of dragons, ceramic ones of fairies, and the obligatory treasure chest of assorted, five-for-a-dollar "gemstones."

"Sorry about that," Zoe said once we were all inside. "That Mr. Rockford worries me. I caught him stuffing white sage into the pocket of his, er, poncho, or whatever that was he was wearing."

"Yes, I'm afraid I might be the reason for that. I'm the one who invited him to come to the witches' academy," Ada-Mae said. "He's looking for something, and I thought that magic might be something exciting for him to focus on. I didn't think he would steal your potion ingredients a day after the first session."

"I'm not sure that teaching that man magic is a good idea. He has no self-control. Imagine what he could do...." Her eyes grew wide, and then she stopped mid-sentence. For such a young woman, Zoe had an old manner about her. "Anyway, what can I do for you? You were in here yesterday, weren't you?"

"Yes. I... um, left my bag here, I think. A bit embarrassing."

Zoe's eyes widened in recognition. "That was your bag? I didn't realize it. I would have called if I had known it was yours." She went behind the counter and fetched out the cloth bag, which was black and covered in magical symbols. "I found it over by the incense. You must have been browsing on your way out." She opened the bag as she came out again. "Looks like the ingredients you bought are all still there, though.

I was closer to Zoe and took the bag from her. I opened it and peered inside, knowing the answer even before I did so, as the bag did not feel heavy enough to contain the statue. "It's not here," I said.

Zoe looked quizzically between Ada-Mae and me. "Sidney thinks I might have left a missing statue in there."

Zoe shook her head. "No statue that I saw."

Ada-Mae fixed me with an "I told you so" look. "Why would I

bring my very important statue out on a walk with me? It's been stolen, as I said."

"Stolen?" Zoe repeated.

"From my apartment."

Zoe looked toward the doorway. The cloak, although semi-transparent, did a good job of blocking the light from outside, and it was fairly dim in the shop. "Have you thought about Howie Rockford? If he'd pocket my white sage, he might steal your statue."

WE LEFT the shop no wiser than when we had entered it. Well, wiser perhaps, but with a growing list of potential suspects and no real way to narrow them down. Between Sam Barlow, Eileen, and Howie Rockford, there were three people who had the opportunity and either a motive or, at least, the inclination to steal the statue. I had to admit that it seemed likely someone had taken Ada-Mae's statue.

We walked straight into John and Jessie as we exited the shop. Actually, I literally walked into John, and there was a fun moment where he held his jaw, and I rubbed my temple. He was quite a bit taller than me, after all. We both apologized to each other before really knowing who we had bumped into.

"Sidney," he said and nodded toward Ada-Mae.

A patrol car was parked next to Maude, and John had his notebook out, which he now had to retrieve from the ground. "Everything okay?" I asked. "Except for..." I reached up and rubbed my temple. He looked unusually worn and worried.

"No," he said. "Now the jeweler a few doors up has been hit. I can't keep up with this. It's like every burglar in Florida has come to Crystal Beach at once.

"A convention, maybe."

He did laugh at my joke. That was a good sign.

"Hey, Sidney," Jessie said, emerging from the jewelry store with a digital camera in her hands. As always, she seemed her usual cheery self. Of course, she didn't have the burden of being in charge during a crime spree. Jessie crossed to the patrol car and opened the door, placing the camera back into a bag.

I noticed as she did so that several cats were hanging around the patrol car, which was weird. One of them, a light-gray Persian, wound itself between Jessie's leg. Another, a slim cat that reminded me a little of my Bastet statue, jumped up on the hood. "I see you've hired some additional *paws* to help with the investigation," I said to Jessie.

"Oh, the cats? Yeah, they've been hanging around ever since we got here. Wish us luck on this one."

"With you and John working together on this, you've got all the luck you need." I waved goodbye to them as we got into Maude.

Pulling out of the parking lot, I thought about our suspects for the theft of the Dargi statue. Sam might have taken it to prevent the success of Ada-Mae's ritual if he had somehow found out about it. With magic, he could have perhaps broken in without leaving any signs. Eileen needed to save her restaurant, so maybe she could have gotten hold of some skeleton key—if Shifting Sands had such a thing—while employed there.

And Howie... well, I had no idea how he would have pulled it off. Perhaps he knew its actual worth, but more and more, he just seemed to be a miscreant who was spinning out of control in his retirement. When we arrived back at Shifting Sands, we were shocked to find out just how bad things with Howie were becoming.

CHAPTER

SEVEN

Wendy Rockford was pacing up and down in the entrance foyer at Shifting Sands Retirement Center when we returned, her hands knitting together in front of her in a nervous gesture that looked a little like prayer. As soon as she saw us enter, she made a beeline for Ada-Mae.

"Oh, Ada-Mae," she said in her soft southern accent, one that brought to mind sewing circles and peach pie and ice cream. *Mmm, peach pie.* I still hadn't had a proper breakfast, and it was now lunchtime. "I'm so glad you're here. I went up to your apartment, but there was no answer."

"We were running an errand," Ada-Mae said, although her tone conveyed the idea that Wendy Rockford had her full attention now.

Wendy's eyes flicked across to me, then to my dad, her expression deepening as she realized she didn't know him.

"Jacob Grace," he said, holding out a hand that she took daintily with a polite smile. "Sidney's dad." Poor Dad—he was having quite the first day in Crystal Beach, but he was playing along in gamely fashion without missing a beat.

"We can..." I offered, thumbing over my shoulder and suggesting that my dad and I could retreat and leave them to it. Although I was, of course, intrigued.

"No, no." Wendy waved my offer away. "Soon, the whole world will know the shame my husband is bringing upon us. But I need to show you. Over at our house."

Just over five minutes later, the four of us walked into Wendy and Howie's single-story house on the Shifting Sands site. Most of the accommodations at Shifting Sands Retirement Center were in the central building near the pool, mostly one and two-bedroom apartments with only a few three-bedroom ones. But there were a couple of small streets of single-story houses, two and three-bedroom ones with a small garden and at least some of the vibe of retiring in suburbia. Ideal for the "younger" married couples, these houses were between the tennis courts and the start of the golf course that dominated the northern end of the site. The 9th and the 10th holes of the course, the furthest from the clubhouse, were quite close to the area of the beach where Cody's Cocktails was located.

We walked into a neat living area, half lounge, half kitchen. It was immaculate, save for a scorch mark along one wall that drew my eye. Wendy must have noticed me looking. "Howie was in one of his 'naturally induced' trances almost two weeks ago, and I came in from the garden to find him trying fire breathing with tequila and the lighter for the gas barbecue. If I hadn't found him, he would have burned the house down."

"Looks like he tried."

"Next morning, he claimed he didn't remember a thing."

My dad blew out his cheeks. "Wow. So, he's enjoying retirement, then?"

I narrowed my eyes at him. "Don't get any ideas, Dad. There's plenty of safe things to do here without trying to burn Ada-Mae's apartment down." Wendy smiled thinly, and I remembered the state she had been in when we had first come across her. "Sorry," I said. "What were you going to show us?"

She disappeared into the bedroom and came out holding a small statue. It brought the Dargi one to mind, although it was clearly different. The faded bronze casting was similar and about the same size. But instead of the vaguely amphibian creature of the Dargi, this was more like a humanoid octopus or squid. It had suckers on its fingers and tentacles coming from the side of its face, like a strange sort of beard. Just as repulsive, though, I felt. Give me a cat statue any day.

I looked at Ada-Mae, who had paled and was staring at the statue wide-eyed. She attempted to speak and failed, then cleared her throat for the second attempt. "It's... um, ancient. Norse, I think."

Wendy seemed nonplussed. "Oh, yes, whatever. It's not the statue I'm worried about, but what is inside it." With one hand at the top and one at the bottom, she made a quick twisting motion, and the statue came apart. She held out the bottom half toward us, tilting it so that we could get a good look. The inside of the statue's bottom half was hollowed out into a sort of bowl, and it was two-thirds filled with some sort of yellow-white powder.

"Oh," Ada-Mae said.

"Oh," Wendy agreed. "Is this what I think it is? He had this hidden at the back of the closet, silly man. As if I wouldn't find it. I don't know much about these things, but let's just say it's a lot more than they ever catch someone with on *Cops*."

"It might not be what you think it is," I offered.

"Then why did he hide it?

"Because it's so ugly?"

Wendy ignored my comment and looked at Ada-Mae. "What am I going to do? Maybe I should turn him into the police myself before it gets any worse. Maybe they'll go lenient on an old fool."

"Do you know where he got it?" I asked.

This time, Wendy looked at me like I was speaking an alien language. "Does it matter?"

Maybe it did. "Does he ever go north up the beach, past the golf course?"

Wendy almost shrieked out her exasperation and frustration. "I never know where that man goes anymore." I felt for her. She seemed at the end of her tether. I remembered the previous morning at Cody's Cocktails and the large number of similar-looking statues lined up behind the bar. We had started with burglaries, but things were getting a lot more serious. Perhaps someone had taken Ada-Mae's idol not because they knew it to be valuable in itself. Maybe they had thought it contained something valuable. Valuable and illegal.

"Does the guy from the cocktail bar... Cody... does he ever come around the retirement center?" I looked at Ada-Mae, but she was giving me almost the same look Wendy was. My dad just looked confused.

Ada-Mae laid a hand on Wendy's wrist. "Look, just hang onto

it for now. Attend the academy tomorrow, and we'll deal with it afterward, I promise. We'll speak to Howie."

Wendy nodded, seeming a little better. The poor woman—she had been coping alone so far with her husband's apparent self-destruction.

"Are you okay?" I asked Ada-Mae a few minutes after we left the house. She had been quiet, lost in her own thoughts.

"Yes. It's just... that idol. The statue Wendy had, the one belonging to Howie. It looked familiar."

"It's like your Dargi idol... the same vibe. But it couldn't have been real if she could just twist it apart like that. Not a genuine antique like yours."

"No," Ada-Mae agreed. "But I think it might be related. A sea god in the wide range of ancient deities." She became animated, a finger shooting up in the air. "Got it! Ri'hek. That's the one. Kind of similar to Dargi, I think. A god who brings the ocean to the land. Or bridges realms, or something."

She cocked her head toward the two of us. "How strange is that? I would love to know where Howie got it."

I balked a little. "From drug dealers would be my guess. The sort of people you don't want to know at all. I think the owner of the cocktail bar near the end of the golf course might have something to do with it. I saw similar statues right there on display along the back of the bar. Perhaps he is dealing drugs in those statues. Selling them like they are souvenirs to keep the police off his scent."

My dad grinned, but I couldn't help but notice some concern in his tone. "What sort of town do you live in here, you two?"

I opened my mouth to protest but remembered the murders that had also happened. "Well," I said, "it's never dull."

"I'm not even convinced that stuff was drugs in the statue," Ada-Mae said.

"What else is he going to hide at the back of the closet?" I asked, channeling my inner Wendy. "Fitness supplements?"

"I'd rather not say until I'm sure. I'm going to call Wendy when we get back and ask her to bring it along tomorrow morning."

"To the witches' academy?" my dad asked. He seemed excited by the idea.

"Yes. We've still got a ritual to perform," Ada-Mae said. "Ideally, tomorrow night. Tomorrow's session will be a busy one, and maybe we'll get to the bottom of all this."

CHAPTER

EIGHT

E rnie had been absent all day. Perhaps he wanted Ada-Mae
and me to get some quality family time with my dad,
which we did, popping over to the Atlantic Diner for a
meal together.

The following morning, Ernie turned up right on time to the
Game of Thrones Room, where Ada-Mae secretly held her Quipley's School of Magic. He politely said "hello" to me and my dad,
nodded to Ada-Mae, and then took a seat next to Judd. Howie
looked almost presentable today in stonewashed jeans and a
smiley-face T-shirt. "Almost" was the operative word.

Something was up. I was sure of it.

I noticed Ada-Mae take Wendy to one side when she and Howie arrived, and Wendy secretly slipped the statue across to her while Howie took his seat, oblivious. I hoped that it wasn't drugs in the statue that my almost eighty-year-old grandmother had taken into her possession.

"Morning, class," Ada-Mae said. "We're going to start today with a little fun with crystals. One rather large crystal, actually, which Zoe is kindly letting us borrow from her shop." Almost everyone looked at Zoe, who smiled uncomfortably at the attention and stared at her hands.

Ada-Mae picked up what was more of a cluster than an individual crystal, a large amethyst structure with perhaps a dozen spurs of differing lengths, all roughly hexagonal around the outside. "Now. As I stand here at the front of the class, I would like each of you to come up in turn and gently place your fingers against it. Then, we'll see if we can make it light up together."

There was an excited murmur throughout the class, although the tone of one or two sounded doubtful. After my exploding cucumber trick, I rather expected everyone to have an open mind on what was possible. Maybe they were worried about an exploding crystal, which would be a little more dangerous, no doubt.

Wendy was the first to go up, and after several seconds, the class could see a purplish glow briefly swell to life deep within the crystal. Maybe a cynic would assume an embedded LED inside the cluster with a button or dial hidden somewhere on Ada-Mae's side of the crystal. For all I knew, maybe there was. Maybe this was just a bit of fun because Ada-Mae had not told me about it or let me know anything about the purpose of the exercise.

Howie was up next. Almost immediately, as soon as he placed his fingers upon it, the crystal glowed. It swelled to several times the brightness it had with Wendy, then faded again. Although she tried to keep stoic, I noticed a little surprise in my grandmother's eyes. This was a test of some sort. I was sure of it.

Soon, it was my turn, and although I wanted to impress, memories of the other day had me breathing slowly to calm myself. I thought I caught a little nervousness in Ada-Mae's eyes as our gazes met. As soon as I touched the crystal, I could feel myself connected to Ada-Mae, clearly sensing her on the other side of it. The crystal flared so bright it pained my eyes to stare at it without me even having to think about it happening. It stayed like that for a couple of seconds before dying away again. There were murmurs of surprise behind me, and when I turned, I noticed Zoe staring at me.

Indeed, Zoe was the next one up, and although the crystal again flared brightly, it was not as blinding as it had been on my turn.

Ernie was next, and there was an embarrassing thirty seconds until I thought I saw a brief flicker somewhere deep inside it. Ernie blushed and cleared his throat before stepping aside, but not before I noticed a hint of disappointment in his eyes. Judd followed, and it surprised me to see that his light was almost as bright as Howie's had been. If this was some test of magical potential, as I was guessing, the ex-astronaut certainly had something inside him. Ada-Mae offered the crystal to my dad, but Jacob declined on the grounds of being an observer.

After that, Ada-Mae talked about potions and rituals without so much as a mention of what had just happened, giving the whole thing the feel of a warm-up exercise. Yet, when the session finished and everyone was about to leave, she called out several names of students that she wanted to stay behind. "Sidney, Zoe, Judd, Howie, and Wendy, if I could have a quick word, please."

We gathered at the front of the class as everyone else left. My dad, bless him, turned to leave, and Ada-Mae called after him. "You stay, too, Jacob," she laughed. "I thought that went without saying." She came over and looked at all of us, finally settling on Wendy. Howie and Zoe were standing next to each other, the younger woman giving him the occasional sideways glare. If Howie remembered being banned from Zoe's store, he didn't show any sign of it.

Wendy nodded to a silent question from Ada-Mae, and my grandmother brought out the statue Howie had hidden at the back of his closet. Howie's eyes went wide, and he appeared to be holding his breath. *Busted!* After a moment of utter shock, his eyes slid across to Wendy. Now he just looked hurt... betrayed.

"This is yours, Howie?" Ada-Mae asked.

Howie didn't answer straight away, and he kept looking at Wendy. Eventually, she wilted a little and looked away from him. "Yes," Howie murmured.

Ada-Mae twisted it as Wendy had done at the Rockford house, separating the two halves and exposing the off-white powder within it. Howie's eyes went even wider. "Look," he said, "holding up a hand. I didn't know that was in there."

"Where did you get it from, Howie?" Wendy asked the question at a high pitch, half-bark and half-scream."

"I... I found it!"

"Rubbish!" Wendy shrieked. I could hear months of frustration at her husband's increasingly erratic and irresponsible behavior now coming to a head for Wendy.

Ada-Mae held up a hand to soothe her. "No, no. It's okay, Wendy. I think he's telling the truth. Where did you find it, Howie?"

"I was nosing around those fancy beach-front properties at the other end of the town."

"Mystic Dunes?" I put in. We knew them well.

"Yes. And... well, there were several like it at the back of one of the properties."

"And you stole one?" Wendy asked.

Howie hung his head a little. "I know I shouldn't have. I just liked them and...."

"What?" Ada-Mae pushed.

"I felt drawn to them."

"There would be a reason for that." Ada-Mae took a step forward and held out the bottom half of the statue toward me. "Sidney, if you would be so good as to touch a fingertip to the powder."

I looked at her like she was a little crazy. Would she want me to touch it to my tongue next? Isn't that what the DEA cops did on those crime-drama shows? No, thank you!

"It's okay, Sidney," she said. "Trust me." She had me there. Whatever difficulties there had been between us in the past few days and however many of her spells I had seen that didn't quite go according to plan, I trusted her. With everything inside me.

I reached forward and touched my right index finger to the powder. The instant I did so, the powder started to fizz, and a thick, dark green smoke wafted up from it. "What the...?" I snatched my hand back, and after a moment, the smoke coming from the powder dwindled to nothing. I looked at my grandmother.

"It's nothing illegal," she said, looking around at the others as well. "Although it is a little unpleasant. The powder is a sort of magical reagent made mostly of powdered bone. Animal bone... probably." She shrugged, leaving the "probably" part to every-one's imagination.

"Uuugh!" I said, wiping my finger on my shirt, then wishing I had wiped it somewhere else.

"Don't worry," she said. "There won't be so much as a trace of it on your finger. It reacts strongly to your innate magic. To any magical potential."

"It was just like the smoke in your stolen idol," I said.

"Yes. There must have been a similar reagent sealed into the Dargi statue. And your magic is so strong, Sidney, that you caused a reaction merely by handling the outside of the statue."

That was right. I remembered that the Dargi statue had leaked the smoke soon after I had handled it. I frowned and looked at my grandmother again. "What does this all mean?"

"I think it means that Sam Barlow and whoever he is working with were getting ready to do a powerful ritual of their own. I believe the statues with the reagents in them were left outside to charge. Either in the sunlight or the moonlight, depending on the purpose of the ritual."

"This puts Sam Barlow in the frame for stealing your statue," I said. "If he realized how powerful it was," I pointed to the two halves of the statue Howie had taken, "then maybe he wanted it for what they were doing."

"Excuse me." It was Zoe, the magic shop owner. "Are we talking about Sam Barlow? 'Savvy' Sam, the realtor?"

I nodded. "And I suspect he's a member of an evil coven of witches."

Zoe appeared thoughtful as if assessing this possibility. She didn't outright shoot the idea down, which was encouraging.

"Which brings me to the test I conducted at the start of the session," Ada-Mae said. "I'm sorry to do things this way and to put what I'm about to put on all of you, but this needs to be done now. And I need your help."

CHAPTER

NINE

"Oh, wow. That looks interesting," Ada-Mae said as we passed the Crystal Beach police station in the Rockford's vintage minivan. Judd's little joy ride would not fit everyone in it this time, so Wendy Rockford was our ride—and, well... getaway driver—for the evening. The sun had recently set, and we were on our way to the Mystic Dunes housing development.

I was next to Ada-Mae in the middle row of seats, with Judd, Howie, and Zoe squashed together in the back row and my dad and Wendy up front. Apparently, Howie's theft of the idol had lost him front-seat privileges in Wendy's book.

Ada-Mae was passing comments on the sea of cats that had gathered outside the police station. As we watched, Jessie and John emerged from the entrance and attempted to wade through them to reach their patrol car. The way all the cats followed Jessie and gathered around her legs, you'd think she had bathed in catnip. My grandmother turned back to me, her eyes narrowing as a slow suspicious grin formed across her lips. "Attempted that love spell by yourself, did we?"

I wilted. *Busted.* To be honest, I had wondered after seeing so many cats gathered around the patrol car the previous day. *Here we go. Be more responsible, Sidney.* Instead, Ada-Mae smiled. "Well, no one can doubt your power. I know I've been hard on you, Sidney. But it's only because I know how great you could be. I promise, once this ritual is done with, we'll make time to work on some spells together."

I smiled back, reaching out and squeezing her hand. "That would mean so much to me." As I turned back to the others in the back seat, I could see Zoe staring down the road, back toward the police station. I looked across at the other two. Howie, who I was pretty sure could not be trusted with magic without supervision, looked like he was lip-synching something as Judd eyed him curiously.

"Hey," I said to Ada-Mae. "Have you noticed how quiet and, well... absent Ernie has been the last few days?"

Ada-Mae shrugged though she wasn't much of an actor.

"I've never met anyone as enthusiastic about magic as Ernie," I said. "He had all the faith before he saw any of the proof." Ada-Mae's jaw remained set, and she stared straight ahead. "I mean, I think it was mostly because he wanted to be friends with you. But all the same, it must be hard to realize he doesn't have any magical potential. Especially when everyone he cares about is in this car right now.

Finally, Ada-Mae shook her head. "I can't think about that right now."

"Soon, though, right?" I prompted. "The things we don't take care of can get lost. You're the one who told me that."

We passed through the middle of town and took the left-hand turnoff onto the road that went past the site of the Crystal Beach Mini-Golf Invitational—the road to Mystic Dunes. Judd already knew all about Mystic Dunes and Sam Barlow, even if he was surprised to find himself on this evening's excursion.

Zoe, Howie, and Wendy had taken Ada-Mae's request surprisingly well, though. "Please break into this place and help me perform a high-level magical ritual" was likely not what anyone had expected after just two sessions at Quipley's School of Magic.

Maybe Zoe, as the owner of a magic shop and someone who clearly had powers of her own, was not so surprised. I suspected Howie was up for anything that might give him a buzz, and Wendy was just hoping to get her Howie back at some point. Perhaps indulging his craziness with other people was better than him doing it unsupervised.

And my dad, Jacob Grace, was as awesome as ever. I felt like we had hardly spent any proper time together since he had arrived. But he was staying for Ada-Mae's birthday, which was coming up next week, so we would make time soon. As the outline of the beachfront properties loomed before us, I cleared my mind of all other worries and distractions. I needed to be on my "A" game tonight.

～

"THEY NEED to improve the security around these places," Howie Rockford said as we settled into the living area in the same house where we had recently traversed a portal that led to a janitor's closet at the Spectrum Space Center.

"And it's notable that nobody lives in any of them still," I pointed out. It was odd, to be fair, that Sam left these places unguarded. There wasn't even an alarm system installed. Ada-Mae had some lock picks in that magical shawl of hers, so we had that advantage, but it was otherwise way too easy to trespass on the properties of Mystic Dunes. All the same, Wendy and my dad had stayed outside in the car, keeping watch for us.

Inside, there were no signs of ongoing or recently undertaken magical rituals in the space like the last time we were here. We opened the French doors at the back of the living room that led out onto a wide area of decking just yards from the lapping waves of the ocean and eyed the space where we would perform the ritual.

The ritual itself was simple. No drawing runes on the decking —or even a protective circle, which Ada-Mae said would kind of defeat the point. Ada-Mae stood with the idol clutched to her chest. And the four of us stood around her, each in a position corresponding to one of the cardinal directions. I was on the northern side, representing fire. Judd was in the east, aligned to the air. Zoe was opposite me in the south, representing earth, and then Howie was in the west, for water. Which was ironic because the sea was to the east. I thought better of pointing this out.

"You all need to lay hands upon me," Ada-Mae said. "Not only so you can lend me your strength, but also, hopefully, so the effects of the ritual will be transferred to all of you. Then you will see whatever the spirits have to show us."

We did as we were told, although the other three placed their hands on her a little more awkwardly since they did not know her as well. When Ada-Mae spoke the ritual words, they were not the sort of rhyming chant that her spells often were. They were more like a speech, an impassioned plea.

"Oh, great spirits of the land and the sea. Spirits of the in-between and of the other side. Hear my voice in this time of great need. We need your guidance. We need your wisdom to show us the way."

I felt a trickle of warmth moving through me, the way a heated seat slowly spreads its benefit through a chilled body. The evening was also warm, with almost no breeze, making the sensation feel even stranger.

"Dark powers use this place for their own nefarious gain," Ada-Mae continued. "We must see their purpose so that we may keep our precious town in the light. We must understand and prepare defenses. Reveal to us their secret plans. Why build where no one else would? Where the sea will reclaim—"

Ada-Mae stopped speaking as the ground rumbled beneath our feet for a moment, the deck shifting, although not enough for anyone to lose their balance. Howie let out a gasp followed by what I thought was a curse word. He removed his hand and took a step back, as did Judd.

"Don't!" I said, feeling the connection and the building power drain away the moment they did so. I already understood what was happening before Ada-Mae spoke.

"There is a dark presence here," she said. "Some spirit or malign force guards this place. It resists us, but if we stay connected, it is not powerful enough to harm us."

Judd and Howie needed no more convincing to lay their hands on Ada-Mae again. I watched as Ada-Mae's forehead creased with concentration, sweat forming on her brow. This was taking its toll on her, so I reached deep inside myself, hoping to send more of my strength to her.

"If you will not tell us their purpose," Ada-Mae said, "then at least show us something of what we are facing."

The moment that Ada-Mae spoke those words, the same greenish mist I had seen twice in the past few days poured out of the idol. Thicker than it had previously been, there was an inner glow inside the mist, pulsing a little like lightning in the heart of a storm system.

It snaked right past me, and as it moved further from the idol, the mist revealed a stream of glowing green particles reminiscent of tiny fireflies. It kept going past the side of the house.

"Go!" Ada-Mae bellowed. "Follow that... sparkle!"

I opened a gate set into the fence surrounding the decking and was first around the side of the building. I could see the Rockford's car and the sparkling trail streaked straight over the top of it and along the road that led toward town.

"Quick," Ada-Mae said as I slid open the vehicle's side passenger door, "follow that sparkle!"

She pointed beyond the windshield, and both my dad and Wendy peered through it and down the road. "What sparkle?" my dad said after a moment.

Ada-Mae put a palm to her forehead. "Of course. You can't see it because you weren't a part of the ritual. Just... just... drive!"

We all hopped into the back of the car without enough time to put our seatbelts on before Wendy darted down the road after something she couldn't see.

CHAPTER

TEN

"We're heading into the center of town," Judd said. We had taken a right at the end of the road onto Mangrove Street, the long thoroughfare that cut right through the middle of Crystal Beach. The sparkling green trail was still making its undulating way along the street in front of us, unseen by the cars and pedestrians it passed.

"I have no idea where it's taking us," Ada-Mae admitted. I thought that it might take us to Sam's real estate office, but we had already passed that turnoff. Unless it was taking us to Sam himself, and he was somewhere in town.

Then, suddenly, the glowing green trail veered left, and Ada-Mae screamed at Wendy to turn. The poor woman veered across the road, earning a long horn blast from a surprised driver coming the other way.

"Ain't this just the best buzz ever?" Howie said from the rear of the car. "We should do this more often."

We were on a long, wide road with trees on either side, and in the dark, I didn't realize where we were until we reached the end of it. Then I saw the familiar outline of the oldest building in Crystal Beach. Or so I had been told.

"The guest house," Wendy whispered. The Rose Garden, to be specific. Rose and Rodney Gantzes' home and business. Tonight, it towered above us all in darkness, its porch and rose bushes eerily lit up by the car's headlights, which Wendy now switched off.

"Rose and Rodney are away," Ada-Mae said. "I saw Rose in the market last week. She said they had no bookings and were going to see family in Tampa for a few days."

"Why would your ritual lead us to an empty guest house?" Zoe asked.

"But it isn't empty." my dad said. He leaned forward, pointing toward a dim light inside one of the upstairs rooms.

"What do we do?" Wendy asked. "Call the police?"

Ada-Mae shook her head. "If whoever is in there is who we are looking for, then I'm not sure that the police can help us." She slid the side door of the vehicle open and stepped out.

I put a hand on her shoulder. "You're kidding me, right?"

Ada-Mae gave me a hard look. She was not about to be dissuaded.

"Then I'm coming too," I said.

"Family breaking and entering time, then," my dad said, unbuckling his seatbelt. Judd, Zoe, and Howie followed, quickly piling out of the van.

I turned to Wendy. "Turn the van around. Be ready to burn it out of here." Wendy shook her head in agreement, but I could see the alarm in her eyes.

Stepping out of the car, I could see the dwindling cloud of green sparkles hanging over the roof of the house. This was our place, and I suddenly felt woefully ill-prepared to face whatever was inside. The brave people around me gave me hope, yet I knew that in any confrontation, they would rely on me being able to make use of my power. To control and focus it. Not to explode vegetables.

I looked down as a black cat appeared out of nowhere and wrapped itself around my legs, before trotting off across the lawn and into the darkness. *Oh well, here we go.*

Like the strangest Scooby-Doo Gang ever, we did our best to stroll purposefully up toward the guest house. Then the flood-lights came on.

They blinded all of us. Howie even collapsed to his knees, clutching his eyes, and Zoe staggered backward a couple of steps, letting out an odd hissing sound. I did my best to stare into it, shielding my eyes as best I could. A familiar voice came from behind the lights.

"Sidney?" called out Chief John Reece. "That you?" The lights, which were fixed to the top of a police car on the far side of the house, dipped a little, so at least we weren't all blinded anymore. "Who else is that? Ada-Mae? Howie? Zoe? And who's that in the car?"

I crossed over toward John and spotted Jessie next to the car too. The car was tucked back on the far side of the lawn, almost in the tree line. At least a dozen cats were around it, several rubbing themselves on Jessie's legs. *Man, when was this dang attraction spell going to wear off?*

"What are you guys doing here?" I hissed.

That took John by surprise. "What do you mean? We're the police. On a stakeout. What the—"

He didn't get to finish as a loud sound from the rear of the property made us all look over. In the darkness, I could see the silhouette of a person running away from the guest house.

"Oh, heck!" John exclaimed, and he and Jessie ran after the figure. As did several of the cats. "Stop right there!"

A moment later, there was a splash, and we all ran after the two members of the Crystal Beach Police Department and their suspect. The fleeing villain had, in the darkness, rushed into the large pond where Rose kept her prized koi fish. We caught up just as John was hauling the man from the pond. He was dripping wet, head to toe, but I still recognized him. The man had sold me a lovely cat statue several days before.

"Got you!" John said, then turned to the rest of us. "This is our burglar. A genuine one-man crime spree.

"Preposterous!" the antique dealer spat. Although after being caught in the act, he needed to make a convincing argument.

"Don't try it," Jessie warned. "We've already been to your motel room just outside of town. A treasure trove of stolen objects."

John looked at Ada-Mae. "Even an ugly amphibian statue. I owe you an apology." Ada-Mae made a gracious shake of the head. "Although I see you found a replacement," he added, nodding to the statue that Ada-Mae was still clutching.

"And the stuff inside isn't even drugs," Howie put in. Helpful but not helpful.

John frowned but appeared to let it go for the moment. He looked at the perp again. "How you knew the location of so many valuable objects in one little seaside town is beyond me, though."

Out of the corner of my eye, I saw a tiny wisp of smoke escape from the idol. The green sparkles drifted across to the suave older man—though not so suave now while covered in pond water—unseen by him, John, and Jessie but witnessed by the rest of us. The sparkling dust settled on some sort of pin fixed to the front of the black zip-up hoodie the antique dealer was wearing. I reached out and pulled the pin free.

"Hey!" he said.

I turned it over in my fingers. It was a gray metal, like dull brushed steel, and shaped like the head of a gargoyle. An ugly thing, all in all. I held it up. "I think it had something to do with this." The man's eyes went wide.

John looked at me like he knew what I was going to say next. "One of those things you don't want to know the answer to," I told him.

He looked at the six of us. "Like why the lot of you are all here so late at night," he said. He sounded serious, but there was a wry grin in there somewhere.

"Yep. Like that."

WE WAITED by Wendy's vehicle while the antique dealer who had single-handedly been responsible for more than half-a-dozen burglaries and thefts during his brief stay in Crystal Beach was put into the back of the patrol car.

"You think that pin is what drew the spell all the way here?" Ada-Mae asked me as we leaned against the car.

I screwed up my face, thinking of the gargoyle-faced pin that had helped the suave antiques dealer locate things of monetary value in Crystal Beach. "I don't know. But I am certain that dark powers made that pin. When I held it, I could feel the strength of that power. I guess if there were no answers at Mystic Dunes for us, then the spell drew us to the nearest source of dark magic."

Ada-Mae looked at the guest house, the spell cloud still hovering over the building. "Maybe that was him and his pin. But The Rose Garden is an old building that I bet has seen a few dark deeds in its time. Maybe there is another reason the ritual brought us here."

"Yes, maybe there is something more to it. I wonder what he was after in there," I mused.

"I'm curious to know that myself."

"Do you think there's any connection to what he had hoped to find and the strange things going on at Mystic Dunes?" I said, pushing my glasses up on my nose.

"I'd bet my witch's hat on it! And I'm not so sure we won't find Savvy Sam in the middle of it. You and I have our work cut out for us, Sid."

I nodded in agreement and traded winks with Ada-Mae before I noticed John coming over. I pushed away from the side of the car, heading him off. "You got your man, then?"

"The arrogant fool left all the evidence in his hotel room."

"And what about the idols at Cody's beach bar? Was he in on it too?" I asked.

"No, those were actually Cody's statues that he collects and keeps out on display. No connection to the burglary." He glanced over at Ada-Mae. "We'll get your grandmother her statue back as soon as we can."

I shrugged. "Take your time. Now that she knows it's not a replica, she wants to find a historical museum to donate it to."

John looked down at me, his eyes smiling but serious. "I owe you an apology, Sidney. Obviously, it didn't turn out to be Sam Barlow. But I was still out of line, speaking to you the way I did."

On instinct, I reached out my hand, my fingers lightly brushing the back of his hand.

"You can make it up to me over dinner...because we are

overdue to celebrate your promotion, Chief Reece," I said with a wink and a smile.

I noticed the twinkle in his eyes as he turned his hand over, so his fingertips touched my own. "That's a date."

ENJOYING the Crystal Beach Magic Mystery Series? Then why miss your favorite characters in Crystal Beach for a single minute when you can start the next book in the series today?

If you love quirky characters, an enchanting town, fun mysteries, a little magic, a talking cat, and a good dose of humor, then you will find yourself binge-reading this series! Turn the page to start the next book.

Next in Series:

Magic in this witch's family has a name: Trouble.

In the bewitching town of Crystal Beach, life is anything but ordinary, and for psychic witch Sidney Grace, the mystery and family drama is just beginning.

For starters, her ghostly grandfather pushes her to uncover the secrets hidden within an ancient guest house. He believes it holds a dangerous magical item, and Sidney's determined to get to the bottom of it.

What's even more disturbing, the sleepy development of Mystic Dunes suddenly finds itself buzzing with new residents. How did they all move in overnight, and what secrets do they bring with them?

If her to-do list wasn't long enough already, Sidney has fallen behind in planning her grandmother's surprise 80th birthday party. With time ticking away, she must conjure up a celebration that will leave her beloved Grams spellbound.

Can Sidney juggle her family's drama, unveil the secrets of the Rose Garden, and pull off the party of the century? Find out in this whimsical and mysterious tale that will leave you spellbound!

Turn the page to join Sidney, Ada-Mae, Mojo and the unforgettable residents of Crystal Beach in Witch in the Middle, the seventh installment of the Crystal Beach Magic Mystery Series.

~

KAREN MCSPADE

WITCH IN THE MIDDLE

A Crystal Beach Paranormal Cozy Mystery
Book Seven

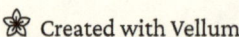 Created with Vellum

FREE GIFT

Receive your FREE copy of **Dog Gone Troubles**, the Crystal Beach Magic Mystery series prequel, and get notified via email of new releases, giveaways, contests, cover reveals, and insider fun when you sign up for my Mystery Book Club mailing list!

Scan the QR Code To Sign Up and Claim Your FREE Exclusive Book

NOTE: If you're already a member of my VIP Mystery Book Club, your email will not be added again.

CHAPTER
ONE

"Don't you just love it when people die?"

The three of us—me, Ada-Mae, and my dad, Jacob—all just sort of looked at Eileen McCann, the owner of the Kelp Seafood Restaurant and Grill in Crystal Beach.

"Um..." my dad said after a long, awkward moment.

"Well, I suppose that depends on who it is," Ada-Mae answered, earning her a "what the heck?" look from me.

"I prefer if it isn't me doing the dying," I said.

We were sitting at a table inside Eileen's restaurant. We had come in for breakfast, as my dad had been in Crystal Beach for about a week and hadn't yet visited the best restaurant in town. Well, the food was good. Eileen was, um...

"My aunt died the other week and left me a sizeable sum of money," she beamed.

"I'm sorry for your loss," I said.

"Oh, I didn't know her. Not really. She moved to Australia when I was twelve."

"But she left you money?" Ada-Mae said.

"Benefits of a small family. We McCann's aren't big on marriage and children."

"You won't be giving up the restaurant business, will you?" Ada-Mae said, sounding alarmed.

"It wasn't *that* much money."

"But enough to leave the cleaning job?" I asked. When Ada-Mae's ancient tribal idol had been stolen the previous week amid a town-wide crime spree, I had, it now pained me to admit, briefly thought of Eileen as a suspect. Mainly because she had taken a morning cleaning position at the Shifting Sands Retirement Center with plenty of opportunity and means to take the idol. Thankfully, we caught the real thief... or Eileen might have fallen under suspicion again when out of seemingly nowhere, she comes into money and can quit her morning cleaning job. Coincidence, I know, but my brain tracks these kinds of details.

"Enough to ensure Kelp Seafood Grill will be running for a while yet." Eileen glanced around the restaurant, where a few of the other tables had customers at them. "I wouldn't sell this place for anything. They will carry me out of here in a wooden box."

Well, there was a cheery thought. Seriously, though, I wasn't sure I had ever seen Eileen this happy and positive. A ray of sunshine where she was often an angry little cloud.

"So, what can I get you?" she asked.

"Shrimp scramble, please," my dad said eagerly. He had been

hearing about Eileen's breakfasts all week and was chomping at the bit to try her food.

Eileen flushed and then put a palm to her forehead. "What is wrong with me this morning? I didn't put the sign out."

We all gave her a questioning look, and she glanced down at the table.

"And I left out the usual menus." Eileen rolled her eyes and shook her head. I hadn't ever seen Eileen giving herself a hard time before. I had, of course, been on the other end of Eileen giving a hard time to someone else.

"Usual menu?" said my dad, disappointment evident at the edge of his voice.

"I'm doing vegan breakfasts all week."

"In a seafood restaurant?" My dad sounded like his day was ruined already.

"Vegans are taking over the world," Eileen said. "Got to stay with the times if I want a business five years from now."

Eileen handed out several menus, and I tried to pick up the mood as I looked at the choices. "Look, Dad. There's vegan eggs Benedict. It comes with avocado and vegan bacon on sourdough toast." Unfortunately, my enthusiasm was not rubbing off. In fact, he glared at the choices on the menu like they were offending him.

"To be honest," Eileen said, ignoring my dad, "I just fancied a bit of a challenge. A chance to create some new menu items. My vegan options have been lacking until now. I might even include the most successful dish as an option on the main menu going forward."

My dad and I ordered the faux eggs Benedict, while Ada-Mae ordered avocado on sourdough toast. As she collected the menus from us, Eileen fixed me with a look. After a few moments, I grew a little uncomfortable under her scrutiny. Even in a good mood,

Eileen just naturally came off as haughty and bothered. But she was all bark and no bite.

"The real reason I forgot to put the sign out and left out the wrong menus is that it's too much for me all on my own," Eileen said. "I'm the waitress and head cook, and I double as the dishwasher. This money means I can afford to hire some full-time help. Are you interested, Sidney? Apart from moonlighting for the police, you were quite a good employee when I did the food truck at the mini-golf tournament."

Okay, the world really was about to end. Something that sounded almost like a compliment slipped from Eileen McCann's lips. Yet, despite how snarky and cantankerous Eileen could be much of the time, a part of me was attracted to the offer she presented. The restaurant was the hub of the town in many ways. Eileen made the best food and had incredible taste, from the color of the decor to the art on the walls and even the table decorations. The Kelp Seafood Grill was a cozy place to be in, and being paid to spend big parts of my day in it was appealing. On the other hand, it was a matter of pure joy that I could afford to say "no" to her.

"Thanks, Eileen. If you had asked me a few days ago, I would have bitten your hand off for a job here. But I've just recently gotten a new job."

Eileen raised her left brow, looking surprised.

Ada-Mae beamed with pride. "Sidney's been hired to write a regular weekly article for *Living It Large In Boston Magazine*."

Eileen's face creased in confusion. "Didn't you work for them already? And aren't they, you know... in Boston?"

Two good points, but Eileen wasn't stealing my thunder out from under me. "It was only a casual arrangement," I replied. "That they might buy the occasional article from me. This is a weekly lifestyle column about living in a van, on the beach, in Florida. It's not paying a fortune, but enough to keep me comfortable as long as, you know... I keep living in my van on the beach and don't have actual rent to pay."

Eileen nodded. For the first time, I thought I saw something like respect in the way she looked at me. "Well, good for you, Sidney." She turned to go. "Food won't be long."

I looked at my dad, who still appeared glum. "It'll be great, I promise," I told him. "Everything Eileen cooks is delicious."

"But it won't be shrimp," he grumbled.

"Cheer up, Jacob," Ada-Mae chided. She continued to regard him as he poured each of us a glass of water. "And no offense, I love having my 'no-longer son-in-law' around, but have you got any other plans for your time off?" There was a way that Ada-Mae said "time off" that grabbed my attention.

She had been having some of the same thoughts as me, I guessed. While I didn't want to question my dad outright, I wondered why he suddenly decided to retire. He had always loved his job, but maybe he was rethinking his life after the divorce. It was a subject I would have to carefully broach with him later.

"You'll stay for my birthday, I hope?" she added.

"Of course," my dad said. "Wouldn't miss it for the world."

Ada-Mae would be eighty in just two days. Maybe I was biased, but I didn't think she looked much older than she did when I was a teenager.

My dad put down the water jug and sighed, his eyes now fixed on the table and not on either of us. "Look, I've been trying to find a way to say this all week. I'm... I've..."

"Yes?" I pushed, unable to stop myself.

"The firm let me go."

As much as I already had my suspicions that something was up with my dad's random visit, I couldn't stop myself from feeling a little shocked. "Why? Why would they do that?"

"Well, you know. Young blood coming through and all that."

"Young blood?" I said without thinking, my face scrunched in confusion. "In finance?"

"Yes, Sidney. It does happen, you know. It's a place for sharp, young minds, as well as experience. Whatever you might think."

I gave my dad a lop-sided smile of apology.

"All the same," Ada-Mae said. "How can they just push you out? And at your age."

My dad blushed at that as a sigh escaped from his lips.

"Surely there's a pension or something?" she added.

"Yes. But I can't get my hands on that right now." My dad wrung his hands together in a kind of nervous gesture. "Look, I'm not about to run out of money or anything. Not this soon. But I need to find another job at some point. I'm... I'm sorry I lied about being retired. I need to find something else to do, though. And I'm just not sure I want that to be in finance again."

I looked long and hard at my dad. This still did not quite compute. Who was Jacob Grace if he didn't work in finance? I wasn't sure my brain could deal with those thoughts on top of magic, talking cats, and evil covens, too. So I changed the subject.

"I haven't seen much of Ernie in the last week," I said to Ada-Mae, my index finger innocently drawing an invisible, ever-decreasing spiral on the table. "Have you?"

Ada-Mae stiffened. In fact, it seemed like she had stopped breathing; she was so still. "No," she said eventually.

I took a sideways glance at my dad. Nothing was ever too sensitive to talk about in front of Jacob Grace. He was one of those easy-going, approachable, unassuming people. Plus, even though he wasn't married to her daughter anymore, he and Ada-Mae would always be close. It was just how things were.

"Put yourself in Ernie's shoes. He's been your—for want of a better word—wingman with magic and everything else that's been going on from before there was any school of magic. He believed you and had faith in you when no one else did. Including your own daughter."

My dad shuffled his feet and nodded in recognition. He knew all too well about his ex-wife's utter lack of belief in and complete hatred of magic. Of course, certain events during her recent visit to Crystal Beach might have made it hard for her to hold onto her disbelief of unseen magical forces, although it very well could have deepened her loathing of wizardry.

I went on. "And then Ernie finds out he doesn't have a shred of magic in his entire body. I can only imagine how... disappointed that made him feel."

Ada-Mae's jaw moved from side to side. "Well, a fraction of a shred, maybe. I mean, every living thing has some magical potential. Although I think the begonia in my bedroom window might have more mojo than Ernie does."

"Maybe don't tell him that, eh? I mean, poor Ernie. After finding he has no magical potential to speak of, his other best friend, Judd, the astronaut, makes it into the witch squad for the Mystic Dunes raid last week. And Judd initially only turned up to Quipley's School of Magic to support his friend."

Ada-Mae huffed, although she sounded a little like a snorting horse. "What am I, a counselor?"

"You're supposed to be his friend. And, more than that, you know he...."

My dad looked back and forth between the two of us, keen to hear what was about to be said. His eyes settled on me as the candidate most likely to spill the beans. "Yes?"

I kept my eyes fixed on Ada-Mae. "How he feels about you."

Ada-Mae's chin jutted stubbornly skywards. "Well, he hasn't said anything."

I felt myself going red in the face. Did my grandmother not notice Ernie's affections? Or was she playing innocent in front of

Jacob? For a woman who could see the unseen, surely, she could see what was clearly right in front of her.

Then I noticed her shoulders relax in some sort of signal of surrender. When she spoke, she mostly hissed her reply, even though no one else was anywhere close to us in the restaurant. "I mean, I like Ernie. I like him a lot. But, well, it's complicated, isn't it?"

She glanced around. Both Dad and I followed her erratic looks at the empty space around us.

"I just... I never know when your grandfather might be listening."

CHAPTER

TWO

*Y*ou look... *passable.*

    "Passable?" I said to Mojo, my highly insensitive cat. "You could be a little kinder than that."

We cats are not very good at lying.

As I finished fiddling with my hair for at least the twentieth time, I turned and gave Mojo a narrow-eyed glare. "Liar."

Before he trotted off, I could have sworn he grinned at me.

I was getting ready in Maude, which made it a little strange that John was coming to pick me up for our date at my camper van on the beach. But what else can you do when your home is also your mode of transport?

I looked at the time. "Shoot." He was due to arrive at any moment now. Although I had been ready for at least fifteen minutes, I felt like I needed at least another thirty to be fully prepared. Why was I so nervous? The two of us had hung out both socially and professionally several times since I had arrived in Crystal Beach, yet our pending dinner date was causing a hundred butterflies to flutter in constant circles inside my stomach. I wished now that I had asked John to pick me up from Ada Mae's, where I could have had her and my father's calming influence, as well as some of that nice herbal tea, to settle my nerves.

Forcing myself to put my shoes on, get out of the camper van and lock up—therefore admitting that I was ready—I wondered what vehicle John would pick me up in. Going on a date in a squad car would be weird, but I didn't even know if he had his own vehicle.

No sooner had I turned around from locking up Maude that a classic, red and white Chevy pickup rumbled along the road. *Ah*, I thought to myself, *of course*. It all made perfect sense. Chief John Reece was a classic himself, a bit old fashioned but still fun and relatable in a way that made my stomach flutter as he pulled up.

John leaned out of the open window on the driver's side and appeared to check me out with a look from head to toe before our eyes met. If it had been any other guy, I might have told him to keep his eyes to himself.

"Evening, ma'am," John smiled. "I'm here to pick up Sidney Grace for a date. You haven't seen her around, have you? I thought this was her camper van."

I laughed, feeling both flattered and a little insulted. "You're not as funny as you think you are, you know," I said, walking around to get into the passenger seat. Hopefully unseen by John, I blushed with pride over the saucy, figure-hugging red dress I had chosen for our date.

"Yes, I am," he said. Then, as I climbed into the cab, he added a little more seriously, "You do look beautiful, though."

I smiled. This was going to be a wonderful evening, and I could not believe I had been so nervous.

We drove into the center of town, then passed through it, heading toward the far end of Citrus Way as it cut a straight path inland and away from the ocean. The Kelp Seafood Grill would, of course, have been the obvious choice for a delicious meal, although everyone who was anyone in Crystal Beach would have been talking about the police chief's date by the next morning. Eileen McCann's place was a hub of activity and gossip. A center of information.

We had agreed we wanted some privacy, and John knew of an Italian restaurant on the way out of town that served a killer tagliatelle carbonara. Well, hopefully not "killer." Since moving to Crystal Beach, I had learned to be careful around careless uses of certain words.

"I hear you got a new job," John said as we headed past the town center along Citrus Way.

This part of town was new to me. Crystal Beach began to peter out along a slow, even gradient as we moved away from the central intersection. There were few buildings, even in the heart of the town, above three or four stories. The sun had recently set in the west, the direction we were heading in, and the sky bled through the distant trees with pink and orange.

"Not so much a new job as a lot more of an old one," I replied. "It's great, though. Exactly what I wanted. A lifestyle column based on living by the beach in Florida."

"Always good when you get to do something you love."

"And it has the incidental effect of preventing me from starving."

John looked between me and the road several times, saying nothing. I knew this, I realized. I knew *him* and what it meant when he did that. The idea of knowing John that well warmed me, the wave of heat spreading from my feet up through my belly.

"Out with it," I said. "I know that look. What do you want to ask?"

"I was just wondering—and I'm asking this as a friend and not the police chief of Crystal Beach—whether you were planning to stay in Maude indefinitely. On that same spot, on the back of the beach?"

"So, you're not planning to have me moved on for vagrancy, then?" I asked with a laugh. My laugh was only about twenty percent nervous.

"You're breaking no laws as far as I'm aware. And, personally, I think you're becoming like a charming feature of that part of the beach."

I laughed out loud... so hard it made me cry. No one had ever called me a "charming feature" before. I wiped the tears from my eyes as we pulled into the parking lot of Deliciously Donatelli's restaurant. I felt certain the tears weren't helping hold my inexpertly applied makeup together.

"I don't know," I finally answered. "As wonderful as Crystal Beach is, I think I'll at least need to take some day trips around the area to do this new column justice."

I grinned to myself as John turned off the engine and pulled on the parking brake. "But you know what? That little spot on the beach is starting to feel a lot like home." I turned to look at him. "Does that make me a weirdo? Shouldn't I want to live in a proper house with four walls and all the comforts of home? Rather than heading over to my grandmother's place every day to use her utilities? I used to be like that. Normal."

John remained looking at me for several long moments, and it made me feel nervous. *Okay, I am a weirdo.*

"I think you're the freest person I know, Sidney Grace," he said. "And I can't think of a thing wrong with that."

The tagliatelle was, as advertised, delicious, and Dominic Donatelli, the owner of Deliciously Donatelli's, was excitable and attentive. He treated John like he was one of his favorite customers.

We sat close to the window, and both chose crème brulée for dessert. John's sugary crust made a crunching sound as he plunged his spoon into the top of it. "I know I'm probably not going to get a straight answer to this," he said with a grin, "but I keep wondering what you and Ada-Mae—and Wendy Rockford of all people—were all doing at The Rose Garden on the night we arrested that antique dealer for burglary." He shook his head and grinned. "I mean, *Wendy Rockford.*"

I idly scraped my spoon along the top of my sugary crust, the occasional fault line appearing where I wasn't quite gentle enough. "That man you arrested sold me a cat statue, you know," I answered without really giving him the true answer he sought.

"I know. He had a stall at the antique market." There was a subtext of "stop being evasive, Sidney," attached to his statement.

"You know you won't want to know," I said. There was one thing between us that could never change. John Reece was a police officer, and magic could only ever have a very limited role in his world. If any. Every time Ada-Mae, I, or anybody else using witchy powers in Crystal Beach turned up at one of his crime scenes, it was a problem. There was no getting around that.

He put his spoon down and slid his hand across the table, finding the fingers of my unoccupied hand and sliding his hand on top of mine. "But I want to see more of you, Sidney. I want to spend time with you. Maybe I'm ready to know."

I looked into his dark, intense eyes, wanting to believe in what he was saying. Sure, he meant it. Deliciously Donatelli's was a place outside the realities and problems of the rest of the world. At some point, however, we would have to pay the check and leave this place.

I took a breath, not sure what was about to come out of my mouth. "What I would like to know is what that man was after in Rose and Rodney's guest house." Hearing myself say this, I realized that this was something that had been bugging me ever since that night.

John's fingers slipped away from my hand, and he sat back in his seat. He didn't look annoyed. Or even disappointed. But I sure missed the warmth of his hand on mine.

"Well, he had nothing in his hands when he tried to flee across the garden," John said. "Who knows if he even found what he was looking for? Because he was quite specific about what he stole—like your grandmother's statue. Or, if he found what he was looking for, maybe he dropped it before he fled once he knew we were closing in on him."

"But what *was* it?"

John gave a small shrug. "I'm sure the Gantzes have valuables. Everyone does."

"Except me," I laughed. "I have Maude, and I have my cats." I grinned. "What more does a girl need, right?"

John smiled, my evasiveness apparently forgotten. "Someone to share them with?"

That stole the breath from me. *John Reece, you terrible, sneaky... desirable... romantic man.* Maybe this could work. Maybe there was a world where I could share everything with the Crystal Beach Chief of Police.

"Yeah," I said, my fingers finding his again. "There is that."

When John dropped me back at Maude, I invited him in for a coffee—the first time I had ever done that because my living space was only about ten feet by six feet—but he declined. Maybe he didn't fancy the awkwardness of me moving around him while I made us coffee in my tiny camper van, but I liked to think that he was being a gentleman. Somehow, that made the night even more perfect. It was perhaps the first time in my life that I had been happy to be turned down. It made me feel special.

I went for a walk along the beach to clear my racing mind or, at least, to let all the crazy thoughts bouncing around in my head tire themselves out. Mojo, Jinx, Abra, and Cadabra were nowhere in sight when I got back to Maude. Which wasn't unusual when the weather was calm. I often came home in the evening to find Maude empty, then the cats would enter through the clever cat flap that John had installed for me a few minutes later. I liked to think they came rushing home because they missed me, but it was usually because they were ready to eat, and the food bowls were empty. In fact, Mojo had told me exactly that.

This time, the four cats trotted over to me as I walked south along the beach, in the direction where the southern side of the town was marked by the new housing development of Mystic Dunes.

"Hi there," I said as Mojo brushed against the back of my legs. "What have you guys been up to this evening?"

Oh, you know, Mojo replied. *The usual. Networking, spreading our influence, and hopefully, forming a new committee.*

I looked down at him for a moment, trying to work out if he was joking. Unless a cat tells you they're joking, it's hard to tell. "Okay..."

Abra, one of my two Siamese cats—the one with the lighter-colored face—ran up to me and leaped straight into my arms. It was sweet, although I was nearly knocked backward on my bottom in the sand.

"Are you all right?" I asked Abra, cradling him to my chest and stroking his head. I glanced down at Mojo. "What have you been making him do?"

Let's just say that Abra is not very good with confrontation, he answered. *But sometimes, it is necessary to get things done.*

I thought about that for a moment. Then, seeing Jinx, the other tabby, chasing a leaf blowing in the wind across the sand and Cadabra stopping to lick the length of his extended leg, I decided that I didn't need to know any more of my cats' business. Instead, my mind wandered back to John.

It had been such a perfect night, and when we were alone together like that, it felt like we belonged together. Yet the further I got from Deliciously Donatelli's, the more I remembered how magic stood between us. Especially the fact that I hadn't felt able to give him a straight answer about why I had turned up at the scene of a burglary with the magic store owner, my father, and several residents from Shifting Sands Retirement Center in tow.

It just wasn't fair. I had finally met the perfect man, and he seemed about the last man I could let fully into my life.

But John said he was ready to know more about magic, Mojo said as he trotted beside me.

Dammit, Mojo, stop reading my thoughts.

Well, they are rather loud, you know.

With my mind turning things over and the gentle sound of the waves crashing into the shore and dragging themselves back out to the ocean again, I hadn't realized that I had walked as far as I had until I looked up and saw the lights of Mystic Dunes twinkling ahead in the distance, just past the creek.

"Well," I said out loud. "That's far enough. Better turn back."

I was just about to do that when I stopped myself and looked up at the lights in Mystic Dunes again. What was wrong with this picture? And then it hit me: If there were ever lights on over at Mystic Dunes during the evening, it was only one house at most. It had never looked like anyone was moved in, and the only house with the lights on, I had always assumed, was the show home. Which meant it was probably Sam Barlow working late. Or, more likely, up to some nefarious magic.

The problem now was that almost every house in the subdivision had a light on. Curious, I wandered a little further and stood on the other side of the creek, staring across at the small housing development by the sea that my mother had almost bought into. What I saw there now was no illusion. Somehow, since being empty just a week ago, Mystic Dunes was, miraculously, completely full.

CHAPTER

THREE

"Full, you say?" Ada Mae said, looking up at me as she lined up her croquet shot. Following the events of the Crystal Beach Mini-Golf Invitational, Ada-Mae wasn't sure whether mini golf was quite the game for her anymore. Instead, she had discovered croquet, which she seemed to fancy more. I wondered if she thought the heavier mallet made for a better defensive weapon.

Upon arriving at Ada-Mae's place earlier, I faced half an hour of grilling over my date the previous evening before we finally headed out for the game.

"Uh-huh," I said. "And Mojo confirmed that this must have happened recently, in the last couple of days at most. One moment it was empty, and the next, what... ten, twelve houses, all with people in them?"

Ada Mae took her shot, sending her ball right through the middle of the hoop without touching the sides at all. The croquet lawn at Shifting Sands Retirement Center was on a raised piece of land that just about enabled us to see over the rear wall and onto the beach. It was a glorious morning with a breeze coming off the sea that kept the excessive heat at bay. Between the cooler start to the day and more than a week of time to acclimate, this was the first time I had seen my dad outside during the day without him sweating profusely under the Florida humidity.

"Mojo said?" he asked.

"Yes. I forgot to tell you, but my cat talks to me in my head."

Jacob Grace studied me for a moment, then shrugged and moved to take his shot. Wasn't my dad just awesome?

"Well," Ada-Mae said, "that is a little worrying. I wonder who these people are who have all moved in so quickly."

"Me too." I thought for a moment, then added the other thing that had been bothering me. "And, you know what, I haven't been able to shake what happened at The Rose Garden guest house out of my head."

"What do you mean?" Ada-Mae asked.

"I just feel that the spell we cast over at Mystic Dunes, the ritual. It worked so well." I met her eyes, trying to make sure she understood what I meant. "I could feel it. I know the fact that the spell led us to The Rose Garden was important. More important than some stupid burglar who stole your Dargi idol."

"Yes, dear, but we've been through this," Ada-Mae said. "That pin or brooch or whatever you want to call it. That thing the antique dealer had that looked like a gargoyle with fiery red eyes was helping him locate valuable goods in Crystal Beach. There was dark magic involved in making it, I assure you. We asked the spell to take us to the source of the dark magic, and that was what it did. It wasn't what we intended, but sometimes that's the way things go with spells. They can go askew. Or they just go with what they can find. Perhaps that's all there was for the spell to find."

"Or..." I said, moving to take my shot and blasting my poor dad's ball right out of the way. "What if there's something else at The Rose Garden? I mean, it is one of the oldest buildings in the town. If anywhere could have a dark history and negative energy seeping from under the floorboards, surely it has to be that creepy old building."

"Sidney!" Ada-Mae admonished me, although I was sure I could see the ghost of a smile there. "Don't be so critical of Rose and Rodney's very successful guest house." She shrugged. "Okay, it is a little creepy, and I guess Rose and Rodney are an acquired taste. Still... don't you think it's too much of a coincidence?"

"But the burglar never left with what he went there to find," I replied. "That's what I'm thinking of. That it isn't a coincidence at all. What if there's some dark item, some nexus of power, still in that building? Rose and Rodney might not even know it was there."

"And what do you propose we do about that?"

I shrugged. "I suppose we could just ask Rose and Rodney. They are back from their vacation now."

I didn't like that idea, though, and Ada-Mae could tell.

"What we need is an excuse to go over there," I said, rubbing my chin thoughtfully. Then an idea came. "Dad, how do you fancy staying in a creepy guest house for a couple of days? It's owned by two of the weirdest people you'll ever meet."

My dad took his shot, missing the pin by miles. Croquet was

not his game. It had to do with angles instead of numbers, so my dad was hanging on by a thread. "Well, when you put it like that...." He straightened and cleared his throat. "Actually, there was something I need to talk to you both about."

"Other than losing your job and entering a midlife crisis?" I said with a grin.

"I am not having a midlife crisis!"

It was hard to look ashamed when I was amusing myself. "I know. It's just fun thinking of it that way. You're, like, the least likely candidate to have one. You know, sports cars, loose women. Discovering leather pants."

"Well, it's funny you should say that...."

I put a hand over my eyes. "No, Dad. I don't think I could take seeing you in leather pants."

"No, the other one."

"Loose women? If that's what you're looking for, Crystal Beach may not be the place for you then."

"Sidney!" Ada-Mae said, interrupting my witty banter. "I think your father may be trying to tell you something important."

My dad nodded toward Ada-Mae. "Well, yes. I have met someone. She's not loose, but she is a woman. And, well..."

"Is she coming to visit us?" Ada-Mae interrupted.

"If that's okay?"

Ada-Mae smiled. "Of course, dear. I'll need to vet her. When will she be joining us?"

"Ah, she'll be at the airport later this afternoon."

"And this is the warning you thought you would give us?" she said with a surprised laugh.

My dad laughed, although his was a little more nervous. "I know. I'm sorry. It's just...." He turned to me, perhaps noticing for the first time how uncharacteristically quiet I was being. "You okay, Sidney?"

"You have a girlfriend?" I gasped. My brain was stuck in neutral, struggling to process this news. Although Jacob Grace was my dad and had been married to Mom for over twenty-five years until their divorce, it was still hard to think of him having things like romantic relationships. I felt like a kid again, surrounded by those fragile, breakable walls that kids unknowingly hold around them.

"Yes, sweetheart," he said, taking half a step toward me, his hands out, although the gesture was defeated by the croquet mallet I held up between us. "I'm sure you will get on with her. Her name's Gillian." He said that last bit as if everyone got on with people named Gillian. Maybe they did; I wouldn't know since I hadn't known any.

I forced a smile onto my face, still not sure how I felt about this. Like Ada-Mae, I guessed a little more notice would have been nice. "Great," I said, forcing my jaw into action, "I can't wait to meet her."

"So, to your earlier point, sweetheart," my dad said. "I was thinking of seeing if they had a vacant room at the guest house tonight. It wouldn't be practical or fair to impose on Ada-Mae any further, especially with my...guest in town."

Oh well, I thought, *there's a sunny side to everything, I guess.*

"If that's not an option," my dad continued. "Gillian has an old college friend she could stay with until I can find us a place."

"Your girlfriend knows someone living here in Crystal Beach?"

"Yes, I'm afraid her friend got snookered by that devil himself... Sam Barlow."

Ada-Mae and I exchanged looks before I turned and glared at my father. "So, you already know about his real estate disaster, but do you know about him and Mom?"

"Yeah. Ada-Mae filled me in after I mentioned the strange man who had broken into your van. I was worried about you."

"Oh. Well, thank you, Dad, but I can take care of myself. But back to your girlfriend. So, are you saying her friend is living in Mystic Dunes?"

My father shook his head and let out a heavy sigh but didn't say another word. His lack of response told me that he was concerned as we were. It appeared he was more troubled by Sam's shady business deals and how he had likely taken advantage of Gillian's friend.

But it was the sudden inhabitation of the new housing development by the sea that was bugging me... and if I read her furrowed brow right, it was bothering Ada-Mae too.

"Hi, Mom," I said, answering my cell phone as I walked out of the back gates of Shifting Sands Retirement Center and onto the beach. I needed to make some headway on the first week's edition of my lifestyle column. Neither my date nor playing croquet were going to help me get the piece done. I didn't even have a proper theme for it yet. I was just getting into my writing groove when my mother rang. "What's up?"

"Me," she answered. "Well, I'm down rather than up. I'm down in Crystal Beach."

"Here? In Florida?"

"Are you living in another Crystal Beach that I don't know about?"

Something heavy dropped to the bottom of my stomach. "Doesn't anybody give any notice these days?" I blurted out before thinking about what I was saying.

"Well," she huffed. "That's not a very nice way to greet your dear mother, Sid."

"I mean... weren't you here just a few weeks ago?"

"And neither is that. I've come down to help my mother celebrate her eightieth birthday. I'm allowed to do that, aren't I?"

"Of course," I said. "Sorry. It's been a surprising day already. Wait... where are you staying?"

"The same place as before, of course, The Rose Garden guest house."

Oh, for the love of magic... How quickly my life could go from idyllic to farcical. Having my father, his new girlfriend, and my mother all staying at the same guest house—now there was a recipe for disaster.

"Look, darling, there's something I wanted to talk to you about. It's... not the sort of thing to talk about over the phone. Are you able to drop by this morning?"

And poof...just like that, there went any chance of me writing my first award-winning article.

CHAPTER
FOUR

I f I wasn't going to get any work done, then I might as well feed my obsession a little. Sam Barlow's realty office wasn't too far out of the way on my journey to The Rose Garden guest house. Well... it was quite out of the way. But when had that ever stopped me from investigating when I smelled something fishy.

The sight of Mystic Dunes full of residents had shaken me, that's for sure. Almost like it had been occupied for ages. I wasn't sure what I was expecting to get from Sam. That was not the point, though. There was something brazen about the almost instantaneous total occupation of the development. Like Sam was thumbing his nose at those of us who knew about the magical powers he had employed in the past.

Or maybe he just didn't care whether we noticed, which was even more infuriating. We were irrelevant to him, ants on the bottom of his Bruno Marc shoes.

Sam was showing a couple out of his office when I arrived. "I'm sorry," I heard him say to a middle-aged man with thick-rimmed tortoiseshell glasses, who looked like he worked in some sort of investment or banking firm. "These beachfront properties are very popular, but I've got your number if anything opens up in Mystic Dunes."

The pair noticed me as Sam's would-be clients stepped onto the sidewalk.

"Apologies, ma'am," Sam said to me with a brazen smile unseen by the other man, "there's still nothing for your mother at Mystic Dunes. I told her she should have snapped up that property while she had the chance."

The man and his wife looked at me like they thought my mother had wasted some golden opportunity.

"That's okay," I said. "It was a little too low-lying for her. A bit like the man who tried selling it to her."

Though I hoped that would wipe the smug smile from Sam Barlow's face, I was disappointed by his lack of reaction. The man who had just left the realty office with his wife backed up a few steps and headed back to their car, looking back like he wanted to work out the source of the tension between us.

"What can I do for you today, Sidney?" Sam said in that thick, slimy voice of his. "Haven't finally decided to stop living in that ugly camper van of yours like a vagrant, have we? Ready to join civilized society? Although I'm not sure we'll have anything in your price range. I'm afraid you'll need a job if you want to get a mortgage or rent an apartment."

"I have a job," I shot back.

"Breakfast shift at Eileen's, is it?" he laughed. "I'm not sure I've got a shoebox small enough to rent you for those wages. Or are we back to conning the old people at Shifting Sands? Good money in speaking to the dead, is there?"

My eyes went wide at that.

"Yes, I heard all about that," Sam said. "Contacting the ghosts of the loved ones of poor old retirees. How low can you get?" He laughed again. "And this is coming from me."

"I never charged anyone for that." I felt a little shaken. Sam was on his game today. "Although a few people insisted—"

"I imagine the IRS would like to hear about that one. I can't believe that *Chief* Reece didn't put a stop to it. Then again, I hear you've worked yourself into a position of favor as far as the local police department goes."

This confrontation was not going at all as I would have hoped. It took all my will power to stop myself from running off down the street, my proverbial tail between my legs. I wanted at least to put my accusation to Sam to see if I could elicit any sort of response.

And something else occurred to me too. The fight-or-flight feeling I was getting was about more than just the fact that Sam's words were embarrassing me and catching me off guard. I could feel the power behind them; the dastardly villain was using his—for lack of a better word and apologies to my oldest cat—mojo on me. There was power behind his words, and the thought that he could use whatever latent force he had to make me want to run away was a sobering thought. But it also made the blood rise to my cheeks in anger.

"Don't you be smug with me, Sam Barlow," I wagged my finger at him, feeling at least thirty years older as I did so. "There's something foul in the way you've filled up all those houses with new residents in just a few days. You're a good salesman, but you're not that good. And I'm going to get to the bottom of what's going on and put you out of business once and for all."

I had been riffing that last bit, but it felt good to be dishing the threats back to him all the same.

"Yes, yes. You're all talk and hot air, Sidney Grace. Just like your grandmother. And your grandfather, for that matter. I did not know him long, but I could always tell he was a blustering old fool. And with no power of his own to back him up."

I felt the push from his words again, something messing with the way I felt inside that was more than just what Sam was saying. "You use magic recklessly, Sam. And it will be your undoing. Seeing as I'm so tight with the police chief of Crystal Beach, maybe I'll bring the amazing turnaround of fortunes of Mystic Dunes to his attention." I almost brought up John's apparent new willingness to accept magic but stopped myself. I would keep that one as a secret ace in my pocket, I thought.

His self-satisfied smile faltered a little, replaced by a glare full of malice, hatred burning within his dark eyes. "I'm sure I don't know what you're talking about. But I would be careful about making threats. I've got powerful friends who can do a lot more than a bunch of aging bridge players and lawn bowl enthusiasts can." He seemed to grind his teeth as he talked, and as much as I had felt the force of his bullying a moment before, it now felt like something a lot darker and more dangerous.

I took an involuntary step backward, and something flashed across Sam's face, like a realization he had said too much or gone too far. The self-satisfied smile returned, although now I could not look at him in the same way.

I reached inside, tapping into my courage, and asked the question that was at the front of my mind. "And what friends are those, Sam?"

~

OF COURSE, I didn't get an answer to my question. Maybe I shouldn't have let Sam know how badly he had slipped up by admitting he had allies with potential powers of their own, but I couldn't help myself. One thing was for sure: Ada Mae was right; Sam was not working on his own. There were more people involved in the dark coven that was operating in Crystal Beach. Although we already suspected a nefarious force, this was the first actual confirmation of it by Sam. My detour to the realty office had not been a complete waste of time after all.

I hurried from there to The Rose Garden, as it had been over an hour since I had spoken to my mom on the phone, and I did not want to keep her waiting too long. I needed to talk to her about my father and his girlfriend to avert a possible confrontation. I also wondered why she had insisted that I head straight over to speak to her. Julia-Mae Grace—she had divorced my dad but had held onto the surname—was notorious for being dramatic about things. For all I knew, she wanted to show me her new Chanel handbag or something.

The first thing I noticed as I walked up the drive toward The Rose Garden guest house was that Rose's, um... roses were not looking as good as they usually did. Much of the flora around the entrance and in the flowerbeds had wilted. Even the grass on the enormous lawn to the side of the house was looking a little yellow. Rose and Rodney had been on holiday, returning a week ago, but it seemed surprising that the well-tended garden suffered so easily or that Rose wouldn't have found someone to look after the flowers of which she was so proud. I resolved not to bring it up if I saw her.

Walking into the foyer of the guest house was much the same experience as always. Rodney Gantz, Rose's husband, was working away on fixing something, as usual. This time, it was some loose carpet on the stairs while Rose occupied her queen bee position behind the reception desk. I opened my mouth to speak, but Rose beat me to it.

"Sidney!" she said, her fingers pressing together a little like a comic book villain plotting their next dastardly deed. "Julia-Mae said you would be over. I feel like I haven't seen you in ages."

"In ages," Rodney agreed from over by the bottom of the stairs.

Rose was speaking to me as if we were best friends. And, although I didn't have anything against the Gantzes, except for the fact that they were a little creepy, Rose's enthusiasm was both unexpected and unsettling.

"Although... I heard you made a visit here while we were away."

Of course, she had. This was Rose Gantz we were talking about, Grand Champion of the Crystal Beach Gossip Contest five years running. Or something like that. She could probably vacation in China and still know everything about what was going on in Crystal Beach.

"Yes," Rose said. "A burglar of all things... in our house!" She held a hand to her chest as if the mere thought was enough to give her heart palpitations.

"Our house," echoed Rodney. His voice, however, did not convey the same amount of horror as Rose's had.

"And, more than that, a full-blown crime spree. We missed out on a crime spree!" Rose sounded mortified about that. "But you and your grandmother were out sleuthing, weren't you? Like, who was it, darling...?"

It took me a moment to realize that Rose was speaking to Rodney and not calling me "darling."

"Miss Marple," Rodney replied.

"No, darling, not like her," Rose smirked.

"Scooby-Doo," Rodney said. The name of the Agatha Christie sleuth and popular children's cartoon spurting in isolation from Rodney's mouth made it seem like he had momentarily lost control of his faculties and was just spouting random words.

"That's it," Rose said, pressing her hands together again. "Scooby-Doo. Just like the Scooby-Doo gang."

I smiled, words evading me.

Rose took my silence as a hint. "Sorry, how rude of me. I will summon your mother right away."

That Rose referred to "summoning" my mother amused me, and I had to stifle a laugh. No one summoned Julia-Mae Grace. Although if anyone could be capable of getting away with it, I guessed it might be Rose Gantz.

"I could head up?" I offered.

"No, it's okay," Rose replied. "Your mother said she would come down when you arrived. I can make a cup of tea if you would like?"

I smiled my appreciation, liking the idea of a nice cup of tea.

"Take a seat, dear," Rose said, jutting a hand toward the chairs and Chesterfield sofas that were arranged around coffee tables right next to a massive fireplace that dominated that side of the foyer. If it wasn't such a dark space, this entrance area of The Rose Garden would feel quite cozy.

Rodney mumbled something to himself, and I didn't quite catch what he'd said. However, sitting down in a comfortable red velvety seat, my brain absentmindedly deciphered what he had said. "Quite cozy," I mouthed to myself. I couldn't be sure, but it seemed like Rodney had said, "quite cozy." Which was exactly the thought that had run through my head. I cast my mind back a minute, trying to remember if I had said those words out loud.

Looking up, I saw Rodney had finished fixing the strip of carpet that came down the middle of the curving staircase. The carpet was the same color as the seat I was in—a deep, almost blood red. He glanced over in my direction as he lumbered, Lurch-like, back around the reception desk to deposit his tools somewhere behind the counter.

A few moments later, my mother appeared down the staircase, wearing an unusually muted ensemble, topped off with a pale-yellow cardigan that screamed "fifty-something suburban housewife." My left brow arched as this was a very different look for my mother. I was used to seeing her in business casual attire with the occasional power suit thrown into the mix.

Rushing over, she threw her arms around me and hugged me tighter than I could remember her having done in years. "Darling," she said, her mouth close to my ear, "I've missed you so much."

I took a step back from her, confused. Don't get me wrong, I love my mother dearly, and despite our occasional differences, we could, at times, be like two peas in a pod. Well, in a different life, back in Boston, where it seemed I had been a different person.

Public shows of affection were just not her thing, and that had me on guard. "It's good you're here," I whispered, realizing I meant it. My mom's relationship with Ada-Mae had long been a complicated one, even before one of my grandmother's magic spells had inadvertently led Julia-Mae to lose her Tupperware business. Her marriage to my dad crumbled soon afterward, and things had not been quite right between them ever since.

The bridge between them was halfway repaired when Julia-

Mae came down to stay a few weeks ago. While competing together in the Crystal Beach Mini-Golf Invitational, mother and daughter seemed to have bonded even though the idea of Julia-Mae in the competition hadn't initially thrilled Ada-Mae. It filled me with hope for my family. I might even have allowed myself dreams of Ada-Mae's eightieth birthday celebrations going smoothly if I didn't know that my father and his new girlfriend were going to be present.

"So, what's going on?" my mother said. "What have you organized for your grandmother's birthday?"

"Well..." I began, trying not to sound awkward. "We're going to have a barbecue on the beach. She loves the beach," I added as justification. "And, um... barbecues."

"What? That's rubbish. I mean, finish with a barbecue on the beach, that's fine. But what's the main event going to be?"

"I don't know," I had to admit. "It's been difficult because I've been waiting to organize something with Ernie, but he sort of vanished into thin air." It was true. Ernie was so close with Ada-Mae—or *had been*—that I had assumed we would organize her eightieth celebration together."

Things with Quipley's School of Magic and the ritual that had led us to The Rose Garden and the burglar had taken up most of my time until last week. Then there was all the correspondence over my new job and trying to write my next piece for *Living It Large In Boston, et voila*, we were almost at the big day.

"Well, that won't do," my mother said. "We will have to track Ernie down. And if not, then we will have to figure something out ourselves. We've only got until tomorrow. Have you even bought a present?"

"I've ordered something at the magic shop in town, The Invisible Cloak. I'll be going to pick it up a little later."

My mother looked a little mollified by that. "Oh, well."

Her indignation gone, she instead looked sheepish, her sudden silence telling, her eyes unable to meet with mine. Julia-Mae Grace had a way of getting you to ask the question.

"What's up?" I asked.

"So... I hear your father has been down for a visit."

Of course, you have. Although, I thought to myself, maybe this might save me an uncomfortable job. I was waiting for her to ask about his new girlfriend because I reckoned she had heard about her too, as weird and awkward as that would be. However, I ended up with the wrong end of the stick.

"It's just... well, I've been thinking about him a lot lately."

"Thinking about him?" I repeated.

"Well... you know what I mean."

No, I really, really don't know what you mean.

CHAPTER
FIVE

I should have told her. I should have told my mom about Dad's girlfriend. But I just didn't have the heart to. I wasn't sure how I felt about my mom thinking that she might still have feelings for my dad, but what I did not want to do was crush those feelings right away.

Sure, my mom could seem hard on the surface, but in some ways, this made it even more shocking on those rare occasions when she crumbled. Seeing her upset was like being a child and having some safe, immutable facet of your existence snatched away. Like pulling down the proverbial walls of security and revealing the harshness of the world beyond. Innocence lost.

I left The Rose Garden, determined to speak to my father and, at the very least, warn him that my mother was staying at the same guest house that he intended to stay at with his new girl-friend. The part about my mother's renewed feelings for him... Well, I thought I would keep that to myself for now.

Secondly, I needed to find Ernie. My mom was right; the lack of detailed plans for Ada Mae's birthday was pretty pathetic. I mean, to make it to this age is a feat, and not to celebrate it would be a true crime. Waiting for Ernie had turned into having nothing planned at all. Although I was sure that Ada-Mae did not have any expecta-tions of a big fuss for her birthday, not trying to do so would look a lot like not caring. It seemed we did not need to have any murders or thefts going on in Crystal Beach for life to feel problematic.

A further complication was the fact that I had let my cell phone run out of charge, so I could not simply call my dad to warn him. I didn't even have a cord with me to sneak a quick charge for a few minutes somewhere at the guest house. I was also almost out of gas, so I jogged back through town in the Florida heat, telling my mom that I had to put some gas in Maude so I could drive her places. Like one did with vehicles.

The nearest gas station was just outside of town, close to the motel where the gentleman thief and antique dealer had stored his stolen goods from the crime spree he had attempted in Crystal Beach. So it was an out-of-the-way trip to fill her up. Maude was a thirsty little lady, though. Like a Lamborghini. But a lot less... sexy. But first, I had to walk back to my parking spot—my home—at the beach.

There was a bit of a breeze blowing in from the sea today, but it wasn't reaching as far as The Rose Garden guest house or the center of town as I crossed through it. I was a hot, sweaty mess by the time I got back to the seafront. I took a left, heading toward Maude, with a trip to Shifting Sands being my next stop. Hopefully, my father would still be there.

I stopped off at Maude, so I could get the charging cable for my phone. As I was about to open up the sliding door on the side of her, I noticed a familiar-looking silhouette of a figure sitting on the beach, looking out to sea. There was another familiar figure sitting next to him—the outline of a cat whose head he was stroking.

Ernie turned as I walked up behind him. Mojo looked up too, a lazy look in his eyes before he spoke. *Wow, the gym at Shifting Sands smells better than you do,* he said. *Don't let the policeman see you like that, or that might be another potential relationship snuffed out before it's begun.*

I ignored my insolent cat, intent on Ernie.

"Hey, how are you doing? I have hardly seen you this last week."

"Sorry," he said as if it was something he should apologize for. "I've been busy, especially the last few days."

I felt I needed to jump in quickly and steer the conversation the way it needed to go before it went somewhere else. Anyway, by now, Ernie knew that I was not someone who beat around the bush.

"Look, I'm sorry about the magic thing. It sucks. I mean, if anyone deserves to have magical powers... And no offense to Judd because I really like him, but who saw that one coming? And Howie Rockford? I mean, come on! That guy's got even less self-control than I have. Or my cat Mojo here." I eyed my eldest cat with a spark of reproach.

Ernie laughed out loud, which made me feel good. Emboldened, even. When I went to speak again, though, he held up a hand to stop me.

"Thank you, Sidney. You're a dear." Ernie had such a rich voice. Authoritative yet kind. I had missed hearing it over the course of the past week. "I'll admit it was a bit of a shock at first. Or a disappointment, I guess. Knowing Ada-Mae has opened a whole new world to me, and magic was an important part of that. But not *the* most important part."

"What do you mean?"

"I guess a part of me felt like not having any magical power meant that Ada-Mae would never like me in the way I hoped she would. Then I remembered that was just plain stupid."

"Yup," I said with a kind grin. "Gramps never had a magical bone in his body, and they were married for nearly sixty years." I smiled at him. "And, for what it's worth, I think you two would make a great couple."

"And yet, I always feel there's an invisible barrier there." Ernie sighed.

"That would also be Gramps," I said. "Because my grandfather might be dead, but he hasn't exactly left this physical world. How could Ada-Mae start a relationship with anyone knowing that he might be watching? Not just in the 'from some remote cloud up in Heaven' sense, either. He's quite capable of popping up and telling his granddaughter how displeased he is about it. Or, as a ghost, perhaps making his feelings known in some other way."

"I never knew your grandfather," Ernie said. "Although I wish I had. From the way Ada-Mae speaks of him, I think we would have gotten along. But I get the sense he was quite passionate. Do you think his ghost would get... I don't know... vengeful? I remember how he helped with Hampton Harper. So... he can manifest himself physically, I assume?"

"Yes, but it takes a lot out of his ghost. And no, I don't think he would hurt anyone... anyone not trying to kill us, that is. Sidney Simpson was very protective of his family, but he was never unreasonable or selfish like that. No, it's more that Ada-Mae would feel like she was betraying him if she knew he was near."

Ernie nodded his head. "My feelings aside, it does not seem fair to Ada-Mae. Whether or not she would choose me if she could."

"And the hard part of it is that Gramps seems to come and go. Which is hard for me too. I get to see him here and there for a few days at a time, and then he is gone, and I never know if or when he's going to come back." I picked up some sand and let it slip back through my fingers, my hands like a makeshift hourglass that could change time just by splaying my fingers a little further apart.

"This sounds bad when I complain out loud like this," I continued. "I should be grateful just for getting to see my grandfather after he has died. Ada-Mae can't, and sometimes I feel a little guilty about that. But uncertainty is one of the hardest things to live with. It's like being stuck in a single moment that feels like it lasts for an eternity, a moment you cannot move past even though you want to."

Ernie tilted his head to one side and favored me with a lopsided grin. "You can say that again." Then his eyes went wide, and his mouth dropped open. "I almost forgot; I need to tell you what I've arranged for Ada Mae's birthday."

Warm relief flooded through me. "I knew you wouldn't let us down, Ernie."

Ernie told me about his big surprise and made me promise to wait to reveal it until he was there, too, then he turned and headed down the beach.

As he did so, I called after him. "I would love it if you two were a thing," I repeated. "You both deserve to be happy." Then I looked skyward and called out. "And I don't care if anyone is listening... Gramps."

Ernie smiled and waved his hand in farewell, walking as he wandered off on more birthday business. I turned back to Maude and jumped when I found the incorporeal form of a ghost standing next to the door.

"As it turns out, I am listening," Gramps replied.

CHAPTER
SIX

"Gramps!" The image of my grandfather's ghost was clearer than I'd ever seen it, almost like he was there. Taken by surprise, I stepped forward without thinking and tried to fling my arms around him. I did, of course, pass right through him and feel a slight chill accompanied by a tingling sensation. It was like that vein of ice that would sometimes sit inside me when I had been out in the snow too long. The kind of chill that would linger for quite some time after I was otherwise warm and toasty by an open fire. It was something I hadn't suffered from since coming to Florida.

"Sorry," I said, jumping back. It somehow felt like a violation of my grandfather's ghost that I had passed through him like that, but Gramps didn't seem to mind and just smiled, waving it away.

"I wish I could take full advantage of that hug," he said. "But I guess I should just count my blessings I get to see you at all."

"It's good you're back," I said. "It's hard not knowing when you'll be here."

"Yes, I heard."

"You heard all of that, huh?"

"A lot of it."

No matter how pleased I was to see my grandfather, that earned him a scowl. "I'm not sure it is fair listening in on people like that, you know. Especially when you're a ghost, and it's so easy to."

"I know," Gramps replied. "I'm sorry. Sometimes it's a little hard not to. When I use up all my ghostly powers to be here, it's a little like I go somewhere else. Coming back is a slow process, much of it hearing and seeing but not being able to tell anyone I am here. It begins distantly so that you're just voices or little, blurry dots a long way off. So I look, and I listen. What else can a ghost like that do except wait to be able to see and hear you all again? And wish I was with you."

"Okay," I admitted. "That was exactly what you needed to say to be forgiven for eavesdropping."

He nodded his thanks. "And I'm back in time for your grandmother's birthday too. Also, listen, I want to talk to you more about those things you and Ernie were just discussing."

I tensed a little at that, but at least he did not seem overly angry.

"But not now," Gramps went on. "There's something even more urgent. Sometimes, the point at which a ghost can show themselves again is the point at which they are needed. It's as if that need is what fully pulls us back. What gives us that last bit of physical presence."

"So, what are you saying, Gramps?"

"I came to warn you, Sidney. You need to go to The Rose Garden."

"But I just came from there," I said. "And I need to get to Dad quickly... before he and Mom run into each other and all chaos breaks loose."

"I know," he said., holding up a ghostly hand to try to stop me as I turned to walk along the beach. "Your father, he's not with your grandmother anymore. He is heading over toward the guest house now."

My ghostly grandpa, complete with one of those lumberjack shirts he always liked to wear, even after they moved down to Florida, and his neatly trimmed gray hair and beard, briefly closed his eyes as if he was concentrating on trying to invoke some ghostly power. "And I can feel it... like something bad is going to happen there. I can't quite say what, but something terrible might come from his visit there. You need to get over to The Rose Garden as soon as you can, Sidney. Like now!"

SIDNEY SIMPSON WAS NOT prone to panicking on a whim, so I took my grandfather's warning seriously and decided to risk jumping into Maude to drive over to The Rose Garden. As soon I started the engine, I remembered I still needed gas, so I had to make a quick stop to fill up the tank enough to keep me from becoming stranded on the side of the road.

All my cats came along on the ride with me, Mojo settling down on the passenger seat beside me. The other three ran about excitedly, occasionally bounding into the front of the camper van to chase something that I, for the life of me, could not see. This was not exactly the safest way to drive, and I wished I had put them away in their little travel carriers before peeling out of my beach spot, but there was no time for that. I was on a mission—gas and then the guest house.

Finally, I made it to The Rose Garden. After pulling up, I saw the familiar sports car driven by Sam Barlow parked outside. I resisted the temptation to ram it. Funny how my mother should come back to town, stay at The Rose Garden, and straightaway, Sam Barlow turns up at the guest house too. Coincidence? Probably not.

I was about to rush up the front steps when I noticed that Gramps—last seen waving me off at the beach—was standing in the middle of the wide lawn to the side of the property. Either he had hitched a ride with me unnoticed, or ghosts were not bound by the same rules of physics that we were when it came to getting around. He always kept himself fit, but there's no way he would have been able to outrun Maude.

"What are you doing?" I asked, quickly skirting around the side of the sickly-looking rose bushes.

It seemed that Gramps hadn't heard me for a moment. He was unmoving, looking up at the top level of the house. If it had been any ghost other than my grandfather, I would have found it creepy enough to warrant running away.

Finally, he noticed me. "Ah, Sidney." He glanced back up toward the top level of the guest house again.

"You should go in," I suggested. "See Mom, even if she can't see you."

"I'm not sure that I can," he said. "I'm not sure I'm strong enough."

"What do you mean?" I asked.

He appeared hesitant to reply for a moment. Or maybe he was

just trying to find the right words. "There's... something in there. Something powerful."

"Evil?" I asked, jumping straight to my thoughts about the burglar and the theory I had that he hadn't found whatever he was looking for at The Rose Garden.

Gramps shrugged. "Evil is a point of view."

"I'm not sure I'm following you, Gramps."

"Well, sometimes power is just power; it's neutral. The good and the bad depends upon what is done with it."

I followed his gaze up to the first floor of The Rose Garden guest house, thinking about the fact that my mother was staying there. "Is Dad inside?"

"Yes, sorry." He shook his head like he was clearing or breaking a spell. "You might want to get in there quickly."

That was when I heard someone shouting. "Sam Barlow!" a familiar voice roared.

"I HEARD WHAT YOU DID, you disgusting man. You should be locked away."

It was my father speaking. He and Sam Barlow were in the middle of the entrance foyer of The Rose Garden. Rose was in her customary position behind the reception desk, although Rodney didn't appear to be about. Which was a first.

The only other person—aside from me—in the room was a man I had not seen before. Presumably, he was a guest. He sat by the fireplace, reading a paper, a steaming hot drink on the end table next to him. He was Caucasian, although with a look that could have come from Eastern European ancestry. His hair was dark, streaked with silver, with a bald spot forming on the top, and he appeared to be approaching middle age. He continued to read the paper, despite the argument going on in the middle of the room, either not bothered by it or studiously trying to pretend it wasn't happening.

No one else appeared to have noticed me come in, and for the moment, I decided to take advantage of that. I stepped slowly and quietly to the side, where I was half-hidden by a tall, palm-like potted plant and a coat rack. As soon as I had done so, a strange feeling came over me, like I was safe and secure, despite the brewing argument happening close by involving my father, a man who didn't ordinarily do arguing.

"I have no idea what you are talking about," Savvy Sam said. "I think you've got the wrong person."

My dad poked a finger into his chest. "Oh no, I don't think I have. You're Sam Barlow, aren't you? Do you know who I am?"

"I'm pretty sure I couldn't care less," Sam said. "But you do need to get out of my face, old man."

"Don't you 'old man' me. I know what you did to my wife. I mean, ex-wife."

Savvy Sam gave one of his smarmy grins that made me want to wiggle my nose and turn his pants inside out, but who knew what might happen if I actually tried it? It wasn't worth the risk, especially if it blew my cover behind my plant hideaway. "You have to narrow that one down a bit, I'm afraid. There have been a few wives." *Then again, maybe it was worth the risk.*

I saw my dad's right fist clench by his side. This might be the time to leap out and make my presence known, to stop this before it turned to violence. Much as I wanted to see Sam Barlow suffer a little, I was sure my dad would not be any good in the fighting department. Yet another instinct within me said that I needed to stay hidden and see what was going on here. The man by the fireplace rustled his paper and turned the page, and Rose watched the two men like a hawk, but otherwise, everything stayed quiet. There was something surreal about the whole situation.

"Julia-Mae Grace," Dad said. "Remember her?"

"Julia-Mae?" Sam said with an overplayed gesture of trying to recall. "Oh yeah. You must be Jeff."

"Jacob."

"Yeah, whatever. Well, you've got no worries there, buddy. I've had my fun already. That thing they say about older women being more experienced—"

Sam didn't get to finish what he was saying because, suddenly, my dad had a hold of the front of his shirt, pushing him several steps backward so that Sam bumped into a chair that was behind him. "I'm not talking about that! I'm talking about the fact that you used magic on her." *How the heck does he know about that?* "What kind of a sick individual uses magic on a woman in that way, huh? Controlling their mind."

Sam pushed my father away and smoothed the front of his suit. He glanced one way toward Rose, then the other way to the man sitting by the fireplace, licking his lips a little nervously. "I have no idea what you're talking about, you crazy old fool." I saw something change in Sam's expression, like he was coming to a decision to do what he wanted to do, disregarding the consequences. "But I do have powerful friends," he said, a heavy weight to his voice I hadn't heard before. "Let me tell you that. I wouldn't even have to end you myself."

"I'm not scared of you," Jacob said. It was still strange to see him this way—so angry and passionate. "You stay away from Julia-Mae, you hear me? And all my family. Or you will regret it."

Behind the reception desk, Rose clapped her hands together, the loud noise cutting through the argument and the otherwise oddly peaceful entrance foyer. "That's enough now!" she shouted. Rose had quite the authoritative voice when she wanted to. I even felt a little chastised where I was hiding behind the giant potted plant.

Suddenly, the man with the paper dropped it onto his lap and looked up, staring straight at me. His face creased in concentration, and he continued to look in my direction for a couple more seconds before giving a slight shrug and picking up his paper again. He still hadn't reacted to the argument, though.

"Now, Mr. Grace," Rose said. "I'm going to have to ask you to leave. You can't come into my establishment and cause this kind of fuss."

Finally, my dad looked a little chastened. "I apologize, Mrs. Gantz."

"Be that as it may," Rose continued, "I'm not sure I can honor your booking for this evening any longer, given your behavior and the fact that your ex-wife—the cause of such disagreement—is already staying here. We are... not looking for that kind of drama at The Rose Garden guest house."

Yeah, sure, Rose, I thought.

At that moment, I noticed that my mother had appeared at the top of the last flight of stairs coming from the rooms on the first floor. My dad noticed, as well, looking up and drawing Rose's attention. Only the man by the fireplace did not see her, reaching over to take a sip of his drink.

Sam grinned that oily smile of his and nodded toward the stairs. "Julia-Mae, nice to see you again."

He winked at my mom and then turned and headed toward the door, walking within a couple of feet of me, yet Sam didn't seem to notice that I was there at all. Were the plant and coat rack that good at hiding me? The light in the foyer of The Rose Garden guest house was not great, I guessed, but it was far from dark. Still, no one seemed to notice me. It almost felt like I was a ghost.

There was a long moment of silence as my dad looked up at

my mother. Just before the door closed following Sam's exit, Mojo slipped through it and rubbed himself against my legs. *Nice job hiding,* I heard him say in my head.

The way he had sauntered over to me, I expected to hear a sarcastic remark about the fact that I was standing behind a plant and a silly coat rack. However, it sounded like Mojo meant it. *Is that why no one can see me?* I asked. The next words made me feel a little ridiculous, but I needed to ask. *Am I invisible?*

Not so much invisible as doing a good job of blending in with magic. Almost as good as a cat can do it. Almost.

Thanks, I guess. I didn't know that cats *could* use magic to do things like that. Then again, I had never really felt that my ability to speak to Mojo in my head was all about me. So it made sense that cats could do other things with magic. I mean, I already knew they could see ghosts. Either way, Mojo had confirmed the sense I was getting that there was something supernatural in the way I was staying hidden.

My mom came down the stairs and stood a few feet away from my father.

The haughty expression on Rose's face softened slightly, replaced by the usual look of interest she had when expecting that gossip was about to fall into her lap.

"Jacob," my mom said. "That was very... chivalrous of you."

"Well," my dad replied, "we may not be married anymore, but you are still the mother of our beautiful daughter. And I will never let anyone treat you the way that man has."

I saw my mother's face soften, her hand coming halfway up in what looked like an involuntary gesture of unmasked longing as she took another step toward him. They were now only a pace or two from each other.

Of course, Mojo said in my head, seemingly oblivious to the tension of the moment unfolding in front of us, *it seems a little hypocritical of you to criticize your grandfather for spying on people when that is exactly what you are doing right now.*

"What?" I said, realizing a moment too late that I'd spoken out loud. Suddenly, everyone in the foyer looked my way, even the man with the newspaper. Understanding that the game was up, I stepped out from behind the potted plant as if I'd always meant to do so.

Before I could try to explain myself, the front door opened behind me, and a woman with a suitcase in one hand and a bag in the other struggled into the entrance foyer. She looked up, saw my dad, and smiled.

Pretty, she had curly dark hair and was probably in her late forties, with the easy but polished look of someone with an exciting, glamorous job, like something in advertising or fashion.

"Hi, honey," she said, trotting up to my father. Then she stood on her tiptoes and kissed him on the cheek.

CHAPTER
SEVEN

I drove my father and his girlfriend to the motel on the edge of town to get them out of The Rose Garden without further incident. Dad sat next to me in the front seat of Maude, and his girlfriend, Gillian Mead, was in the back with my cats crawling all over her. She looked quite uncomfortable about that. Gillian was a little younger than Dad but, thankfully, still quite a bit older than me.

"Did you know she was coming so early?" I asked, still thinking of my mother's face when Gillian had turned up. Julia-Mae could sometimes be a person to feel sorry for. Yet there had been a certain tightening around her mouth and a dilation of her eyes, which had done something quite terrible to my insides.

"Like I said," my father answered quietly, although he didn't need to whisper as it was easy to have a conversation in private due to Maude's noisy engine—my old girl did like to make a fuss about getting places. "I thought she would get here later. She decided to surprise me a bit early. She had her friend pick her up and bring her to the guest house after I texted her about staying there. She was trying to be romantic, I think."

I glanced in the rearview mirror. I supposed Gillian had meant well, and my father did deserve someone nice. "She seems nice enough. Not a cat lover, though. It's just... that could not have been more awkward back there."

"I thought your mother acted with dignity."

"I think she was in shock. Just wait until that passes."

I had been joking. Well... kind of. My dad did not seem to take it as a joke, though, and he ground his teeth.

"We're not married anymore, Sidney. It's been quite some time, you know. I am allowed to move on. And it's not like I did this on purpose."

My dad's speech had the sense of something prepared, like he had been rehearsing it since we got into Maude. He sounded like he was feeling guilty about it. I knew him well enough that he did not want to hurt Mom. Maybe he didn't even think it was possible to do so. But Jacob Grace was a considerate man, so he would always be careful to avoid the possibility if he could. "I know," I said.

Looking in the mirror again, I could see that Gillian was tentatively trying to stroke Jinx, who was imposing himself all over her.

"Jacob, honey," Gillian called out from the back. "Why didn't we stay at that charming guest house again?"

"Dad's banned," I called out mischievously.

Jacob looked sharply at me, and I tried to subdue my smile with little success. "What? The ladies love a bad boy."

"Why?" Gillian called over the noise of the camper van.

My dad's eyes flicked across to me again. He seemed reluctant to reply, so I thought I would do it for him. "He was standing up for his family. Like a good man does. It's a long story, but that's the short of it."

"Oh... okay. Well, that's good to know... I think. I'll have to tell my friend we've moved locations, but I can do that at the little get-together tonight. Jacob, you'll still be able to drop me off tonight, right? I know you want to spend time with your family."

"Yes, of course."

After a few minutes of driving in silence, my dad spoke again. "I like Gillian. She's fun. She's got... energy."

"Eww. Not sure I need to know that much."

"I don't mean *that*. I just mean that she's... revitalizing me. And I need that."

I reached across and squeezed my father's arm. "That's good." I was a little surprised to realize I meant that.

Maude pulled into the parking lot of the Tropical Oasis, which seemed like an oxymoron upon closer inspection. It was certainly rundown, just short of seedy looking. The sign in the parking lot was straight out of the fifties and was bringing down the cool factor of the neighborhood. But wasn't that retro look coming back into style? Maybe they were onto something by keeping the old sign around. Anything to make the hotel look somewhat passable.

"This is where that antique thief was staying, wasn't it?" my dad asked.

It's the closest place you aren't banned from," I replied with a grin.

Jacob winced and turned back to his new girlfriend. "We're here, hun!"

Yeesh. Was my dad this cringe-worthy before?

"Really?" Gillian sighed. "Oh, okay. Thank you for the ride, Sidney. It was lovely to meet you."

"Sure. You too," I said, then watched as the pair of them moved off toward the main entrance. I was just about to pull away when I noticed someone was sitting next to me in the passenger seat.

I let out a small shriek before I realized who it was. "Gramps! Do you have to do that? Scare me to death when you arrive?"

I noticed, as had been the case back on the beach, just how clear and visible Gramps was compared to before and to other ghosts I had seen. He really could have been standing there right in front of me, and I wondered whether this difference had to do with Gramps or with me. Maybe I was getting better at seeing ghosts.

"Sorry," Gramps said. "I didn't want to distract you when you were driving. Or, you know, superimpose myself over Jacob."

"Yeah, thanks. That would have been more mind-blowing than distracting."

He glanced over his shoulder to where Gillian had sat in the back of Maude.

"She is—"

"I'm sure she's very nice," I cut in, surprising myself at how protective I was being of this woman I'd only just met. "Did you hear what Mom said?"

"No. I couldn't go into The Rose Garden, remember?"

"I think she still has feelings for Dad."

"Oh, dear."

"That's putting it lightly. Look, I need to get into town. Can we drive and talk?"

Gramps nodded, a little too enthusiastic about the idea. "Sure. I've been practicing this."

"Practicing what?"

"Well, interacting with solid material is a little tough. It takes a lot of effort for me even to sit here and be moved alongside Maude."

"Oh." I hadn't thought about that. But it did make sense, I guessed. I remembered how some of his previous physical interactions had seemed to drain him until he faded away.

"So," Gramps went on. "It's actually easier for me to float along in a sitting position at the same speed as the camper van. It just takes practice to stay in the right place. Start driving, and I'll show you."

I pulled away, keeping half an eye on what was happening with Gramps. He wobbled in the seat a little, attempting to match the speed and slight directions I made as I pulled out of the parking lot. It was quite impressive, though.

"I'm not sure I've ever seen Dad as angry as he was with Sam Barlow today," I said after we had been driving for a few moments. "I found out Ada-Mae told him about Mom and Sam."

Gramps nodded. "Maybe not her finest moment, but...."

"What?"

"It really got to her. You know, what happened to Julia-Mae at the golf competition. The way she was a victim of that man's despicable magic. Your grandmother likes to let everyone think she is as tough as old boots, but...."

"I get it. Still, whatever terrible thing you thought was going to happen, I think we're safe from that now."

Gramp's silence was telling. He slid sideways in the seat as I turned Maude so that, for a moment, he was bisected by the door. Which was unsettling. He slowly corrected his position, sliding sideways again to end up right back in the seat beside me, although now I got the sense of him hovering above the seat, making him look much taller.

He glanced over at me as though there was nothing weird happening at all.

"Does this silence mean that we're not really safe for now?" I asked.

"Remember how I couldn't go into The Rose Garden?"

I nodded. "Yes, but what does that mean?"

"That wasn't Sam Barlow. Or the argument between him and your father. That wasn't what kept me out. I'm worried there's something more at The Rose Garden. More going on there than meets the eye, maybe."

"Well, you're just full of cheery news today, aren't you?" I winced. I just wanted Ada-Mae to have a nice birthday.

"There's something in that guest house, Sidney. I don't know if it's a person or a thing, or... something else."

"What doesn't fall under a person or thing?"

"I don't know, but you need to check it out."

I slammed on the brakes as a car in front of me suddenly stopped at a crosswalk. Gramps's ghost flew through the windshield, his body sailing right through the car in front of us until he landed in a sitting position in their back seat. Fortunately, no one else was sitting there with him ... because even if they couldn't see Gramps like I could, I felt certain they would feel his ghostly presence.

Realizing what had happened, Gramps glanced back over his shoulder and backed up in some weird parody of reversing an invisible car. If one could parody that.

When he arrived back in the seat next to me, I spoke again, carrying on with our conversation without missing a beat. "I need to check it out, do I?" Sometimes, having magic powers felt a lot like being at everyone else's beck and call.

Gramps shrugged. "I just think it's important, Sid."

"It makes sense, though," I admitted. "The antique thief with the magic brooch was trying to find something at The Rose Garden when he was caught. I don't think he found it, either. Maybe that's what you're sensing."

"Maybe you should speak to your grandmother. Get the whole Scooby Gang together."

I had to smile at the Scooby Gang reference this time around. "No. It's her birthday tomorrow. Let's give her a few days off from... all of this.

"And I know someone else who might help. As it happens, I was on my way there anyhow."

CHAPTER

EIGHT

I headed back into the center of town to pick up Ada-Mae's birthday present from The Invisible Cloak. Walking through the distinctive curtain at the entrance to Zoe's shop was like walking through a veil between worlds. I found that the store was empty, aside from Zoe, who stood behind the counter, and one other person, who was leaning over the counter from the other side.

I smiled when I noticed that the other person was Jessie. The two women were deep in conversation, their foreheads inches from each other. Jessie jumped up when she heard me come in.

"Oh, hi, Sidney," she said.

"Hey, Jessie," I replied. "Didn't know you shopped here."

"No... well, I, um...."

Behind Jessie, I saw Zoe smirk. It shouldn't have been such a tough question.

Jessie pointed toward the door. "Well, I had better get back to work. Crime never sleeps and all that."

"See ya later." Zoe winked, and I noticed Jessie's cheeks blush. It appeared that my lame attempt at an attraction spell wasn't even necessary to help Jessie in the dating department. If I wasn't so happy for her, my own cheeks would have blushed from embarrassment too.

I watched Jessie hurry out and then turned back to Zoe. "Things must be quiet today for the Crystal Beach Police Department, eh?"

"If there're no murders or burglaries, they just don't know what to do with themselves," Zoe replied with a laugh.

"Is it in?" I asked, approaching the counter.

"Yes. Came in first thing." Zoe reached behind the counter and pulled out a package wrapped in brown paper.

"Thank goodness. Imagine not having my grandmother's present in time for her birthday."

Zoe found a bag for me to put it in as well. "Does Ada-Mae have plans?" she asked.

Even though no one was in the shop, I instinctively leaned forward and lowered my voice. "Well, Ernie has arranged something. A birthday cruise timed to watch the space launch tomorrow evening."

"Ooh, that sounds fun."

"You should come," I said. "All are welcome. Especially Quipley's students."

Zoe shrugged and looked at the floor. I liked the young magic shop owner but was still getting used to the way she often swung between seeming quite confident one moment and rather bashful the next. "Oh, I don't know."

I knew exactly the incentive, however, and glanced back to the doorway where Crystal Beach's deputy had just exited. "Jessie is coming."

Zoe gave me a "mind your own business" look. Not that she suppressed the smile that came with it. "Maybe I can make it."

Silence fell between us for a moment as I tried to figure out how to say the other thing I had come in to ask.

"What?"

"I kind of have a favor to ask. And it's a big one."

"Sure."

"Please say no if you've got any doubts."

Zoe rolled her eyes and huffed a little impatiently. "Just shoot."

"I'm... um, I'm running my own MRM tonight."

"MRM?"

"Yeah, Magic-Related Mission. I need to look for something at The Rose Garden."

Zoe crossed her arms, and I knew I now had her full attention.

"I think the burglar was after a magical item at the guest house on the night he got caught, something powerful, I suspect. I just... I never felt that the spell we did at Mystic Dunes was only leading us to the burglar.

"I think maybe it was leading us to whatever he was after. Something important, maybe. And now Mystic Dunes is suddenly full of people, and it feels like whatever Sam is up to is about to happen. We need to find out what is in that guest house. It could help us."

I stopped, realizing I had sort of blurted out all my thoughts at once.

Zoe looked thoughtful and chewed on her bottom lip for a moment before speaking. "You really think things are happening?

"I do," I nodded.

"Because... I don't know. I don't feel like that at all. Things feel calmer to me than they have in ages. And I'm usually quite sensitive to magic happening in the town. It's my only real power, sensing magic. It's why I run a magic shop."

I found it hard to believe that Zoe's powers were as limited as she was claiming, remembering how powerful she had appeared to be during the crystal test at Quipley's School of Magic.

"But... Mystic Dunes," I said. It felt like the name of the development had become a popular refrain for me, yet I was sure there was some bigger purpose to the place than just ripping off a few home buyers.

Zoe nodded, so I thought she got what I was saying. "Yeah. Even Sam, with all his extra magical help, is not that good of a realtor. But that doesn't mean anything is about to happen."

I failed to hide my disappointment, and Zoe noticed, her face softening. She had pretty features, which she hid behind a lot of dark-colored makeup. "But I'll come tonight. Of course, I will. Is Ada-Mae coming to?"

"No. Like I said, I'm kind of running my own mission, and I wanted to do it without her knowing."

Zoe lifted an eyebrow at that.

"It's not that I'm going behind her back," I added hurriedly. "But I feel she needs a few days off from things. And maybe you're right. Maybe it isn't anything. I need backup, though. Gramps would come, but some force is keeping him out of The Rose Garden. It might be this thing or power, whatever it is, that's doing that."

"Gramps?"

"Well, yeah," I said, remembering that Zoe may not have been in on the whole "my dead grandpa is still hanging around" thing. "His ghost has kind of been helping with things."

"Ah, right."

This felt like one of those "only in Crystal Beach" conversations.

"I met him when he was still alive a few times," Zoe said. "He was nice. I bet it's good to have him still around."

I smiled gratefully and went on. "So, my mom is staying there. It shouldn't be too hard to find a good reason for me to be there."

"And me?"

"We'll figure out something. But my mom doesn't know, and it needs to stay that way. She hates magic."

Zoe looked surprised. Considering what she knew of my other family members, it was a sensible reaction.

"I'll do all the searching," I said, "but I need you to back me up. Especially with those keen senses of yours."

Suddenly, the veil at the front of the shop flew open, and my mother walked in. Her sudden presence in a magic shop made me feel awkward, considering the conversation I had just been having with Zoe. "Ah, here you are," my mother said. "I've been looking for you everywhere. Then I remembered you had to pick up your grandmother's gift." She said the last word like a pungent taste had filled her mouth.

"Yes, sorry for the fast exit. I just, you know, thought I should get Dad out of there."

Out of the corner of my eye, I noticed Zoe looking between the two of us, confused. At the mention of my father, however, my mother was already starting to tear up, even blubbering a little.

I rushed over to comfort her but tripped on the way, falling into a display of gemstones and scattering hundreds of them across the floor of the shop.

"Oh no! Zoe, I'm so sorry." I hopped back and forth, caught

between the desire to pick up the mess I had created and the need to comfort my mother.

Zoe rushed out from behind the counter and waved me toward my mother. "It's fine, Sidney. It was a slow day, anyway. This will keep me busy for a while. I'll see you later, yeah?"

Outside the shop, I guided my mother toward Maude, which was parked nearby. I opened the passenger door and helped her up into the seat before running around to the other side.

"Can we go to the beach?" my mother asked, sniffing. "I think I need to sit down by the sea. Maybe close to... Where was the place I nearly bought a house again?"

It wasn't that long ago, and that she couldn't even remember the name of it was a testament, in my opinion, to just how addled her brain had been. Blooming Sam Barlow and his evil magic.

"Mystic Dunes?" I said in a way that suggested it had not been a huge part of my vocabulary in the weeks since she last visited.

"Yes. I know that buying there would have been a mistake, but I like that end of the beach. It feels... wild to me."

"Wild" wasn't a thing I tended to connect with my mother, especially seeing as she had moved as far into the center of New York as she could after splitting with my father. "Sure. We'll head there."

I drove almost all the way down to the Mystic Dunes development, parking as close to the beach as I could. We both kicked off our shoes and walked down to sit at the back of the beach, just across the narrow creek from Mystic Dunes.

We were quiet for a while, my mother with her arms wrapped around her knees. Looking around, feeling a cool breeze on my skin, I saw that my mother was right. There was something a little wilder about this end of the beach. It almost had an energy to it.

"Are you okay?" I asked.

"Sure. Just a little blindsided at the guest house. I need to get it together, though. I cannot ruin your grandmother's eightieth birthday."

Who are you, and what have you done with my mother? I thought before chastising myself for failing to recognize her better side.

My mother looked over at Mystic Dunes. "When your father and I divorced, I thought it was a chance to take some time for myself, you know? There were things I felt I'd missed out on as a mother and wife in suburban Boston. High-end shops, sophisticated friends. Culture. All those things my mother and father never appreciated or understood. Or your father, for that matter. Although, at least, he tried. I was upset about the things I had missed out on."

"But..." I said, helping my mother along when she paused.

"I'm not upset anymore. I realized I wasn't missing out after all. Because the things I thought I wanted were not important. Only the things I left behind were.

"Now, your grandfather has passed away, and your father has found someone else. The things I care about the most...are slipping away from me."

Her voice shuddered as she forced back her tears.

We were quiet for a long moment, and I didn't know what to say. I knew what I wanted to tell her, like how letting magic into her life might make things easier. But I sensed it wasn't the right time and, anyway, I didn't even know how to start.

"Your father has every right to move on. Of course, he does," my mother continued.

"But you wish he wasn't doing it at your mother's eightieth birthday celebration," I said with a small, ironic laugh.

"I know that Sam fella was a snake and that buying at Mystic Dunes would have been a terrible investment." She stopped to wave a hand toward the nearby development. "Although a lot of people seem to disagree with that suddenly. It was a pleasant dream for a while, though. Being wanted again. Living by the sea in a beautiful town, close to my mother and daughter."

I followed the irresistible urge to reach out and squeeze my mother's arm. "None of that is impossible, Mom."

"But won't I always be just a little apart from the rest of you? You all have this thing, this magic that binds you together."

A huge flood of relief washed through me, grateful that my mother had opened the door to the conversation I wanted to have. "That depends on you more than anyone else. Ernie, grandmother's friend, made me realize that earlier today. Magic isn't only about power. It's a state of mind. An open mind. A way of living. And it is there for everyone."

"Good day to you, ladies."

We both jumped and looked around as those words came from a man that had approached unseen behind us. He had a rich, accented voice. Eastern European, perhaps. It belonged to a broad-shouldered man with a square jaw and a deep tan. Black hair was flecked with silver here and there, and there was a bald patch on top, although he carried it off a little more flatteringly than most men. A little overweight, the newcomer nonetheless had an athletic build lurking somewhere below the surface. He looked middle-aged, perhaps around the same age as my mother.

"I'm sorry to startle you," he said. "I came over to say hello."

I realized this was the same man I had seen earlier. He was the man sitting in the chair in The Rose Garden while my father and Sam argued in the middle of the foyer. I remembered how he had ignored the argument, continuing to read his paper.

He pointed his thumb over his shoulder, indicating the development behind him. "I have recently bought a house over at... how you say?

"Mystic Dunes," I filled in. Totally not obsessed with the place.

"Yes, Mystic Dunes. And I'm keen to meet new people in Crystal Beach. My name is Nikola Vorak."

Nikola extended his hand, and both my mother and I stood up to shake it, each of us introducing ourselves as we did so. I noticed that his grip was firm and his hand warm.

"Ah. Sisters, no?" Nikola said when he had heard that we both had the same surname.

My mother giggled appreciatively, though it seemed a bit of a cheesy line to me. "You bought from Savvy Sam?" I asked.

It took Nikola a moment to register what I was saying. "Mr. Barlow? Yes. Yes, I did."

"You know nearly all those properties were empty a couple of weeks ago?" I said.

"I know. I was lucky to get one before... how you say? They were all snapped up!"

"Which one is yours?" my mother asked.

Nikola pointed to the nearest house. "Number One, if you believe it."

I could see from where we were, quite close to the buildings, that there was a large plaque next to the door of the house with the number "1" painted on it. Looking further, I noticed the other houses now had address plaques on them as well, although I could not recall them being there before. Perhaps they had been put up right before people started moving in.

"Well, it is nice to meet you, ladies," Nikola said. "Hopefully, I will see you around town, no?"

"I'm only visiting, I'm afraid," my mother said.

He looked disappointed, and I failed to suppress a little protective feeling toward my mother. *Hands off, buddy!*

"Well, maybe," I said, giving my mother a reassuring smile. I realized how nice it would be if she could stay around longer, maybe even move to Crystal Beach with all of us.

We watched Nikola walk back toward his house for a moment, then my mother said, "I thought I would spend the day with your grandmother tomorrow. Keep her occupied until the party."

"Good idea," I said. "Will you be at the guest house tonight, though? I wanted to visit."

"Sure, I can be."

"Might be late. After dark."

She shrugged her agreement but then paused, narrowing her eyes. "Wait a minute. Are you up to something? Something to do with magic?"

Oh no, busted.

But my mother's smile relaxed. "It's okay if you are, you know."

Again, what have you done with my mother?

CHAPTER

NINE

T he entrance foyer of The Rose Garden guest house was
quiet and almost entirely dark when Zoe and I walked
into it later that evening. Only the glowing embers
coming from the fireplace provided any light at all, just a little of it
casting across the chair where Mr. Nikola Vorak had been sitting
earlier in the day.

"We're not that late, are we?" I said to Zoe. "No Rose or
Rodney."

Zoe whispered to me. "Maybe they're upstairs in their rooms.
Will that make it harder, do you think?"

"Maybe. But at least we don't have to answer any questions right now." Rose always had a box full of questions for everyone.

We headed upstairs quietly, finding my mother's room not far past the top of the landing. She opened the door to my cautious knock and looked Zoe and me up and down, taking in the dark clothes we were both wearing.

"Well, don't the two of you look just like a pair of criminals?"

"Mom!" I said, both insulted and embarrassed.

"I always dress like this," Zoe said with a shrug. Which was true.

My mother stepped aside. "Come on in, then. Do you have time for a drink before... whatever you are doing here? I'm pretty sure I don't want to know, do I?"

Zoe looked at me, confused. "I thought we weren't—"

"Mom's working on being cooler now."

My mom cocked her brow at that. "Hey, I was always cool." Then, after catching a look from me, she corrected herself. "In my own kind of way."

"Have you seen Rose and Rodney, Mom?"

"Not since dinner. And, by the way, I think I will dine out in the future. Rose's cooking is just boiling things to within an inch of their life."

"If there's a chance they are out of the way, we should try to find what we're looking for now," I said. "There's an item in this house... most likely."

"Most likely?"

"Something which might have great power and could be connected to dark forces at work in Crystal Beach."

I sounded like a trailer for a TV show and could see my mother struggling with her new openness to the whole magic thing. To her credit, she continued to stay engaged in the conversation. "Dark forces? What are these dark forces up to?"

Maybe I liked it better when my mother hadn't been that interested. "Well... that's what we would like to find out."

"Except for fixing golf tournaments and selling dodgy condos," she added with a laugh.

"And stealing space technology," Zoe put in.

"But there must be something more they want," I said, speaking to myself and my own convictions.

"Must there?" my mother said.

"Surely."

"I don't know. Power, prestige, money. That's what most people want. And it sounds like the sort of things they have already."

Annoyingly, my mother was making an awful lot of sense.

"Not that I'm saying someone shouldn't stop them," she added. Possibly a reaction to the crestfallen expression I could feel dragging my face downward. But then she went a little too far, doing an imaginary pom-pom wave like a cheerleader. "Goooo, Sidney!"

Well, at least she was trying.

"Let's move," I said, turning to Zoe. "Have you got anything? Any feelings?"

Zoe closed her eyes. "It's very vague, I'm afraid. I feel like there is power all over this house. But this place is also old, and old homes have power and presence. Like they hold a residue of what has come before." She nodded back out toward the hallway. "Let's move. Maybe I'll get a better sense of what it is out there."

We left my mother's room and continued to move carefully along the hall. There was the sound of a television a few doors further up, and seeing as it had a number on it, I assumed it was just another guest in their room.

Then, at the other end of the hall, we came to a short set of stairs leading up to the left.

"Up there," Zoe said.

"You sure? The burglar was looking on this level."

Zoe looked back down the corridor and shrugged. "I admit I'm not sure at all. There's a strange vibe in here. It's... distracting."

"You've been in here before, though? It didn't always feel like this?"

"It's been quite a while since I've been inside here," Zoe admitted. "And I wasn't actively trying to use my powers then. Sorry, I can't be more helpful."

I put a hand on her shoulder. "No, that's fine. It's much better than me just blundering around. You stay here, yeah? Keep a lookout while I check what's up there."

When I got to the top of the stairs, I tried the door handle and was pleasantly surprised and a little worried to find it open. "Careless," I muttered to myself.

Walking into the room, half of it was cast in the bright moonlight from beyond a dormer window on the opposite side. From what I could see, the room was surprisingly small—one main living room with a little kitchenette against the wall to one side. There were a few chairs and an old cathode-ray TV set on a rickety-looking table.

As a guest house, The Rose Garden was all about rustic charm, yet there was something a little sad and run down about the owners' private space. Which didn't add up to me.

I looked around for a light switch and then decided it might be safer to turn on the small lamp with a dusty, cloth-covered lampshade. I looked around for a good minute or more, not seeing anything that stood out to me as a potential magic item. I was considering going back and getting Zoe when a voice made me jump out of my skin.

"It's down there," Gramps said.

I whirled around and saw Gramps sitting in one of the chairs. "Will you stop trying to scare me to death?"

"Sorry."

"Wait," I said. "I didn't think you could come in here?"

Gramps just shrugged. "Apparently, I can. Whatever was keeping me out is not here right now. I can sense that something is here, though." A finger pointed toward the floor. "And it is down there."

"But Zoe said it was up here."

Maybe it's both, came a new voice, this one in my head. I spun around again to see a familiar shape trotting out of the shadows: my cat, Mojo. I took the opportunity to turn a slow, dramatic circle, my arms flared out and my palms up. "Anyone else hiding up here?"

For the moment, silence greeted my inquiry.

"Are you following me?" I asked my cat.

Thought you might need a hand.

"What do you mean by 'both?'" Gramps said to Mojo.

Well, obviously, my grandfather could hear my cat too. Somehow, I wasn't surprised. Mojo did a leisurely walk into the middle of the room and stopped in the center of a faded Persian rug that was gold and deep scarlet. His head sort of nodded downward in what was an oddly human gesture. When I said nothing, he did it a couple more times, becoming increasingly impatient.

Houston to Sidney.

"Oh!" I said at last and moved over to pull the rug back.

She gets it at last.

Moving the rug revealed a trapdoor, sitting flush with the rest of the flooring, the handle set back into the wood.

Gramps's ghost stood up to look. "Well, slap me with bread and call me a sandwich."

I pulled back the trapdoor, revealing a steep set of steps into a dark space below, a room adjacent to the floor below where Zoe stood guard..

"Up here and down there," Gramps mused.

Suddenly, Mojo let out a loud hiss and scrambled back toward the dormer window. Almost at the same time, I noticed a shadow moving around the outer edges of the room. Tracking it, I realized that no physical object was making the shadow. The shadow was the object.

"What's that?" I asked.

Whatever it is, I don't like it. Mojo hissed louder.

"A supernatural security system," Gramps added, and I could hear the fear in his voice. "You're in danger."

The shadow lunged into the middle of the room, and Gramps moved between the shadow and its intended target—me. The two of them wrestled for a moment, the shadow taking on a vaguely humanoid form as it did so. I could see Gramps's vivid, ghostly form fading a little with the effort of fighting it.

The shadow spirit won out, grabbing Gramps by his wrists and slinging him with impossible speed to vanish through the dormer window and far beyond it.

"Gramps!" I screamed.

The shadow barely paused before moving to envelop me, filling my head with hundreds of spiteful voices at once. It was a suffocating feeling, like being trapped in a tiny space, and after a moment, I realized it was getting harder to breathe.

"Mojo, help!" I squealed.

I can't fight it, Sidney, Mojo replied. *But you can if you try.*

I dropped to the floor, narrowly avoiding falling into the secret room that had just been revealed. Fighting this terrible, all-encompassing force seemed an impossibility, but I reached inside myself and tried to force it away from me, as all my flailing and pushing with my arms was not doing a thing.

My first effort did nothing, so I calmed myself, despite becoming quite desperate for air. I formed an image in my mind of a solid wall that could push the spirit away from me. For a moment, I felt the shadow spirit bend, but on the point of breaking it, the last of my will crumbled away instead, and I knew the thing had me. All was lost.

CHAPTER
TEN

Suddenly, there was a face above me, at once familiar but, at the same time, strange and feral. It was like a cross between a person and a wild beast from some nightmare fairytale, all teeth and hair and drooling terror.

The spiteful voices in my head turned to screams, and the shadow released me, enabling me to breathe again. As I watched, the shadow shrank away into the corner of the room, still screaming, until it became nothing. My head snapped back around, looking for the feral beast that must have saved me, but all I could see was Zoe looking down at me, concern etched on her face.

"Are you all right?" she asked.

"Yeah, I think so. Thanks."

"I heard the commotion," Zoe said and glanced across the room. "Oh, your cat is here."

I thought about quizzing Zoe about the feral beast I had seen during the fight, but I just wanted to get on with our search and find what we had come looking for. I rushed over to the window to see if I could find out what had happened to Gramps. Scanning the yard, there was no sign of him, and then I saw Sam Barlow pulling up in his flashy sports car.

"Sam is here! Mojo, Zoe, do you think you could hold him up if he tries to come upstairs?"

What am I supposed to do? Mojo said.

"Be a cat," I said. "People love cats. Maybe play with some yarn or something."

I'm going to pretend I didn't hear you say that. Mojo ran past me and downstairs.

Zoe turned to me. "I'm going to assume he said 'yes.'"

Zoe disappeared after Mojo, and I made my way down into the secret room, finding the switch to a dull bulb that illuminated a tiny pentagonal space only ten feet across. It was full of books and an impossibly large amount of spell paraphernalia.

Out of place among all of that, there was a house address plaque propped against the wall on top of a low bookcase. The plaque was familiar, looking very similar to the number "1" plaque I had seen on Nikola Vorak's house earlier in the day.

"That's the one!"

I jumped a little again, although I was getting used to Gramps appearing and trying to scare the heck out of me. Looking around, I saw he had appeared again behind my left shoulder.

"I didn't know what had happened to you," I said.

"Yes, sorry about that. I landed halfway between the main road and the beach. You took care of that thing, then?"

"Zoe did," I said. I thought about telling him about the beast that had been there, too, but it seemed like too much conversation with our prize right in front of us.

"Oh. Good for her. That Barlow idiot was walking in when I got back."

I nodded. "Zoe and Mojo are on it. Hopefully. Why would an address plaque be the thing I'm looking for? But now that I'm here and looking at it, I agree with you. This is what I wanted to find."

"That's what the Mystic Dunes spell was leading you all to?"

It was. Looking at it, I felt attracted to the thing and reached out my hand to touch it.

Gramps's ghost sucked in an airless breath between his teeth. "Sure you want to do that, Sid?"

My hand stopped, though only for a second. It didn't matter if I wanted to do it; I was going to do it. I felt a powerful jolt go through me the moment my fingers met the cold slate of the address plaque, forcing my eyes closed and throwing my head back.

Through my closed eyes, I could see a vision of somewhere else, although this place looked a little distorted, like looking through a fisheye lens. The longer I stayed in the moment, the more I felt like I was actually there in a modern, familiar-looking house. As the seconds passed, I became sure that it was one of the newly built houses at Mystic Dunes. Someone walked into view, close to me, before turning to reveal that it was Nikola Vorak. He was holding a large glass of what looked like red wine.

I became aware that there were other people there, milling around behind Mr. Vorak, a little out of focus from my point of view. Sound slowly entered the vision as well, the noise of many voices speaking at once. A bright clinking sound. Glasses, perhaps? This was a party. Mr. Vorak, the keen new resident of Mystic Dunes, was having a party, possibly to meet his new neighbors.

My view moved with the host as he passed through the living area, through a set of French doors, and onto a deck. A few feet of dunes and the ocean were in front of him, the way into the development and the parking lot visible to the side. Nikola Vorak raised a glass and a figure on the balcony who, up until that point, had stood with his back to the host, turned and clinked glasses. It was Sam Barlow. The same Sam Barlow—and please, let there only be the one—who had supposedly just arrived at The Rose Garden.

Perhaps what I was seeing was not current. Maybe this had already happened. Was this a window into the past? Or an event in the future? Or something else entirely?

Nikola turned to face those gathered inside, back through the open doors, and raised his glass. "To Mr. Samuel Barlow, a great realtor," he said in that thick, oddly adorable accent of his. "Who has brought us all together in this wonderful place."

"And at a very affordable price!" shouted out an unseen voice inside, to a general murmur of approval.

"Exactly!" Nikola called out and turned back to a beaming Sam Barlow.

Even through the vision, I could feel the dragon in my stomach waking in anger, the bubbling acid burning my throat. To the side, a car pulled up. A rental vehicle, judging by the logo on the side. My father got out and moved around to open the passenger door. His girlfriend, Gillian, got out, lightly kissed my father on the lips, and moved out of sight toward the front of the building.

A moment later, I heard Nikola Vorak's doorbell ring. I expected my vision to follow him as he went to answer the door, but instead, it lingered. My father stood by the side of the car, looking at Sam Barlow, who didn't appear to have noticed him yet.

Even though it was nighttime, and he was a little distance away, I could see the rage simmering in my father's eyes, the same rage that had burned my insides moments before. Yet everyone knew I could be an emotional person, sometimes led too rashly by my feelings. On my father, it was an alien expression.

He stalked over to stand just below the deck, and Sam Barlow finally noticed him. "What are you doing here?" my father hissed at him.

Sam grinned that self-satisfied grin of his, glancing back to make sure no one was within earshot, and then leaned forward. He made an encompassing gesture, the wine sloshing about in his glass. "I made all this happen. That's what I'm doing here." I could hear the venom in his voice.

My dad's outburst at The Rose Garden earlier in the day had put him in Sam's crosshairs, and he needed to be careful. I suddenly feared for him. Feared that something bad had already happened and that this was what I was being shown. "I'm someone in this town. You would do well to remember that."

My dad pointed a finger up at him. "You're not untouchable, Sam Barlow," he growled. A couple of people inside the party heard his raised voice and came outside to see what was going on. They had an audience now. I noticed that Rose and Rodney were among them, which only confused things further, as they did not appear to be in the guest house right now, even though Sam Barlow was.

"You will get your dues," my dad went on, "trust me. People like you always get what they deserve in the end."

He glanced inside, perhaps considering whether he needed to go and extract Gillian from the party, but in the end, his shoulders just slumped a little, and he returned to his car. I waited for Sam to throw some insult or retort to his back, but none came, and the vision quickly faded. My head whipped forward as I opened my eyes.

"What happened?" Gramps asked as I found myself back in the small, secret room again. "You went rigid for a moment."

I looked down at the address plaque. "This thing, it's... I don't know. Like a spying device. Kind of. I think."

"Spying on who?"

"I had a vision of a man Mom and I met today. He lives in Mystic Dunes. I was just in his house, I think. He was having a party, although I'm not sure it was happening right now. Maybe earlier. Or maybe it hasn't happened yet."

To his credit, Gramps only looked confused for a moment. "So, Rose and Rodney are spying on Mystic Dunes? Do you think they are part of this bad coven? In league with Sam Barlow, maybe?"

I realized I didn't want to believe that. As creepy and weird as they were, I liked Rose and Rodney Gantz. But this hidden evidence of witchcraft, not to mention the fact that Sam Barlow kept turning up at the guest house... All was not as it appeared with the two guest house owners.

"Might be," I replied, shaking my head. I was still trying to get my mind around all I had just discovered and the vision I had seen. Was it even real at all? "Rose and Rodney were in this vision, as were Sam and my dad." I glanced back up the steps. "Anyway, we will worry about that later. Let's get out of here."

I started toward the steps and then looked back at the plaque. "I bet Ada-Mae would love to study this thing."

"What if it works two ways?" Gramps said. "If someone could look back at you?"

I grabbed a cloth bag that was lying nearby and picked up the plaque again, stuffing it into the bag. "Not if I put it in this... let's hope. Either way, I think Rose, Rodney, and Sam Barlow will realize someone has been here, and it's not a big stretch of the imagination to guess it was me."

Back in the room above, I put the trapdoor down and pulled the rug over it. No point in making it look too obvious, though.

"I don't think Mom should stay here anymore," I said to Gramps. "Not with what we found down there and the evidence of magic."

I stuck my head out the doorway and peeked down the hallway. Zoe and Mojo were at the far end, close to the top of the stairs.

"Any sign of Sam?" I asked as I got closer.

"No," Zoe whispered. "What did you find?"

"I'll tell you later. We need to get my mom out of here first."

I went back and quietly knocked on my mom's door. "We need to get you out of here, now," I said in hushed tones when she answered. "No arguments, please."

Much to my surprise, she nodded her agreement. "One minute for me to grab a few things."

"One minute," I agreed. "We might come back tomorrow, but you cannot spend the night here, okay?"

My mother disappeared back inside, and Zoe beckoned me over again, pointing to where Sam Barlow's legs could be seen extended in front of a chair by the fire. The same one Nikola Vorak had occupied earlier. "I didn't notice him at first," she whispered.

"Mojo, do you think you can distract him? Just so we can get out?"

I could sneak into the kitchen and make a noise, Mojo said in my head, then disappeared down the stairs, taking a right past the reception desk. I heard a door close quietly behind me as my mother came out holding a cloth bag over her arm. I hadn't realized Gucci made cloth shopping bags.

A few seconds later, there was a loud clattering coming from the direction of the kitchen. Sam Barlow, however, did not move. Then, after another pause, there was an even louder crash, but still, Sam remained in the chair, unmoving.

Mojo slipped out of the kitchen, dashing by where Sam was sitting, then came back to us. *He is sleeping, I think.*

"Must be tiring work being a scoundrel," I whispered.

Then we snuck down the stairs, cringing at every creak of the old floorboards. We went across the foyer and past the unconscious Sam Barlow, an almost-empty glass of wine that looked like the one he had been holding at the party, now resting on the table beside him. He did not appear to stir at all as we hurried back out into the evening air of Crystal Beach.

CHAPTER

ELEVEN

Ada-Mae's eightieth birthday started off as an incredible day. The sky was a vivid blue that deepened even further toward the horizon, and the Atlantic waters lapped peacefully on the beach. There was a slight breeze, and although the typical Floridian humidity arrived eventually, it was a day for getting out and doing things.

Ada-Mae spent much of the day shopping in Orlando with my mother. This had the sense of being more for Julia-Mae than her less-shopping-inclined mother, but what it was really about was the two women reconnecting. And also keeping my mother and father, with his new girlfriend, as far apart as possible for as long as possible.

At four o'clock on the dot, we all gathered on a small jetty and boarded a boat for a cruise down the Florida coast. Ernie, Judd, Wendy, Howie, and several other residents from Shifting Sands Retirement Center joined the festivities. Zoe had found her way to the jetty too. My mother was on the boat along with my father and Gillian. However, the new couple seemed more interested in each other than the Florida coastline, quietly moving away from everyone on the boat. But I really didn't want to dwell on that too much. When the boat returned to the beach after the launch, there would be a barbecue, which would be catered by Eileen.

The only people who were conspicuous by their absence were John and Jessie, the two members of the Crystal Beach Police Department. Though I felt disappointed that they weren't able to join us, I vowed not to let my feelings get in the way of our celebration because I wanted my grandmother's eightieth birthday to be a special occasion she would always remember.

However, despite enjoying the evening, I found myself a little distracted, wondering whether Gramps was going to turn up. More than that, I was debating whether I should tell Ada-Mae he was back. Maybe not yet. Who knew that ghosts could be so complicated, huh?

I wandered off to one side of the boat, sitting on a bench close to the stern, and looked back toward the beach, which was a thin line some ways behind us. As much as I loved living in Crystal Beach, I felt a sense of relief about being a little away from it for a few hours, even if only offshore, heading toward the horizon. More questions and complications waited for me when we got back. Well, for all of us, really.

Tomorrow I would tell Ada-Mae about the mission to The Rose Garden, unsure whether she would admonish me for not involving her. Either way, however powerful Ada-Mae kept telling me I was, I knew she was the best good witch in Crystal Beach, and she needed to know what was going on. Just not tonight.

As I sat there thinking about everything, I heard someone approaching the railing at the side of the boat, just around the corner from me. The edge of the cabin behind me kept them out of view.

"Thank you for organizing this," I heard Ada-Mae say. "You are a good friend, Ernie."

"Oh, I don't know about that," Ernie replied. "Coming out to watch a rocket launch sounds a lot like doing what I would want to do, not something special just for your birthday."

Ada-Mae laughed gently, and I stood up, leaning around the corner to spy on them.

What? My curiosity sometimes outweighed my moral compass.

A warm flush of excitement went through me as I saw that Ada-Mae had taken Ernie's hand.

"I'm sorry if you felt left out recently," Ada-Mae said. "I got fixated on—"

"Important things," Ernie put in. "You have a lot on your plate. What sort of a man-child would I have to be—?"

"A regular, normal man-child, like everyone else," Ada-Mae jumped in. "And that is allowed, you know."

"I admit it was a blow to realize how little aptitude for magic I have." He held out a hand and wiggled his fingers. "There are a lot of things I would have swapped for some of that in these old things. But not your friendship. Never that."

Ada-Mae's smile faltered, and the two of them turned more fully toward each other. To see what was going on, I had to lean out a little further, pressing against the nearby safety rail.

"What is it?" Ernie asked her.

"You are my best friend, Ernie. It would not do to lose that because I didn't take enough care of our friendship. Of you. But... things are complicated."

Ernie waved her words away. "I'm too old to make things complicated for anybody. It's okay, I get it."

"But. If they were not so complicated... I would, you know."

I stretched myself as far as I could across the railing to avoid missing anything. That's when I realized that I was actually leaning on a gate with a catch that my hand had just pushed to the side. The thing flung open, and I went toppling forward over the side of the boat and headfirst into the water.

"Sidney!" I heard Ada-Mae bellow as I resurfaced. "Stop the boat. Someone, stop the boat!"

I looked up to see Ernie reaching for a life preserver. Ada-Mae held out her arms toward me, and I felt a force pulling me through the water to keep me from getting too far behind the boat. A few seconds later, the boat slowed to a halt, and a life preserver came down, with Ernie holding the other end of the rope.

Although grateful to be rescued and impressed by Ada-Mae's ability to pull out the right sort of magic when needed, I felt my cheeks flush. *Nice work, Sidney. That's what I get for spying on people.* Ada-Mae hustled me below deck with as little fuss as possible. Zoe joined us in the small cabin with seating around the side and an almond-shaped wooden table in the middle. Between the two of them, they worked a spell to dry me off.

Beyond the embarrassment I still felt, I decided it was the perfect time to give Ada-Mae her birthday present, although I was originally going to wait until the beach.

"Zoe got a hold of this for me," I said.

Ada-Mae opened the box wrapped in black paper with silver stars and decorated with a purple ribbon and bow, her eyes lighting up to see the miniature cauldron I had bought, which came with its own miniature gas-fired burner.

"For making potions on the go," I said.

Ada-Mae threw her arms around me. "It's perfect, Sidney. So thoughtful." She looked at both me and Zoe. "You are becoming such an accomplished witch, Sidney. And the two of you should work on projects together. But please let me know the next time you plan a dangerous mission together?"

Zoe looked as surprised as I was. How did Ada-Mae always seem to know everything? *Oh yeah... witch.*

"But I'm very proud of you both."

Then my grandmother headed off to make me a hot chocolate to warm me up, leaving Zoe and me alone for the first time since the previous evening. My mind raced a little, wanting to ask about what I had seen when she rescued me, but the previous evening also seemed quite far away. Almost like a dream. There was enough doubt now about what I had seen in that highly stressful moment in a dimly lit room. It could wait.

Instead, I said the other thing that was on my mind. "I'm sorry Jessie isn't here."

Zoe did that shy looking-at-the-table thing. "I'm sure I don't know what you mean. I'm here to help Ada-Mae celebrate her birthday." Then she met my eyes and lifted her eyebrows. "No John here, either."

Touché. "Yes. I wonder if there was some police business. Nothing too serious, I hope. We could do with another quiet week or two around here."

Zoe nodded her agreement. "Here, here." Then she stood up. "I'm going to find my drink. See you for the rocket launch."

As soon as Zoe had gone, Gramps materialized on the seat opposite me. This time I didn't even flinch.

"Gramps! I didn't know if you could join us on the boat."

"I was just waiting for the right moment," he said. "I should be strong enough to manifest properly so that your grandmother can see me too."

"You can do that?"

"I can... but it will exhaust me again," Gramps admitted with a smile. "And... then I do not think I will be around for a while."

"Why not?"

"Because I need to give your grandmother some space."

"You were listening up on deck?" I asked.

Gramps nodded at my still-damp clothes. "As were you."

I blushed.

"You made a good point the other day," he went on. "For your grandmother to move on, she needs to know I am not looking over her shoulder."

"I didn't mean—"

"I know, but this is the best solution."

Ada-Mae walked back into the cabin, a mug of hot chocolate in her hand, and stopped. "Sidney?" Her voice was hoarse.

I knew, of course, that Ada-Mae was not talking to me. I got up to give them some privacy. "I should—"

"It's fine," both my grandparents said together. Then they looked at each other and laughed.

"Really, stay, Sidney," Ada-Mae said. "It's okay. You are an important part of this."

I took my hot chocolate and stayed sitting opposite Gramps's ghost as Ada-Mae took a seat next to him.

"I'm going away now, my love," he told her.

"I guessed as much," Ada-Mae replied. "Do you know if you will be back?"

Gramps glanced over at me. "One day."

Ada-Mae nodded, looked down, and sniffed. To me, she seemed both smaller and younger suddenly. Gramps's ghostly hand moved over hers, and I could see through it, realizing that he was already beginning to fade with the extra effort of being visible to Ada-Mae.

"Should I get Mom?" I asked.

Both shook their heads. "She's not ready for this," Ada-Mae said. "Not so soon. There will be another time, hopefully."

They looked at each other for a long moment, then Gramps spoke again. "This is me telling you to move on and live your life."

"I'm sure I don't know what you mean," Ada-Mae said weakly.

"I'm sure you do. From here, nothing you ever do or say can lessen what we had. You know that. The only thing that will ever change how I feel about us is if you make yourself miserable because of me."

Ada-Mae's hand reached up toward Gramps's quickly fading face, one hand close to his incorporeal cheek. "I love you."

"Goodbye, my love," Gramps answered, leaning over to kiss her on the cheek before he faded.

I felt a tear trickle down my cheek. I wanted to hold onto this beautiful moment between them, remembering the love they would always share and how that love could never be bound by time or space.

ADA-MAE and I arrived back up on deck, and Ernie turned to greet us. "Just in time for the launch," he said, turning to point at a bright ball of light just above the distant horizon.

As it continued to move into the sky, Judd came over with a birthday cake, a single candle on it. We all sang "Happy Birthday," and Ada-Mae blew out the candle while, just out of the corner of my eye, I saw the faint outline of a familiar ghostly form drift off into the setting sun. After we finished the cake, I noticed the boat had turned and was making its way to the shore.

"Look," my father said as we neared the shore. I can see the light of the barbecue." He rubbed his hands together. "I can't wait to try some of Eileen's famous seafood at last."

Zoe stood close to me and pointed toward the beach. "Look, John and Jessie are on the shore. They are in their uniforms too." She nudged me. "No one ordered any inappropriate entertainment for Ada-Mae's birthday, did they?"

I laughed. "Stop! Although, if things in Crystal Beach stay too quiet, maybe they will have to start moonlighting."

The boat pulled up to the small jetty we had left from earlier. John and Jessie walked out onto it, John catching the rope and securing the boat to the dock.

"You missed out on all the fun, you too," I said as we opened the gate on the side of the boat.

John smiled back at me, but it was a thin smile devoid of his usual warmth. Behind him, Jessie's face was impassive, almost like stone.

My father and Ada-Mae stepped up behind me. "Everything okay?" Ada-Mae asked.

"Yes, you didn't eat all the crab already, did you?" my father joked.

He was the first to jump down, turning to hold out a hand to Ada-Mae, but Jessie grabbed his arm and, in the blink of an eye, slapped a pair of handcuffs over it, grabbing his other wrist to secure the second one.

"Jacob Grace," John said, "You are under arrest for the murder of Samuel Barlow."

The smile dropped from my father's face. "What?"

"You have the right to remain silent," John went on. "Anything you say can and will be used against you in a court of law...."

❧

SIDNEY KNOWS her dad is not guilty of murder, but who killed Sam Barlow? Was Jacob intentionally framed or in the wrong place at the wrong time? Is there a connection between the savvy realtor's death and the strange things happening at Mystic Dunes? And how will this all impact Sidney's budding romance with Chief Reece?

Turn the page to find all the answers in the next magically mysterious and spellbinding paranormal cozy mystery,
A Grave Mistake

Next in Series:

Welcome to Crystal Beach, an enchanting town with a dangerous secret.

With another resident now six feet under and her dad's neck on the line for murder, Sidney knows there's been a grave mistake. Now, this witch must act quickly to clear his name and reveal the real danger lurking in this cozy beach town.

Guided by her grandmother's wisdom, Sidney evokes the spirits to ask for guidance. But a surprise spectral figure joins the séance, and Sidney must convince this unlikely helper to aid them in solving the murder.

To complicate things, her father's arrest strains her relationship with the chief of police, and navigating these murky waters won't be easy. Though Sidney yearns to rekindle their romantic connection, family comes first, and Chief Reece isn't going to budge for love.

Can this psychic witch find a way to peer into the past, revealing the clues she needs to locate the real killer? What secret does her magical feline unearth in the garden? And can they discover the evidence needed to free her father?

Turn the page to join Sidney, Ada-Mae, Mojo, and the unforgettable residents of Crystal Beach in A Grave Mistake, the eighth installment of the Crystal Beach Magic Mystery Series.

~

KAREN MCSPADE

A GRAVE MISTAKE

A Crystal Beach Paranormal Cozy Mystery
Book Eight

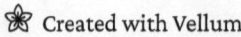 Created with Vellum

ONE

Did that really happen? Did my father just get arrested?

I couldn't think. I was numb. Everyone looked at me, but I just couldn't process any of it.

It was strange, though, the way everyone was looking at me at this moment—even Mom and my grandmother, Ada-Mae. It seemed they thought I might have the answer, the solution to the fact that my father was being hauled away for murder.

Almost as shocking—although not nearly as distressing—was the fact that Sam Barlow was dead. No matter how badly I thought of the man, he seemed larger than life and invincible in his own way. My nemesis.

Which could, I suppose, be one reason why everyone was staring at me. But I hadn't done it. Geez, I had seen him alive and well the previous evening at the Gantzes' house. Several witnesses —although one was my cat and the other was the now evaporated ghost of my grandfather—could swear that I hadn't laid a finger on the man. Neither physical nor magical. Not that I would even know how to hurt someone with magic. I did not use my gift that way.

Yet it was an equally crazy idea that my dear, gentle father could have killed Sam. Of course, there was that vision I had received when I touched the plaque with the house number on it, the one that matched Nikola Vorak's house at Mystic Dunes. I hadn't yet asked anyone who was there at the party for a list of attendees to verify if my vision was real.

Still, when you took it together with the unexpected confrontation between Sam and my dad at The Rose Garden.... Well, it seems everyone knew that Jacob Grace had an ax to grind with Savvy Sam. Especially since Rose, the town gossip and possibly a purveyor of dark magic in league with Sam had been present, both at the party and during my dad's confrontation with Sam at the guest house.

"I'll... handle this," I said, backing away from all the expectant faces looking at me on the beach. Zoe reached out to me as if to offer her help, but I waved her away. "It has to be a mistake."

I hurried along the beach to where Maude was parked a little south of the Shifting Sands Retirement Center. Night had fallen now, and a slight breeze had picked up, rustling the palm trees in a way that sounded unfriendly, almost threatening.

I can't believe your father would be capable of murder, Mojo said, appearing out of the shadows at the same time as he spoke in my head, making me screech with fright.

"How do you know about that?" I demanded, a hand to my chest. I shook my head as I opened up Maude's side door. "Never mind. I've got to get down there, to the station. But, yes, of course, my father would never murder anyone. Not even Sam Barlow."

No, I meant he isn't capable of murder. He doesn't, you know, seem to have the disposition. Murderers are usually pretty clever.

I turned around and glared at my cat. "My dad *is* clever! He was a partner at an accounting firm, I'll have you know.

One of Mojo's paws came up in what almost looked like a placating gesture. *Okay, okay. So, your dad could kill someone?*

"No... that's not... just hush up, okay?"

Geez, touchy.

I didn't even dignify that with a reply, although Mojo jumped up and made his way to the passenger seat before I could close the door. He was coming, too, I guessed.

"WHAT DO YOU MEAN, 'I can't see him?'" I raged. "He's my dad, John."

Chief John Reece looked up from the report on his desk and stared at me. "He's also a murder suspect, Sidney. Unless you're planning to take over as his lawyer, then you can't see him yet."

"He can't have done it," I said. "When did Sam even die? *How* did Sam die?" It was still strange to think that Sam was dead. It just didn't feel possible. He had seemed so... untouchable.

"I cannot discuss any details of an ongoing investigation with you, Sidney. I'm sorry."

John's big, dark eyes looked earnest enough, like they always did, yet somehow that was even more frustrating. I stood at the counter just inside the police station and realized I hadn't been there since the night that Jessie was attacked and Eduardo Fitch had been killed in his cell. Maybe the same cell that was holding my father. I realized that I knew too much about this police station as I counted how many times I'd been here since I arrived in Crystal Beach. Too many. It wasn't even like I could use the excuse that I was kind of dating the police chief, as we hadn't got to the point yet in our relationship where we roleplayed him "taking me in for questioning." At this rate, we weren't ever going to.

I batted my eyes, pulled a little at the neckline of my dress, and let some fingers drift over toward his arm.

"Oh, come on, John. It's only me."

John snatched his arm back and cleared his throat. "My name is Chief Reece. And yes, it is *you*. The suspect's daughter. Now, go home, Miss Grace. Maybe call in the morning."

Miss Grace...? "Now, look here you—"

Keep it PG-13, came a feline voice in my head. I looked down to see Mojo loitering just inside the doorway. *You're already skating on thin ice here. Just saying.*

John noticed too. "Your familiar's just walked in," he said acidly.

Well, that was uncalled for. I was about to ignore Mojo's advice and give John a piece of my mind when Jessie walked out from the cells. She would be more of a soft touch. "Jessie!"

A hand went up like she was stopping traffic. "Not now, Sidney. Go home."

I gave a frustrated little shriek and pointed at John as I backed toward the door. "He didn't do it. You know he didn't do it."

～

It was well into the evening by the time I got back to Shifting Sands. I headed straight to Ada-Mae's apartment, where my grandmother had taken Dad's girlfriend, Gillian. When I walked in, my mom was comforting her on the couch. Despite the horrible events of the evening, that sight warmed me inside a little. It would have warmed me in any event, just seeing my mother do something selfless like that, especially for my father's girlfriend. But because I now knew my mom had feelings for him again, it seemed an even kinder gesture. Ernie had answered the door, and Judd smiled at me from the dining table as I entered the living area.

Ada-Mae was in the kitchen, making cocoa for everybody. It was her specialty, with grated cinnamon on top, although she appeared to have left off the marshmallows in recognition of the somber mood.

"I'm sorry about your birthday," I said to her.

She smiled, although it didn't quite reach her eyes. "It was about eighty percent a good birthday, and I'll take that on my eightieth one. If I get to a hundred, then I will expect everything to be perfect. Any luck at the police station?"

"John—sorry, *Chief Reece*—stonewalled me. Even Jessie wouldn't talk to me. Then again, there was that time she was determined to pin a murder on me. Not always as sweet as she looks."

Ada-Mae nodded toward Gillian, who appeared to be leaking uncontrollably from all her facial orifices. My mom was doing quite an impressive job of being comforting while avoiding the worst of it. "Gillian can't provide an alibi. She was at a party at Mystic Dunes." Ada-Mae finished with a raise of her eyebrows. Anything to do with the shady waterfront development that Sam Barlow had been involved in raised eyebrows with us witches. If you asked me, it was not a mere coincidence that Mystic Dunes always seemed to be connected to the strange things going on in Crystal Beach. "Apparently, she has a friend who has just moved there."

"Uh-huh," I said. "I... um... saw it in a vision."

Ada-Mae's eyebrows rose even higher.

"Dad dropped her off, then had another public face-off with Sam Barlow."

Ada-Mae sucked on her upper lip. "Well, that's not helpful."

She handed me a couple of mugs and nodded toward the two women on the couch. I glanced around before I took them over. "Zoe didn't come back with you?"

"No," Ada-Mae replied. "She went back to her shop to gather supplies."

"Supplies?"

Ada-Mae almost looked sheepish for a moment. "Not that I don't have every confidence in you, dear, but I didn't expect you would have much luck at the station. Not tonight. But I want to get ahead of things... if we can."

"Okay?" I was equal parts intrigued and wary.

"I think we should ask the spirits for guidance. Well, when I say 'we,' I mean 'you.'"

CHAPTER
TWO

F ive of us sat around the table in the center of Ada-Mae's living room. Ernie and I had pulled the big, flowery fabric-covered sofa over to one side so that we could bring the round dining table right into the middle of the room. As soon as we had finished setting up the room, Zoe returned with the supplies Ada-Mae had requested. The two quickly unpacked the herbs and incense, and Ada-Mae began her preparations.

Earlier, Ada-Mae had extended the offer for Gillian to stay at her modest one-bedroom apartment. After all the stress she endured with Jacob's arrest, Ada-Mae didn't feel right about just sending her off when there was a real murderer on the loose. Ada-Mae then insisted that she try to lie down and rest in her bed. But Gillian had wanted to return to the motel room she and my father had rented since all her things were there.

"I expect the police will want to talk to me tomorrow," she had said, "so the least I can do is look respectable when they do." Her face crumbled then. "I feel so awful about what's happened to Jacob... like I am somehow responsible. Why did I have to go to that..."

"There, there, now, dear. Don't you blame yourself for this. That's not going to help Jacob or you. What's done is done, and we'll figure this out," Ada-Mae consoled Gillian as she rubbed her shoulder.

Judd had volunteered to give her a ride back to the motel, removing another magically active individual from being present at the séance we were about to attempt. When my mother insisted that she wanted to join in, and Ada-Mae agreed almost cheerfully to her request, I pulled my grandmother aside to speak to her in private.

"Do you really think that's a good idea?" I asked. "We'll be light on power, anyway. I think it's great that Mom is more open to things... I really do. But that's why I don't want her to have a negative experience."

Ada-Mae gave me a reassuring grin back and patted my arm. Perhaps, it might have seemed condescending coming from anyone else, but my grandmother had a way of being, well... grandmotherly. "Power won't be an issue, dear. We're not trying to contact anything too horrible. With spirits, more often than not, it's how you handle them. If you try too hard to control them, then they will just clam up and give you nothing. And there isn't much that's harder than compelling a spirit to tell you something that it does not want to." She patted my arm again. "And, anyway, you're all the power we need. Don't forget that you've been contacting spirits for the residents of Shifting Sands without any help from me. A séance is just a more organized way of doing that."

This was true, of course, although I had been too busy for the last few weeks to find any time for that. Connecting people with their willing loved ones was one thing, but reaching out to an unknown spirit for guidance on a man's murder was surely something else. I wanted to help my father—I had rushed straight down to the police station to do that—but I wished I wasn't always at the center of these things... mainly because I still wasn't sure that I knew how to harness my magic, and I didn't want to mess things up.

"Couldn't you take the lead on this one?" I said. "You're so much more experienced than me."

"I won't always be around, though, Sid. Trust my experience when I say that you need to lead this séance."

Ada-Mae grinned and moved away to place a large, half-burned candle in the middle of the table. Gramps's final-sounding goodbye the previous evening had rattled me, and she knew that. He had a habit of turning up when needed since I had arrived in Crystal Beach, and I had relied on his help in exploring the Gantzes' secret magic room the previous evening. I realized that maybe there was a little tough love going on right here from Ada-Mae, gently pushing me to stand on my own a bit more. It did not make it any easier, though.

With Mojo watching from the back of the sofa, the five of us took our places around the table. Ada-Mae lit the half-melted candle, which heated an incense burner above it. Within moments, the smell of essential oils, mixed with certain herbs that Zoe had added after crushing them with a pestle and mortar in Ada-Mae's kitchen, filled the air.

Now, we were ready to start the séance.

"SPIRITS OF CRYSTAL BEACH," I said with my eyes closed, holding hands with Ada-Mae to my right and my mother to my left, "we reach out to seek your guidance. Please let us know if you are out there and if you will be able to assist us."

"It's quite important," my mother added.

I opened my left eye to see that her own eyes were screwed so tightly shut it looked painful. A look of concentration creased her forehead so deep that she would have changed her skincare regime right there and then if she could have seen it. I wondered whether this was an expression of nervousness about being involved in her first séance or whether it was more concern for her ex-husband. Probably both.

"Jacob Grace has been wrongly accused of murder," I continued. "We seek to clear his name and identify the real perpetrators of this, um... terrible deed. Well, fairly bad. I mean, it would have been worse if he was a nicer person."

"Ahem." It was Ada-Mae trying to get me back on track. I could have sworn I heard Ernie giggle, though.

Suddenly the table started rattling, like we were in the middle of an earthquake, although nothing else in the room was affected. My mom shrieked, and we all opened our eyes. Looking across at my mom, I knew what her expression meant. She had wanted to believe, to be a willing and full part of this, yet years of prejudice against magic were a hard thing to get over. Julia-Mae had never truly admitted, not in a clear, irrefutable way, that she had been a victim of Sam Barlow's immoral spell. She had always left a little room in there for denial.

My mom snatched her hands back from me and from Zoe on

her left, then she looked around at the rest of us. "Who did that?" she asked as the shaking stopped. No one answered. She already knew that it was none of us, but she leaned backward and looked under the table anyway.

"It's alright, Mom," I said. "But please keep holding hands. We need to keep whatever spirit comes within the circle."

She nodded and did as I asked, her eyes wide.

"Let's not try too hard to make judgments right now, Sidney," Ada-Mae said. "This is a general appeal for information and help. Whatever we feel to be the truth of things, let's not prejudice the opinions of any spirits that might try to help us."

A fair point. And annoying as he was, I would never have wished Sam Barlow dead.

That's nice to know.

My head snapped up to look over at Mojo, who had been observing proceedings from the back of the couch. He was standing up, his back arched, his hair on end. He did not look to be in a happy place. But more to the point, it was not his snarky but familiar voice in my head.

What's nice to know?

That you didn't wish me dead. Although kind of useless, considering the way things worked out.

"Sam...?" I said, looking around. Although, no one was visible except for the people who were already in the room.

Ada-Mae's eyes flicked across to me. "Is... is he here?"

Yes. You did just call me.

I was trying to call a spirit to help find out who killed you.

Didn't know you cared.

I don't.

Well, apparently, I'm the most qualified to find out who killed me.

My dad has been arrested, and I need to prove he's innocent. That's all.

"Is that him? Is that Sam Barlow?" my mom said. I could hear a touch of fear in her voice. "Tell him to tell the police that Jacob didn't kill him."

Oh, but your father did kill me, Sidney.

"No, he didn't!" I cried out loud. "That's a lie."

"I know," my mom said. "That's what I was saying."

Well, who else could it have been?

You mean you didn't see him kill you? So, you don't really know?

"Does he know anything that can help, Sidney?" Ernie called across the table. "Ask him how he died."

This might be easier if I borrowed you for a moment. Do you mind?

What do you mean…?

There was an extreme and sudden explosion of cold throughout my being, the feeling you get when you've been out in the cold too long and feel a little sliver of ice deep inside your body that doesn't want to warm up. My body went rigid, and my head flew back so that I was looking at the ceiling. When my gaze dropped back down to take in the people around me at the table again, I was a passenger in my own body, no longer in control of it. Sam's spirit was inside me.

"I want all of you to hear this," Sam Barlow said.

I did not know what the others were hearing, but from where I was, it was like we both spoke at exactly the same time, Sam's voice laying over my own. "As far as I am concerned, Jacob Grace killed me. He threatened me right before I died."

"Sam?" Ada-Mae said.

"Sam?" my mother echoed.

We turned to look at her. "Oh, hi, Julia-Mae. You're looking nice today."

My mom turned pale, and I tried hard to fight back against the force that had control of my body. *GET. OUT!*

You called me, and then you let me out of the circle, Sidney. I was dead and gone, and then you just brought me back. Can't a dead guy have some fun?

I didn't mean to bring you back.

Well, maybe I will stay around long enough to watch your father go down for my murder. Maybe he'll get the death penalty.

"Sam?" Ada-Mae said.

Against my will, my head turned to look at her. I felt my face form into a sneer. "Ah. If it isn't the head of Quipley's School of No-Hopers. You're all out of your depth here, you know. My death won't change that."

My grandmother's face barely registered the insult, and from inside my body, I felt proud of her for that. "Listen, Sam. As a ghost, you can go to places we can't go and see things we can't see. You could help Sidney find out the truth about what happened to you. Whoever the real murderer is."

"No way!" the two of us called out together. At least we agreed on something. My slight regaining of control was what I needed to force him out of my body.

Hey! he said, now only as a voice inside my head again. I felt him pushing to get back in, but he was much weaker now.

Wow, I'm exhausted now.

I turned from the table and could see him, his ghostly form bent over on Ada-Mae's carpet, trying to stand up. He was very faded, the way Gramps would be when he had over-exerted himself.

"Come on, Sam," Ada-Mae said, now talking to my back, as she probably thought Sam was still in my body. "Together, you and Sidney can do things the police cannot do, either. It might be your best chance of finding out what happened to you."

You did too much, I told Sam, grinning down at him. *Ghosts only have a little spectral energy to work with, and it takes time to recharge.*

Well, that's... annoying, he gasped.

207

"At least tell us how you died," Ada-Mae said to my back as I stood over the ghost's fallen form. "We don't even know that yet."

Sam was getting fainter by the moment. He glared back up at me, his hatred as palpable as when he had been alive. *I was poisoned,* he said. *Your father poisoned me to death.*

I turned back to the rest of the room as Sam finally vanished.

"He says he was poisoned," I told them. "That's somewhere to start." I looked between my mom and my grandmother. "Anybody think my father is a likely poisoner? Because I don't."

CHAPTER

THREE

"Sidney?" Chief John Reece, as he had pointedly reminded me the last time we spoke, rubbed his eyes as he opened the front door of the police station. He looked like he hadn't slept for days, his eyes red-rimmed with dark shadows under them and his hair all disheveled. Even so, he still looked quite edible, although I wasn't supposed to be thinking like that. "Do you know what time it is?"

"It's eight in the morning," I said, "and high time you released my father."

John's face went from tired and confused to disapproving in

an instant. He squared his shoulders, blocking my way in as if I might try to charge him suddenly in some crazy prison break. "Well, some of us were up late last night. Murders come with a lot of overtime."

"I want to see him," I said, trying my best to meet his gaze, which was hard because he was a lot taller than me.

I expected a flat refusal, but the tired look returned to John's face, and he stepped back from the doorway to let me through. "You will have to talk to him through the bars of the cell. I am not letting him out of there until he becomes the county's prisoner. We don't want...."

A repeat of the Eduardo Fitch incident. That's what John was about to say. Then he remembered who he was speaking to. Eduardo Fitch had been arrested while suspected of the murder of my childhood sweetheart, Ben Chalmers, during the Crystal Beach Mini-Golf Invitational. As it turned out, Eduardo had been a potential witness to the actual murderers but had been killed by one of them while in the custody of the Crystal Beach Police Department.

For a moment, John looked almost apologetic as he nodded me toward the cells at the back. But mostly, he looked tired. As I walked through, there was no sign of Jessie.

"Hey, Dad," I said with my best reassuring smile. Jacob Grace looked a little too comfortable in his prison cell, lying on his bed against the pillow, his arms folded behind his head. To be fair, the cells at Crystal Beach Police Station were a little nicer than the ones I saw on TV. More like well-presented budget hotel rooms you couldn't escape from.

When my dad looked up, he flashed me a smile, showing he was thrilled to see me, but I could still see the strain of the situation in the creases above his brows. "Sidney, sweetheart!" He got up and came to the bars, peering back along the corridor toward the front office where John was watching us, presumably in case I had smuggled in a nail file. "I didn't know if I would be allowed visitors yet."

"Well, it helps when you've been dating the Chief of Police," I said loudly enough to earn a satisfying scowl from John. My dad looked a little dismayed at that. Okay, maybe it hadn't been the smartest thing to say. "How are you doing?" I asked, moving things along.

"As well as can be expected. The chief and his deputy have been very decent, all things considered." He leaned toward the bars, his earnest eyes only a foot away from mine. "But you've got to know that I didn't do it, Sidney."

I was a little surprised he even felt the need to say it. "Of course not. Obviously, there's been a grave mistake, and I'm going to uncover the truth and get you out of here."

"I mean, the whole thing is very confusing. And I feel like such a fool for making myself look so guilty by arguing publicly with Sam Barlow."

"Believe me, he was an easy man to argue with. Still is."

Confusion creased my dad's forehead, but he carried on. "It just made me so mad... what he had done to your mother. Men like him...." He shook his head as if to clear it, then met my eyes. His were a clear, watery blue, and their gaze held me now as strongly as they had when I was a child. "I know I never had the most exciting job or was the most exciting, dynamic role model for you."

I tried to interrupt, to protest, but he held up a hand to stop me. "There is a little fire in me, though, Sidney. If a person hurts someone I love or does anything that might cause them to suffer... Well, there's this sort of red mist that descends over me."

It was not the time to bring it up, of course, but my dad had just admitted to still loving my mother. Maybe not romantically, but enough that those protective instincts had kicked in when he heard about what Sam Barlow had done to her.

"But I'm not a killer, no matter how angry I might get in the heat of the moment. And I certainly couldn't do anything premeditated, like murder someone in cold blood."

I reached out through the bars, and my dad's fingers entwined with my own. "I'll sort this out, Dad, I promise. None of us will stop until we find out who really killed Sam Barlow." I smiled sadly. "Who knew I would be so keen on getting justice for that evil rogue's death, eh?"

Wondering why John hadn't already shouted at me for reaching through the bars, I turned to see that Jessie had joined him at the end of the corridor. She handed him a piece of paper and leaned in to speak to him so that I couldn't hear what was being said. John now looked up and noticed what I was doing.

"Hey," he shouted, "hands away from the prisoner!"

Normally, I'd return the lawman's order with a playful gesture like sticking out my tongue, but I hadn't heard John shout quite like that before. There was a fierceness to it, almost like fury, which had both me and my dad letting go at the same time.

John rushed up to us, the paper still in his hand. He waved toward the door with it. "Time to go! Visiting time is over."

"What have you got there?" I said, recovering a little of my poise and narrowing my eyes.

John's eyes went wide, and he tried to put it behind his back, but I followed it, bending over and circling him while he protested until, finally, I caught a glimpse.

"Preliminary Toxin report?"

John sighed and looked over at my dad. "It's from a bottle we found in the toiletries bag in your motel room, Jacob. The final results aren't back yet, but it's looking like the bottle contained the same poison that killed Sam Barlow. Between that and the fact that there is a well-known and public feud between you—"

"He's being set up, John," I said. "He's not dumb enough to just leave the bottle right there for you to find. I mean, how gullible are you? Was it labeled 'Poison,' just in case you missed it?"

For Chief John Reece, that was the last in a long line of "last straws." Before I knew it, he had a powerful hand clamped over my shoulder and was marching me away from the cells. As we went back through the office and passed Jessie, she seemed to be pretending not to notice us.

I turned as I reached the front door, a whole new plea on the tip of my tongue... well, more accurately, just another variation of the ongoing one. But John spoke first.

"Look, Sidney. I think, given everything that's going on... that you and I need to cool things, okay?"

Of course, it wasn't like I was expecting we were going to be heading out on any dates while he was building a case against my father for murder. In fact, it seemed a little presumptuous, and at the same time, it set off a painful little knot in the center of my chest. "Well... yeah," I said. "Until we get this all cleared up, sure."

John's eyes told a different story. "Right, Sidney. It's just... you're always in the center of trouble here in Crystal Beach. And with my job, sometimes it gets a little too complicated."

"We've been through this before," I huffed.

"And yet, as soon as I've got a handle on it, it all just seems to get so much more difficult again."

IT WAS STILL EARLY, and the businesses in the center of Crystal Beach were opening up as I left the police station. I had driven

Maude there but didn't feel like I wanted to drive her anywhere now—not to the beach where Mojo and the rest of my cats would be, nor to Shifting Sands. Just walking and being alone for a little while was what I needed. The chance to wrap my head around what was happening and how quickly things were falling apart.

I didn't think about where I was walking to until I got there, suddenly finding myself standing outside of Sam Barlow's realty office. I reached out my hand and turned the knob on the door. It was locked, empty inside. As far as I was aware, he hadn't yet replaced Ben Chalmers, so likely there was no one to open it up. That suddenly felt so sad to me. As much as Sam's office had seemed like enemy territory, it had also been a fixture of the town, as much as The Kelp Seafood Grill... or The Rose Garden, come to think of it.

It seemed such a terrible, terrible tragedy. I was feeling over-whelmed by grief and felt tears pricking at my eyes. My legs felt weak, and I staggered a little, sitting down with a heavy flop on the sidewalk right outside his office. My head was in my hands, and I was crying, but I stopped abruptly, sniffing away my runny nose as a wave of cold air enveloped me. I looked up, and if anyone was watching me, it would appear that I began speaking to empty air. "Sam Barlow, you despicable monster," I said.

A familiar voice floated into my head. *I never knew you cared so much about me, Sidney. I'm touched.*

"I don't," I continued to speak out loud. "You've done some-thing to me, to my emotions. Stop it."

It's a little like sitting on your shoulders and being able to reach into the back of your head. I like it.

"I don't." Getting to my feet, I stepped out into the road, twisting this way and that as if I might shake him loose. "Get out!" I shouted at the top of my voice, loud enough that a woman around fifty yards down the street stopped and looked at me. She had been heading in my direction, but now she crossed the road, even though there wasn't any sidewalk on the other side, only a grass median. I didn't blame her.

My crazy antics did the trick, however, and now I could see Sam Barlow's ghost grinning back at me from the sidewalk in front of his shop. *How did you come back so fast?* I asked, now remembering to use my inner voice. *You used up your spectral energy last night, and now you are here again this morning. It took my Gramps days, even weeks, to return after he exerted himself.*

Sam shrugged, but his grin was a smug one. *Maybe it's because I was such a powerful warlock in life. Hey, I could just take up haunting you and bugging you full time, couldn't I?*

Do that, and I'll find a way to exorcise you for good. Just see if I don't. I sighed and regarded the unwelcome specter in front of me.

What? he said, looking like he was worried he had some spectral hotdog mustard on his upper lip or something else embarrassing.

Assuming that it isn't just your dislike of me holding you here, I wonder why you are still hanging around and not already in whatever horrible afterlife it is that evil warlocks like yourself end up in.

I would have thought that was obvious. I want to see your murdering father go down for killing me. That's my unfinished business.

I took an inward breath that Sam Barlow appeared to hear through our psychic connection. I couldn't believe I was about to say this...

I think we should work together.

If there was something I knew about Sam Barlow, it was that he was a man who didn't look surprised too often. But his ghost did right then, his eyes narrowing at me suspiciously. *On what?*

Getting to the bottom of who killed you.

Your father killed me. Why would I help you try to get him off?

If he killed you, then that's what we'll find to be true, I answered. *So, what's the harm in being sure? Whatever you might think of me, Sam, I've helped solve more than one murder since I've been in Crystal Beach. And those robberies too. But I don't expect you to believe me when I say that my dad could never murder anyone, let alone with poison. So why don't you prove me wrong?*

I could see Sam's spectral brain—if there was such a thing—turning my offer over. Time to lay it on a little thicker and hope I didn't vomit in the process.

As you are a ghost and *such a powerful warlock, I'm not even sure I could get to the bottom of things without you.*

He did his best to look like he wasn't going to agree for several seconds, but I felt certain that I already had him. *Okay, but I'm not betraying my coven members to you. I might be dead, but I'm still pretty invested in seeing you and your dinosaur-age cronies get beaten. There are things coming to Crystal Beach which, whether or not you will ever see it, will be best for the town.*

Well, *that* was both cryptic and interesting. I would not push my luck right now by pressing him further, but there would be time to work on him later... I hoped. "Deal," I said out loud.

"Yes, Sam always had the best deals."

I turned around to see a woman in her fifties who I remembered seeing around town. She had a concerned, sympathetic look on her face, and she reached up a hand to touch my shoulder.

"He was the best realtor and such a man of the town. It's hard to believe he's gone," she went on. "I saw you there looking into his office, and you looked so sad, so heartbroken. Did you know Sam well?"

This woman was evidently one of the few who didn't realize that my father had been arrested for his murder. I knew it was only last night, but news spread fast in Crystal Beach. "Well," I said, looking up at Sam's ghost, who seemed very amused by this turn of events, "I did not know him for long, but it felt like I had known him for a lifetime."

The woman nodded and smiled sagely at that, but the way Sam's grin slid from his face at my comment made me feel better.

Just as the woman walked away, my cell phone rang. I had updated my ringtone with an excerpt from the music for Disney's *Fantasia*. Since I was living in Florida now, just over an hour's drive from Walt Disney World, it felt appropriate. But the ghost of Sam Barlow rolled his eyes when he heard it.

"Ada-Mae?" I implored. "Any news?"

"Not yet. Did you learn anything at the station? I thought you would have come by my apartment by now."

"Chief Reece has a stick up his you-know-what about the whole thing, so not a lot of help there. But I saw Dad, and he's as well as can be expected." I glanced up at Sam Barlow. "I've, um... been starting my investigation, sort of."

"Well, I need you to head back to Shifting Sands when you can. Meet us in the Game of Thrones Room."

"In the Game of Thrones Room. Why there?"

"Quipley's, of course," Ada-Mae said, mentioning the name of the magic school she was running. With my father arrested for murder, however, attending lessons did not seem like the best use of my time.

"You're kidding, right?"

Ada-Mae answered as if she had been expecting my reaction. "It will be worth it, I promise. And if you can find and bring Sam Barlow's ghost, please do so, dear. I know he might not be back from wherever ghosts go when they exhaust themselves, and... well, all the other reasons we don't really want him around. But for what I'm planning, he could be helpful."

CHAPTER

FOUR

T arrived at the Game of Thrones Room, the strangely titled
multipurpose game room at Shifting Sands Retirement
Center, just in time to find most of the class in attendance.
Among them was Zoe, the magic shop owner who had saved my
life two nights before at The Rose Garden. The same night that
Sam Barlow had been killed. Although everything happened
quickly and with great confusion when I was attacked by some
sort of malevolent spirit that was left as a magical trap guarding
the Gantzes' secret sanctum, I saw something else present as Zoe

saved me—some sort of bestial presence that briefly superimposed itself over the young woman's face. Once my dad was free from this bogus murder charge, I wanted to find out more about the thing that revealed itself that night.

Also in attendance were Howie and Wendy Rockford, as well as Ernie and Judd. I had not been expecting my mother, though, who beamed at me from one of the front seats next to Zoe. Ada-Mae was at the front of the gathering, and it looked like she was arranging the ingredients for a spell.

"Hey, Sidney!"

It was my mom, patting the seat next to her like she had saved it for me. It felt like I was in some weird dream where your mother was your nerdy, over-zealous classmate, and your grandmother was the teacher. Stranger than an episode of *The Twilight Zone*, I shook my head to clear the confusion as I approached the aisle where my mother sat.

"How's your father?" my mom asked as I reached her side.

"Still in jail," I replied with a wry grin and hopefully an undertone of "So, what the heck are we all doing here instead of being out there trying to prove his innocence?" I have expressive grins, okay.

Ada-Mae noticed me and beckoned me over. She glanced over my shoulder before she spoke. "Did you find Sam?"

"I did." I looked back toward the swinging doors at the entrance. Sam's ghost was loitering just inside them, looking like a new student who didn't know where to sit. "And he's here." I leaned a little closer and, assuming that sound worked the same way with ghosts that it did with the living, lowered my voice to be sure he wouldn't hear. "I don't like bringing him here, though. He may be dead, but he's still the enemy. He seems as loyal to his coven now as when he was alive. Anything he learns here, he might find a way to communicate it to them."

Ada-Mae nodded. "It's a risk we might have to take."

I scanned the ingredients she was preparing on the table. It looked like an array of at least half a dozen herbs she was grinding together using a giant pestle and mortar. I caught the scents of both lavender and rosemary in the air. "So, what are we doing here?"

"Something that might help our investigation. To be safe, we'll draw on the energy of the whole group at once. Sam is aware of your magical power and my power. What I don't want him to know about is our other most talented members. Let's try to hide them among the whole."

"What do you need Sam for?" I asked.

"Just tell him to come over and place his hands in the smoke when I nod toward the door."

I was about to head across and do that but paused for a moment and regarded Ada-Mae. "You're being..." It took me a moment to find the word I wanted, as I did not want to appear mistrustful. "Um... mysterious."

Ada-Mae smiled but didn't look up again from what she was doing. "Sometimes... well, often, magic is all about focusing as much intent as possible. At other times, it's more about taking latent energy and, well... letting that energy find an answer for you."

I laughed. "I'm not sure that makes things any clearer for me." *And sometimes I wonder how I'll ever know as much as you do,* I added as I turned back and walked over to Sam.

What is this all about? Sam said. *You better not be wasting my time.*

It's Quipley's School of Magic, I said. *I told you this before we came.*

But what is it? I thought it was some sort of coven meeting. He pointed to the refreshments table at the far side, which had various jugs of juices on it, along with some pastries and sandwiches. *You have snacks,* he went on, sounding incredulous. *And rows of chairs. I mean, where is the pentagram? And no one is even wearing a robe.* He pointed toward Howie Rockford. *Except maybe that guy. I'm not sure what he's wearing. The point is, you might as well be having a PTA meeting or beginning some sort of quilting project.*

"I think that one happens in here on Thursdays, the Shifting Sands Quilting club," I said.

He let out a little ghostly sound of annoyance in my head. It was like music to the insides of my brain. *How did the lot of you ever prove to be a thorn in anybody's side? I've said it before, and I will say it again. You guys are screwed when things really go down in Crystal Beach.*

Yes, so you've said before. I wasn't letting Sam's ghost get a rise out of me.

It occurred to me, not for the first time, to wonder whether ghosts missed those pleasant physical sensations like eating. Because, if they did, I was tempted to find a nice *pain au chocolat,* just so I could eat it in front of Sam. Pettiness, however pleasing it might have been, was not what was called for, however. Well, maybe just a little....

We don't all have to embrace the clichés, you know. I haven't yet seen one of these people riding a broomstick. Although I did once see Howie slow dancing with a mop on the beach.

Sam raised an eyebrow.

I nodded over toward the seats. *Robe guy.*

Oh.

Anyway, Ada-Mae sent me over to tell you to put your hands in the smoke when she nods toward the door.

Why?

She didn't tell me.

Sam balked. *Do I look like an idiot?*

Um...

How do I know she's not conjuring up some spell to get rid of me?

I made an exasperated sound and noticed that several of the other gathered "students" were watching me as I stood there, silently conversing with the door. I was getting impatient with Sam's attitude and his unwillingness to help us find the person who killed him.

How would getting rid of you help us prove my dad's innocence?

Sam crossed his arms and looked at me, then his gaze drifted toward the table. *Smoke, you say?*

Uh-huh.

His eyes went to the ceiling. *Won't she set off the smoke alarms?*

Only certain types of smoke set them off. I'm sure that Ada-Mae has thought of that. She will nod toward you when she's ready.

Sam gave a reluctant nod, though I could tell he planned to do as Ada-Mae instructed.

I hurried back over to sit next to my mother. "Any word from Dad's, um, girlfr... you know, Gillian?" I asked her awkwardly.

"Not yet," my mom said, not showing any outward signs of irritation toward the woman. "Judd took her home last night. No one has mentioned her this morning."

"I expect the police will interview her," I said. "Maybe... maybe there's something Gillian can say that will help." I was reaching, and I knew it.

Ada-Mae cleared her throat and brought the meeting to order. She had a way of doing so quietly while at the same time projecting her voice. I sometimes suspected there was magic involved in that.

"Thank you, everyone, for coming this morning," Ada-Mae began, "I know that many of you wouldn't have expected this to go ahead with everything else that is happening, but if something is important enough to us, we always find a way.

"I was just telling my granddaughter something about magic that took me many years to understand." Ada-Mae nodded down toward the prepared ritual on the table in front of her. "That sometimes magic and casting spells is not so much about bending things to your will as it is sitting back quietly and listening for what the world has to tell you."

She glanced over toward the door briefly—although she didn't nod, and there was no smoke yet, so Sam's ghost stayed where he was. 'I'm afraid I'm going to be a little secretive about the ritual that we are about to work on. In this case, the intent is mine alone. But every one of you in the room, no matter your level of power—and power is not necessarily the most important thing in what we are about to do—is going to be a help in finding the answer I need."

There was a soft murmuring among those gathered in the rows of seats. Ada-Mae was often a little obscure—or even just plain random—in how she talked at Quipley's. A little like an eccentric professor, I imagined. She was never quite this vague, though. I looked toward the door where Sam was standing and noticed that he was paying rapt attention, the scornful look now gone. Interesting.

Ada-Mae struck a match and lit the herbs and the rest of the potpourri-looking mix that she'd placed into the fancy brushed copper altar bowl. I was sure I had seen it for sale in Zoe's shop. A birthday present, perhaps? "Okay," she said, "I need everybody to take slow, deep breaths and clear their mind."

Awesome, I thought, *meditation*. My mind needed a little peace right now.

"As you breathe in," Ada-Mae continued, "I want you to note the scent of the herbs and the other ingredients being burned to make the smoke. Breathe them in deeply and consider how they smell. Do not ponder on it hard but let your mind drift along on the question. Or, if you do not want to think about which herbs they are, then think instead about how their smell makes you feel. What does it remind you of? Just let your mind wander freely on these thoughts."

My grandmother's voice was almost a lullaby, and I could feel my eyes getting heavy. But then I noticed Ada-Mae look over toward the door and nod.

I half expected Sam to be hesitant or, at the very least, look doubtful. Quite to the contrary, his ghost almost drifted across the room and straight to where Ada-Mae was standing like some magnetic attraction drew him. I could not see his face as he moved his spectral hands forward into the slightly purplish smoke, which curled around them, almost seeming to cling to them as if he weren't a ghost.

Ada-Mae spoke again. "Oh, spirits of wisdom, whose knowledge is far greater than ours could ever be, please hear my plea. I beseech you to grant me the knowledge I seek, not for my own advantage, for the good of others."

In front of me, Sam flickered momentarily. For one crazy second, I thought he had been right in his earlier suspicion that Ada-Mae's spell was intended to banish his ghost. Then he appeared again, his ghost clear as any had ever been to my spiritually attuned eyes. The smoke seemed to billow upward in ever greater amounts, and I caught sight of my grandmother now, her arms trembling as she held them out from the other side of the table. Her eyes were closed deep in concentration, the tight expression on her face suggesting that the spell was not the gentle wait for information that she had claimed it would be.

No one else around me seemed to notice as Ada-Mae shook harder—all her body now trembled—and in my sudden panic, I was halfway to my feet when the sprinklers in the ceiling erupted.

Looking around at everyone gathered in the communal lounge area near the entrance to the Shifting Sands apartments, I could not see Sam Barlow's ghost anywhere. I had lost sight of him in the swift and damp exit from The Game of Thrones Room. Though I felt relieved that Sam wouldn't have a chance to be smug about Ada-Mae accidentally setting off the sprinkler system, at the same time, I hoped he hadn't actually been banished either. Especially since whatever this was supposed to be had been a big waste of time. Now, I would need Sam's help more than ever to understand what was going on and discover how he had been killed.

"We may have to find a new venue to hold our Quipley's classes after this," Ada-Mae said when I walked up to her and my mother, whose immaculately styled hair was now plastered to the side of her head. "Administrator Jessop was not thrilled. He found the altar bowl with the smoldering herbs, and I think he figured out what we were doing in there. I may not be allowed to book any of the communal spaces in Shifting Sands ever again."

"I was worried about you," I said. "I thought this was going to be a gentle spell, but you were trembling violently before the sprinklers came on."

Ada-Mae nodded. "Yes, I'm sorry about that. But on the bright side, I think I know what killed Sam Barlow."

"Poison," I grumbled, frustrated that we weren't out doing something more to find Sam's killer. "We already knew that."

"Yes, but the ritual determined it was hemlock."

Okay, that was something. A bit of an old-fashioned poison, but also probably not the hardest thing for someone to get.

"And it should have been as simple as that," Ada-Ma continued. "But there was something else...." Her eyes went distant for a moment.

"What?" my mom said, which was what I had been thinking.

"I don't know. It wasn't just hemlock. There's more at play here than a simple poisoning. Dark, dangerous forces were involved in Sam Barlow's death."

CHAPTER

FIVE

I needed to head to The Rose Garden, Rose and Rodney Gantzes' guest house. The scene of the crime. Even though Ada-Mae's ritual provided something useful, I was still a bit impatient at the lack of concrete progress. So I knew heading over there and looking for evidence of hemlock was necessary. Who knew, but maybe they would have a potion bottle lying around that was labeled "Hemlock."

However, I couldn't bring myself to face the guest house... not yet. And I could not quite figure out why. I didn't want to think that I might be sad about Sam Barlow's death—although I would have never wished him dead, no matter the dastardly things he had done. Of course, the creep was still clinging onto some kind of life in his ghostly form. No, I did not feel too sorry for him.

Why, then, did I not want to head to the most obvious place to look for clues? Was it some fear that I was avoiding? I could not ever imagine that my father would have killed Sam, yet some strange, alien-feeling knot was sitting in the middle of my chest. *I am the beginnings of doubt, Sidney,* I heard it whisper. Well, everything else spoke privately to me in my head, so why not my innermost paranoia?

Instead of heading to The Rose Garden, I did what I always did when I needed to clear my head—I walked barefoot along the golden sands of Crystal Beach. Passing Maude, Mojo ran out from the shade of a tall grassy dune and joined me as I walked along the beach.

I don't see the attraction of walking on this horrible stuff, Mojo said, flicking sand from his front paw. *And taking off those flappy shoes of yours to do it. If I could wear silly shoes when I walked on the beach, I would.*

And all those years, I had wondered what cats thought about.

The two of us walked in silence for some time until, big surprise, we came upon Mystic Dunes. It wasn't the first time I had ended up there without realizing that it was where I was headed all along. The first thing I noticed as I walked up to it was that Mystic Dunes felt very different from the way it had when I had first arrived.

It had gone from having no one living there to being fully occupied in the span of a week or two. Of course, it would feel different. Now that it was full, it seemed a brighter, happier place. It had felt so sad, so lonely, before. Sinister, even, despite its gorgeous location right by the sea and the high-end luxurious houses, many with outdoor spaces overlooking the water.

Some residents were out on their back decks enjoying the warmth of the Florida sun or enjoying a drink as a cooling breeze made the day's heat a little more bearable. Another was in their front yard watering flowers. It was all so pleasant, so normal. Mojo and I had stopped right in the middle of it, and I looked up, realizing that I was in the spot in the development that I had seen in my vision two nights before. Nicola Vorak's house.

Suddenly, his front door opened, and two familiar figures walked out. Rose and Rodney Gantz noticed me standing there and came over, Rose beaming away at me as if she didn't feel anything in my world could possibly be wrong.

"Sidney," Rose said, a paragon of polite conversation, "what brings you over here?"

"I could ask you the same thing," I replied a little too defensively.

Rose seemed unflustered and nodded back toward the front door they had just exited. "Rodney left something at that nice Mr. Vorak's house when we went over for drinks the other night," she replied.

I put my hands on my hips. "Oh yeah? What was that?"

"His reading glasses."

On cue, Rodney held them up. "Reading glasses," he repeated helpfully.

"You sound quite suspicious, Sidney," Rose said. "Everything okay?"

Harrumph. "Well, my father's being accused of a crime he didn't commit. All peachy apart from that."

Rose's face fell into a perfect mask of sympathy. "I know, and it's terrible news about Sam Barlow. But it's hard to believe that your father, or anyone in your family, could do such a thing," she said. Rose *sounded* sincere, but somehow, I didn't quite buy it.

"But we all saw the way he was behaving with our own eyes,"

Rose continued. "I think he must have been jealous of Sam because of... you know, what was happening when your mother stayed in Crystal Beach before. Everybody saw it, Sidney. He was so full of rage over it."

"Sam Barlow and my mother were not a thing," I said, grinding my teeth together as I spoke. "And I've got a feeling you know that. I bet you also know Sam was up to some pretty dodgy things too."

I was expecting some sort of reaction from Rose, even if it was just a brief twitch of the mouth. Surprisingly, the reaction came from Rodney instead. I looked up at him as an unfamiliar grin spread across his flat, sullen features. My eyes caught his, and for the first time, I felt the full weight of his gaze. It wasn't his usual vacant stare. And that smile... it made the hairs on my arms stand on end.

"I understand you were at The Rose Garden a couple of nights ago," Rose said. "I'm sorry we missed you. Your mother checked out unexpectedly the same night. Which is a shame. We will miss her."

I detected some hidden meaning in Rose's words, a flurry of subtext heaven. If there was any doubt about it before, I now knew that the Gantzes and I were on different sides of the magical divide in Crystal Beach.

I did not know what to say, and Rose glanced down at Mojo, who sat next to me, staring up at both of them during the entire exchange. "Don't be a stranger now," Rose said cheerily, and they both walked toward the exit of the little development.

Wow... so, those two are weird, Mojo said. *You picked up on the super weird vibes, right?*

"Yep."

And you got the bit where she basically spelled it out that she knew you were in their sanctum the other night, right?

"I did." I looked back toward Nikola Vorak's house, noting the familiar address plate on the door—the same as the one I touched in the Gantzes' sanctum that gave me the vision of the argument between my father and Sam. Hmm... maybe they had just come around to pick up Rodney's reading glasses. But if those two were a part of this unwelcome covenant, then there was every chance they had a deep connection to Mystic Dunes, especially considering their address plate's similarity to the number plaque on Nikola Vorak's house. However pleasant and friendly his new place might appear on a beautiful morning in Crystal Beach, it had been built on land that was liable to sink into the sea, and it still felt like terrible things might yet happen here. Or maybe, they already had.

Aye. That's right there, missy. I wouldn't trust anything that goes on in this place, either.

Although the voice had appeared in my head, I looked around to see where the words had come from. This ghostly voice was not Sam Barlow's or Gramps's, nor was it any other ghost I could remember speaking to since coming to Crystal Beach. And with the little sideline I started at the retirement center connecting people with their dead relatives, there had been quite a few.

"Who said that?" I asked out loud. "Show yourself."

It's the guy over there in the party outfit, Mojo said in my head. I followed my cat's gaze through a gap in the houses to an area of vegetation sticking out into the water. It had a tiny Everglades vibe. There, right next to the water, was a ghost. *Yes,* yet another one. But this one resembled a gentleman whose outfit was quite bold and flashy.

CHAPTER
SIX

I stood there as the ghost continued looking at me. He smiled, but no more words came into my head.

It was hard to be sure from where I was, but he appeared to be advancing in years, although still younger than most of the residents of Shifting Sands. He wore some sort of colorful coat. Not a modern one, probably not even one that belonged at any point in the twentieth century, but a much more historic-looking uniform-style jacket with large brass buttons and tassels. It was brightly colored, predominantly purple, with bits of green, red, white, and black. I stood by my initial assessment of "flashy."

The ghost had black hair and a black mustache and beard, both with the sort of oily sheen that suggested something had been used to style it. The mustache was long, curling, and bordering on the absurd. His hair was tightly bound into a single plait that hung over one shoulder, and he wore shiny black boots and a tricorn hat that stood out from the rest of the outfit.

I suddenly realized, as I was taking all this in, that I was also slowly drifting toward him while Mojo followed behind me. Now, a little closer, I saw he wasn't so much sitting at the edge of the water as floating just a few inches above it.

Well, hi there! He said in the same ol' sea dog accent that had first come into my head. *And who might you be?*

I was now almost directly in front of him. "My name is Sidney," I said out loud. I nodded down at Mojo, standing a cautious couple of steps behind me. "And this is Mojo."

Well, pleased to meet thee, landlubbers, he said with an affectation that reminded me of cartoonish portrayals of eighteenth-century pirates. *My name is Admiral Avery.*

I looked up and down at his colorful attire. *Nice outfit.*

You're thinking it's a bit colorful for any admiral ye've ever heard of, he stated.

I had been thinking exactly that. Perhaps it was obvious I might have been, but I also remembered that this ghost had earlier plucked the thoughts right out of my head when I had been standing maybe twenty yards away from him. That wasn't how it usually worked with ghosts or with Mojo. I usually had to project the intention of my voice at them for them to hear me.

Not for me, lass, Admiral Avery said, reading my surface thoughts again. *I were a telepath in life, and some o' that seems to have stayed with me in death, so it has. Anyway, you were wondering about the coat?*

I was.

I never belonged to any navy, aye, it's true. I was more on the other side of them... um... a privateer, if ye will.

"So, were you... a pirate?"

"Aye, some like to call it that. But the coat makes me look very fetching, does it not? It's one thing I hung onto when I retired from the sea. Always liked to wear it when I were running me bar.*

You had a bar too? I asked. Was it in Crystal Beach? There aren't many bars here. I'll probably know it.

Admiral Avery smiled, although it seemed a bit of a sad smile to me. *Oh, ye wouldn't know my bar, lass. It's not in any place ye will be able to find it. Unless ye know where to look.*

Well, that was mysterious. I had to admit that he had me intrigued. I glanced around at Mystic Dunes and the smart, new houses that spoke of an idyllic existence by the sea. No one else was outside of their houses that I could see right now, but it had a friendlier feel now, a more positive energy about it. Admiral Avery was the first ghost I had seen here, as there were none before, not even back when it had been empty and a more ominous place to be. The only previous ghost I had seen close by had been Ben Chalmers, who had appeared to me a few hundred yards away at the mini-golf course.

Admiral Avery took a step or two forward, so he was almost on land. He then turned and pointed his ghostly hand out toward the sea, gaudy gold rings visible on his fingers. *My bar were the finest establishment for rum and great music in Crystal Beach.*

Was it a floating one? I asked. Like on a boat?

Nay, he answered. *It lies about fifty feet that way, beneath the waves.*

I stared out to sea but could not see anything of what might lie below the water's surface. *Is that why you're haunting this place? I asked. Because your bar is here?*

Aye, lass, Admiral Avery said. He looked around at all the houses that had been recently built at Mystic Dunes. *Forever beneath the sea. Just like these will be soon enough.*

I nodded my agreement. *Tell me about it. I think bad people are intending to do bad things with this place.*

Ye feels it too, aye? Admiral Avery said. *The power in this place? It's always been this way... since before my time.*

I wondered when "before his time" was. I had doubts that he was who he said he was or belonged to the time period he suggested. I waited for a comment on that, assuming he would read my thoughts, but none came. What I did know, however, was that as soon as Admiral Avery had spoken of the power of Mystic Dunes, I felt it more keenly than I had at any other point before. How special this place was and how... *old* the energy here was.

My bar was always a place of magic, so it was, lass. I can even take ye there now if ye wanted. Show ye what I mean.

I'm sure that, as a child, the TV had played a safety infomercial about not going to underwater bars with strange, flashy pirates. Or if there wasn't, then maybe there should have been.

All the same, the idea appealed to me. Even though I had only just met this ghost, I was already quite taken with Admiral Avery. But a trip to his underwater bar wasn't going to help me with my investigation into proving my father's innocence. After my conversation with Rose and Rodney, I felt more strongly than ever that I needed to get into The Rose Garden and investigate further. With them walking home, I might be missing my best opportunity to poke around there.

That's okay, the admiral said, obviously having read my thoughts again. *I can teleport ye there, lass, to the Rose Garden Guest House.*

"You can do that?" I said out loud, shocked enough to briefly forget how odd I would look to anyone watching me.

Like I said, there be a lot of power in this place, and I've been making use of it since I was alive. And that was quite some time ago now.

Won't it exhaust you, though? I asked. *All the other ghosts I know vanish for long periods of time after expending so much energy.*

Admiral Avery smiled knowingly. *Oh no, not me. And not in this place. But do come back and see me again soon,* he said. *It's lonely here, and there be no one else who can hear me. Well, no one else I want to talk to, anyhow.*

That was interesting, and I filed the thought away to follow up and see who else around Mystic Dunes could hear Admiral Avery. Time was of the essence, though.

"Yes, I will," I said aloud, looking down to see if Mojo wanted to join me.

I'm not sure I like the idea of this ridiculous individual teleporting me anywhere, Mojo answered, *but I'll come if it's real fish for dinner tonight.*

Deal, I answered and felt the admiral's amused presence in my head again. He had heard Mojo, too.

"How do we do this, then?" I asked. But before I even finished my question, Mystic Dunes faded below me.

CHAPTER
SEVEN

I had always imagined teleporting as being in one place at one moment and suddenly in another place the next. That was what had happened with the portal we had crossed through between Mystic Dunes and the Spectrum Space Center in pursuit of Ben Chalmers's killers.

This was not, however, what happened when Admiral Avery teleported me from Mystic Dunes to The Rose Garden Guest House. Instead, I was suddenly lifted off the ground like a human-sized rocket and shot high into the sky above Crystal Beach.

Well, above something that looked *a lot like* Crystal Beach.

One reason I knew it wasn't really Crystal Beach was that I started screaming the moment my feet left the sand, yet no sound came out of my mouth. Looking down, the ground below me was hazy, its colors all muted and blurred, a bit like watching an old TV set with a poorly tuned antenna. I was flying high above the land, moving in a straight line from where I had been standing by the ocean at Mystic Dunes, now heading toward the center of town, with The Rose Garden lying somewhere between the two.

Mojo was clinging to the leg of my thin cotton pants, his expression one of unbridled horror that I had not seen on the face of a cat before. Yet I could not feel his claws digging into me, so maybe, like sound, pain was not a thing in this in-between place.

Looking past Mojo and tracing the beach northward, I saw where the Shifting Sands Retirement Center was. I noticed a tiny bright spot in the middle of it and instinctively knew it was Ada-Mae. The glowing whiteness was this "other" place's way of representing the magical power she possessed. In the middle of town, there was another bright spot, and I thought I could approximate that position to where Zoe's magic shop, The Invisible Cloak, was located. As I watched, the light representing Zoe seemed to pulse with a more purplish color briefly, then turned bright white again.

Looking down, I could see The Rose Garden as it started to get closer, to where I could identify the individual roof of the place growing larger as I descended. The old guest house glowed slightly differently, its insides swirling like oil moving around on the surface of water. A couple of similarly colored spots—Rose and Rodney, I guessed—could be seen less than a ten-minute walk from their guest house. I would not have long to look around once I got inside.

Finally, I glanced back toward Mystic Dunes, seeing if I could get any ideas on whether any magical individuals lived there and whether they glowed in the same way as Ada-Mae or Zoe—or more like the Gantzes and their guest house. What I saw there was something else—a mix of the dark, swirling oil, the white, and even the purple that was like Zoe's magical light. But what stood out most was that the entire area of Mystic Dunes was covered with this mixture of light. As the admiral had hinted, there was great potential and power there.

And then, my ride was over, and both Mojo and I were dropped into the reception area of the guest house. The cat slid down my leg and stumbled about drunkenly for a few moments before finding a little stability on his four feet. *Never again,* he said. *Teleporting is NOT for cats!*

Yeah, that wasn't quite what I expected, either. Ernie would have loved the rocket ride here, though.

That's because he's crazy! Mojo looked up at me, and I noticed his eyes were crossed but decided it was best not to bring it to his attention.

Looking around, the place was eerily quiet and empty, and I wondered if they even had any guests visiting.

We should head to their private quarters now, Mojo implored, and I concurred that it seemed the best place to start. The second floor, where most of the guestrooms were, sounded quiet as we hurried along the hallway and up into their uninspiring little living space. It should have been a reassuring thought that there appeared to be no one else around to see us, sneaking around as we were. Still, I found my skin crawling, my hackles raised like that sensation when you feel someone creeping up behind you.

We don't have much time, Mojo said. *Where do we look?*

I looked down at the rug covering the entrance to the sanctum. "Well, there's an obvious place."

Didn't you nearly die last time you tried going in there?

I pulled the rug away and opened the trapdoor before I could change my mind about it. "Thanks for reminding me."

No guardian spirit came for me this time, and moments later, I was down in their sanctum. It looked almost the same as before, except for the house plaque I had touched to witness my father's argument with Sam Barlow was no longer here. I had taken it to show Ada-Mae and then buried it on the beach beside Maude as part of a protection spell for safe keeping. I glanced around quickly, with little time to rifle through any drawers or other hidden places.

"I can't see anything," I called back up to my cat a minute later.

What are we looking for?

"I don't know, any sort of evidence that the Gantzes were involved in Sam's death. Or, at least, that they might have framed my father." It still felt odd that I was thinking this way about the kookie older couple. "A vial containing hemlock would sure be helpful."

I didn't actually believe we were going to get that lucky. Then again, if there was something I was coming to understand about witches and warlocks, it was that the heady sense of power could sometimes lead to a little complacency.

Nothing in the sanctum looked like it might be useful, and I was conscious of the time. Unless they stopped or took a detour, Rose and Rodney would likely be back in less than a few minutes. "Where else would they hide the poison?"

Mojo was waiting at the top of the short flight of stairs as I crawled out of the sanctum and closed the trapdoor behind me. I noticed that all the surrounding cabinet doors were open in their living quarters. How the heck had my cat done that? *Well,* he said, *it's not up here. Maybe in the kitchen downstairs? Or the bar?*

The bar at The Rose Garden was just a small section behind the reception area. "You check the kitchen," I told Mojo. "I'll do the bar." After pulling the rug into place, I quickly closed all the opened cabinet doors, still wondering how my cat had opened them all.

Downstairs, Mojo rushed off into the kitchen in a way that was eerily reminiscent of just a few nights ago when Sam had been killed. I shook my head to clear the déjà vu and ran behind the reception desk, looking at all the different bottles and other articles set onto the small bar area. It didn't even have any draft beer, only bottles in the fridge and a few typical bartending tools —a wine and bottle opener, drink stirrers, and a few cocktail glasses. Nothing was jumping out at me. Turning back around, I nearly jumped out of my skin when I noticed a figure sitting in one of the chairs by the currently unlit fireplace. "Sam!" I shouted. "What in the ghostly realm are you doing? You scared me to death."

Sam was in the same chair that he had died in, looking toward the cold fireplace, and he did not turn around when he spoke to me. *It happened here,* he said. *This is where I died.*

"You were already dead, I think." It was an admission I had wanted to make to him ever since I had first contacted his ghost. "Zoe and I were here that night, trying to find out things about your coven. We took mom with us when we left. All of us walked right past you, assuming you were just drunk and asleep. Maybe you weren't already dead then? If I had checked and called an ambulance...."

Sam held up his hand and wiggled his ghostly fingers to stop me from going on further.

There was that guilt thing again. I supposed it made me a good person, but it still felt like Sam Barlow did not deserve to be murdered. If only I could have saved his life that night, my dad might not be in a police cell right now.

You were here that night? I never even sensed you.

"Uh-huh. I was here for... um..."

Well, I still say it was your father. But how did he get here to put the poison in my drink? I thought the question Sam asked was as much for himself as it was for me. *Or did he do it when we were arguing? Although, I don't know how that could have been possible. I brought the drink back here with me from the party. I don't recall leaving it unattended. It is a mystery, I'll admit.*

I realized this was the first time Sam had given me any real detail about the evening he had died. I probably should have tried harder to pry these details from him earlier. All the same, I needed to keep searching, so I bent down and started opening the cupboards and drawers behind the reception desk. "Well, that's what I'm trying to find out. You could always help, you know."

The third cupboard I opened had another of the house address plaques in it. This one was for Number "2," but otherwise just the same as the one that had given me the vision and those already fixed to the houses in Mystic Dunes.

I was reaching for it, wondering if this might also lend me a vision, one that could help the investigation, when something else caught my eye. A small, empty bottle, only big enough to hold maybe an ounce of liquid. Could this be it? The bottle that might have contained the poison? I reached out to pick it up and suddenly went rigid.

One of my visions kicked in, and I could see a pair of hands covered in black leather gloves. The hands held the same bottle I had just picked up, although it had liquid and swirling little bits as if something had been mixed into it. I was seeing things from the perspective of the person holding the bottle, and they were crouched down behind the counter, just as I had been. Now they stood up, revealing Sam Barlow—the real, living Sam Barlow, not his ghost—standing over by the fire, looking into it and swaying a little drunkenly. There was a drink on the counter nearby, a tumbler with what might have held a mixed drink. The gloved hands wasted no time in tipping the contents of the bottle into the drink before they ducked down again.

Suddenly, I was back in the room, and the vision had passed. I stood up again and spoke out loud. "They were here, Sam. Whoever poisoned you was here that night."

The ghost looked around, then got up out of the chair and crossed over toward me. He looked at the bottle in my hands. *What's that?*

"It's the bottle that was used to poison you," I told him. "I... I saw how it happened when I touched this bottle."

Sam's eyes narrowed. *You can do that?*

"I can. I saw the hands of the person who poisoned you. You must have placed your drink on the reception desk here. I saw you standing and looking into the fire, and they tipped a small bottle into your drink. Something finely ground into a clear liquid — hemlock, I'm guessing."

I remember putting the drink there, but not for more than a minute. Hmm, I thought that whiskey seemed a little... bitter. I was already drunk, though, to be honest.

"What? And you drove over here? So irresponsible. You could have killed someone."

Sam's ghost glared at me. *Dark Warlock, duh! Sometimes I even littered. Bad to the bone, you know.*

I held up the bottle. "Back to the point, though. Whoever killed you was already here. What's the chance my dad could have done that?"

Sam shrugged slowly and reluctant. *Not impossible, although I left the party almost immediately after he verbally attacked me.*

And how do you think my dad would have arrived here without you knowing? Besides, I would have known he was here. I was upstairs with my mother and Zoe while she packed her bags.

If you're trying to suggest that Rose and Rodney did it, they were still at the party when I left.

That was a good point. They were my prime suspects, but if what Sam was saying was true, they weren't his killers—my vision showed the poisoning happening here, right behind this bar.

Suddenly, there was a noise outside the front door. The Gantzes were coming home, and I was about to get caught. I quickly shoved the bottle into my pocket, hoping Ada-Mae could figure out what had been in it.

Sam's ghostly form changed suddenly, his face distorting to look more... spectral. His ghost suddenly shot across the foyer and slammed into the door, shutting it before it could be fully opened. Still, he disappeared with little effort, his ghost literally evaporating through the door.

I took the moment he had bought me and leaped over the reception counter, my trailing foot catching it so that I half-landed on my face on the other side. Shaking the pain and the dizziness away and with no time to stop, I got to my feet and ran into the kitchen, hearing the front door open somewhere behind me and Rose Gantz call out. "Is somebody there?"

In the kitchen, Mojo was standing with his upper body in the fridge, snacking on a plate of fish. *That* did not look like searching for evidence.

Come on, my inner voice hissed, *we don't have time for that; the Gantzes are back.* Mojo took one more bite of baked fish and then joined me as we rushed out the back door.

There wasn't a rear entrance to the property, only through the main driveway, but the guest house did have an extensive garden for those staying there to relax in, with a pond and an arbor with roses trained all over it. Heading past the pond, Mojo and I found some thick brush to hide in until we felt it was safe to creep past the house and off the property.

I can't believe you were in there snacking while you were supposed to be finding evidence, I fumed. *And they will probably notice that someone—or some cat—had been at that fish.*

What can I do? I'm a slave to my nature.

He did not sound in the slightest bit repentant. *Luckily, I might have found something.*

Me too.

Well, why didn't you say so? Was it in the fridge?

No, it's right behind you.

I nearly jumped out of my skin, spinning around so fast I fell over, the pain in my knee complaining loudly. "What?" I whispered in a panic.

Mojo slinked past me to some pretty, white flowers growing in clusters right next to the pond. *Here, we cats call it, "Don't eat it, or you'll die number twenty-three."*

Huh?

You humans call it water hemlock.

Amazing, I said, my eyes wide. *Should I pick some? For evidence?*

Fine. Just don't eat it.

I broke off a stem and looked at it, rolling it around between my thumb and forefinger. *But because they have it growing here, is that proof enough to take to John? I mean...does it just grow wild here?*

I heard what amounted to a telepathic sigh from Mojo. *I'm a cat. I'm not sure I should have to tell you all this.*

Nothing like being lectured by something that stares hard at you when it goes to the toilet in the litter box. *Just indulge your stupid owner, okay?*

Hemlock grows wild—although not usually in well-kept gardens—in all but four states in the U.S. Can you guess which sunshine state is one of them?

CHAPTER

EIGHT

"Wow, what incredible timing," I said as Chief John Reece pulled up at the police station and exited his vehicle just as I arrived in Maude. I had been in a bit of a rush and hadn't quite applied the brake quickly enough, overshooting the space and knocking into a wooden sign that said "Reserved for Chief of Police" on it. Oops. I leaned my head out the window as he walked towards my vehicle. "You are exactly the man I am looking for."

"I haven't got time for you today, Sidney," John answered, passing me and glancing back at the tilting parking sign, perhaps considering whether he at least had time to pull out his ticket book and cite me. It was a little like the time we first met. Only then, it was my grandmother who had been locked up in one of his jail cells and not my father.

Either way, I felt that his dismissal was rather rude. He didn't even know what I wanted yet. "Really? I didn't think you would be so busy, what with the Sam Barlow murder case being all done, dusted, and solved and all that."

John stopped and turned around, his eyes narrowing at the sarcastic tone in my voice. Like a fish on a hook, he jumped at the bait. "It may surprise you to hear this, but there is a little more to police work and building a case than just pointing at someone and saying, 'Hey, you did it!'"

John shouldn't try to do sarcastic; he wasn't very good at it. "Exactly." I stepped up to him as if I had been invited to do so and pulled a piece of hemlock taken from the garden at the guest house. "Do you know what this is?"

John could not have looked less interested in the bundle of what looked like dried weeds, but he reached out and took it anyway. "Ah, flowers. How nice of you, Sidney." I had to admit the sarcasm was improving a little. "When you buy someone flowers, though, they're better bought from a flower shop or at least a gas station convenience store." He looked at the bundle of stems with the little white flowers. "Rather than, what, something you ripped out of someone's garden?"

Okay, technically, that was true. "How would you know?" I bit back. "Don't remember you ever buying me flowers."

He sighed a little sadly and turned to head into the station. Somehow, that sad look enraged me even further.

"It's hemlock!"

That made John stop, and he turned around, his brow furrowed. "Uh, why would you give me that?"

I let out an exasperated gasp. "Hemlock, John. Come on! Doesn't ring any bells, does it?"

John regarded it again, then his eyes went wide. "How did you know about...?" He let out an exasperated groan as if what he was about to do was the last thing he wanted. "All right, you better come inside."

Hah!

"Best make it quick, though. I'm expecting someone."

I followed him inside and tried to continue on with him behind the desk, but he turned around and pulled the hinged part of the counter back down in front of me, doing his best to illustrate the barrier it formed between us. Deputy Jessie sat at her desk toward the back of the office and looked up when she saw me, favoring me with a slight smile. She looked tired, disheveled, and altogether sad. It tempered my anger just a little as I turned back to John.

"Okay," he said, "let's have it. How did you know that Sam Barlow was poisoned with hemlock? And please explain in a way that doesn't make me want to arrest you and throw you in the cell next to your father."

Yeesh, I hadn't thought of that. "Do you know where I found this?" I said, snatching the bundle of hemlock back from John and shaking it in front of him.

"I would certainly like to know," he said. John stopped and glanced behind himself. "In fact, the more I think about it, we should probably have this discussion in the interview room and with a recorder running."

I took a step back from the desk, suddenly a little panicked. Not because I was worried about being in the interview room or in a jail cell myself, but because being there would put an instant stop to my efforts to prove my father's innocence. Maybe coming here was a mistake. I was glad that I had not followed him behind the counter. Although, if I had to make a run for it, I did not fancy my chances of getting into Maude and driving off before John caught up with me, even with the head start the counter would give me.

"I found it growing in a flower bed at The Rose Garden Guest House," I blurted out.

John's right eyebrow rose a fraction, but otherwise, he didn't seem all that impressed. "Well," he said with a shrug, "doesn't it grow naturally?"

"Not in Florida," I snapped back at him. "Mojo—"

John's jaw worked itself from side to side a little. "What? What were you about to tell me about your cat?" He almost seemed to dare me to speak of talking cats and magic spells at this moment. Another time, I might have taken him up on that dare, but this was too important.

"There are four states in the U.S. where hemlock does not grow naturally," I told him. "And one of those is Florida."

John shrugged. "Plenty of plant species can be invasive."

"But hemlock?" I said, my voice almost rising to a shout before I caught myself. "Your victim was killed by hemlock. Surely the fact that it is growing in the garden of someone who knew him should be of interest to you?"

John's cheeks turned red. Apparently, he didn't like me telling him how to do his job. Long moments later—perhaps after a quick count to ten—John spoke again. "Okay," he admitted. "Maybe something I could look into, but right now, it doesn't change our current set of circumstances. Not yet."

Just as he said that, the door to the police station opened. A man and a woman in corrections uniforms entered. The woman looked at a clipboard. "Here to pick up Jacob Grace for transport to county custody?"

John threw me a worried look like he thought this turn of

events might set me off. Maybe it should have, but the sudden panic gripping me made me want to curl up in a ball rather than spur me into some rash action. In fact, a part of me wanted to run past the two correction officers and jump into Maude, then drive as far away as fast as I could—maybe all the way out of Crystal Beach and back to my old life in Boston, like doing so might somehow turn back the clock on all this. That was better than seeing my father put into the back of a prison vehicle and driven away. I knew that there would be a sense of finality to seeing that, even though he was still far from a trial or a verdict... or the potential sentence that might follow.

"Sure," John said. "We've been expecting you. We will have him with you in a moment if you want to head around to the side door?"

The woman nodded and turned to her partner before heading back outside.

"Look, Sidney, I don't..." John said. Suddenly, his voice was full of the sympathy and concern that I realized I had missed from him. John's coldness since my father had been arrested had been more painful than I realized. It was understandable, and I knew it, but only in those rare moments when I could look back at things objectively or from his point of view. But it was still painful. "I don't think you should be here to see this. Come back later, maybe. We'll talk about the hemlock more then."

It sounded exactly like the sort of thing he would say just to get rid of me—an empty promise. Still, I nodded dumbly and turned to leave. I felt tears stinging their way free, and all the fight seem to drain out of me. In my heart, I was convinced that Rose and Rodney Gantz were somehow involved and that my father was not capable of murder. But, in that moment, the tiny bundle of hemlock I had brought with me seemed so insignificant against the wheels of justice turning as inevitably as they were.

I hurried outside before John could see me crying.

"Sidney?" said a familiar voice, and I looked up to see my mother's face, full of concern. "You're crying. What's the matter? Is it..." she gestured toward the corrections vehicle parked to one side and the two officers now heading out of sight along the side of the building.

Gillian, Dad's girlfriend, was with her.

"What are you doing here?" I asked them both.

"I was coming in to give my statement," Gillian said. "And Julia-Mae kindly came with me for moral support." She looked over at the transport vehicle, as well. "Are they taking him away now?" she asked, her voice becoming even more brittle than it had been already.

"Maybe we should head away for a moment," I suggested, "maybe grab a coffee. Then come back a bit later when they're ready for you."

Gillian shook her head fiercely, and so did my mother. "No," Gillian said. "He needs to know we are here for him."

My mother nodded in agreement. "Absolutely. Let him see us here. And you, too, Sidney. Tell him you're still working to set him free. He needs to know that."

I nodded and stood with the two women. About a minute later, the correction officers came out with my father handcuffed between them. Both John and Jessie followed them.

"We're here for you!" my mother called out. Oddly, given all the difficult emotions of that moment, I felt a brief stab of something that might have been joy. She really, truly did still love him. My mom was there to support Gillian, but at the same time, she loved her ex-husband, and not only because he'd found a new girlfriend, as I had originally assumed.

My father smiled when he saw us, and the absurdity of the whole situation struck me hard again. No one could have looked less likely to belong in handcuffs between two corrections officers than Jacob Grace. I was glad I'd stayed to watch this now because it had fortified me further. Afterward, I jumped in Maude and hurried off to see Ada-Mae. Between the two of us, we could still figure this out.

~

"Hmm," Ada-Mae said, holding up the bottle to the light by her window and looking at it. "This power of yours, the ability to get these flashbacks or whatever they are when you touch something. Very impressive. Very... powerful."

My grandmother sure sounded fascinated and maybe even a little jealous if I didn't know her better. But none of that was relevant right now.

"It's the bottle that was used to poison Sam, I'm sure of it," I said. "Not that I can prove it. I'll bet it's been wiped clean of any evidence. Whoever used it wore gloves, and we won't find any hemlock in there now."

Ada-Mae rubbed her chin thoughtfully. I had driven straight to Shifting Sands after leaving my mother and Gillian at the police station, and we were in the living room of her apartment. Ernie and Judd had offered to "make lunch," apparently, and there were some rather worrying and loud noises coming from the kitchen while they were preparing it. Now and then, one of them popped out to see what was going on and to check on us.

I knew both men were interested, of course, in the investigation's progress, and I could tell by their protective behavior they were also concerned with the fact that Sam Barlow's ghost was present. Yet again, Sam had quickly recovered from the spectral energy expended in briefly distracting the Gantzes back at the guest house. I had to admit, I was a little jealous on Gramps's behalf about how quickly Sam could recover. I had seen so little of my grandfather's ghost because, every time he had helped us, it had cost him dearly and taken him a long time to recover the spectral energy needed to reappear to me.

Sam was currently sitting on the couch, as far as ghosts could do such a thing. However, he occasionally got up and paced around the room, looking doubtfully at various objects that Ada-Mae possessed.

Ada-Mae would notice when he actually picked something up as, from her point of view, it would float in the air, and she would snap, "Put that down, now, Samuel Barlow!"

"I'm not sure that what may or may not have been in this bottle is the thing we should be most interested in," she said, still holding onto it.

"No?" If it was the bottle used when Sam was poisoned, it had to be a key piece of evidence to the case. If only we could extract that evidence from it.

"No," Ada-Mae agreed, either not hearing or ignoring the confusion in my tone. "The question now becomes if this was the bottle that poisoned our Sam here," she waved a hand around the space, clearly not sure where he was currently, "then what is the bottle that they have in evidence at the police station?"

Fair point. I had forgotten about that.

She called out to the room, facing more toward the table, with Sam's ghost sitting directly behind her on the couch. "We have a job for you, Samuel Barlow, if you want to find out who your actual killer is."

Sam rolled his eyes petulantly, stomping his foot on the floor, which, of course, only I could hear. He had mostly been attempting to look disinterested in what was going on and had been unusually quiet. However, his behavior now made me think he was having doubts about the official version of events concerning his death.

And what's that? he grumbled.

"He's listening," I said, then glanced at him with a wry grin. "He's desperate to find out how he can be useful."

That earned the glare from Sam I expected it to.

"We need you to sneak into the police station," Ada-Mae said, "and get us a photograph of the bottle of poison they have stored in evidence."

"How would we even know where..." I protested.

Before you arrived, Sidney, I performed a spell to try and uncover some new clues in the case. The only thing that revealed itself was the location of the bottle of poison at the police station. Until now, I didn't realize why I needed to know."

Just at that moment, Ernie appeared from the kitchen. "Did you say something?"

I sniffed the air. There was a slightly foul, burned edge to it. "Is the food ready?" I asked. It had been a busy morning, and I was hungry, although I wasn't sure I wanted to expose my stomach to whatever they had created. Ernie was fine with barbecuing, but it seemed that was where his culinary talents ended.

Judd appeared behind Ernie. "We, um..." he said. I noticed the ladle in his hand had some black-looking rice clinging to it before he hid it behind his back.

"We were thinking we could treat everyone to lunch at the Atlantic Diner," Ernie offered.

"I'm up for that," I said.

"Not you, dear," Ada-Mae said. "You're going to be helping Sam."

"I'm pretty sure I'll get noticed sneaking into the station."

"I'm counting on that," Ada-Mae answered.

CHAPTER
NINE

The plan was simple: use my feminine wiles to distract the Crystal Beach Police Chief while Sam snuck in to take a picture of the bottle of poison they had in the evidence locker with Ernie's digital camera. Sam was a ghost, of course, invisible to most, but the camera was not, and a floating camera might attract some attention.

I swung by the magic shop to pick up Zoe on my way back to the police station, as there was also a deputy to be distracted. In my more confident moments, I liked to think that I could have been capable of distracting both of them. Still, I was grateful to have the backup. Not that Zoe was pleased about the idea, but I begged and pleaded and shamelessly played the "My dad's in jail for a crime he didn't commit" card. My feelings of guilt over this were going to be put on hold until this ugly mess was over.

"Howdy police-boy-man-daddy-o," I said as I strode confidently through the door of the police station. *Man, I'm bad at flirting.*

John looked up and saw me. He looked surprised but not as instantly hostile as had often been the case in the last few days. I headed for the far side of the counter as Zoe followed me in, and hopefully unseen behind her, the door lingered open a second or two longer than it should have while Sam—visible only to me—crawled in on his hands and knees, keeping the camera low and out of sight for now.

"Zoe!" Jessie called out, jumping from her desk and crossing over to the counter. "Everything okay? Are you here to report a crime?"

Next to Zoe's legs, Sam crawled through the gap underneath the hinged section of the countertop.

"Have you come to speak about the hemlock?" John asked me.

Now *that* was a good idea. I should have led with that rather than my weak attempt at flirting with the man who had arrested my father for murder.

"I haven't gotten out to The Rose Garden yet," John continued, "but I will. I guess Rose and Rodney should at least know that they have it growing on their property."

I scoffed. "Even I know that Rose loves gardening. She will surely already be aware of it." I was about to lay into John about the need to question them both properly when I remembered I was there to distract him while Sam got his photo rather than argue and get myself thrown out before he could complete the job.

John sighed. I could see how exhausted he was. "I hate that this is happening, Sidney. I really do. I've been feeling so bad about it."

"A date?" Jessie said to Zoe. "Sure, I'm free tomorrow night. About eight?"

Apparently, Zoe was panicking even worse than I was. John looked over, frowned a little, then turned back to me again. Behind him, Sam suddenly popped into view and started to slowly pull out the top drawer of a filing cabinet, where Ada-Mae's spell revealed the bottle was hidden. I failed to keep myself from glancing at him and the camera, which, if either of the police officers in the room turned around, would be suspended in mid-air in front of the cabinet.

John caught my look and started to turn around. In a panic, I reached up and caught his cheek, pulling it back around to keep him looking at me. "I get it," I said. "You're only doing your job."

His body seemed to relax a little as if he had been waiting for —*hoping* for—this absolution from me. Our eyes met, and I saw a deep sadness where there had only been an impenetrable wall over these past few days. At that moment, I knew for sure how much I loved John Reece. And also, as things stood, how could I ever love the man who helped put my father away for murder? These contradictory feelings were pulling me in two directions, trying to tear my heart into pieces.

"You know what I wish more than anything?" John said.

"What?"

Sam was now holding up a clear evidence bag and was positioning it to take the photo. However, someone hadn't thought to make sure the flash was off, and there was a sudden flare of light.

John started to turn around again, and I reached out a second time, grabbing his chin in desperation, but not only to keep him from discovering the camera.

"What, John? What do you wish for? Please... tell me."

For a moment, our eyes met again, and John's mouth fell open just a fraction while, at the same time, his right hand slid across the counter, the tips of his fingers finding my free hand.

A quiet scraping noise finally broke the spell, and John pulled away from me and turned to look behind him. Sam wasn't there, though. Somehow, he had put the evidence bag away and shut the cabinet. Glancing around, I saw he was now ducked down by Jessie's desk.

John looked back at me again, his eyes now narrowed, his suspicions clearly raised. Then I noticed that Zoe had kept Jessie distracted in a different way. The deputy was leaning across the counter, her arm extended, her palm up. The index finger of Zoe's right hand was tracing a gentle line across Jessie's palm. Zoe was reading her palm, a skill I did not know she had.

"Well, this here shows me that you have a long lifeline. And I see that your love line starts off faint but starts to become more defined right about here...."

Jessie takes a deep breath and asks, "So, what does that mean?"

Zoe meets Jessie's eyes. "It usually means you will soon meet your true love... or might have already."

Chief John Reece cleared his throat. "Deputy, we should probably get back to work, don't you think?" he said, with all the guilt of a man whose fingers had been touching my hand only a moment ago.

Jessie pulled back suddenly, her pale cheeks flushing hotly, while Zoe's eyes went straight to the floor. It seemed like you could have been zapped from the electricity in the air between them.

Thinking quickly, knowing that Sam still needed to get the camera out of there, I pointed to one of the fluorescent lights in the middle of the ceiling. "Did you see that flash? I think your lights are flickering. Might want to replace that before you're left in the dark here. You should get LEDs," I babbled on. "A much greener option, and they last way longer."

Sam came scuttling out from behind the counter. Then, after I took Zoe's arm, we backed toward the door. It seemed I would not find out what John wished for more than anything, after all. Shame.

Outside, the day's light now nearly gone, Sam was chuckling to himself, thrilled by the buzz of what we had just pulled off. Zoe stalked away toward town, her eyes fixed on the ground.

"Wait," I called after her. "I'll give you a ride."

"I'll walk," she snapped.

"What's the matter?" I asked, still not quite down off my own high from our accomplishment. "You even got a date."

Zoe whirled at that, and lined by the last rays of the setting sun, I saw something flash briefly in her eyes, her face a mask of animal rage. "You made me deceive her," she snarled. "Making up a palm reading on the spot like that."

I snickered. "Was it something like, 'I see a great love in your future?'"

"It's not funny, Sidney," Zoe half-growled at me.

"I'm sorry," I said, now realizing just how upset she was. "It had to be done."

"Don't say you're sorry when you're not. Things got intense in there. And that's a dangerous thing with me. It should never happen." She waved a dismissive arm and turned to leave. "I'm done with you. Leave me out of your stupid schemes from now on."

Iss-ues, Sam said as Zoe disappeared into the hazy grayness of the magic hour.

"Zip it!" I told him out loud as we went to get back into Maude. "And what sort of idiot forgets to turn the flash off?"

TEN

"See how the little bottle floats in the air," Judd said with a giggle. "That's so funny!"

Sam and I arrived back at Shifting Sands just as the three retirees rolled out of the Atlantic Diner, Ada-Mae wrapped in her magical shawl. A late lunch had turned into a long dinner, and apparently, Judd had indulged in one too many glasses of his favorite bourbon.

Standing outside the entrance to the diner, with its seaside motif of carved wooden wave crests and beach umbrellas, Ada-

Mae squinted at the tiny screen on the back of the camera. "It's a different bottle."

"Well, it can't be the exact same bottle," I said, "but it looks pretty similar."

"Almost," Ada-Mae replied. "But not quite the same."

I knew my grandmother well enough to pick up on the emphasis in her words. The differences she saw were significant. "And what does that mean?"

She looked up and around the reception foyer, just outside the diner. "We need to print that photo out."

"The office at the front desk will have a printer," Ernie said.

"After the incident in The Game of Thrones room," Ada-Mae said, "we're not too popular with management. But I think Howie has a photo printer. And we're going to need some Quipley's members. There may be a spell to be done." She started toward the entrance but paused. "Speaking of which, where's Zoe?"

I felt the weight of shame settle on my features. "She's... upset."

"Why?"

Sam, who until that point had been observing our conversation with a look of mild amusement, snickered. I tried to ignore him. "Things got a bit... intense when we were distracting the Crystal Beach Police Department."

Ada-Mae stared at me for a moment, like she was trying to decide whether she wanted any more information than that.

Also, Sam said to me, *she's got some serious stuff going on with her. You saw what happened to her eyes, right? I mean, I've done some dark magic, but... that was something very strange.*

Ada-Mae turned away again, and I continued to ignore Sam. Even though he was right. I had pushed away my concerns when she had saved my life the other night, but Zoe was more than she seemed, and I would need to deal with that at some point.

WHEN WE ARRIVED at the single-story retirement residence of Wendy and Howie Rockford by the golf course toward the northern end of Shifting Sands, Howie was on the roof. Not on the roof in a "fixing a loose tile" or "cleaning the gutters" sense, especially as it was dark now and altogether a bit late for that. Instead, Howie was sitting cross-legged on his roof, a flashlight balanced against his leg, lighting his face from below. The only thing he was wearing was a pair of swim trunks. His eyes were closed, and his arms were extended, palms resting on his knees in a typical meditative pose.

"Evening, Howie," Ernie said from below like Howie was where Ernie might usually expect to find him. "Can we use your printer?"

"Sure," he replied without opening his eyes. "Wendy's inside."

Ernie nodded his appreciation, and then Judd knocked on the door.

"If you would come down when you are ready," Ada-Mae said. "There might be a spell to be done."

Howie's eyes shot open, and he got up so fast I thought he might fall from his perch on the roof. "I'll come now," he said. "Wasn't doing anything important."

"Do you want me to get you a ladder?" I said, searching around for the means that Howie had used to get up onto the roof but not finding anything.

"I'm good," he replied and started to climb down a pipe, slipping almost straight away and falling into a flowering bush.

"Are you okay?" I asked.

"Fine," Howie said, rising up in the middle of the bush.

As Wendy answered the door, I watched Howie pulling flowers from his hair, really looking like the hippie he thought he was. I shook my head to stop my laughter before hurrying inside.

"Howie," Wendy scolded. "Will you stop hanging about in the azaleas and come inside, please?"

Wendy led us into her office, where we printed the picture out on the biggest piece of paper that Howie had. Then gathering around one of the couches in the living room, Wendy served up a pitcher of peach-flavored iced tea, perfect on this stifling Florida evening that seemed to overcome the house's air conditioning.

"See," Ada-Mae said, pointing between the enlarged floating bottle in the picture and the life-sized one I had taken from behind the reception desk at Shifting Sands. "The lid on this one is a slightly different shade."

"Could just be the way it's come out in the picture," I said, feeling the need to play devil's advocate until I could understand what Ada-Mae was driving at.

"And the ridges where you grip it," she added. "In the picture, they are wider and further apart."

"Because the picture is bigger! Can you get to your point, please?"

What does it even matter if the two bottles are not exactly the same? Sam said, hovering right behind my left shoulder.

"Sam even agrees with me," I said.

"Oh," Ada-Mae said, standing up from where she sat on the couch, her homemade shawl swinging around her as she glanced behind where I was standing, this time almost looking Sam's ghost straight in his spectral eyes. "And Samuel Barlow knows everything about magic, does he?"

I was more powerful than you, you dotty old fool, he griped back, even though she could not hear him.

Ada-Mae looked at me. "Probably going on about what a powerful warlock he was, is he now?"

I inclined my head. "Pretty much."

"Didn't help keep him alive, though, did it?"

That was uncalled for.

If we were talking about anyone else but "Savvy" Sam Barlow, the man who'd held my mother under his magical snare, I would probably have agreed.

"What people like Sam Barlow never understand," Ada-Mae went on, now looking at the rest of us, "is that magic is as much about knowledge as it is power. It's not just knowing one or two big spells or summoning a powerful spirit to make you look stronger than you are.

"Magic is a way of life. A way of looking at the world and understanding how it works. Because magic is about harmony and also about change. If you can't see the difference in things and understand what it means. Well, you know almost nothing."

I gulped. As much as all that had been meant for Sam Barlow, I felt even more so that it was meant for me. This felt like a Quipley's lesson right here in the Rockfords' living room.

Ada-Mae held up the picture. "If this bottle in the evidence locker at the police station looked completely different to the one found at The Rose Garden, then we would have nothing. If it looked exactly the same, then maybe we could say that there is a link between the two, but it still doesn't prove much for us. Maybe they were bought separately from the same place. "But the slight differences between them tell me something important."

What? I glanced back to find Sam enthralled, his spectral hands almost gripping the back of the sofa.

"This bottle," Ada-Mae looked at me, "the one being used in evidence against your father, has been magically manufactured. But whoever did it had to do it in a hurry. So, they did it wrong.

"This explains the slight differences between the two. They've used a replication spell. Maybe they even cast the spell in the guest house with the copy intended to appear in Jacob's overnight bag. That is potent magic but almost impossible to get completely right when creating a copy so far away from the original.

"It's also probably weaker. All replication spells will fade over time, but a good caster could make it last months, likely years. But a poor copy, cast to appear some distance from the original, they'll be lucky if it lasts a few weeks. Who knows, maybe just days?"

"How can we know if that's the truth?" I asked.

Ada-Mae held the picture in both hands at arms-length in front of her. "Well, it's not very ethical. But we could speed up the end of the replication spell, making the bottle in evidence disappear. That's essentially tampering with evidence... both unethical and illegal."

I actually heard Sam clap his spectral hands together behind me. *Right! Now you're talking my language.*

WE SAT in a circle in the middle of the Rockfords' living room. All the members of Quipley's were present except Zoe, so there was a small gap in the circle. That was where Sam sat.

"Reach over, Sam," Ada-Mae said, "touch the photograph. Your powerful link to the original item is what's going to help us dispel the copy."

Sam looked at me. *And then your father will go free.*

I nodded at him and spoke my answer out loud. "He didn't kill you, Sam. He was set up, and now you know he's innocent."

Sam slowly nodded his agreement. If I hadn't known better, I might even have thought I saw tears welling in his eyes. *They betrayed me, didn't they?*

"It must have been them."

Sam reached out toward the picture, which was in the same altar bowl that had been used in The Game of Thrones Room earlier in the day. Somehow, it had appeared out of Ada-Mae's shawl.

We'll speak soon, Sam said, holding my gaze. *I'll tell you what I know about the coven and Mystic Dunes.*

If we hadn't been about to destroy the falsely planted evidence that had put my dad in jail, I would have stopped the ritual and insisted he tell me right there and then. Instead, I nodded to Ada-Mae that she should proceed.

She sprinkled some ground incense on the picture lying in the copper altar bowl, the powder passing through Sam's ghostly hand to rest on the image, then spoke an incantation.

"For what is real and what is not, we come to undo a spell and foil a plot. For change is king, and nothing lasts... the false bottle shall vanish when the spell is cast."

The picture beneath Sam's fingertips burst into flames spontaneously. Still, Sam kept his hand there as the photographic paper discolored, curled, and then finally became ash.

"Did it work?" Judd asked in the silence after the flames had died.

"Well," Howie put in, "apart from the spontaneous flame, that was a bit anticlimactic. Especially after all the smoke and the sprinkler system theatrics at Shifting Sands."

Ernie chuckled, letting go of what seemed like a long-held breath at the same time.

"He's gone," I said. The rest of the room, Ada-Mae included, turned to look at me. "Sam's gone."

"He was our connection to the magically replicated bottle and the poison," Ada-Mae said. "Perhaps the part he played in the spell drained him. I'm sure he'll find his way back."

I hope so, I thought. Funny how I had been looking forward to the point that I would never have to see Sam Barlow's ghost again. Now I had gotten my wish, and I desperately wanted him back. What he knew could make all the difference in the fight I felt sure was still to come.

CHAPTER

ELEVEN

"I want you gone."

Chief John Reece was standing outside Maude. It was the next morning, and I was barely awake. What with the spell and everything, it had been a late night. I had been rudely awakened by a loud rapping on Maude's side door and opened it to find a furious-looking police officer glaring at me. Behind him, it was a beautiful morning on the beach, the waves lapping gently against the shore, just a hint of a breeze skipping across the surface of the sand, and the cry of seabirds adding an astonishingly soothing melody.

"Huh?"

"This van," John said, "you can't park it on the beach."

"That's what Sam used to say. But it's a free country."

"It really isn't," John said. "I could cite you right now. You've got twenty-four hours to find somewhere proper to live, Miss Grace. Next time I catch you sleeping on the streets of Crystal Beach, the van gets impounded. Do you hear me?"

Chief John Reece turned to stalk off.

Wrapping my covers around me, with just a long shirt on beneath it, I shuffled to the edge of where my slide-down bed filled the side opening of the camper van and called after him. "What's got into you this morning?" I hoped that I already knew.

John obviously thought I did. He turned around and jabbed his finger toward me. "I'll tell you, although I'm sure you already know. We went to hand over evidence to the district attorney's office this morning, only to find a crucial piece of it missing."

"Huh?" I was terrible at looking innocent.

"And wouldn't you know, it went missing after you and Zoe came into the station yesterday." John was seething, unable to stand still. The muscles on his neck were flexed, his thick shoulders rolling as if he was dying to let out his anger. He needed a session with one of those punching bags at the gym to let it all out.

"Zoe didn't do anything," I said. I knew I shouldn't, but guilt drove me to defend her.

"I don't know that I believe that," he said. "And I don't know if Jessie ever will." My stomach sunk at that. "However you did it, magic or otherwise, I know you stole that evidence, and that is so far beyond the lowest of the low, Sidney. I've been more patient than most would be with the witches of this town. But I've had it. With the lot of you. And especially you, Sidney Grace."

His finger came up again. "Do not give me another excuse to put you in jail. Or, even better, why don't you head back to Boston? I think it would be better for the both of us."

And with that, he stalked back to his patrol car, parked along the street. I wasn't sure what I had expected. John didn't have to be a genius to put our visit and the disappearance of the evidence together. Still, I wasn't prepared for such a visceral reaction so early in the morning.

My stomach hurt at the thought of... well, whatever we had started building truly being over between us. But maybe the worst thing was that I totally understood John's angry outburst and his ordering me to leave. Still...

I jumped from Maude, the blanket still wrapped around me, and shouted after him just before he slid into his vehicle. "When's my dad getting out?" I called out to him.

John turned back, and for a moment, I thought he wasn't going to dignify my question with an answer. Then his shoulder slumped a little, and he called back. "He's out on bail already," he said. "For now."

So my dad really was free. At the moment, that was what mattered the most.

WITH HER FATHER out of jail, Sidney is on the hunt to find the person responsible for Sam's murder. But where will she and her felines live now that Chief Reece has kicked them off the beach? What secrets will Sam reveal about the coven and Mystic Dunes? And what are Rose and Rodney hiding besides the hemlock growing in their garden? Is Admiral Avery just a flashy seafaring ghost or does he have something important to share with Sidney?

Turn the page to find all the answers in the next magically mysterious and spellbinding paranormal cozy mystery, ***Tangled In Magic***

Next in Series:

Welcome to Crystal Beach, an enchanting town with a dangerous secret.

As Sidney and her magical felines search for a new place to call home, a peculiar creature roams the beach under the cover of night, setting Sidney's supernatural senses tingling. And more disturbing trouble is heading this witch's way.

A woman close to Sidney's heart vanishes without a trace, leaving behind a chilling puzzle. Is there a connection between her disappearance and the enigmatic beach creature? To find out, Sidney must harness her own magical abilities, as even Ada-Mae's spells are no match for the task at hand.

As the mysteries deepen, an old seafaring ghost emerges with a forewarning, hinting at an impending catastrophe that threatens Crystal Beach. History may be doomed to repeat itself unless Sidney can piece together the cryptic clues in time.

Can this gifted psychic witch untangle the web of strange events, connect the dots between a baffling death, a woman's vanishing act, and the elusive beach creature, and decipher the ghost's ominous prophecy before it's too late to save her beloved town and the people she holds dear?

Turn the page to join Sidney, Ada-Mae, Mojo, and the unforgettable residents of Crystal Beach in Tangled in Magic, the ninth installment of the Crystal Beach Magic Mystery Series.

∾

FREE GIFT

Receive your FREE exclusive copy of **Hash Browns And Homicide**, the series prequel, and get notified via email of new releases, giveaways, contests, cover reveals, and insider fun when you sign up to my VIP Mystery Book Club mailing list!

Scan the QR Code To Sign Up and Claim Your FREE Exclusive Book

KAREN MCSPADE

TANGLED IN MAGIC

A Crystal Beach Paranormal Cozy Mystery
Book Nine

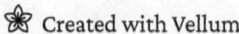 Created with Vellum

CHAPTER

ONE

T he full moon above us had snuck up on me. It always
seemed to do that wherever I was. One day, it would be
a sliver in the sky, a little curl like the one the boy fishes
from in the DreamWorks logo. Next, it would be a looming,
mysterious presence, sometimes bright and stern overhead,
sometimes a massive orange or dirty yellow ball lurking near the
horizon.

For many, the presence of the full moon is desirable because it
pushes back the night and the shadows where scary things might

hide. Yet there is something alien about it, too... something magical.

Not the friendly, well-intentioned magic I had been learning from Ada-Mae. Neither was it the dark magic of witches and warlocks with malign intent. It no more belonged to the likes of Sam Barlow and his coven than it did to me and Ada-Mae. No, the magic of the moon was wild and untamed. It was its own kind of magic, uncaring of our lives and petty grievances. The gravitational pull of the moon moved entire oceans of water across the face of the earth. So, what effect could it have on just one individual under its sway?

Tonight, though, the moon poured benevolent light on the small gathering by the pool at the Shifting Sands Retirement Center. We were happy—myself, Ada-Mae, Judd, Ernie, my mother, and, thankfully, my father. A few other residents had drifted over to join our little celebration party, Wendy and Howie Rockford foremost among them. Howie was even behaving, having turned up in cargo shorts, a cotton shirt, and sandals rather than in some state of undress, as was often the case.

However, I felt my father's smile seemed a little painted on. Prison, a murder charge, and the possibility of the rest of his life in jail for a crime he had not committed had shocked him. I could tell that without him having to say it, which wasn't surprising. Maybe that's why he had moved away from the group. I sat beside him as he removed his shoes and dangled his feet in the swimming pool. He cradled a glass of champagne from a bottle that my mom had bought, although the glass was still full as if he had barely taken a sip.

"You okay?" I asked.

"Sorry," he said. "You know I'm not much for parties and... well, social events. Doubly so when they are in my honor."

"You don't have to apologize. You've been through a lot."

He glanced back at the gathering. Mostly made up of people who cared about him, even though some had not known Jacob for very long. "It's just—and I don't want to sound ungrateful here—but this all feels a little premature. I'm not off the hook yet, and that charming policeman of yours still seems convinced I killed Sam Barlow."

The mention of Chief Reece stung a little. I was worried that our relationship—if it had ever amounted to enough to actually call it that—was over. I mean, the last time we met he basically told me he was going to run me out of town. Which was a little Wild Wild West, I thought.

All the same, I found myself defending John. "He's a good cop," I said. "And you were set up pretty good."

"By the Gantzes, you think? Those funny people running the guest house?"

"Looks that way from what we found. Or, at least, I'm sure they were involved."

"But why?"

It was a good question, although I wasn't precisely sure what my dad meant by it. *Why him?* Probably because his arguments with Sam made him an easy target. After my dad, I was the next person known to have a "beef" with Sam, so maybe I could have ended up in that jail cell if it hadn't been my dad.

Why Sam? Well, that was a more interesting question. Sam appeared to have drunk the coven Kool-Aid, and it had taken him a long time to come around to the idea that they could have betrayed him. I kinda got that: Why kill someone who was so on board with the program?

"No sign of Gillian yet," my dad said, pulling out his cell phone. "I should call her and see where she's at. No offense, but as beautiful as your new hometown is, it can be a little dangerous."

I smiled at that. "None taken. All the most beautiful things are at least a little dangerous."

Thinking I should leave him to his conversation with Gillian, I stood up and returned to be with Ada-Mae, my mom, and the others. I noticed that Julia-Mae was watching Jacob as I approached, her expression a little hard to read.

"Though your father's release is great news," Ada-Mae said when I reached her, "we still need to prove who did it and get the police off his back."

"We're thinking Rose and Rodney, though, right?" I said.

Ada-Mae shook her head, though not in disagreement. "I just can't believe that the Gantzes would be capable of murder. I've known them since we moved here. Rose especially. Strange as they are, it's hard even to think they could have been mixed up in Sam's shady business at Mystic Dunes. Although, Rose always seemed to have a higher opinion of that young man than I did."

"Well, we stretched ourselves just getting Dad out of jail," I admitted. "Sam seems to have left us, maybe even for good. And, as much as I hate to admit it, he became a real asset. Once he realized he had been betrayed.

"Plus, John is out for blood with us. With me, especially. In fact, with the first excuse he gets, I'm either going to end up in jail or with Maude impounded... maybe both. And now I think Zoe, one of our most powerful witches, is done helping us."

"Well, I can help you with one of those," Ada-Mae said. "Tomorrow, bring Maude over and park her in the parking lot here. It's not a long-term solution, maybe a week or so, but it'll give you some time. I'll clear it with the administrator."

"Administrator Jessop, you mean?" I gasped. "The same man who hasn't yet forgiven you for setting off the sprinkler system in The Game of Thrones Room?"

Ada-Mae waved a dismissive hand. "It'll be fine. His memory only lasts as long as one of Ernie's rocket launches."

"I can't get an answer." It was my dad. He held up his cell for illustration as he joined us from the side of the pool, a worried frown creasing his features, which were usually smooth and youthful looking for a man of his age.

"She's staying with her friends, right?" I questioned. "The ones over at Mystic Dunes?"

"She didn't want to be alone at the motel after I was arrested," he explained.

"Fair enough," my mom said. "I'm sure she's fine. Just busy."

I wasn't sure whether she was being dismissive because she didn't want Dad to worry or whether she didn't mind that Gillian wasn't there. Julia-Mae had been supportive of Gillian while Jacob had been locked up. But the mom I knew, love her though I did, had always been a little... well, for want of a better word... selfish. Or, at least, she seemed at times to be more concerned with herself than others. Except when it came to me and Dad. Then, we were always a priority.

But since she had visited Crystal Beach that first time for the Mini-Golf Invitational after being hexed by Sam Barlow, I thought I had seen a change in her.

Or maybe it was that she and Ada-Mae had reconnected again and become closer than they had been since before my grandmother and grandfather had moved out of Boston. Either way, I needed to get used to giving her more credit.

My dad shook his head in response to her placating words. "I called her earlier after they let me out. I didn't get any answer then, and she hasn't called me back since."

"Look," I said, "it's a bit late to go over there now, and we've all had a bit of champagne. But maybe I'll pop over to Mystic Dunes in the morning, huh? Make sure she's okay."

I LEFT the party after that, suddenly tired. If this was to be my last night on the beach in Maude, at least for a while, I wanted a little time to sit in the doorway, stare out at the sea, and hear the waves breaking against the shore. I liked to close my eyes and let that calming, reassuring sound wash over me. I'd leave the window open a little so that I could fall asleep to it. As close as Shifting Sands was to the beach, it wasn't quite close enough for that, and I was going to miss it.

As I meandered the roughly ten-minute walk back along the beach to Maude, I noticed something a little odd, something I probably wouldn't have seen had it not been for the extra light of the full moon, casting a mysterious light on the crashing waves and the gently swaying palms at the back of the beach. Paw prints.

Not all that odd by the mere fact of them; my cats—who had become more accustomed to running along a sandy beach than any other cats I had ever heard of—left their paw prints behind all the time. Their feet, however, were dainty little things, while these prints were big, even for a sizable dog. And they were strangely spread out—not the shorter, even spacing of a dog trotting along, nor the wider, more uneven spacing of a canine at full speed. It was as if this creature had bounded in great leaps, its weight pushing down hard on the sand, splaying the resulting print and probably kicking up a lot of the sand as it did so. More like how a big cat might move when chasing its prey, I figured.

Yeesh, that's creepy! Still, as far as I was aware, a lion or tiger on the loose was highly unlikely in Florida.

So I shrugged and pushed on toward the camper van and my cozy bed. The prints appeared all the way past the van and continued further up the beach as far as the bright moon allowed me to see. I wondered if my cats had seen what left the paw prints, and I made a mental note to ask Mojo when I saw him.

Unlocking the side door, a movement out of the corner of my eye made me turn. A shape was moving at the edge of what was visible—maybe thirty yards down the beach. All I could see was a silhouette hunched over as it ran south along the beach toward Mystic Dunes, moving with a sort of half-leaping gait that was not exactly what I had imagined from the prints... but close enough.

Fear lanced through my chest. What was this thing that was loose on the beach? It looked big—person-sized, at least. As the vague shape disappeared into the night at great speed, I remembered the fact that Gillian was... well, not missing, but still out of contact.

There was no way I was heading after it, though, and I could not have kept up with it, even if I had wanted to. All I could do was lock myself up tight in Maude and hope the cats would be home soon, all safe and accounted for.

CHAPTER
TWO

I fell asleep before any of the cats came back and woke in the morning to find Mojo's face about three inches from mine.

Glad you woke up before the high tide washed us all away, he chastised me. *You're so lazy. All you do is sleep.*

"This coming from the cat," I scoffed. I lifted my head a little to check that he wasn't alone. All his brothers—Jinx, the other brown tabby tortoiseshell, and my two Siamese cats, Abra and Cadabra—were there. "You're all here," I added with a sigh of relief.

Only just. We nearly died. And here you were, sleeping!

"What happened?" I asked, not yet awake enough to take Mojo's criticism personally.

There was a monster. A monster came running up the beach.

"Yeah, I think I might have seen it. I saw its tracks, for sure. Great big paw prints. But that was last night. Hours and hours ago. Why didn't you wake me sooner?"

I'm not sure if cats can look flustered, but my question caused some twitching of Mojo's nose and whiskers that made me think the oldest of my cats was uncomfortable.

We...

"You what?"

We hid, okay?

"For what," I laughed, "the last ten hours?"

Well, we needed to be sure it was gone. It was Jinx's fault. He's a complete coward.

Hmm, right. "Sure, all Jinx's fault."

I was tempted to enjoy the moment and Mojo's rare bit of discomfort a little longer, but there were more pertinent things we needed to discuss.

"Well, what did you see? What was this thing that had you all running for cover?"

None of us hung around long enough to get a real close look. And it was nighttime.

"You're cats. Can't you see well in the dark? *And* it was a full moon."

Cadabra's the slowest, Mojo went on, ignoring my line of questioning, *and he said it was very hairy. A bit like a dog.*

The slowest? With cats, apparently, it was a case of "if you fall behind, you get left behind."

"So, it chased you?"

It was running like crazy along the beach, so we didn't wait to find out for sure. But dogs and cats... we do have a history, you know.

That was a fair point.

And, oh, how it howled.

"Howled?" I was surprised I hadn't heard that, although the waves had been crashing loudly against the beach, perhaps reducing the distance over which a sound like that could be heard.

Yes, right before it ran toward us, it howled. I've never heard a sound so terrible in my life. Worse than any other dog howl I have ever heard.

Something had clearly rattled my usually ice-cool and acerbic cat, and I didn't like it. We already had enough problems in Crystal Beach without giant howling dogs terrorizing the beach.

Still, one issue at a time. I needed to check on Gillian and make sure she was okay. But first, there was someone else I wanted to speak to, and I needed to get moving if I wanted to catch her before she went to work.

"Argh!" Jessie screeched, reaching for the weapon at her side before realizing it was me. Then, with a relieved sigh, she added, "Go away, Sidney."

On second thought, I shouldn't have hidden in the bushes outside the police station. It was just that I didn't want John to see me loitering. As a precaution, I had parked Maude some ways up the street. I already had all my cats in the van, so I could head over to the parking lot at Shifting Sands later, as Ada-Mae had suggested.

"I'm not here for me," I said as Jessie shut her car door and walked toward the police station. John's car was already there, and I glanced nervously toward the entrance of the building, knowing that there was no way I could follow the deputy in. "Or my dad. It's not about that."

"I don't care," Jessie said, walking around the car.

"Please!" I hissed as loud as I dared. "I'm here for Zoe."

That stopped her, although her expression remained wary, the angry crease in her forehead deepening. "Why doesn't she come and talk to me herself?"

"She doesn't know I'm here. In fact, she won't talk to me, either."

Jessie sniffed judgmentally. "That's happening a lot, isn't it?"

Ouch. I had come to see Jessie for Zoe because I felt I owed her that. But I was almost as uncomfortable with the idea of the smiling, easy-going deputy—who I had become fond of and who not so long ago had feelings for me—thinking badly of me as I was with John doing so. I tried to hold my tongue, but you know, my name is Sidney Grace, and well... discretion has never been my strongest attribute.

"My dad was in jail for a murder he didn't commit, Jessie," I shot back.

"So you say. But do you even know he didn't? Do you know it for a fact.?"

"I do. I just can't..."

"Prove it? Is that what you were going to say? Yeah, a pesky thing that proof. But we police officers are kind of bound by it... because it's the law, Sidney."

"And that's why we had to go around you. You're not equipped for this, for the darkness settling over Crystal Beach."

Jessie sighed, deflated a little, but didn't look any less angry. "The thing with that magic you all claim to have such a great relationship with is that those of us who don't have it are just expected to take it at face value. Do you know how hard it is for the police to do that? And then you lie and deceive us. You use our feelings to cheat the system rather than having a little more faith in us to get to the bottom of things."

As Jessie spoke, the last of the anger seemed to drain from her. Now she just looked sad, those big, expressive, dark brown eyes glistening wetly in the sunlight of a bright Florida morning.

"If you have something like magic on your side, then the responsibility to be fair in how you use it is double," she added.

She wasn't wrong, and I knew that before ever walking into the police station the other evening. But he was my dad. Zoe, though...

"I just want you to know that I put Zoe in a difficult position the other night. That's all. The last thing she would ever have wanted to do is deceive you. Especially since she..."

She likes you. I didn't have to say it. I could see that Jessie knew. Her bottom lip started to curl. More into a ghost of a smile, but at least it was something.

"Still can't figure out how the two of you did it from the other side of the counter, even with those special powers of yours. It's bugging John, too. He was going to get a warrant to search your van and Ada-Mae's apartment, but figured there wasn't much point."

As if summoned by the mention of his name, Chief John Reece appeared at the door to the station. He glared down at me, then at Jessie, who had turned at the sound of the door. "You coming in, Deputy?"

Jessie nodded and glanced back at me before heading inside. I waited for another rebuke from John, some accusation that I was casting a spell over his deputy or something. But nothing came. In fact, he didn't even give me a second look before heading back inside.

CHAPTER

THREE

W ell, that went better than I thought it would. Jessie had kind of listened to me, and I had at least a small hope that I helped Zoe's cause.

Now, it was time to see to my other obligation. I returned to Maude and drove over to Mystic Dunes.

Gillian's friends were next-door neighbors of the friendly man who had come to see me and my mother on the beach, Nikola Vorak. He had hosted the party for the new residents of Mystic Dunes, the same party where guests witnessed my dad arguing with Sam Barlow, making him a suspect in the realtor's death.

I hadn't thought too much about that fact until now. Why had Mr. Vorak been the one to host the party? Did he have some connection to Sam Barlow and the whole project I didn't know about? Or maybe he was just sociable and enjoyed hosting parties.

I tried to recall what the guests had said during the vision I had the night of the party when Zoe and I had sneaked into the Gantzes' living quarters at the guest house. Nothing incriminating, as far as I could recall, just a bunch of people pleased with their bargain price seafront properties. Although, now that I thought about it, the very idea of a housewarming party for the whole development was quite strange. But no stranger than the fact that the whole place had filled up at once, I guessed.

Then, there was the fact that Rose and Rodney were in possession of a large house address plaque identical to the one on the front of Vorak's home. When touching it activated the vision, I thought that it was just another of my magic powers presenting itself. Which was a little arrogant, I realized, to think of that way. "Just another power," like everyone had this stuff happening to them. Things had been moving so fast since I arrived in Crystal Beach that I'd become a little desensitized to the fact that I could do incredible things with my magic. When things slowed down, I promised to practice proper gratitude, humbleness, and so on.

But what if the vision I had seen was the purpose—the function—of the address plaque? What if it was a spying device? Then maybe Rose and Rodney were using it to spy on Nikola Vorak. Of course, I had also seen a plate for number two—the house where Gillian was now staying. The vision had been different for that, though. More of a memory of something that happened on the night of Sam's death, seen through the eyes of the killer. Still, that didn't mean that these plates could not be some sort of spying device. Maybe it only meant that I didn't fully understand them.

And if they were spying devices, then who knew if there wasn't a corresponding number somewhere at The Rose Garden for every house on Mystic Dunes? In my book, Rose and Rodney were looking more and more guilty. They had to be the ring-leaders of this evil coven of witches, and there was some yet-to-be-enacted plan for the development and possibly for all its residents.

In fact, it occurred to me as I drove there that maybe I should warn Gillian and the friend she was staying with about these spying devices. But I decided against warning them. I was more likely to sound crazy to them than anything else. *Concentrate on one thing at a time, Sidney.* Check on Gillian and make sure she's okay. Judging by what Dad had looked like the previous evening, I think he still needed the support and comfort she could offer.

Taking a left off Mangrove Street, I headed down the road that became ever more like a dusty track until it reached Mystic Dunes —at first sight, a shining, unexpected jewel right next to the ocean. But what else was happening there?

I parked in the open area—what one might consider visitor parking, although there was no sign to that effect. Getting out of Maude, I looked up at Mr. Vorak's back fence and the deck area overlooking the sea.

Rather than a money pit that might any day collapse into the ocean—and the pet project of an unsavory coven of witches— Mystic Dunes appeared benign and kind of beautiful. Even for someone who grew up among the early twentieth-century redbricks of Boston and not these modern, faux New England-style luxury builds. It was strange to travel almost the entire length of one side of the country and find someone making more expensive knockoffs of period houses made famous in your home state. There was something about them that sold a dream even I would have loved to believe in.

Maybe it was magic that made me feel that. Maybe there was some glamour or other spell cast on this place to make it appealing, even irresistible, to potential buyers. Or maybe it was just the more conventional magic of the sea, the Florida sun, and a subtle yearning I had for things to finally settle down and become normal again.

Are you okay staying here? I asked Mojo silently. I don't expect I'll be long.

You don't need backup? he asked.

I'll be fine, I answered, signaling toward the other cats. *You keep an eye on these guys.*

Mojo seemed to have recovered from the scare of the previous night with the giant leaping dog on the beach. The others—my two Siamese cats, in particular—were still rattled and restless, though.

I had to pass in front of house number one on the way. The two houses were right next door to each other, as Sam—or whoever had designed the development—had done quite a job of packing them like sardines into their respective lots.

The houses were carbon copies of each other, the residents not yet having much chance to stamp their individual marks on the outside of their homes. The same black doors with a tiny porthole window beneath the same miniature porticos with the same little shrubs poking out of the gravel beside the short front path. The same black slate plates with the house numbers engraved on them and lined in gold paint.

I eyed house number one out of the corner of my eye as I walked by, then arriving next door, I tentatively reached out and touched number two's address plaque. Nothing but cold stone there, and I didn't know if I was disappointed or relieved about that. I pressed the buzzer. Without even a bit of fence between the front of the two properties, they really were the closest of neighbors. Nikola could just step out of his front door and take a single stride to be in front of number two. And vice versa. They were so close to living on top of each other that they might as well be living in the middle of a big city.

I smiled at the irony of that thought and was still smiling like some kind of idiot when a woman who might have got on very well with Howie Rockford answered the door.

About Gillian's age, her brown hair hung in long dreadlocks. She wore baggy striped trousers and a multicolored knitted tunic. The arms sticking out from the oversized sleeves had at least twenty friendship bracelets on each wrist. How many friends could one middle-aged lady have?

"Come in, come in," she said, stepping back and sending several friendship bracelets sliding with a wave of one arm. "Welcome to our home."

I had a strange feeling, like maybe somehow, I had been expected. Or maybe she just greeted everyone who arrived at her doorstep like this. Who knew? Indeed, Mystic Dunes was quite out of the way, so maybe she was even glad to get any visitors at all.

"My name's Sidney," I felt the need to explain. "I'm Jacob's daughter. My father was..."

"Yes, yes," she nodded with the enthusiasm of a jack-in-the-box without letting me finish. It seemed the rumor mill in Mystic Dunes was running on overdrive.

She led me through the front foyer and into the living area. Although its layout was a mirror image of Nikola Vorak's, the decor and furnishings could not have been more different. Heavy drapes hung across all the windows, and several candles provided what light there was, even though it was a bright Florida day outside.

There was a man in the room, about the same age and in similarly Bohemian dress as the woman, sitting in a cross-legged meditation pose. The real features of his attire were a colorful waistcoat, an old Japanese-style "Rising Sun" headband, and rose-tinted, round glasses, the type worn by John Lennon back in the sixties.

He beamed at me through smoke drifting up from an incense stick. "Sidney!"

I jumped, not expecting to hear my name coming from a stranger. Perhaps Gillian had told them about me, or maybe they had somehow seen a photo, and that was why they recognized me. All the same, the enthusiastic greeting by these total strangers felt surreal. My fight-or-flight instinct was kicking in, shivers dancing between my shoulder blades, and I now wished I had brought Mojo in for backup, after all.

"We've been looking forward, so looking forward to meeting you," the woman said, signaling for me to sit down on a sofa covered by a tie-dyed throw. "You're a witch. A witch, I hear!"

"Yeah, big-time powerful, too, man," the man added in a lazy drawl.

I was still having trouble wrapping my head around the fact that these people were friends of Gillian, the neatly turned-out businesswoman who, lovely though she was, just exuded common sense. Maybe they had gone to school together or something and only just reunited again.

"I... um... I don't believe we've met?"

"I'm Lennon," the man said.

The woman held out a hand, letting out a little gasp as I took it. "And I'm Janis."

"Wow," I said, shaking my head in disbelief. "Really... uh, cool names."

"We renamed ourselves in keeping with our new lives here in Mystic Dunes. You dig?" Lennon told me.

"O-kay."

"Well, Neil and Regina aren't very hip, are they?" Janis said by way of explanation.

Grinning weakly, I thought it best to move things along. "I was looking for Gillian. I understand she might have been staying here since my dad's, er... trouble. He's tried to get hold of her a couple of times, but she hasn't gotten back to him."

Janis's brow furrowed, but it was a little harder to determine Lennon's reaction in the darkened room and with the tinted lenses of his glasses.

"We haven't seen Gillian since last night," Janis said. "We thought she was going to the party for your dad, and we were expecting her back, but... Well, we thought she and your father... You know, you know." She raised her eyebrows suggestively.

I was one hundred percent sure I did not know... and it would stay that way. "No, she never turned up at the party."

This seemed to shake Lennon, who had remained in his meditative position until that point. He straightened his legs and hoisted himself up to sit on the sofa. "Do you think she's okay?"

I did not know whether to say anything about the strange sighting of the huge dog-thing on the beach the previous night. They might have been more receptive to my talk of magical spying devices than I assumed they would be unless all the hippie clothes, incense, and excitement about my witchiness were just a thin veneer. It could be that way with people and magic at times. It was a lovely idea at first, but some found it hard to truly believe despite their best intentions, while others ended up frightened when the reality of it hit.

"Do you think we should call the police?" Janis said when I hadn't replied after a few moments.

"No!" I snapped on instinct. If my dad's girlfriend was now missing when the police were still very interested in him for Sam

Barlow's murder, it could put him further under a microscope. Also, what if Sam's killers had her? John and Jessie were not equipped for the sheer force of power now threatening Crystal Beach, and worse, they might tie me and anyone else who could help by arresting my dad again.

The sixties power couple were looking at me with shocked expressions. They needed a little more than my desperate "no."

"I should look for her some more before we bother the police," I said, recovering. "They're busy trying to find Sam Barlow's real killer."

I watched their eyes for any raised eyebrows at the mention of that, but neither gave anything away. It seemed they were just genuinely worried about their friend.

I turned to leave, realizing the thick, incense-filled atmosphere was getting to me a bit, anyway. "I will let you know as soon as I find anything out."

Leaving their house, I was trying to decide where to investigate next. Should I search the stretch of beach between Mystic Dunes and where Maude had been parked the previous night—where I had seen evidence of the creature with the huge paws? Or maybe it would be better to head back and seek Ada-Mae's advice on the whole thing. It meant worrying my dad, too, but maybe we were already at the stage where that needed to happen. *Yes,* I needed help with this.

I was back at Maude and about to open the door when a familiar voice—unmistakable, even though I had only met him once—called out to me. *Yar, landlubber!* said Admiral Avery. *I would have a word with thee.*

CHAPTER
FOUR

T he ol' sea dog and bar owner was where I had seen him before—in an area that was not quite sea and not quite land. This time, he was standing up, with a sense of urgency about him, beckoning me over.

I glanced at Maude, wanting to get on with my plans to find Gillian, unsure of my assertion that involving the Crystal Beach Police Department was not necessary yet. *No,* I should hear what Admiral Avery had to say. Aside from the fact that it would be plain rude to ignore him, he had already shown incredible power in teleporting me across the town as he had. On top of that, he resided close to Mystic Dunes, and it was possible he might have some information I needed to know... to stop whatever darkness was threatening Crystal Beach.

"Hello, Admiral," I said respectfully as I approached. "Thank you for getting me across town so quickly the other day. It was very helpful."

Aye, you're welcome, lass, he replied, then looked about, his eyes darting from right to left. *Do ye have time for that drink?*

"Well, not really. My father's girlfriend has gone missing, and I need to find her."

He fingered his beard. *Aye, that be a problem.* The Admiral was wearing an eyepatch below the tricorn hat, and I tried to remember whether he had been wearing it the last time I saw his ghost. I didn't think so.

"By the way. Did you happen to see a giant dog or some large animal anywhere around here last night?"

Can't say that I did. But the people at number five have a nasty little chihuahua. Evil little thing that yaps at me every time I see it. Say, are you sure you can't spare time for that drink?

I shrugged. "Guess a quick one can't hurt. No alcohol, though, please. I'm driving."

Deal! he said with an eager grin. The admiral reached out and touched my arm, much as he had when he had sent me to The Rose Garden Guest House. His touch was again disorienting, and the world appeared to fold in on itself, but not before I felt a brown tabby tortoiseshell presence rub against the back of my leg.

Oh my, oh my. Where are we? Help me. I'm going to die! Mojo's voice kept up a rapid-fire pace in my head, bringing me back to things, although I did not feel I had been unconscious. What I remembered was not pleasant, though. Admiral Avery's colorful, flashy old naval officer appearance had turned into something out of *Pirates of the Caribbean*, his face a faintly glowing skull, the hand holding my arm turning into long, skeletal fingers. It was rather frightening.

And even more alarming, he had dragged me underwater. I couldn't believe my senses as I looked around, but sure enough, that's where I was. Where *we* were, as Mojo was right next to me.

On the plus side, I wasn't drowning. In fact, I was sure I had taken a breath or two while recovering my bearings. A powerful urge to try another experimental breath came over me, and when I did so, my lungs did not fill with water.

It's okay, I thought toward Mojo. *We can breathe.*

I know that, Mojo huffed. *But it's still horrible. I'm a cat. We do not do water.*

Looking at him, I almost laughed. The ends of his thick fur were floating free in the water, and he looked so... dare I even say it... innocent and sweet.

Sorry 'bout that, came Admiral Avery's voice again, and I looked across to see him sitting on a bar stool. *It's easier just to do it than have to explain.*

I wouldn't have minded an explanation or at least some kind of warning, but I decided not to push the point. I floated in front of the Admiral, amazed at being under the water, a little silver fish darting past me into some bright orange coral, long tendrils of seaweed swaying back and forth from the ocean's floor. Looking up, I could tell we were not too far from the shore. In fact, the distorted shapes of the buildings of Mystic Dunes were still visible through the ripples above me.

What was more interesting, though, was what was surrounding me. Glowing the same faint blue as Admiral Avery had in his ghoulish form, an entire bar stretched into the distance.

Somehow, both there and not there, it appeared to float among the sea grass and crustaceans. There were plenty of round tables, each with a scarlet cloth and a candle burning on it. There was a low stage, just a half-step up from the sea floor, and a long bar with stools where the admiral was now sitting.

"Your place?" I asked him, relieved to see that he now looked less frightening, more like his normal flashy ghost-like self, as he appeared when I saw him from the shore. Well, apart from the eye patch, which seemed to have switched eyes, and a plastic parrot that now appeared on his left shoulder. "The one you told me about?"

Aye, he said, his salty lilt so proud it was almost a purr.

"What happened to it?" I asked. "Why is it underwater?"

Well, you'll need a drink for that one. We both will.

I raised a watery eyebrow and, when the admiral didn't appear to understand what I was getting at, brought my arms up and waved my hands through the water, undulating them like a swimming fish.

Admiral Avery slapped a ghostly palm to his pale forehead. *Argh. A dolt, I be.*

With a wave of his arms, a huge rectangular-shaped area drained of water, leaving the bar area dry with water hovering above it and all around us. I looked up at our new ocean ceiling, as a wave of dizziness washed over me, and I quickly glanced back down at the admiral to get my bearings.

Mojo looked worse than he had when we were in the water, his wet fur flat and dripping. I probably didn't look that much better, but at least it was cooler down here without the Florida humidity. Admiral Avery walked over to the bar, and I followed him. His ghostly form disappeared behind the barnacled remains of the old mahogany wood bar, coming up with an ancient bottle of amber-colored liquid in his hand.

Rum is traditional, he said, shaking the seawater out of a pewter tankard.

"No alcohol, for me," I reminded him.

To a sailor, rum not be alcohol, he argued. *It be life.*

"How long has it been down here," I tried. "Might it be past its best date?"

Nay, liquor only gets finer with age. He gave a sly wink as he popped the cork—a sound which strangely echoed back off the surrounding walls of water. *Like we admirals.*

I continued to look doubtfully at the drink once he had poured it into the tankard but, under an expectant gaze, sniffed it and took a sip. It was good, much better than I had expected... for liquor that was stored beneath the sea for who knows how many decades.

"Delicious... if a little salty. I'm afraid I can't have any more, though. Like I said, I'm driving."

Admiral Avery turned his attention to Mojo, a wooden bowl having appeared in his hand. He glanced about. *I'm afraid we don't have any water that isn't, er... salty. Or milk.*

I'll have the rum if she isn't finishing it, Mojo replied. *I'm not driving, and I feel like I need it.*

I held up a hand when Admiral Avery moved to take my tankard and looked at Mojo, who had hopped up onto the remains of the bar. "Alcohol is poisonous for cats. Even a few laps of that could kill you."

Mojo huffed like he was disappointed I had just saved his life. *Well, I didn't know that.*

"Anyway," I said to the admiral, trying to move things along. "You were going to tell me how your bar ended up"—I spread my arms out wide—"here."

Well, Florida is very low-lying, Mojo said and looked pointedly at me. *I know that even though I'm only a cat. Wasn't it just claimed by the sea?*

Aye, the admiral said, *the sea did claim it. Though not in the way ye thinks.* He looked around, pointing to the seabed beyond the bounds of the bar area and the rather large air pocket he had made for us.

Bars do not exist on their own now, do they, lass? he went on. *We need customers, and they come from a town.*

"There was another town here once?" I asked. "One before Crystal Beach?"

That there were, lass. Only a small town, much smaller than Crystal Beach, and this bar lay on the western edge of it. He pointed east, out toward the deeper parts of the ocean. *It did not extend for much more 'n two hundred paces in that direction and was maybe twice as wide as yonder housing up there.*

"So, the town was a little larger than Mystic Dunes?"

Admiral Avery nodded eagerly as if I had just stated something important. *Pretty much.*

"So, why did it sink into the sea? Or... not sink?"

The best way to describe what happened to Coral Point would be to say that it were washed away.

"Coral Point," I mouthed to myself, trying out the unfamiliar name. And yet—maybe because of where I was and who I was with—it felt right to say it, like speaking the words might somehow unravel the mystery of it. Coral Point.

I looked back to the Admiral, his eyes now huge and sad. "A wave seventy-foot high. Everything gone... just like that. A whole town destroyed."

I looked through the sea wall at the surrounding ruins, catching glimpses of what remained of the town between the swaying seaweed, discerning what was left behind and what part of it appeared as part of the admiral's ghostly reconstruction. I could see how all the parts that were now missing could have been torn away by such an event and shook my head in sorrow. A tsunami. Most likely caused by some underwater earthquake or volcanic eruption. Such bad luck for everyone living here.

Not bad luck, the admiral said, doing that thing where he read my thoughts again, reaching in unbidden. I needed to ask him to stop doing that. But not right now.

We were quiet for a moment, and then I asked the question I guessed he expected of me.

"Why wasn't it?"

Admiral Avery did not reply, his eyes moving from side to side as if he were considering something important. Maybe it wasn't the expected question after all.

I'll let ye decide for yerself, he said eventually, as if deciding something. *Ye has a library in this town o' yours?*

I nodded and then realized that I hadn't noticed. Surely Crystal Beach had a library, though. Considering that my livelihood revolved around writing, I was a little disappointed in myself that I didn't already know the answer to that question.

Well, let's just say I have a feeling that history is in danger of repeating itself.

I growled out my impatience. "Can't you just tell me?"

Admiral Avery's head snapped up and looked beyond where I stood, up through the water toward the houses of Mystic Dunes. *Sometimes,* he said, distracted by his thoughts, *ye has to see... to understand it. Being told is not enough.*

"Have we been swimming?" I heard the familiar, accented voice, although I did not place it until I turned around and saw Nikola Vorak walking up from the beach.

One moment, Mojo and I had been in that magically protected space beneath the waves; the next, we were on the edge of the small parking lot where I had left Maude. Disorientated again, I glanced back at the water. There was no sign from the shore of what lay beneath it.

"I believe a bathing suit is traditional. Or, a bikini, if you prefer," he added, then looked down at Mojo, an intrigued smile playing across his lips.

I glanced at my damp clothing and then toward Mojo's flattened fur that he was desperately trying to groom. Compared to Vorak's attire—beige slacks and a checkered, short-sleeved shirt—I guess we did look like a bedraggled mess spit out from the sea.

"I... we... it was an accident. Sometimes, it's a little hard to tell where the sand ends and the water begins when you're daydreaming. And... uh, Mojo goes everywhere I go, so..." I said weakly. Then, moving the conversation away from my own embarrassing state, I pointed past him. "Have you been enjoying the beach?"

"I take a walk on the beach every morning," he replied with a smile. "Why move next to the sea and not make the most of it?"

There were a lot of questions I wanted to ask Mr. Vorak. *Do you know the house address plate next to your front door is magical?* That would be a start. I wondered if, being at number one, he was the first resident to agree to move in. Why had he done that? Did he know Sam or Rose and Rodney before he moved here?

The question that came out my mouth, though, was more urgent than any of those. "You didn't see a woman on the beach, did you? Gillian Mead? She's been staying with your neighbors."

Looking at Nikola Vorak, I noticed that besides the bald spot that was threatening the top of his head, he *was* quite a hairy man. Dark chest hair billowed out from the gap at the top of his shirt where the top two buttons were undone. Suddenly, I found

314

myself fixated on that spot as I waited for him to answer my question.

Are you thinking what I'm thinking? Mojo's voice piped up in my head.

I glanced at my cat, catching him staring at Mr. Vorak's chest as well.

Well, the thought had occurred to me that we might be dealing with some sort of were-creature. A "shifter," as they were now often called. Not something I had any experience with or could even be sure was a real thing. Until not very long ago, I hadn't known for sure that there were such things as ghosts, either. And last night, the moon had been full...

But no. His slacks and shirt were neatly pressed. In fact, he hardly had a bead of sweat on him, so I wondered if he had already lived in a warmer climate before moving to Crystal Beach. He didn't even look like he had been on a walk along the beach.

In all the werewolf films I had seen as a teenager, the creature's clothes were ripped in the transformation. Vorak didn't look like the type to want to sully or destroy his clothes. He seemed too polished for that, giving off those "cultured" vibes that some Europeans just seemed to naturally exude.

"I am afraid not," he said, answering my query. "I have seen no one on the beach. I can help you look, though."

I held up a hand. *Thanks, but no thanks.*

"Or you are welcome to come into my house to dry off. I may not have spare clothes to fit you, but... well, we can see."

I waved away this second offer, too, although I did rather fancy a look around the inside of his house. "Very kind of you, but I have more clothes in my van, and..."

I left the thought unfinished, although Nikola Vorak did not seem to mind, bidding me "good day" and saying he hoped we found Gillian okay. I just wanted to get back to Ada-Mae, my father, and the others. We needed to pool our magic together, as I was coming to realize that my running around Crystal Beach was not likely to achieve much. Or maybe speaking to the police was the right thing to do after all. I needed Ada-Mae's guidance. Or even just her presence.

Admiral Avery's tale of a town wiped out by a tsunami had rattled me. What was it he had said...? *I have a feeling that history is in danger of repeating itself.*

I stepped inside Maude and drove her back across town, trying to ignore the sensation of my wet backside soaking into the seat. When I arrived at Shifting Sands, I parked in the back lot, as Ada-Mae had instructed me to do. I pulled on the parking brake and looked over my shoulder to see Mojo passed out in the back seat from what I assumed was the equivalent of post-traumatic stress syndrome—flying and swimming weren't natural, even for my magical feline. So I turned on the air conditioner and left Mojo to dry off in the van.

Heading up to Ada-Mae's apartment, I grappled with how I wanted to explain to Ada-Mae the great tumult of bad feelings that were swirling around inside me. The sense of foreboding that Sam's death, Gillian's disappearance, the giant dog-thing on the beach, and Admiral Avery's warning all added to something terrible and imminent happening in Crystal Beach.

I hadn't, however, expected Rose and Rodney Gantz to be sitting in the living room when I got there.

CHAPTER
FIVE

I looked between the guest-house-owning couple and my grandmother several times, my mouth open but no words coming out. Finally, gathering a little of my wits, I looked around. "Social visit, is it?"

Rose and Rodney both looked at me sheepishly for a moment, then stared at the floor. Maybe it should have been gratifying to see the two of them apparently cowed this way—particularly the unflappable Rose—but it was, instead, disturbing. I turned my attention to Ada-Mae, noting the sound of tea being made in the kitchen.

"Rose and Rodney," she said to me, clearing her throat as she did so. "Well, they've come to us for help."

"Help with what?" I shot back. "Making sure my father stays in jail this time?"

Inside the kitchen, cups clattered, and the sound of the kettle raised in pitch.

Ada-Mae, usually so sure of herself, appeared nervous in a way that was different from the Gantzes. "They, um... they say they had nothing to do with that."

The pitch of the kettle grew just a little higher, a little more insistent.

"The people with a hidden evil sanctum underneath their lounge say that they had nothing to do with trying to frame my father for murder, and you just believe them?"

"'Evil sanctum' is a bit strong," Rodney said. Those might have been the most words I had ever heard him say that were not a direct repetition of what his wife had said.

"To be fair, you broke into our private quarters to discover the sanctum," Rose added, still keeping her eyes mostly on the floor. "*And* we didn't call the police or report you for it."

"Well, aren't you just saints?" I said, surprised a little at the intensity of the sarcasm coming off my own words while the kettle hit boiling point in the kitchen. Not that my mocking words weren't warranted, of course, but I was feeling much more resentment than I probably ever had. It was not a pleasant feeling.

"I feel we're getting off on the wrong foot here," Ada-Mae said, raising a hand and stepping forward between me and them as if picking up on the growing feelings inside me. At that moment, the whistling died as the kettle was taken off the heat. My mom's head popped through the doorway that led into the kitchen. "Who's for tea?"

Rose looked up. "Yes, please."

Rodney nodded as well.

"Sugar?" she inquired.

"Do you have honey?" Rose asked.

Julia-Mae looked at her mother for an answer while I repressed the urge to make a comment about Rose not already being sweet enough.

"In the cupboard," Ada-Mae replied.

"We'll bring it out on the tray," my mom said to Rose and Rodney, "Let you do your own." Then she glanced at me. "Tea?"

"Um..." I wanted to say "no," but I was quite thirsty and was hoping to get the residual taste of the sea out of my mouth. "Yes, why not? We're all having tea together like nobody died or framed anybody for murder or got mind-controlled into buying a house and playing mini-golf really well. How nice." There was that disdainful undertone again. Must try to keep a lid on that.

"However difficult things get," Ada-Mae said to me, with the air of someone reminding a forgetful student, "we don't have to forget the niceties. Civility stops the world from descending into chaos, you know."

I preferred to think that good people fighting against evil kept things in the universe in alignment, but this time, I held that sarcastic tongue of mine.

"Rose was one of the first friends I made when I came to Crystal Beach," Ada-Mae continued, nodding across to the couch and smiling. "She was friendly and approachable when I did not know anyone here. And she was like a rock when your grandfather passed." Rose smiled weakly back, and Ada-Mae looked at me. "Things are not always as straightforward as you would like them to be, Sidney. They are rarely one way or the other way entirely."

Well, that seemed like an excuse for bad behavior to me,

although also one I might have used myself. I waited to see where she was going with her little speech.

"Before you came in, Rose was explaining how they came to be involved with the coven here in Crystal Beach." She looked at Rose. "Perhaps you should repeat it for Sidney's benefit?"

Rose nodded. Ada-Mae took a seat next to the dining table, so I followed suit, although I stayed sharp and kept my wits about me. As far as I was concerned, the enemy had just walked straight into the heart of our base of operations, so we were vulnerable right now.

"A few years back," Rose began, "we were running into financial trouble with the business."

"The pandemic?" I asked.

"Pandemic," Rodney agreed with a nod.

"We were looking at selling The Rose Garden," Rose said. "Maybe even having to move away from Crystal Beach. And then Sam told us about the coven."

Rodney laughed a deep, scoffing laugh that seemed to echo off the walls for a moment.

"Exactly," Rose said as if Rodney had stated some point. "We thought that the whole 'magic' thing sounded absurd." Rose glanced up apologetically at Ada-Mae then. "We had always thought that you were, you know... in a..."

"Secret cult," Rodney put in.

"Yes," Rose agreed awkwardly. "We never dreamed this magic you spoke of was a real thing. Maybe if we had, we would have come to you when we were in trouble."

Ada-Mae smiled but shook her head. "The magic we have... I'm not sure it could have helped. Not in the way you needed right then."

Rose nodded as if she knew what Ada-Mae was getting at.

"You're right. The hole we were in, only dark magic was going to turn our fortunes around."

"You do not know the power of the Dark Side," I said, a hand cupped over my mouth to emulate the voice of the most well-known Dark Lord of the Sith. No one else seemed to get it, although maybe that was only because they weren't *Star Wars* fans.

Rose simply ignored me and continued with her story. "At first, it was like a gift. All our problems were solved, and business picked right back up again. Sam did well, of course. We had already seen that. Any other realtor who tried to set up in town never stayed for more than a few months, yet Sam always thrived.

"Yes, there were downsides, but they seemed small. For one thing, the meetings were creepy, and the whole thing had a slightly... absurd Hollywood air to it. I kept expecting someone to pull off their robe and start laughing at us all for falling for their antics. But we did not know any better, and, at least at first, no harm was done."

Just then, my mom and dad walked in, wheeling the silver tea trolley with them. I wondered who else was helping my mom in the kitchen, assuming it was Ernie. She wasn't much for food prep, and judging by the array of sandwiches and baked goods on the cart, it was obvious she had some help.

I couldn't figure out why Rose and Rodney were being treated like honored guests. The silver tea trolley had not come out the whole time I lived in Crystal Beach.

Rose's tale paused while my mom and dad handed cups of tea out, and a long explanation followed about what was in the various sandwiches—from just cucumber to pimento and cheese. I clasped my hands over my bouncing knee and tried to appear patient while all this was happening.

Once everyone was settled and before Rose started up again, I asked a question that had been bugging me. "Who else is in the coven?"

"Well, it was a bit like a secret society," Rose said. "We knew Sam, of course. Otherwise, everyone wore robes with long hoods, so you rarely saw anyone's face. When I got a decent glimpse of someone, I didn't recognize them. I thought maybe they weren't from here. A neighboring town, perhaps? Or from the city.

"There was one coven member, a leader named Pantaloon, who spoke with a strange voice, neither male nor female sounding. They were in charge, or at least they tended to lead what we did. Everyone deferred to him... or her, and we called them 'The Head.'"

"Yup," I said. "Nice and creepy."

Rose inclined her head in agreement. "There are a lot of strange practices you can ignore when it's saving your business and your home."

She had a point there. Still... "Like Sam casting spells on people to make them buy a property?" I said and nodded to Julia-Mae, who was stabbing her fork into some Victoria sponge cake. "As he did with my mom and Mystic Dunes?"

Rose looked ashamed then, and I almost felt sorry for her. Even Rodney shifted uncomfortably. It nearly stopped me from going on, but not quite.

"Like Ben's murder?" The words came out a little strangled. I waited for Ada-Mae to speak a restraining word or two, to rein me in. But she watched us mildly, perhaps accepting that this was something that had to play out. I wasn't as bothered now as when I walked in, not as shocked. My words were no longer coming from quite the place of resentment they had at first. But this pair had come to us for whatever reason, and these things needed to be said. If possible, answers had to be found.

"We were not in on that," Rose said. "Not really."

"Not really?" That was going to need some clarification.

"I helped with a portal connecting a house in Mystic Dunes to the Spectrum Space Center," Rodney said. "That was all."

Rose reached out and placed a hand on her husband's arm. "Rodney here is the one with all the magical power between the two of us. I'm pretty useless, I'm afraid."

Rodney shook his head and patted his wife's arm back, disagreeing in the way people do when they know they are disagreeing with the truth. It would have been endearing under different circumstances. Still, it was a revelation to know that Rodney had all the magical power. I was fairly sure he did not have any power in any other aspect of their relationship.

"We knew nothing of what was going on with CAD-Astra," Rose elaborated.

"I assumed your status as coven members was much higher up," I said.

"Only in that we were friends with Sam," Rose corrected.

"Strange, because he insists he knows nothing of what's going on in the coven, either." That was a slip, and it caught their attention, both of them looking at me curiously.

"Insists?" Rose said after a moment. "When did you last speak to Sam?"

I considered my reply for a moment. Did I want to tell them I had been working with Sam Barlow's ghost? Sure, they seemed to be coming clean right now, but what had we learned from them that would be useful to us? Only their denials of being involved in any of the things we were really interested in and the fact that no one knew who anyone else was. In any event, it didn't matter in the whole scheme of things.

"Ah, you've seen his ghost," Rose said. "What does he know?"

My eyes narrowed, and she caught my meaning straight away.

"Seriously, Sidney. I know you didn't have time for him and

that he was far from the most moral individual, but Sam was our friend. We wouldn't have a home if it wasn't for his help. His death was a shock to us, and"—Rose shrugged apologetically at Jacob—"we genuinely believed your father had done it."

"And now?"

"Now, we're worried it is someone else in the coven. And that we might be next."

Which, of course, was why they were sitting in Ada-Mae's living room, nibbling on sandwiches with the crusts cut off. But then, there was a problem with all of this...

"Sam was killed with hemlock, though," I said. "And there is hemlock growing in your garden."

Rose paled and put her sandwich down. "That was the poison that killed him? I didn't know. Yes, I found water hemlock growing near our pond yesterday. Had to look it up as I did not recognize the flowers."

"Because it doesn't grow in Florida," I said. "It would have to be carefully cultivated to survive here."

"Or someone used a little magic to help it along," Ada-Mae said.

Rose and Rodney looked thoughtful and distant. After a moment, Rose shook her head, though not in disagreement. "That is probably the correct assumption, but who? I doubt Sam grew the hemlock that killed him."

"What does Mystic Dunes have to do with the coven?" Ada-Mae asked, moving things along again.

"Mystic Dunes was Sam's baby," Rose answered. "Although, I think he got the tip on the land from another coven member. The coven also helped conjure false reports about the state of the site and its likelihood to... you know..."

"Fall into the sea." My mom said, peering down into her cup of tea.

Or be consumed by it. I remembered the vision that Admiral Avery had given me. What had he said? *I have a feeling that history is in danger of repeating itself.*

"Exactly. At first, we assumed the whole Mystic Dunes project was just some money-making scheme, and we thought this was why Sam was involved."

"But?" I prompted.

"Well, there is clearly some magical energy centered on the site. Once the shells of the buildings were up, coven meetings always happened there. That's where we did the harder spells, like the portal. And now, almost everyone who lives there now is a coven member."

"I thought you never saw anybody's faces?" I said.

"We don't, and we haven't had an official meeting since everyone moved in, either. But Sam told us it was mostly coven members moving in. I think he was just glad to see them all sold and the money rolling in, but..."

"But...?"

Rose looked at Rodney, a brief twitch at one corner of his mouth that seemed to show agreement of some sort. "Well, we both felt he seemed unsettled when it happened. Like Sam was getting everything he wanted but, at the same time, realizing the price. Or... I don't know. You could just tell he was having reservations about things... because he... well, he lost his powerful edge in the end. He even told us to stop attending the meetings."

Not something he had shared with me, although our association had been one of convenience for much of it before being cut short after we dispelled the false evidence against my father.

"Is he okay?" Rose asked. It seemed like she was truly concerned for her friend. Or was she a talented actress? It was the latter; I was sure of it. Was this whole visit and their seemingly helpful admission only a smokescreen to throw us off their real intentions? I wanted to keep these two on the "bad guy" list—if for no other reason than without them and with Sam dead, we didn't have any bad guys to focus on. The coven, this evil cabal of witches and warlocks, would be just as faceless as it had once been.

"I haven't seen him in a few days," I admitted. "He helped us with a spell and..."

I could see the disappointment on their faces. "Ghosts can wear out their spectral energy," I explained. "But it usually comes back. And speaking of ghosts," I remembered, "thank you for that guardian spirit that nearly killed me."

Rodney shrugged, although he had the good grace to almost sound apologetic when he answered, "You were breaking in, Sidney. And"—he said with a proud smile glowing on his face—"I conjured that one up all by myself."

I was not going to congratulate anyone for any rogue spells or hexes, not today.

"And what's the deal with those house numbers?" I said. "You've got address plates that match the numbers on the houses at Mystic Dunes."

Rose nodded. "Simple portals."

"Simple?" I scoffed. There was nothing simple about magically connecting two remote points together and sending someone between them. For all my lack of understanding of magic, I still knew that.

"Well," Rose said, "that's what The Head calls them. They were made to be an easy way to move between Mystic Dunes and other places, but no one is supposed to use them yet."

"Well, they did," I said. "A portal was used to murder Sam."

"I'd love to meet this 'Head,'" Ada-Mae said.

Yes, that makes two of us.

"So," I said, "with Sam dead, you want out, and you think... what? That we can protect you?"

They both nodded.

"The thing is," I said, taking no pleasure in what I was about to tell them. "Your safest place is to stay in the coven, at least for now."

All the other adults present gasped. In Rose and Rodney's place, I would want out too, but I knew I was right. "We still don't know enough. Your coven and 'The Head' are so powerful. We need to know more if we are ever going to take them on and find out who really killed Sam. Not to mention what is happening at Mystic Dunes."

"Well, that last one," Rodney said. "It is going to happen soon."

"How do you know that?" I asked.

"There is a big coven meeting and ritual planned there in three days," he replied. "All of this, whatever it is leading to, we are sure it will happen then."

Oh, dear. That's not very far away at all, I thought.

CHAPTER
SIX

I wondered where Ernie was, as he had almost always been a fixture at Ada-Mae's apartment since I had arrived in Crystal Beach. Just before everything had gone crazy with Sam's murder and my dad's arrest, Gramps had given his blessing to Ada-Mae to seek companionship. I had hoped to see her friendship with Ernie develop into something more.

During the chaos of the last few days, I hadn't found the opportunity to see if that was happening at all, so I worried that Ernie's absence might be significant.

"Where is Ernie?" I asked my mom as Ada-Mae saw Rose and Rodney out.

Julia-Mae gave me a wry smile. "As usual, you might want to ask your grandmother about that. She's always in the know, one step ahead of everyone else with everything."

I thought about how, once upon a time, those words might have sounded bitter coming from her mouth. Now, my mother just sounded amused.

"She did say something about him 'making preparations,'" she added. "Along with Judd, the astronaut fellow."

That sounded like spell stuff to me. So when Ada-Mae returned, I inquired about what was going on and why I wasn't already in on it.

"A location spell," Ada-Mae said. "Remember your missing dog?"

I did, indeed. About five years ago, a pedigree puppy called Sapphire was stolen from right under my nose back in Boston. If we hadn't been able to find the dog, I would have lost my job at *Living It Large In Boston* magazine for sure. With the help of one of Ada-Mae's location spells, we not only tracked down the puppy but also uncovered an insurance scam.

Of course, the same spell inadvertently led to my mom losing her opportunity to become the Boston area Tupperware Queen, a hard fall for her that she held Ada-Mae responsible for. Which, in turn, was the start of a sequence of events that ultimately led to my mom and dad's divorce and a somewhat strained relationship for years between her and Ada-Mae.

Anyway, moving on. I'm sure any old spell could have caused such a family disaster. "I do remember it," I said.

"Same sort of thing. Jacob has something of Gillian's. A necklace. We're going to use that item to try and locate her. It should be fairly straightforward. I've been refining the spell since Boston.

I will need some extra ingredients from The Invisible Cloak. If I give you a list, could you take Maude to get them?"

I nodded and took a page from a floral-scented notebook Ada-Mae used, as she shunned digital devices like cell phones as "having no spirit to them." I wasn't looking forward to facing Zoe again. Rightly so, she was pretty mad at me. Time was of the essence, though, so I took a deep breath and headed out.

Stepping out into the intense Florida sunlight, the first thing I noticed was that it wasn't... well, *intense*. Instead, I was met with a gentle breeze. As I made my way to Maude, I thought back on the conversation with the Gantzes.

Rose and Rodney had stayed at Ada-Mae's apartment for quite some time, reluctant to return to the guest house and the reality that they were involved in a coven they did not want to be a part of anymore.

It had been weird to go from seeing the Gantzes as a slightly creepy but lovable part of the Crystal Beach community to, essentially, becoming the enemy. Switching back again so soon was even harder. I needed to keep an open mind about other possibilities, though. They gave us some details about the coven. But something wouldn't let me let them completely off the hook.

The lowering sun conveyed that the afternoon was already fast escaping as I drove Maude back into town, past the police station, Denny's Donuts, and the Kelp Seafood Grill, right to the central crossroads where Eternity Foods was on one corner of Citrus Way. I parked right outside Zoe's magic store and looked for the open sign on the door.

You want me to come in with you? Mojo asked from the passenger seat, which he had taken to occupying.

"No," I said with a sigh, appreciating the offer, even as I steeled myself for a frosty welcome. "I'll be okay."

Good, Mojo said. *I was only being polite. Magic stores give me the creeps.*

I entered through the net-like veil—the "invisible cloak"—at the door. It was there to keep insects looking to escape the heat of the day from getting into the shop, but the effect of walking through it was always like heading into another world. A quite literal lifting of a veil into a whole new world of magic.

As usual, the light was low inside, and an incense stick burned near the counter, but there was no sign of Zoe.

She must be in the back storeroom, I assumed.

I pulled out the piece of scented notepaper and looked for the ingredients we needed. I found everything I needed—mostly aromatic herbs to create a landscape of scents that would help to bring the participants together, tuning everyone into the same way of thinking.

When I was done, I returned to the counter, but there was still no sign of the young Goth-witch store owner.

"Zoe?" I called out. "Are you in?"

Nothing. So I called out again, a little louder this time. "If you're not here, Zoe, I'm about to steal stuff!"

Still no answer. Had she popped out somewhere and forgotten to put out the "Be Back Soon" sign? It did not seem all that likely. But now I was in a bind. I needed to get these ingredients back to the retirement center because they couldn't start the ritual without them... or me. We were meeting at the Rockfords, apparently, so time was of the essence.

Any other time, maybe I would have left an IOU, although some ingredients needed to be weighed, so I wouldn't know exactly how much I owed Zoe. Seeing as how things were between Zoe and me right now, leaving the store without paying would look bad, and I did not want to give John one more reason to either throw me in jail or run me out of town. Not now.

Well, ideally, not ever.

Maybe I could leave some cash. I searched in my purse and found a twenty. That was enough, surely? Probably too much, but right now, I shouldn't be splitting hairs. I took a pen from the counter and was about to write a note to Zoe on the back of the scented shopping list when a noise from somewhere beyond the counter stopped me.

It sounded like someone was moving around back there, perhaps knocking into things in the stock room as they did so. That, or Zoe had a problem with some enormous rats.

"Hello?" I tried. "Anyone back there?"

Well, if it was a burglar, they were well warned I had heard them. Nice job, Sidney. I thought about what magic spells I might have to cast to defend myself if needed. The problem was that my magic really didn't work that way. What little I could do in the spur of the moment was not the stuff that could overcome a desperate criminal. Oh, to have the guardian spirit of Gramps looking out for me again. Even if it meant his ghost popping in unannounced and scaring me half out of my wits.

"Go away!" a familiar voice called out from the direction of the storeroom, but that wasn't the voice of my Gramps.

"Zoe? Are you hiding from me?"

"Not exactly."

What was that supposed to mean? Was I not welcome in her shop or something? And why couldn't Zoe tell me that to my face? *I'm not that scary... am I?*

"I need spell ingredients. It's really... important."

"Just take them. It's fine."

Hmm... what the heck is going on? "You okay?"

"Just... please go."

Now, if my name were not Sidney Grace, I might have done just that. Although I would have felt the need to leave the twenty behind me on the counter. However, my "stranger things" radar was going "blip-blip-blip," and I was going to have to walk behind the counter and check out what was going on.

More sounds came from the back storeroom as I walked around the end of the counter. This time, it sounded like more of a metallic clanging sound.

Stranger and stranger...

A beaded curtain separated the main part of the shop from a small, dim corridor with two doors along the length of it. One, right in front of me, was open all the way and led to some stairs that presumably went up to Zoe's apartment above the store. The other at the end of the hall to my right was slightly ajar, with a slice of artificial light coming through the opening. I could see a freestanding section of shelving, which I guessed was used as the storeroom.

"I can hear you coming through the beaded curtain, you know," Zoe called. "Why can't you ever... argh!" She let out a sudden sound somewhere between a cry and a gasp. When she continued, it seemed like she was struggling to talk. "Why can't you ever take a hint and mind your own business, Sidney Grace?"

As I reached the end of the corridor and pushed the door open, I said, "Because I care too much." *Okay, and because I'm super nosy.*

Whatever I might have expected, it did not prepare me for the sight that greeted me.

Zoe was on the floor in the corner, handcuffed to a metal radiator. She looked away from me, her eyes cast down toward the floor.

"What happened?" I asked. "Did someone rob you and leave you handcuffed here? You don't have to be embarrassed, Zoe. How else would you get free if not with some help?"

I remembered Zoe was a powerful witch with years of experience in the craft beyond my own. Maybe she would have figured it out.

"Sidney," Zoe said. I could still hear the protestation in her voice. She wanted me to leave.

I was having none of that, though, and I stepped forward.

"No!" Zoe snarled, looking up at me. Seeing her eyes and the almost feral expression on her features, I froze. They were animal eyes, almost amber, and her jaw was set in a warning growl, her incisors prominent over her lips. "Get back!" she growled from somewhere deep inside.

"You're..." I knew the words I wanted to say, yet despite all the magic and the many strange things that had happened to me in Crystal Beach, I had to force them out. "You're a werewolf."

Zoe sunk down, all resistance to my presence having now left her. "We prefer canine shifter nowadays."

CHAPTER
SEVEN

"You do realize the shop is open out there?" I asked Zoe. "Anybody could have wandered in. Plus, how long were you going to stay handcuffed to the pipes there? At some point, someone—probably John or Jessie—would notice that you didn't close up for the night and come in to see why."

Perhaps I should have lingered longer on the "You're a canine shifter, what the heck?" bit. Ghosts and witches were one thing, but I still deserved the right to be surprised by some parts of the supernatural world, surely? Then again, maybe it was a sign of the emerging adult inside thirty-year-old me that these practical business concerns were among the first things I thought of.

Despite her now bestial appearance, I could tell that Zoe looked ashamed. "I panicked," she said. "Not great, I know, but it never comes on this early, not usually."

She had a point; it was only late afternoon and still a few hours away from sunset. Of course, for werewolves, the moon was the real issue. I hadn't noticed whether it had shown any pale, daytime presence anywhere in the cyan sky above Crystal Beach yet. However, I had always imagined that it was the bright full moon of nighttime that would bring out the beast, as it were.

"That was you on the beach last night, wasn't it?" I asked. "Giant paw prints? Reports of a giant dog?"

In her sitting position, legs drawn up protectively, Zoe seemed to shrink back against the wall as she heard my words. She glanced up at the handcuffs. "That's why I've got these. I was caught out yesterday, too, and it was much later than this. I, um... have a cage in a soundproof room in the apartment upstairs. Which is why I never have company. I've been searching the local news all day, half-expecting to find out that something terrible happened."

"You scared my cats, but that's all I've heard." That was kind of a lie. I wondered whether to mention that Gillian was currently unaccounted for and straightaway decided to keep it to myself. Sure, she had been keeping a pretty big secret from me, but I knew that if Zoe and I were ever to be friends again, I had to show her a little more respect than I had, including telling her the truth. But she didn't need to be worrying about Gillian right now. Her disappearance could be a complete coincidence.

"Besides," I added as if trying to cover my own thoughts, "it was refreshing to see Mojo shaken up a little. He's usually so annoyingly sure of himself."

Zoe smiled weakly, showing prominent fangs. "I've been carrying these cuffs around all day, just in case, but I still didn't expect it to hit me this early and so hard. It was all I could do not to turn instantly when I heard you in the shop. I've been better at managing my changes around the full moon recently."

"It's a full moon tonight?" As a witch, I probably should keep better track of these things—in fact, I'm sure Ada-Mae would have had a tut or two for me if she were present—but hey, I'd been busy, okay? It'd been non-stop murder and intrigue since I got to this supposedly sleepy seaside town.

"Yes. There's the potential for a shifter to change involuntarily for several days on either side of the full moon. But the better your control over it, the less that's a problem. I usually only change on the full moon itself now. If it's cloudy, sometimes, not even then. That's part of why I got caught out yesterday. It was a day before the full moon, and that shouldn't have been a problem."

I wondered how long Zoe had been "afflicted"—if that was even the right word for it. But I figured it wasn't the most urgent topic of conversation.

"There's something coming in a few days," Zoe continued. "A planetary conjunction. I think maybe this is enhancing the power of the moon already."

Well, that was interesting. A planetary conjunction in just a few days' time—again, I needed to be more celestially aware. Remembering what Rose and Rodney had said about the upcoming meeting they felt might be a culmination of the curse at Mystic Dunes or whatever the plan was, I started working on connecting the dots.

Even I knew about the strong gravitational and tidal effect of celestial bodies, particularly the moon, which Zoe was claiming was right now a lot stronger than usual. Combine that with Admiral Avery and his stories of tidal destruction... Well, too many dots were all working hard to draw themselves together.

I took Zoe in. Her hair had sort of puffed outward a little on either side of her head as if pointy wolf ears were trying to push their way through. I guessed they would if she were fully turned.

"You should go," Zoe said, "before I change all the way. Lock the door behind you and the front of the store, too, please. Just take whatever you came in for." She grinned with some effort as if working hard to keep what was inside her repressed. "It's on the house."

Her expression collapsed again, and she looked miserable. I had sometimes experienced some loss of control with my magic. Things happened without me meaning them to, but I couldn't imagine my whole body trying to drastically change on me for several days each month. *Well, now that I think about it, I am a woman. Wow... it does make sense now.*

Geesh, concentrate, Sidney. Focus on the issue at hand. It looked like poor Zoe never even remembered what happened when she wolfed out. Looking at the cuffs and wondering if they could even hold her in place, I considered whether there might be anything I could do to help her. Something magical.

"Maybe I could help?" I half-reached toward her, and Zoe flinched. "Take some of the burden and help you control it?"

Zoe's look was wary... skeptical, even. "No offense, Sidney, but that sounds like a terrible idea. You're wicked powerful. I'll give you that. I've never seen anyone with your power, the way you can tune into different abilities almost at will... I don't even think you understand how special you are."

Ah, a girl could blush.

Zoe was lisping a little as her lower incisors had suddenly grown by almost half an inch. "And thatsth part of the problem.

You're like a wild, uncontrollable forth. It theems like ethry time you yooth magic, it could go either way."

Ouch.

I was a little stung, I had to admit. It sounded like she was calling me a reckless time bomb. Maybe it was the wolf talking.

"Let me try," I pushed. "Maybe we could at least keep a lid on things long enough to get you upstairs and into your... cage."

Zoe glanced at the cuffs hooked around the pipe, maybe having the same doubts as me about their ability to remain in place once she fully turned.

"Okay." She pushed a small key into my hand. "But don't releath me until you're sure it'th working."

She reached her hand out to me, and our eyes met. "It will be a thock if you've nether felt it before," she warned. "You're throng enough to take it, but it'th not just about magical thrength. It'th also about your ability to focuth through really hard dith-tractionth."

"I can focus," I said, and when I took Zoe's hand, it was like a bolt of lightning zapped through me, suddenly forcing my whole body rigid. I had expected some mental process, some deliberate act of my will to accept a little of her burden, to make it easier for her to control the change long enough to get her safely upstairs.

Instead, it was like an invasion, something hard, powerful, and wild trying to force its way into my head. Several seconds passed, and I realized I had been holding my breath. Somewhere at the edge of my consciousness, I—we—ran through a midnight wood, the light from the full moon dancing among the trees, leaving only the shadows behind us. Running through the dense woods was glorious, and I—we—felt so connected to every sense within me, full of the thrill of the hunt. We, the pack, were never more alive than when we stalked our prey and ran free, masters of the night.

I blinked my eyes open, not even realizing that they had been closed.

Zoe was looking at me, her expression saying, "Now you understand at least a little, don't you?"

I remembered what she had said outside of the police station the other evening, how it was dangerous when things got intense for her. I got a little of that now, remembering the intoxicating thrill of the hunt—at once pure freedom and something feral and dangerous and... out of control. I also noticed that Zoe was a little less wolf-looking than she had been a moment before, those protruding lower teeth having receded almost back to normal.

"Now?" I asked, holding up the small key I still had in my other hand.

"Now," she agreed, and I reached forward to release her.

CHAPTER
EIGHT

When I got back to Shifting Sands, I headed to the Rockfords' single-story residence near the golf course. I found a note on the front door asking me to head out to Cody's Cocktails, the bar at the end of the beach. Only a bunch of retirees would not have thought to text me with that kind of information.

The sun was getting close to the horizon by the time I arrived at the beach bar. This was the place where John and I had shared our first date. It hadn't really been a "date" at the time—our first official date had been at the Italian restaurant on Citrus Way,

Deliciously Donatelli's. Yet, looking back, this seemed like the place we had first connected. With a long sigh that seemed like it exhaled something from deep within me, I wondered if we would ever "connect" again.

The beach bar looked quiet and empty as I reached it. Only the solar-powered lanterns that hung in an undulating line around the top of the bar were glowing faintly as their sensors picked up the receding of the sun's glow. Cody, the surfer dude owner of the bar, popped up from out of sight, a cleaning cloth in his hand and wearing the same red and yellow Hawaiian shirt I had seen him in on my last visit.

He beamed at me. "Hey, Sidney, man!"

Not the last time I checked. Still, I wasn't going to correct him, especially as I remembered wrongly suspecting him in the whole missing statue debacle. And seeing his innocent face now was making me feel bad about that.

"Hey, you haven't seen a gang of septuagenarians and octogenarians pass this way, have you?" Then I remembered that my mom and dad were with them, too. "And two people in their fifties..."

"Quinquagenarians."

I guess I deserved that, even if I wasn't thrilled about the owner outdoing the writer on the vocabulary front. "Yes, those people."

Cody pointed toward the beach, a little past where some of his tables and seating extended onto it. "They're waiting for you. Whatever it is, it looks like it's going to be gnarly. Ada-Mae said I can come and watch, so I'm closing up early.

"Wait." He reached behind the bar and came back up with a flambeau—an unlit torch on the top of a long piece of bamboo. It was almost as tall as me. "You should take this." He grabbed a lighter and lit my torch, which burst to life impressively so I could feel the heat of it against my cheeks.

"Thanks," I said.

"I'll see you in a minute," Cody nodded. "Try not to let them start without me."

Carrying the flaming torch with me, I couldn't help but feel like I was on the way to something momentous. Like in the *Survivor* series, where they all carried torches... although having your flame extinguished meant you were out of the tribe. But I knew that Ada-Mae would always be an integral part of my tribe and that I belonged here. I continued walking and watched the flame flicker in a breeze that felt cool against my skin.

I could see a little further down the beach now to where everyone else was, several flickering torches dancing like fire spirits. From a distance, they appeared suspended above the beach. I heard a rustling coming from somewhere to my left, among the palm trees and unruly undergrowth that fought with the sand for territory here at the wilder end of Crystal Beach. The sound made me stop, a little alarmed, but when I looked over, I saw two familiar shapes slinking out of the shadows. I recognized the two outlines before they fully formed into the people I knew.

"Ada-Mae, there you are," I said to the shorter and slightly rounder of the two outlines, watching as her shawl swayed around her in the ocean breeze. "And Ernie, too," I said to the second figure approaching. His outline was familiarly tall and long-limbed. For a man approaching eighty, he still had a powerful build, though, and moved in an easy, unhindered way.

Even in the fading light, I could tell just how much Ada-Mae was blushing, which I enjoyed a little. "Oh... Sidney. You're here. We were... discussing things." She held a glass up, which I could see—by the light of my torch—contained a peach-colored cocktail, presumably acquired from Cody's bar. "And having a little drink... um... to celebrate this beautiful sunset."

I cast a doubtful eye west toward where only half of the sun now clung to the horizon, inevitably losing its daily battle to hang onto the edge of it. "That's good."

With a look from Ada-Mae, Ernie nodded toward me and hurried off to join the rest of the group a little further down the beach.

"It's not what it looks like," Ada-Mae said as soon as he was out of earshot. "We really were, er, just discussing things."

As amusing as this all was, I felt a swell of affection toward my grandmother, who so often took so much on her own shoulders. I reached out and squeezed the top of her arm. "And if anything else was happening," I said, "then it would be nobody else's business but yours and Ernie's. You're allowed to still have a life, you know. And it's not like Gramps didn't give his blessing."

Ada-Mae didn't stop blushing, but she managed a small smile. "I know. It's just... well, I've had a good, long, and happy relationship with your grandfather already. But here we are, your father and mother divorced, Jacob's new girlfriend missing, and you having to sacrifice what you had with John for your father's sake all because of the witchy shenanigans I've roped you into in this town.

"Doesn't seem fair for me to, you know... go flaunting anything in front of you all."

"Flaunt away," I said, impressed by her use of the word "shenanigans." Everyone was out-vocabularizing me tonight, while I just seemed to be making up new words. "The idea of you and Ernie together only makes my life better."

Ada-Mae smiled gratefully at that. "You've got everything, I trust? You seemed to be a little while. And no Zoe?"

"That's something to explain later," I answered, at the same time holding up my bag of spell ingredients. "Mom will have to step in for Zoe after all. But I got everything we need. So let's do this. Let's see if we can find out where Gillian is."

I was stunned at what awaited me when I reached the space within the wide circle of the flambeau torches. The area contained a pentagram Ernie and Judd had set up for the spell. It was made of colored ribbon tied between metal stakes driven deep into the sand to keep them in place, sketching out the five-pointed star and also the sacred circle that encompassed it. The pentagram was huge—at least thirty feet across—and there was a reason for that. Within the space was a detailed map of Crystal Beach.

Although all the pieces of the map were just objects, random things chosen to represent buildings and the town's best-known locations, the overall shape of it was so familiar. The job was so well done that I instantly understood what I was looking at.

I noticed a Saint Bernard dog ornament taken from the hutch in Ada-Mae's apartment represented Crystal Beach Police Station. I wasn't sure if the particular animal they chose was intentional—either way, it certainly was an interesting choice. But if it was an attempt at solidarity for the Grace family and the Crystal Beach police, I guess I could laud their sentiments.

Most of their picnic set had been used for other locations. These included a bowl for the Kelp Seafood Grill, a cup for The Rose Garden, a salt shaker for The Invisible Cloak, and a wine glass for Cody's beach bar. The pink-painted wicker picnic basket itself occupied the position of Shifting Sands Retirement Center, while the houses of Mystic Dunes were a collection of assorted cutleries.

"Amazing," I said across the circle to where Ernie and Judd looked pleased with themselves. Then, I greeted my mom and dad, who had been deep in conversation when I arrived. Both of them seemed different somehow. My dad still looked tense, but for a man who had all the current worries he did, he looked younger than he had in years. There was a sense of peeling back time, maybe as much as a decade on him.

And Mom seemed to be loosening up, too. It was like she had been a tightly wound ball, both in her personality and appearance. The metaphorical ball of string was not so much unraveling as slowly fraying, the threads becoming fuzzier and puffing outward. Her above-the-shoulder blonde haircut was not as neatly brushed, the collar of her blouse rumpled, and she was wearing flip-flops. My mother in flip-flops of all things!

Cody arrived just as my dad produced Gillian's necklace and handed it to Ada-Mae. Judd, Howie Rockford, Julia-Mae, and I all donned cloaks, although Ada-Mae stayed in her favorite shawl. The five of us found our spot around the pentagram—one at each point.

The space outside the burning torches was, by comparison, almost black by the time we settled down to start the ritual. The necklace was put in a crystalline amethyst bowl and placed in the equivalent of our current location on the pentagram map—close to the wineglass.

Ada-Mae mixed the herbs and other ingredients that I technically hadn't paid for in a small metal bowl. I was pretty certain the bowl appeared from one of the inside pockets in her shawl. Closing her eyes, Ada-Mae placed her hands over the bowl, mouthing some words I could not hear nor lip read, then she stood up and moved to each of the torches on the outside of the circle. She flung a small handful of the mixture into the flame each time, resulting in a greenish flash and causing the flame to give off an astonishing amount of smoke for what had been thrown into it.

That smoke stayed within the circle of the flames, billowing in toward the rest of us—not just those sitting at the points around the pentagram but also my dad, Ernie, Wendy, and Cody, who were all crowding around to observe.

"Rad," Cody observed as the scented smoke surrounded him.

At this point, I noticed how much the wind had picked up outside the circle of torches. The long fronds of the palm trees were blown parallel to the ground, the trunks bending a little in agreement with them. At the same time, a miniature sandstorm scoured its way along the beach, breaking around our smoky sacred space as it slammed into it. Serious weather was hitting Crystal Beach almost out of nowhere, the dark shapes of clouds billowing up threateningly above the sea and blotting out the moon. I hoped this weird weather was helping Zoe, now safely locked away in her self-built "cage" in her apartment, because it was making me nervous.

We hadn't even properly begun the ritual yet, but I could feel the presence of great power coming forth to meet the intent of what we were about to do. This wasn't just about Ada-Mae's refined location ritual. I caught my grandmother's look as she returned to her position around the pentagram. It was unsettling to her, too, almost like the town itself was reacting to the magic.

The smoke settled like a haze across the top of the map of Crystal Beach, giving it an eerie quality. The five of us began to chant. "Dod o hyd i'r perchennog." The same low chant I had heard while peering through the window at Ada-Mae's and Gramps's house in Boston when she was helping with my puppy problem. Only Ada-Mae was good at pronouncing the unfamiliar words, so the rest of us stumbled through them, making the whole thing sound like a minor cacophony. Yet it did not matter. The heavy crystal bowl with the necklace in it moved almost immediately. It would most likely have taken both my hands to lift it, yet it rose from where it had been sunk into the sand, its base now hovering a centimeter or two above the beach.

The crystal bowl drifted sideways, sliding along the map. I realized that much of Ernie and Judd's lovingly constructed representation of Crystal Beach would not be needed. Poor guys. The bowl crept along what was both the beach in reality and a representation of it on the improvised map. Smoke seeped behind the crystal—or perhaps pushed it along—urging it toward its destination.

We all watched with bated breath, the atmosphere inside the circle of the torches quiet and intense despite the chaos going on outside of it, like being inside the eye of the storm. I could feel the desire of undefinable forces beyond our safe space trying to get inside with us as we continued the ritual. I didn't know what would happen if they did, but the thought was equal parts terrifying and exhilarating.

For a moment, the bowl paused and teetered as if to settle back down. Its position marked a spot only a few hundred yards along the beach, and I tensed, ready to spring up and race to see if I could find Gillian buried there. My heart pounded with worry about whether she was alive or dead.

But the bowl moved again, tipping forward a little as it gathered momentum, racing along the front of Crystal Beach and past Shifting Sands toward the southern end where—surprise, surprise—the Mystic Dunes development was located. For a moment, my heart leaped with the idea that Gillian had found her way back to the home of her hippie friends, where at least she was safe. Before the end of the beach, however, the crystal bowl unceremoniously plopped itself down roughly in front of the former site of the Crystal Beach Mini-Golf Invitational.

"That's it!" I said. Looking around, I realized we had all stopped chanting some time ago. High above our heads, the clouds swirled, reaching downward in misty wisps like the beginning of a tornado.

"We will need to dispel this carefully," Ada-Mae said. "And quickly," she added, casting an eye up toward the descending funnel above our head.

"We need to go there," I said, fascinated by the crystal bowl, which now seemed to glow hypnotically, pulsing in a soothing rhythm. Before I knew what I was doing, I reached out to touch it. "I could run and get Maude," I said, my voice a little distant, the words automatic and unthinking. "The quicker I get there, the better."

"No!" Ada Mae called out, trying to stop me as my fingers stretched out to touch the rough crystal. But she was too late.

The tips of three fingers of my right hand brushed the edge and experienced a hard, fast vibration that ran straight up my arm and into the middle of my body, somewhere deep in my center. Out of the corner of my eye, I saw the cutlery that represented the houses of Mystic Dunes all shift and turn at once on the sand, avoiding each other in a swift, almost choreographed ballet. Within a couple of seconds, they had formed into the unmistakable outline of a skull, and then the world spun.

CHAPTER

NINE

Gillian screeched as I appeared out of thin air about two feet above the ground right next to her, dropping to land with a painful thud and a naughty word that escaped my lips. I was one of those people—and this was most probably the writer in me—who felt that if people were going to use curse words, then they should at least use them at the proper time and in the right way. Precision in language mattered, as did precision in intent—magic had taught me that.

Right now, spitting sand out of my mouth, I felt I had enough justification to put fifty cents in the swear jar.

"Sidney!" Gillian cried out, one hand clutched hard against her chest. For a moment, I worried that having finally found Gillian, I might need to carry her straight to the hospital.

Glancing north, back toward the other end of the beach where I'd just teleported from—which was becoming an unsettling habit—the distant swirling clouds looked to be retreating. And I could see the wind was dying down. It was like the power of the ritual had spent itself in moving me perhaps a couple of miles along the oceanfront.

"Did you just appear out of thin air?" Gillian asked, clearly horrified.

"Yes," I said. "Sorry about that. I didn't know it was going to happen."

"When you were all talking about magic and what have you," she said, "I thought you were... you know, exaggerating."

"No, no," I said a little impatiently, wanting to get to the important business of where the heck Gillian had been while we were all worrying about her. "Magic's real, witches are real, ghosts are real, and so forth."

"Oh..." Gillian replied but said no more on the subject.

"So everyone has been looking for you. We thought you had gone missing, and no one seemed to know where you were."

As the clouds above us receded, the moon slid into view again, and I could make out Gillian's expression as she stared out to sea for a moment. "I needed time to think."

I took a little breath and tried to see things from Gillian's point of view. She and my father had not been together for very long, and all the goings-on since they came to Crystal Beach had probably been a lot for her to deal with. "I get that," I said. "But it would have been nice to know you weren't dead. Especially as my father has recently been accused of murder. His girlfriend going missing was not exactly helping his case either, you know. Not to mention that he's been worried about you. Even your friends didn't seem to know where you were."

Gillian cocked her head to one side, a confused frown emerging onto her elegant features. "Friends?"

"Yes, Lennon and Janis, or whoever they are. At Number Two Mystic Dunes."

Gillian shrugged in a rather offhanded way. "Oh, I don't think they're my friends."

O-kay... That one shocked me a little.

Before I could figure out a response, Gillian spoke again. "Look, I don't want to upset anyone, and your father is a good man." She managed a smile. "And he's definitely not a murderer. But I think whatever this is between us isn't going to work. In truth, I'm not even sure why we were together in the first place. Like... I can't even remember how we first met. I think it's just best if I head back home."

"Look, I know it's been a rough time," I began, "but—"

Gillian cut me off with a hand gesture that I imagined had silenced a boardroom or two in her time. "My mind is made up." Her voice softened as she went on. "Will you tell him for me? To be honest, you know him better than I do. I just think it will be better coming from you."

"But he will have questions," I protested.

Gillian shook her head and stood up. "I don't think he will." She looked around her at the moonlit beach. I genuinely don't even know why I'm here."

With that, she turned and walked toward the back of the beach. A part of me wanted to go after her and tell her to stop being so selfish, to have the guts to face my father herself. This was all very unsatisfying, and I had heard no real explanation for where she had been all this time. Gillian hadn't even had the courtesy to answer her phone or reply to a message.

From the way she spoke to me, I didn't feel I would get any answers, either. And from the sounds of it, she might not have the answers herself... which got me thinking. Something strange seemed to be happening with her. I stood up to head back along the beach myself when I realized I didn't even have my phone on me to call my father as I had placed it out of the way during the ritual and had been snatched away from there without a chance to grab it.

Geez, I thought as I trudged back along the beach, it would be nice if teleportation gave you a return ticket.

I DIDN'T HAVE to walk too far before a huge pickup truck came racing along the road behind the beach and screeched to a halt. It was big and black, with flame decals along the side and roof and a thick roll bar, which my father and Ernie were clinging to, standing up like they were *Dukes of Hazzard* extras chasing off "out-of-towners" in that old TV show. It was a bad enough idea for Jacob to be up there, and it was a minor miracle he hadn't fallen off along the way. But I had to restrain myself from telling Ernie to "get down from there right now."

At least Ada-Mae had taken the passenger seat while Cody and his wavy blonde hair sat behind the wheel.

"Everything okay?" Ada-Mae called out. "What happened? Where is she?"

Ada-Mae stepped out of the truck, showing deftness for her age, as the truck had big wheels and a high suspension, and the ground was some ways down. Ernie moved to the side of the truck's rear, but neither my dad nor he made any move to get down, both eying the distance to the ground with what looked like skepticism. I wondered how on earth they had both gotten up there in the first place.

"Are you alright, Sidney?" my dad asked. "It was like you got sucked into the bowl."

"It was Ada-Mae who thought you might have been teleported," Ernie said.

Ada-Mae looked grim. "I did not design the spell to do that. If only I had ever been powerful enough to do that on purpose."

"It's Crystal Beach," I said. "And whatever this conjunction is. It's overcharging spells."

"Seeking out magic," Ada-Mae said in agreement. "We must be careful now with whatever magic we decide to use in the coming days."

"Whoa, did you see what happened to the map of Mystic Dunes?" Cody was coming around the front of his truck.

"The skull?" I had. It happened after I touched the crystal bowl.

"If ever we need proof of the malevolent power of that place," Ada-Mae agreed. "So?"

I realized she was pushing the question about Gillian. I shrugged and shook my head, a little amazed by what I was about to say. "She's fine. Been walking around Crystal Beach, I think."

There was almost a palpable sense of disappointment, which I kind of understood. No one wished ill of her, yet we all seemed to have been through such a fuss for someone who could have just let us know she was okay. For one thing, I could have been working more on making sure my father stayed a free man.

"She doesn't want to be with me anymore," he said from the back of the truck, "does she?"

I had hoped not to have to do this in front of everyone else. It felt more like a private thing. I gulped. "No."

He smiled ruefully. "It's okay. You know, I can't even quite remember why we got together in the first place."

Huh. "She said something like that, too. Maybe even exactly that."

"I mean, I literally can't remember our first date or how we even came to know each other. A mutual friend? Some event? I..."

I could see the worry on his face, the distant look that showed concern for the fact he could have forgotten something that should be easy to remember. But in the end, he shrugged in a sort of "oh well" gesture.

Ada-Mae and I looked at each other, both thinking the same thing. In fact, we both breathed out the word at the same time. "Magic."

"Gillian even told me that the people at Number Two Mystic Dunes were not her friends. When she said it, I thought she meant they had a falling out or something. But..."

My dad looked between us, his expression confused, although I knew he was sharp enough to get what was being implied. He just didn't want to believe it.

Ada-Mae turned to Cody. "We might need a ride somewhere else. Would you mind? I know you probably need to get back and open the bar again."

Cody waved her away. "No way. This is the most fun I've had in ages."

CHAPTER
TEN

The Tropical Oasis Motel appeared as if it was straight out of a horror movie. Its sign was very much mid-century modern, meaning the motel had been there since at least the early nineteen-sixties. It looked like it hadn't benefited from an awful lot of love since then. The only saving grace of the whole scene as we pulled up there—the three of us in the rear grimly hanging on for dear life—was that the thunderstorm that had threatened earlier had not materialized, so there were no jagged forks of lightning illuminating the scene from behind.

"You think she came back here?" my dad asked me.

"From what she said, she wasn't going to stay with her supposed 'friends' in Mystic Dunes. And, well, she asked me to... you know, let you down gently for her. So unless she managed to book herself on the next flight out of Orlando International, she would have needed somewhere to spend the night. And, seeing as the room was already booked and paid for here..."

Or maybe she was still wandering the streets of Crystal Beach. Who knew?

My dad held up a key. "I've still got this. Shall we head straight to the room?"

I wondered if maybe we should go to the reception desk and get them to buzz the room. I was desperate to have my suspicions confirmed, though, and what if Gillian said she didn't want to talk to us? She might assume we had come in force to get her to take my father back.

I waved for the others to stay where they were as Ada-Mae rolled down the cab's window. "Be careful now."

Gillian had not seemed dangerous, just confused, but I nodded my affirmation.

There was no answer when we knocked on the door, although we could tell there was a light on inside. After two attempts, I tried the handle, ignoring a quiet protest from my father, who was feeling just as nosy as I was.

"Gillian?" I called out, poking my head in. I could see the length of the room, and there was little in there save for a cabin-size suitcase on the bed. At the far end, the door to the bathroom was ajar, and I thought I could hear running water beyond.

Panic took hold of me again. There was something wrong with this picture.

"Sidney!" my dad warned, grabbing at my shoulder to stop me

from charging in before losing his grip on the thin, mint-colored cardigan that was there to cover my shoulders.

I dashed through the room and burst into the bathroom, seeing that the cold water tap on the sink was running. Glancing to my right, I saw Gillian sitting on the edge of the bathtub in white linen slacks and a long-sleeved violet tunic top. The woman had an effortless chic older mom style. I had to give it to her. More importantly, she seemed well, apart from the fact that she was staring at the running water, a single tear running down each cheek.

It took her a moment to notice me, even though I had made a dramatic entrance into the bathroom. She looked up a little bleary-eyed just as my dad followed, almost running into me.

"Hi, Gillian," he said a little awkwardly.

She looked up at him and smiled apologetically. Or that was the way it looked to me. "I'm sorry," she said, looking at Jacob.

"That's alright," he said. "I get it. I actually feel the same. Or I don't feel it... if you know what I mean. Something was done to us, Gillian, by some evil person."

Gillian's expression melted into a frown, quite like it had back on the beach. "No, I don't mean that. I mean, the fact that I planted that evidence against you, Jacob. It was me who set you up. I was the one who put the bottle of poison in your toiletries bag."

SOMEONE OR SOMETHING has a nefarious plan for Crystal Beach. Is Gillian connected to the mysterious "The Head" of the coven or is she merely a pawn in their wicked game? Can Sidney help Zoe control her shifter powers to protect those she loves? How can Sidney find a way to prove to Chief Reece that the murders in

Crystal Beach are connected to a dangerous magical force? With time running out, can Sidney cast a spell to save her family, the town she loves, and find a way back into back into John's heart? Or is this witch going to find herself dead in the water?

Turn the page to find all the answers in the next magically mysterious and spellbinding paranormal cozy mystery, ***Charmed and Dangerous***

Next in Series:

**Welcome to Crystal Beach, an enchanting town with a
dangerous secret.**

Peril and uncertainty loom heavily over Crystal Beach as a cataclysmic event threatens to wipe out Mystic Dunes and its residents. Only one witch possesses the power to halt this impending disaster - psychic Sidney Grace. But is she ready to face such a powerful and deadly force?

As time ticks away, Sidney faces a daunting task—convincing the Crystal Beach police that magic and ghosts are real—and that's not something they teach at Quipley's School of Magic. Fortunately, Mojo, her magical feline, lends a paw in this battle to save their town.

Can Sidney harness her magical abilities and unravel the mysteries—a strange death, the enigmatic beach creature, and the ghost's chilling prophecy—before it's too late to avert disaster?

Turn the page to join Sidney on her most perilous mission yet in Charmed and Dangerous. Don't miss the electrifying tenth installment in the Crystal Beach series.

KAREN MCSPADE

CHARMED AND
DANGEROUS

A Crystal Beach Paranormal Cozy Mystery
Book Ten

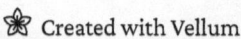 Created with Vellum

FREE GIFT

Receive your FREE exclusive copy of **Hash Browns And Homicide**, the series prequel, and get notified via email of new releases, giveaways, contests, cover reveals, and insider fun when you sign up to my VIP Mystery Book Club mailing list!

Scan the QR Code To Sign Up and Claim Your FREE Exclusive Book

CHAPTER
ONE

Jacob looked stunned, as he should be. He seemed to stagger a little, stumbling back against the door to the bathroom as if this revelation from Gillian had taken some of the strength from him. "Why would you do that? Why would you plant evidence to make me look guilty? What did I do to deserve that?"

"I... I don't..." Gillian stammered.

I could see the confusion on Gillian's face. She knew something had been done to her, but she couldn't quite wrap her head around it.

"It wasn't me. But, at the same time, it was," she confessed.

Rage filled my thoughts for whoever had done this to her. The recklessness of messing with someone's mind this way. As if I hadn't seen enough proof already that we were truly dealing with someone—or something—who would stop at nothing to achieve what they wanted.

Gillian looked up at me, then across to my dad. "I need to make this right." She straightened and turned to the door. "I'll give a statement to the police. It's the least I can do." I saw a lump make its way down the line of her throat. "I will tell them I planted the bottle of poison in your toiletries bag. That I framed you."

I put a hand out and squeezed the top of Gillian's arm. I didn't really know this woman, and her entire relationship with my father had been manufactured, most likely by a mind control spell. Yet I felt a swell of warmth and gratitude toward her right then. By going to the police with a confession, she might very well end up under arrest herself, and we all knew it wasn't her fault. But would the intransigent Chief Reece see things that way? He who would not take any more rubbish about "magic" in his criminal investigations.

"Unless they've got someone in the cells, I doubt there will be anyone in at the station," I said. "We've got a bit of a nine-to-five police force here in Crystal Beach."

My dad nodded his head. "It can wait until morning then, huh?"

～

ONLY GILLIAN and I went to the police station the following morning. I felt that both my dad and I marching in there with Gillian between us would look like witness coercion... or something to that effect. In fact, Gillian had offered to go in on her own, but I couldn't let that happen, either. It seemed like a friendly face should be there in case they immediately threw her into a cell.

John's reaction when I walked in through the front door of the station was a sort of "here we go again" eye roll. I had to bite my lip a little and remember how, from his point of view at least, I had almost—okay... actually—made their only piece of physical evidence in this murder investigation disappear.

As we walked through the door, he pointedly ignored me and instead spread his wide, too-delicious smile for Gillian's benefit. "What can I do for you?"

"I've, um... come to confess."

Well, that wiped the smile right off his face. I enjoyed seeing it fall a little more than I should have, although Gillian probably shouldn't have led with such a dramatic opener.

"Confess to...?"

"Planting evidence that would make Jacob Grace look guilty of murder."

"But she didn't know what she was doing at the time," I added quickly.

The depth of John's frown could have given the Grand Canyon a run for its money. He turned to look straight at me. "This has got to be the lamest—"

"It's true!" Gillian insisted. She had virtually screamed the words, shocking the Crystal Beach chief of police into silence.

From where she had been warily observing the proceedings from her desk, Jessie got up and slowly made her way over.

John turned a little red and hadn't responded yet.

"But why?" Jessie asked, reaching the counter. "Why would you frame your boyfriend? What did he do?"

"Well, he wasn't really my boyfriend. I mean, he was. I just didn't really have any choice in the matter."

Both officers' eyes went wide.

Not helping things, Gillian.

"It's magic!" I cut in, desperate to divert Gillian's car crash of a confession.

"Everything always is," John said. "Isn't magic the most convenient—"

"It is magic," Gillian insisted. "I don't know how, and I never would have believed it before. But..."

John crossed his arms and looked back and forth between the two of us. "And how do we know this isn't 'magic' at work right now?" He pointed to me and then to Gillian. "How do we know you haven't hexed her to come in and say this?"

"Whatever this is," Gillian said, "it goes back to Boston. To when I first met Jacob."

"Your father," John helpfully pointed out to me.

Thanks. Didn't know that one. "Who doesn't have a magical bone in his body."

"Jacob and I didn't know each other," Gillian said. "And I would never have expected to meet. We are completely different people, yet we began a whirlwind romance out of nowhere."

"It happens," John said, his arms still crossed defensively in front of him.

"It was only a matter of weeks ago, but I can't even remember how we met," Gillian said. "And then there are the 'friends' I visited in Mystic Dunes. I realized yesterday that I didn't even know them until a few days ago. Something very strange is going on, Chief Reece."

"Well, that is quite weird," Jessie agreed.

John looked over at her disbelievingly as if she was taking our side in the "it was magic" argument. His shoulders relaxed a little, his arms slipping out of their crossed posture and sliding down to his sides, but the suspicious frown remained.

"Okay. Let's say I'm buying the whole 'magic and mind control' thing," Chief Reece said to me, his icy stare drilling into me. "What's to say, after what happened with your mom, which our murder victim Sam Barlow may well have been responsible for, this isn't revenge on your part?"

He gestured to Gillian. "That you didn't find a woman to cast a spell on, then bring her to Crystal Beach to ultimately provide your father with an alibi?"

I knew he was reaching now. "First of all, I haven't left Crystal Beach this whole time, and you know that. If I could even do a spell like that, I couldn't do it from several states away.

"Then there's the fact that our execution of the plan would have been terrible. Wouldn't it have been easier to have Gillian as an alibi all along rather than at some party? Then we wouldn't have had to—"

I stopped myself just in time, realizing I was about to go too far.

"Make a crucial piece of evidence disappear?" John filled in for me.

I could tell that he wasn't going to get over that anytime soon. Nonetheless, I could see his brain working over what I had said. The ultimate sense in it. Maybe I should have let him get there on his own, but my heart wasn't going to allow that. It had things that needed to be said.

"And look at me, John. Do you really think that's who I am? Who Ada-Mae is? Are we the kind of people who would set up an elaborate murder revenge plan? A crime of passion is one thing. If Dad was there and he had attacked Sam out of anger for what he did, that's one thing. But this...? It's—"

"Insane." It was Jessie finishing for me this time.

My eyes met John's. His were dark and serious, yet there was a glassy quality to them, too. I fancied I could almost hear his thoughts. He didn't really believe in his heart that I was capable of it. Not someone he had so clearly cared for.

"Who, then?"

"Someone that Sam was working with, probably someone at Mystic Dunes. We have our suspicions, but we can't prove anything yet."

"We?" Jessie said with a slight laugh that was not unkind. "The 'Shifting Sands Murder Club,' is it?"

I liked the sound of that and, shrugging, gave a slightly guilty grin. "The usual suspects, yes."

"Zoe?" There was an edge in Jessie's voice then.

I tilted my head one way and then the other. "Maybe. She's been going through some stuff."

Jessie, an open book at the best of times, failed to keep the concern off her face.

Then, remembering Rose and Rodney, I added, "And luckily, we got a little help on the inside of this conspiracy."

John looked alarmed. "Conspiracy? I don't suppose you want to give us a heads-up on what you know?"

I did. I wanted to tell him everything. Having the local law enforcement on our side would be good. Yet something had been broken between me and John in all of this. I knew he had only been doing his job when he arrested my father, but the way he cut me off hurt me deeply. And more than that, how he flip-flopped with magic, which was now such a massive, important part of my life. He believed only when it suited him to do so, then was ready to be suspicious of every motivation of those who used magic. Like we could not be trusted.

Then again, a lot had happened in Crystal Beach that could cause a person to distrust magic. And either way, this was bigger than me and John. Something terrible might be coming, and he needed to know about it.

"I'll tell you everything. But there is someone I need to see first," I said. "Can we meet you somewhere in about thirty minutes?"

"Where?" John asked.

Thinking of the nearest place I knew that was close to where I planned to go next, I said Donatelli's before I even thought about its significance for me and John.

He stopped for a moment, clearly surprised. "Okay, yeah," he said. "Donatelli's it is."

I pointed to Gillian. "And this lady? Free to go, I guess. Seeing as she wasn't responsible for what she did?"

I could see John wrestle with that one for a moment. The police chief in him, the man who was under pressure to put *somebody* behind bars while people were being murdered in his town, wouldn't mind charging somebody with at least a little obstruction. Instead, he gave Gillian an earnest look.

"You're free to go if you wish. I won't stop you. But I do need you to give us more details or perhaps agree to speak to us by video call sometime in the next day or two. Jessie here can get that scheduled for you."

I saw Gillian's visible relief. "Sure, I'll do that. I thought you were going to ask me to stay. No offense to any of you, but I can't wait to get the heck out of this town."

Fair enough, I thought. Crystal Beach is a bit too mysterious for some people.

CHAPTER

TWO

Perhaps I should have stayed and explained things to John and Jessie at the station, but from the moment I woke up that morning, I had been desperate to check in on Zoe.

I offered Gillian a ride to the stop for the Greyhound bus in the next town over—it seemed the least I could do—but she graciously declined. Despite my best efforts to reassure her to the contrary, I think she was still feeling bad about the whole "evidence planting" thing and the fact she could not remember how the manufactured vial of poison had come into her possession. I was sure her lack of memory about that was not Gillian's fault or an accident.

So I pulled up in my cornflower blue and white camper van outside The Invisible Cloak on Citrus Way to find the sign on the door turned to closed. Everything looked dark inside despite already being past the time when Zoe usually opened the store.

I reached out and tried the door handle, which was locked. When I had left the previous evening, I had taken Zoe's key to lock up with, as we didn't want anyone wandering in to find a werewolf locked in a cage in the apartment upstairs. After locking the door, I slid the key through the mail slot. Which I was now regretting.

Taking a quick look left and right along the street, I saw it was still pretty quiet this early, with no one within about three shopfronts of me. I squatted down and called Zoe's name twice through the mail slot.

When no one appeared at the door after a minute or two, I worried even more and tried to figure out what I could do. My fingers, resting lightly on the doorknob, slipped idly down to the lock.

Hmmm... I wonder.

My fingertips ran lightly across the outside of the lock, coming to a stop with my index finger across the hole. Calming myself, letting the few noises of the street in the early morning fade into the background, I tried to push my senses beyond the end of my finger. I imagined the workings of the lock inside, then tried to bridge the gap between imagination and reality.

In my mind's eye, I felt like I could see the spaces. I pictured what I could recall of the key from the door the previous evening. What was its shape, and how would it fit into the lock to make it turn?

My eyes were closed, and I knew I would look highly suspicious to anyone walking past, but I worked to keep my heartbeat calm and my focus inside the lock. Reaching out from the end of my finger, I filled those vital spaces with intention and energy, solidifying this force so it would be rigid and strong enough to turn the metal parts of the lock.

The beat of my heart set the rhythm, climbing as the moment arrived, and I gave my finger a sharp twist to the right.

To my amazement, there was a click, and the door slowly swung open. I had done it!

"What were you doing?"

I opened my eyes to see Zoe standing there, the key gripped between her fingers. A weak laugh escaped my lips as I forced them into a smile. Oh well... I tried.

"Oh, hey, Zoe. I was worried. Wanted to make sure you are okay."

"How did you get in? I found the key on the floor and was just about to unlock the door when it opened. Did you make a copy?"

"Uh, no. I... I did it with my mind. I think..."

Zoe's eyes widened. But she didn't say anything. With everything that happened, my obviously expanding magical powers were likely the last thing she wanted to deal with.

I tilted my head to get a good look at her in the light pouring in from the open door. She didn't look okay. She looked like she had fallen out of a tall tree and hit every branch on the way down. Several clumps of her hair defied gravity, the bags under her eyes relatively duffel sized. I even noticed three thin parallel scratches along one cheek.

Zoe saw me notice the scratches, and her hand went self-consciously to them. "Oh, they'll fade," she said with a weak smile. "One of the benefits of my, er... condition. You won't be able to see them by lunchtime."

I tried my most reassuring smile back. "When I saw the shop was closed up..."

"Yeah, I don't think I'll open up today. Yesterday was too close. I'm going stay up in my apartment today, close to my cage."

I hated hearing Zoe say that. There was something entirely miserable in having to lock herself away in a cage, of being scared to leave her apartment. "That's no way to live, Zoe."

She shrugged—a tiny movement that hinted at lethargy and defeat. "It's only a few days a month, and all of us girls have a few days a month when we're not much fun to be around. Mine kinda just doubles because the two never seem to line up for me."

I smiled supportively, trying to be as laissez-faire about her situation as she was trying to be. I couldn't quite do it.

"Seriously, though," she went on, "this moon at the moment is the worst I've ever experienced. Next month, I'm hoping things will be better again."

We were standing at the entrance to the shop, Zoe blocking my way into her domain. I got that. She had always been alone with this, possibly for years, so she was used to doing the safe thing and shutting everyone else out.

"You don't have to do this on your own anymore," I said.

Zoe's grateful smile looked a little impatient at the same time. "It's okay. I'm used to being alone, Sidney. It's who I am."

"Or maybe it's what the wolf has made you into?"

Zoe took half a step backward and started to close the door. "Thanks for your help last night and for coming round to check—"

I wasn't having any of that nonsense, so I stepped forward into the gap, stopping the door from closing. "Look, Zoe, there are people who care about you. I was at the police station just now, and it's clear that Jessie—"

Zoe interrupted, holding her hand up to silence me. When she spoke, her voice was a bit harsher. "No, you look, Sidney. I know you mean well."

"I can help you, Zoe. And, more importantly, we need you. Crystal Beach needs you out and about right now, not hiding away where you're no use to anyone. Something terrible is coming, Zoe, and I don't know if we can fight it without you."

Zoe smiled, but it was more like grudging respect given to a worthy adversary, underscored with a fair bit of frustration. "You're like gum deep in the treads of a pair of walking boots, Sidney Grace."

Well, that was a new one, and I wasn't entirely sure what proportion of it was a compliment and what was an insult. "You need to open up," I insisted more quietly. "Let people in. Give them a chance."

"Everything okay here?"

I turned to see that Jessie had pulled up in her squad car unnoticed by either of us while we stood bantering in the doorway of Zoe's shop. The deputy's concerned frown didn't go unnoticed, and to be fair, our postures and my position halfway through the door while Zoe had clearly been in the process of trying to close it didn't exactly look the best.

Jessie saw Zoe's face, the magic shop owner too slow in moving her hand to cover the scratches. "Zoe? Has something happened?"

I took a step back from the doorway. "Now would be the time," I said quietly to Zoe, although probably still loud enough that Jessie could hear it.

The deputy looked at me uncertainly, unsure of my role in whatever was going on. I could see it from her point of view: I had been at the station not long before, conveniently delivering proof of my father's innocence to them. Why was I now holding an intense-looking conversation on the doorstep of the magic shop, with the closed sign up when it would usually have been open?

"The chief's waiting for you at Deliciously Donatelli's," Jessie told me. Her voice continued to match her suspicious look. "I just dropped him off there."

Jessie turned to Zoe. The defensive look Zoe had been wearing almost all the time I spoke to her had now melted away. Her face was open—vulnerable, even—as she looked at Jessie.

"Can you come in a moment, Jessie?" she said. "I've got some things I need to tell you."

CHAPTER

THREE

I left Maude outside The Invisible Cloak and hurried toward the opposite end of Citrus Way, crossing to the other side where Deliciously Donatelli's was the last building. The sky-blue horizontal wood cladding made the restaurant feel like it was closer to the sea than it was.

John was sitting at a table on the patio outside, sipping a coffee, and he didn't see me coming. So much so that he spilled his coffee when I called out, "Hey!" as I approached him from behind. Some coffee spilled down the front of his pristine shirt, and he jumped up, slapping at the burning liquid with a napkin.

"Sorry!" I gushed, reaching my arms out uselessly as if to help.

"It's okay," he said, waving for me to sit down. "I've got a clean shirt back at the station."

"You seem, um, a little jumpy," I said as I sat down.

A self-conscious smile crossed his face and then disappeared. I wouldn't have ever described John as "timid," as this was the man who had glared at me every time I came anywhere near the police station. The one who had basically threatened to run me out of town. But the flash of a smile crossing his face made me wonder where his mind was at that moment.

Before he had a chance to reply, we were interrupted by a waitress. John ordered another black coffee—second time lucky, eh?—and I browsed the milkshakes, choosing salted caramel. I felt I needed a sugary kick to get me through the explanation ahead.

John was grinning as the waitress left.

"What?" I said.

"Don't you think it's a little too early for milkshakes?"

"It's never too early for milkshakes. Or cake. Those are just stories made up by people who... I don't know, sell bran muffins and oatmeal or something."

John's grin widened further. I'd forgotten how good it felt to make him grin, and I allowed myself to blush a little and do that coy thing I had definitely never practiced in a mirror.

He reached out and tapped the table—a little half-gesture where, for a moment, I had thought his fingers would find my hand. "Look," he said, "before you share whatever you've got for me, I just wanted to say something first."

Here we go, I thought, excitement welling up inside of me as a warm vibration rippled through the middle of my chest. I nodded seriously and tried to school my expression.

"I wanted to apologize."

Yes, yes, yes.

"For one thing, I've been a little harsh on you."

You have, Mr. Reece. You have, indeed.

"I definitely went too far, threatening your home in Maude on the beach there. I noticed you moved."

I nodded. "The Shifting Sands parking lot."

He chuckled lightly. "Private property. Touché, Sidney."

"Why, thank you."

"Although I don't know how you swung that, I understand Ada-Mae has not been Administrator Jessop's favorite person of late."

"A good chief of police is always up on the gossip at the local retirement center, huh?"

He chuckled again. "Very true. Not as good a view in the parking lot as on the beach road, I'll bet. If you want to move back, I won't be enforcing any vagrancy laws, I promise."

I smiled graciously. "Very good of you."

My response didn't have the desired effect, and John's face fell. He didn't look so much "serious" as sad.

"You know, I'm not from around here. Did I ever tell you that?"

He hadn't. I wasn't sure why he hadn't, although I guessed I'd never asked. I supposed I had always just thought of Officer—and then Chief—John Reece as belonging to Crystal Beach.

"I'm from Atlanta originally. That's where I went to the police academy and then out on the beat as a cop."

"Wow," I said. "Pretty different than Crystal Beach, I bet."

"Well, yes and no. I moved down to Florida after being shot on duty."

"Shot?"

I hadn't exclaimed that out of doubt, merely shock. All the same, John provided proof, leaning back in his seat a little and pulling up the bottom of his coffee-stained shirt. There, maybe three inches above his hip, was a scar shaped almost like a star. A small, pale anomaly in the otherwise perfect olive skin of a nicely taut stomach.

"Not so bad," he said. "Went straight through and didn't hit anything vital. I bled a lot but was pretty fine otherwise. It was one of those moments, though, you know? Got me asking myself, 'Do I want to give my life for this job?'"

"You decided 'yes,' I guess?"

"I decided 'not there.' Not chasing different criminals and mostly speaking to different people every day. If I was going to serve and protect, I wanted to do that in a small community. Yes, maybe a little because it might be safer, but more because I wanted to know the people I could end up taking a bullet for."

"So. you came to Crystal Beach?"

"Yes, quiet, friendly little coastal town where I could make a difference in people's lives in small ways. Or... that's what it used to be like."

John paused and looked down at the table. I feared he was leading up to another "Sidney's trouble" speech.

Some apology, Chief Reece.

"Not that we never had crime before. Mostly done by people passing through. Robberies, even drugs at one time. But Marie Beauchamp's was the first murder I dealt with here."

"And it's been non-stop ever since," I agreed. Might as well put it out there.

"Look, I'm not sure what you're about to tell me, Sidney, but I do know that Crystal Beach has changed recently. The Crystal Beach that I see and have to deal with. I'm not blaming you, but the magic you, Ada-Mae, and the others are involved with is a part of it."

"Not *our* magic," I stressed. Ours was the magic that fought against it. I wished he could see that.

John shrugged a sort of "okay, okay" agreement but was determined to get to his point. "I just... I've realized these last few days that this is a really important time in the town I've made my home. The town I love. And I need to be its police chief first and foremost.

"I know that treating you the way I did when your father was arrested was not fair to you. But, looked at another way, if I hadn't let myself develop feelings for you, maybe we wouldn't all have been in that position in the first place."

"I still don't think I get what you're trying to say," I said, although the painful feeling in my chest was an indication I understood the general theme.

He laughed one of the most charming, self-deprecating sorts of laughs I've ever heard in my life. "Me neither. But I'm sure that what you're about to tell me is going to involve lots of magic and ghosts and other such things. And, in recent weeks, I've come to understand that a part of my job now as the chief of police in Crystal Beach is being open to those possibilities when investigating crime here. "So, if I'm going to do that with perfect clarity and neutrality, I don't think I can let myself have fuzzy feelings for a witch."

"Because you did?"

"Because I always have. And I have to stop."

Hearing him say those words was utterly horrible, mostly because I understood at some level that what John was saying made perfect sense. Plus, the way he had said "fuzzy" in that southern drawl of his was absolutely delicious.

I nodded once, curtly without being too harsh, while I pushed back tears and tried not to be too obvious when blinking them away. "I understand," I said. And that was that.

My milkshake came, which I drained like the proverbial recently jilted do while sitting in front of daytime soap opera TV and polishing off a whole tub of Ben & Jerry's by themselves. Then I told John everything I knew.

And, a little annoyingly, he was right. It included plenty of magic. Not just mind control, but magically conjured evidence and murder through portals. It also included those ghosts he had predicted.

I saw John fighting to suspend his disbelief when I told him I had been hanging out with the ghost of the murdered Sam Barlow. Seeing how we had been great enemies when Sam was alive, it was quite a big one for him to accept, I guess. Figuring that ghosts were hard to put in jail, I admitted that Sam had been the one to help us steal the poison vial from evidence. John, trying to keep up, had to keep checking with me that the vial was not real and had been "conjured" conveniently into the hands of Gillian, who was then hexed into planting it in my father's toiletries bag while under the influence of a mind control spell.

Mind control was the one thing John accepted easily, having already seen some evidence of that during the Crystal Beach Mini-Golf Invitational.

I skipped past Zoe being a shifter, as it didn't seem relevant yet, and, hopefully, she was revealing that one to the town's deputy as we spoke. Sam was not the only ghost, of course. I told John about meeting Admiral Avery and his tale of a cataclysmic tsunami that wiped out the small town that now rests under the sea, along with his dire warnings that something similarly terrible was about to befall Crystal Beach.

"You see," I finished, "although I don't know why Sam was murdered—and neither does Sam—I think that setting my dad up was all about distracting me, Ada-Mae, and anybody else looking too closely at what was happening in Mystic Dunes. That place is at the center of this. It has been all along. Remember how even that portal over to the space center was there? Even CAD-

Astra was involved in some way with whoever is really behind Mystic Dunes."

"But I thought Mystic Dunes was Sam Barlow's baby?"

"It was. But he had at least one silent partner putting in the money to make it happen. Sam was a warlock, and he misused his powers. He thought he was on the inside of this, but ultimately, I don't think he was. Maybe he was just a pawn for the real bad guys."

"And you say you have someone on the inside?"

I grinned at that one. How could I not? "You're not going to believe this."

John scoffed. "There's been plenty for me to get my head around. I'm sure I can take one more thing."

"Our people on the inside are Rose and Rodney Gantz."

John's eyes went a little unfocused, and he blinked several times, staring past me out onto the street. Finally, he turned to face me again. "Okay," he admitted, "I did not see that one coming."

CHAPTER
FOUR

You two looked cozy sitting there.

I had just crossed the road and was watching Chief John Reece head back on the other side of the street, allowing myself—a little dangerously—to dream of a more cordial relationship between the two of us again. *Steady on now, Sidney.*

The sudden voice inside my head almost made me jump out of my skin, and I looked around for a moment, identifying that voice a moment before I spotted the familiar spectral figure.

Sam Barlow's ghost was leaning against the front window of a nearby shop, his hands in his pockets, trying far too hard to look casual. To the untrained eye, it appeared to be an illusion or that the glass was thick enough to hold his frame. Remembering the efforts of my grandfather's ghost to "sit" convincingly in Maude's passenger seat, I knew straight away that Sam's pose was a constructed one designed for making an entrance.

"I didn't know if you'd be back," I said. I managed to sound ambivalent, although my feelings at the sight of the dead realtor were complex. As he had in life, he looked smug and wore a self-satisfied smile it would be nice to wipe from his face.

The mind control that Gillian had recently been victim to reminded me of the hex placed on my mother. I had always assumed that Sam was directly responsible for that. But recent developments seemed to indicate he wasn't working alone, that he was also a victim of magic more powerful than his own.

In some ways, it was a relief to see him. Having a ghost as clearly powerful as Sam on my side had helped to keep my father from being wrongly charged with murder and sent to county jail. We might need more of that help soon to keep Crystal Beach on the map.

Can't keep a good guy down, Sam replied. He used his foot to push off from his perch against the window, leaving a cool area of condensation behind him, which quickly faded.

I made a point of rolling my eyes.

What? Sam said, doing his best to look offended. *We are the good guys, aren't we?*

This time, I remembered to use my inner voice, seeing as we were on one of Crystal Beach's most public streets.

Oh, it's "we," now, is it? I thought you were just here to find out who killed you.

I realized, a little to my own dismay, that I wanted Sam to say this wasn't the case. Not that I was a naïve person who thought life was merely a Disney movie, but I guess I was hoping that the time spent around me and Ada-Mae had brought about some epiphany for Sam. Silly or not, I wanted him to be contrite, to have genuinely changed his ways.

Well, yes. Revenge first, obviously. He looked at John, who was almost out of sight further down the street. *Wasn't he mad after that evidence went missing? I mean, I know our police chief isn't the brightest spark, but I thought he would have put two-and-two together over you throwing yourself shamelessly at him at the police station and that vial of poison vanishing. I was expecting he would follow my suggestion about actually enforcing those vagrancy laws.*

Nope. He was still an ass. I had to hold my tongue about the "throwing myself at the chief" thing," as I would only be rising to his bait.

We're past all that. I tried to sound nonchalant as if Sam hadn't been spot on about John's fury leading to threats upon my residency status. In fact, an idea suddenly popped into my head about how Sam's ghost could make himself useful.

A lot's happened while you've been gone. I turned to head back down the street toward The Invisible Cloak. *Come. I'll catch you up while we grab a friend.*

JESSIE WAS GONE when I returned to Zoe's magic shop, and the store was open, with the owner behind the counter. The dramatic difference in her from the haunted-looking person who answered the front door earlier was clear. Things had gone well with Jessie, I gathered.

So, you two are friends again, huh? Sam said, a hint of bitter disappointment in his tone. *Everybody's just getting the happy ending they wanted around here, aren't they?*

I hadn't, of course, told Sam anything about Zoe's shifter situation during our quick catch-up session along the street. It wasn't my place to.

"Fair warning," I said quickly to Zoe, "Sam Barlow's ghost is back, and he's standing right next to me. You know... in case there were things you wouldn't want to say in front of him."

I felt Sam's intrigued spectral gaze upon me.

A moment too late, I noticed that Zoe had a customer who was browsing among the spirituality books. They gave me an alarmed look and promptly left the shop.

"Sorry," I said with a grimace once they were gone.

Zoe waved my apology away. "It's okay. I know a perennial browser when I spot one." She glanced, eyes unfocused, at the spot next to me. "And seeing as the end times are on their way, I guess it doesn't hurt if a dead man knows I'm a shifter." As she finished her sentence, her face suddenly transformed into the head of an angry wolf and then returned to normal. If Sam could blink, he would have missed it.

Instead, Sam slapped a hand silently to his chest in a mock show of offense. *We prefer "recently deceased."* Then he turned to me. *Has she gotten back together with Jessie? Despite the ugly face she just flashed me, I'm getting less of those "frustrated" vibes from her.*

Once again, Sam's insight was proving uncanny. Or had he been back a little longer than he had let on?

They were never together in the first place, I shot back, making my inner voice speak through gritted teeth.

"Look," I told Zoe, "I don't want to mess with your business or anything, but it would be good to have your help today. Plus, you know, we could practice what we talked about. I think I can help you with the effect the conjunction is having."

Zoe stepped out from behind the counter. "To run my business, I need a town full of people to buy my stuff. And, anyway, I can feel the power building already today. I'm too wired to just stand around here all day."

Yes! This was the Zoe I needed on my side today. Well done, Jessie, I thought. The deputy had achieved something I could not, even with all my magical and mystical knowledge.

Zoe moved to the door and changed the sign to "Closed."

Well, aren't we just like a proper Sherlock Holmes story, maybe with a little Dr. Jekyll and Mr. Hyde thrown in for good measure? Sam said, looking at Zoe for the last part. He kind of ruined the moment for me. *Off to fight the evil forces with magic and ghosts and werewolves.*

Sam, I said. *Please don't narrate us.*

"Where are we going?" Zoe asked.

"Rose and Rodney's," I answered.

Sam shook his ethereal head, as he had done when I told him about Rose and Rodney turning up at Ada-Mae's. *Still can't believe those two turned. They always felt, like, super important in the coven. I thought they were more in favor of it than I was. To be honest, I was even beginning to think they were the ones who had killed me. Not that I could figure out why, as we always seemed to get on well. But when you said that hemlock was growing in their garden...*

As for myself, I could not understand a coven where no one else seemed to be sure where anyone else stood within it. I had a strong sense that some mysterious figure was in charge. But who? Who was in charge? What a way to build a coven where you couldn't trust anyone else.

"Sam here," I told Zoe, "is going to help us with some spying."

Can you ask her to stop that? Sam said as we stood in the middle of Rose and Rodney's living area upstairs at The Rose Garden.

For at least the fourth time since we had been there, Rose was waving her hand up and down in the space next to me, passing it through the ghost of "Savvy" Sam Barlow.

"Oh!" she said with a shrill little shriek. "My fingers just went cold that time, I'm sure of it!"

Probably poor circulation, Sam huffed. *She is getting on a bit. Honestly, I always thought Rose was clever. I mean, Rodney's got the real magical power, but I thought Rose was the brains. You see things differently from the other side, I guess.*

I was sure he was seeing the same thing I was.

There were five of us, including Sam, as Rodney was present, and Zoe had come upstairs, too. The last time the two of us had been in this room, Zoe had saved my life from a magical trap that guarded the secret sanctum hidden below the rug. This time, though, the rug had already been cast aside, and the trapdoor opened.

Rose finally got herself together and adopted a more somber expression. "I'm sorry, Sam. We had nothing to do with your death and knew nothing of the hemlock growing outside, I promise. Or that this was behind the reception."

Rose held an address plaque in her hands, the twin "number 2" for the house in Mystic Dunes where the hippie couple Lennon and Janis lived. The supposed friends of Gillian.

Being a ghost and invisible to all but those who, like me, had the rare ability to see them, Sam was the perfect choice to head through those portals and do a bit of spying.

Rose had devised an idea to make the whole thing even more effective. On one side of the small room, the ends of a fold-down dining table were up, and a midnight-blue tablecloth with gold embroidery of moons, stars, and mystical symbols had been laid over the top of it. Four chairs for myself, Zoe, Rose, and Rodney were spaced evenly around the table, with a heavy-looking crystal ball in the middle next to the house address plaque.

The living people in the room were close enough to hold hands. For a moment, I could not see Sam, but then he slowly rose through the middle of the table, his head momentarily occupying the same space as the large crystal ball.

Woah, he said spookily. *I feel a presence in the room. Samuel Barlow, you devil, are you here?*

"Take this seriously, will you?" I scolded him out loud so that even his former coven allies would know he was misbehaving.

I'm nervous, Sam admitted. *You're not the only person who can see ghosts, you know. These might be powerful people you are sending me to spy on.*

What are they going to do to you? I replied—just to Sam this time. *Kill you again?*

Sam's expression became deadly serious. *There are worse things than death, Sidney. A powerful enough warlock or dark witch could send my spirit to a plane of eternal torment.*

That sounded like a tale old warlocks made up to scare the younger ones into doing their bidding. Still, I guessed Sam was better suited to know the possibilities on the darker side of things than I was.

Well, I replied, *you're checking out number two first. There's something up with them, for sure, but my bet is still on Nikola Vorak for head honcho or Grand Pooba... or whatever he's called.*

Sam didn't look so sure. *Because he's at number one and a sociable person who likes to get everyone together? Bit obvious, don't you think?* He shook his head. *No, Nikola and I got on too well. He wouldn't have killed me. Although, I know he did invest a lot into the project...*

I saw confusion and doubt begin to play on Sam's ghostly face. This was not the time for it. "Focus, Sam," I said out loud without thinking. "That's why we're doing this, to find out some answers."

Sam placed one spectral hand on the crystal ball, and the other hovered above the address plate. The rest of us chanted a low, rhythmic sequence of sounds in a language I did not understand, which Rose had provided us with.

Rodney's low baritone voice rumbled throughout the room, which I could feel somewhere deep within my solar plexus. It had a hypnotic effect, so I soon felt my eyelids growing heavy and closing. When I opened them again, Sam had already touched the plaque and vanished through it.

Now, looking through the crystal ball, the rest of us could see what he saw.

He was in the hallway of #2 Mystic Dunes. I recognized it from my own visit to Lennon and Janis's house. Sam moved to the lounge, carefully stepping inside and moving to one side of the open doorway.

To my surprise, the living room was not at all as I had last seen it. Where before it had been dimly lit with candles and incense burning—even a lava lamp over to one side—now it was brightly lit by natural light flooding in from the floor-to-ceiling windows of the sliding doors that led outside. The colorful, mainly tie-dyed throws covering the furniture were also gone from the faux leather furniture. Lennon and Janis were no longer dressed as sixties peace festival rejects. Instead, both of them were smartly presented, Lennon in a shirt, waistcoat, and tie, while Janis wore an emerald dress smart enough to be worn to a Hollywood movie premiere.

With no sunglasses present, I could see their eyes now. There was a sharp intelligence to both of them. The couple sat side-by-side on the couch, speaking to another person sitting in a single chair across from them. I quickly recognized Nikola Vorak, dressed in his trademark polo shirt. He sipped from a cup of something hot and steaming.

"You wanted to address some concerns, Nikola?" Janis said. Like her appearance, Janis's voice had changed, now cold like a frozen metal pipe in the depths of winter.

"Don't you think it's a problem?" Nikola Vorak said. "It looks like that Boston woman has gotten her memories back. It's only a matter of time before that leads the police here."

"A matter of time," Lennon echoed, his voice rich and confident. "There isn't much of that left for Crystal Beach."

"But Jacob Grace should have been at county lockup by now," Nikola Vorak said. "The police were not supposed to be looking for anyone else in connection with Sam Barlow's death."

The image in the crystal ball flickered momentarily. Through the connection we had with Sam and maybe my own ability to sense him as a ghost, I felt his shock and pain. The sense of betrayal at hearing what Nikola Vorak said was certainly hard for Sam to hear.

"I still think—" Nikola Vorak began, but Janis cut him off.

"We've been over this, Nikola." Her voice had the patience of a schoolteacher, although the iciness remained. "Sam Barlow was the only one with the power to stop things mid-ritual. He had to go. And he was the perfect person to make Jacob Grace look guilty, so it had to be then."

Nikola Vorak nodded a slow, reluctant agreement. "I know."

"Although you have a point," Lennon went on. "A distraction could be useful right now to ensure the police are kept busy for the remaining hours until it is too late."

"Another murder?" Nikola Vorak asked.

"Another murder," the man agreed.

"And as we did the deed last time," Janis said, "it's your turn to contribute."

"And after this, I will get the benefit of the ritual?" Nikola Vorak asked. "You know I cannot wait any longer."

"Once the ritual is complete," Janis said, "everyone left within the binding circle will benefit."

Suddenly, Lennon put up a hand to silence the other two. He looked around the room briefly, then straight at Sam. All of us around the table gasped when we saw those dark, coal-like eyes staring at us from within the crystal ball.

"Someone's here," Lennon said.

I watched, holding my breath as Sam panicked and tried to move out of the lounge and back down the hallway toward the portal.

"Stop!" Lennon called. As he did so, the view in the crystal ball went fuzzy around the edges.

Sam turned to see all three of them standing in the middle of the lounge, arms raised out toward him. I could suddenly feel their energy as they pulled Sam's ethereal form toward them.

"Is that you, Sam Barlow?" Lennon said. I saw how Nikola Vorak's eyes went wide at that. "It was a bad idea to spy on us. Now we'll have to send you somewhere where you can't make trouble."

I felt the wave of utter terror that went through Sam as though our spirits were somehow connected, and then I jolted into action. "Zoe, Rodney... help! Let's get him back through the portal. Now!" I cried out.

I felt the strong power of my adversaries join their magical forces with mine, reaching through our connection with the crystal ball and the house address plate to pull Sam back toward us.

The warlocks' power being employed on the other side of the connection was immense, however. It was like trying to drag a block of granite, except the block of granite was pulling back.

Somewhere between them, Sam Barlow's ghost, his spiritual essence, was getting pulled and stretched and otherwise cruelly mishandled. Because we were connected, I could feel the effect that was having on him, understanding that ghosts could, after all, still experience our earthly emotions at times.

"He's got help," Lennon told the others. "He's... joined forces... with..."

I saw Rose and Rodney's eyes go wide and asked myself the same question they were no doubt asking themselves. Were they about to be identified? Panic took over. No doubt, our enemies already knew what side Ada-Mae, I, and many others were on. However, we still needed Rose and Rodney to be our secret people on the inside. And, more importantly, I did not want to get them killed.

In that moment of panic, I reached out and attempted to bring Sam back through the portal and close it. I summoned all my witchy powers, channeling centuries of magic that had been passed down through my family until I pulled Sam free from their treacherous grip. Both the crystal ball and the dim lamp in Rose and Rodney's living room exploded at the same time, leaving us all staring at the spot where I now indicated that Sam was standing.

The room went dark, save for a little light creeping around the edges of the blackout curtain that covered the dormer window. A moment later, having overreached myself, everything also went black for me.

CHAPTER

FIVE

"We need to tell them! We need to tell them that someone is going to be murdered!"

I awoke screaming, my legs dangling over the end of the short, two-seater couch in the Gantzes' living room.

All the faces that had been sitting around the foldout table with me were gathered, looking down at me with concern. Well, apart from Sam Barlow. His ghost was there, too, but he looked more amused than concerned. I could tell that what had happened over at #2 Mystic Dunes had taken its toll on him, as his spectral image was fainter and even flickered a little, his grin faltering to a wince now. His determination to enjoy my discomfort was impressive, even through his own.

"How long was I out?" I asked, trying to rise. "Has anyone told John yet? The police need to get over there and... stop... Why are you all looking like that?"

The three worried looks above had all turned even more gravely serious.

"They had already found him when we called," Rose said.

Fear gripped my chest in an iron vice. Who had Nikola Vorak killed for them? My mind whirred at a sickening speed through the possibilities. Not my father—*please, no.* Please, not Ernie or Judd.

"Who?" I asked hoarsely.

"Nikola Vorak," Zoe said.

Well, that didn't make any sense to me. I didn't wish anyone dead, but if it had to be anyone... Of course, Nikola Vorak would not murder himself.

I sat up, fighting a minor bout of dizziness. "So, they're going to arrest the two not-hippies, right? And if they're in jail tonight, then there's no ritual. Job done."

"They can't," Rose said.

"They can't," Rodney agreed.

After another second of utter confusion, Sam put me out of my misery. *He took his own life.*

I looked over at the ghost and echoed his words out loud to the room. Then I followed up with, "Why?"

"I think that is what they meant," Rose said, "by it being Nikola's turn."

"And if someone takes their own life," Zoe said, "then the police will still be kept busy with that. Paperwork, working with the coroner. No time for investigating anything else today."

"But he wouldn't kill himself," I said. "Did he sound like a man ready to take his own life to any of you? What possible reason could he have? Surely, the police can see that."

Lennon and Janis probably killed him, Sam said. The amused look from before was gone. I could tell that, even if Nikola Vorak might have been in some way complicit in Sam's death, the ex-realtor was still cut up about his passing. *But that doesn't matter, not if they did a good enough job of making it look like suicide.*

"But John and Jessie are cleverer than that."

He left a note.

"A note doesn't prove anything."

It does when it says he couldn't live with his terminal diagnosis any longer.

"Terminal?"

Rose nodded. "Nikola confided in me a little over a week back. He traveled every week to a clinic in Orlando. The medical records will be there if the police request them."

"In a boat," Rodney said obscurely.

Zoe picked up his thread. "The story is that he rowed out to sea and shot himself. Witnesses heard the shot and, reportedly, he was the only one out there."

"Geez," I said, "how long was I out?"

"A bit over an hour," Zoe said. "Things moved quickly. I don't even know how they could have arranged everything so quickly and in daylight. But they did. Their magic is powerful."

I sat on the couch for a few minutes, trying to shake off the last dregs of fog from my brain and wrap my mind around Vorak's death. No one said anything as I processed everything that had happened since Sam went through the portal. Suddenly, another thought jumped into my mind.

"Hey, if I was out for an hour, why didn't anyone take me to the hospital?"

Zoe smiled at that. "You just needed time and a little of our energy to bring you back."

I might be back, but I felt like I had lost an argument with a train. My body was aching all over, and I felt tired beyond belief.

You saved me, Sam said. It wasn't a "thank you," merely a statement. *I owe you, Sidney Grace. Whatever you need. Except for being nice to you, of course. I have my limits.*

You're welcome.

Suddenly, Rose shoved another crystal ball into my hands. It was smaller than the one that had broken during Sam's spying. "If you're talking to Sam Barlow again, do us the kindness of asking him to put his hand on this. Then, we can all be involved."

I looked up and down between Rose and the crystal ball. "Uh... okay.

"But I can't believe they killed another of their own," I said. "I'm having a problem understanding why they would do that. Aren't they going to need the power of the whole coven for this ritual they are planning?"

Like I said, Sam said, *Nikola had a lot of money.* I noticed that his words now appeared in a smoky kind of writing within the crystal ball, flickering into existence a little like a magic eight ball. The others read what he was saying.

Sam nodded his approval and went on. *Maybe that made up for a lack of magical talent. They might not have ever needed him for the ritual.*

"So, what was Nikola Vorak getting out of this if he was going to die soon anyway?" I wondered.

"Not dying?" said Rodney, and it was a cunning insight. If Vorak had the money but not any true power, he could have made a deal with the coven in exchange for his life. In essence, maybe Vorak had paid them to heal him.

"We need to know exactly what this ritual is for," I said.

"Besides perhaps flooding our town. What's the purpose of doing this? Sink Mystic Dunes and claim the insurance money?"

As far as I know, Sam said, his words flowing against the inner surface of the ball. *Those two were not on the deeds. Nikola and I owned all the properties between us. Everyone else who moved in recently was set to buy their houses, but upon Nikola's insistence, we let them move straight in.*

"Wait a minute...are you saying that you never actually sold those properties? And why let everyone just move in without closing on the homes?"

We needed to gather the coven's power quickly, so it was best to allow them to move in prior to closing. But now that Nikola and I are... well, transformed into a new realm, as it were...I assume the closings will be handled by our attorney.

"Ha!" I exclaimed, pointing my finger in the air. "I knew you weren't *that* good a realtor."

Well, that was harsh, Sidney Grace, floated through the inside of the crystal ball.

I kinda deserved that.

"What about the library?" It was Zoe.

"What do you mean?" Rose asked.

"Sidney is right. We need to know more about the ritual they're planning and its purpose. If this has happened before near Crystal Beach, perhaps there is a historical record of it. Or, I don't know... something. Any idea of a deeper purpose for the ritual might help us defeat it. As it stands, we'll be hamstrung in any attempt to counter it magically because we only know bits and pieces of the plan. And I don't think that Sam will tell us. Maybe because he doesn't know the real plan, either?"

Clever doggy, Sam said, and I moved my hands to cover up the words before Zoe could see them. Then I glared at him.

Don't be... you know, you.

Moving on, I addressed the room, "There's not much time," I said. Being unconscious for an hour meant we were already into the afternoon.

"Then let's get the police in on this," Rose said. She waggled her finger at Zoe and me. "If either of you two ladies have any sway over the members of the Crystal Beach Police Department, now would be the time to make it pay off."

"You realize we've got a dead body in the locker at the police station?" John said as I met him outside the library on the eastern part of Citrus Way between the crossroads at the center of town and the sea, with a couple of palm trees to either side of the entrance. Jessie was there, too, and I had turned up with Zoe and the invisible Sam Barlow in tow. Rose and Rodney had stayed behind, as we still hoped Lennon and Janis didn't know they were involved in our efforts. It was best they stayed home and not be seen about town with us.

"It's a suicide, though, isn't it?" I replied.

John eyed Zoe for help. He had gleaned enough already to guess that we didn't think so. "Apparently," he grumbled, hating being one step behind.

"If you want a shot at catching—or at least stopping—the real killers and at saving Crystal Beach, then you need to help research any extensive flooding events near this town. Historical ones, possibly going back a long way."

Jessie came up and slapped John lightly on the arm. "Come on, Chief. Might as well go with it."

"I have a feeling that I'm already outnumbered here. If the town needs saving, duty calls." John said.

Inside, we all breezed past a shocked librarian who had probably never had so many people in the library at one time. John waved a hand at her and said something about "police business... don't mind us."

All the local historical records and documents were at the back and smelled mustier than any other part of the library. It included microfiche access to the *Crystal Beach Times*, the local town newspaper that now only ran in an online version.

"Do we even know where to start?" John asked.

"Anything that could reference a historic flood or have a title related to the history of this area would be best," Zoe suggested.

It was amazing how much mind-numbing information one town could be responsible for. And it was all collected here, at the back of a single-story building that currently had nobody else in it but us.

Maps, directories, tax records—it was like history intention-ally didn't want those with a low attention span poking around in it. Eventually, I gave in to temptation and crossed over to the microfiche reader.

I didn't know if the *Crystal Beach Times* would go far enough back for our purposes, but I was feeling drained by the effort of pulling Sam's ghost to safety through the portal earlier, and the silence in the library was trying to put me to sleep. The one time I had worked a microfiche reader as a kid in Boston had been exciting—the canister of tiny film, like something out of a spy movie, blown up to a much larger size in a magical box in front of me. Maybe it would have some of the same "wow factor" as an adult.

Impressively, the earliest editions of the newspaper on record went back to the early nineteen-twenties, which, I quickly learned, was shortly after the founding of the town. Remembering Admiral Avery's flashback to the tsunami that wiped out the settlement close to Mystic Dunes, I was sure the cataclysm must have happened before then. Nineteenth century, more likely. Maybe even early in that century.

So if the town named "Crystal Beach" had not existed until the nineteen-twenties, then whatever was here before would have had a different name. Perhaps the earliest editions of the *Times* newspaper might mention that, at least.

There was nothing of interest at first, and I drifted into the nineteen-thirties, wondering when it might be time to give up on the newspaper research. Then I found an article covering the celebrations for the town's tenth anniversary.

Scanning through it, there was still no hint of any previous settlement or cataclysmic events, but I did see something else about halfway down the page.

I turned to the closest person, who happened to be John. "Hey, come look at this."

John came over, and I pointed to a picture taken in a familiar part of the town where some buildings I recognized were the same ones still standing today. It was just off the crossroads in the center of town, an area where the sidewalk was wide and markets were held.

In the picture, people had gathered for the anniversary celebrations, and about a dozen had posed for a photo in front of a stage covered in garland. I pointed to two people at one end of it. "See those two?"

They were a man and a woman, both smartly dressed. But their clothes made them look out of place, like they belonged to a time at least thirty years before the picture was taken.

The other women in the picture mainly wore simple hats of varying kinds, and several had furs draped around their shoulders, long necklaces that almost hung down to their waist, and high-heeled shoes. Many of the men wore fedoras; some were in dungarees, and others were in snappy suits with the tight cut of the time.

John said it before I even had a chance to point it out. "They stand out from the crowd."

"They sure do."

The woman wore a dress pulled in at the waist that splayed out and fell to cover all but the very end of what looked like booted feet. The hat she wore was wide and flat. The man's suit fell longer at the back, and he wore a top hat, too.

"Out of their time," I added.

John looked at me, puzzled.

Zoe, who had been working nearby—between hushed, excitable conversations with Jessie—stopped to look over our shoulders.

"Oh my," she said. "Is that...?"

"Yep," I said.

"Who?" John asked, getting impatient.

"It's Lennon and Janis," Zoe said.

"Who?" John repeated.

"The neighbors of the dead man you pulled off a boat less than two hours ago," I told him.

John did a sort of double take, looking back and forth between me, Zoe, and the screen.

"Yes, it's them," Zoe confirmed before John had a chance to protest about how crazy that sounded.

I spun to the top of the newspaper and the date of printing, which was in 1935.

"That's nearly ninety years ago," John said.

Noticing the rest of us gathered around the microfiche, Jessie came over, too, just as I spun down to the picture again.

She tapped the screen. "They look familiar."

"Mystic Dunes?" Zoe said.

"Yeah. Like the hippie-looking couple that lives there. Straight out of the sixties, those two. Just moved in. So, what's this, some sort of dress-up history event?"

"No," I said. "It's a newspaper article from the nineteen-thirties." I looked pointedly at John.

He always got there in the end. "How's this possible?" he asked. "They look just the same. If this photo is accurate to the time, they would have to be a hundred and twenty years old now, or close to it."

"Oh," Jessie said. "They definitely looked younger than that."

"Ancestors, perhaps?" John tried.

"Both of them?" I said doubtfully. "Seriously, except for the clothes, they look just the same."

"That's it!" Zoe exclaimed, snapping her fingers. "That's what this is all about. This ritual of theirs."

I got what Zoe was trying to say. I just wasn't sure I believed it. "Prolonging life? Immortality? No way."

"Yes, way," she insisted. "Life for life. They organize a catastrophic event above a nexus of power, and the spell or the ritual channels the life forces of those they take. That's how they are able to prolong their own lives. It's dark, difficult stuff, and it needs incredible power to do it, not to mention a handy way to kill a lot of people at one time. But that's what Mystic Dunes is. It's a nexus of power right beside a way to take a lot of lives at one time with a giant wave."

"So, Lennon and Janis have been here before, you're saying?" I tried to wrap my head around the magnitude of what Zoe was explaining. "So, they organized the last tsunami that wiped out the settlement that was here before Crystal Beach?"

Zoe nodded. "And that bought them... maybe two hundred extra years of life."

I shivered. "How old do you think they are?"

Zoe tapped at the screen and the picture of the town's ten-year party. "And when a new town sprung up next to their magical nexus, they probably came back to ensure no one built on the ground they needed. Although looking like this and never aging, I guess they had to leave at some point and return to avoid suspicion and scrutiny."

"And then," I carried on, "they started running out of years. Or they just saw a new conjunction coming and decided it was time to renew their magical life force."

Nikola Vorak actually came to me as soon as I had bought the land at Mystic Dunes several years back, Sam said. He had been sitting quietly through all this, looking mostly bored while the rest of us researched.

"Nikola Vorak was sent to invest as soon as Sam bought the land," I said for the others' benefit, then turned to Sam. "Was that around the same time when the coven began?"

Sam nodded.

"He says yes."

John and Jessie looked confused until Zoe explained. "She's talking to Sam Barlow's ghost." To be fair, they still looked confused after that.

"So they've been planning this all along," I said, "but they had to maintain a presence here, have influence. As soon as someone bought that land like Sam did, they got their representative, Nikola Vorak, to put a large financial stake into its development."

"Nikola Vorak," Zoe said, "who I bet the coven promised eternal life, safe from the illness that was killing him."

So Rodney wasn't too far off. Nikola Vorak had likely done this in order to be cured and continue living.

"Oh well," I added. "At least now we know what they're up to. And what we are up against. I think it's time we bring the big guns in on this."

I took out my cell phone.

"Big guns?" John asked.

Bless his heart, he thought that he and Jessie were the "big guns."

"Ada-Mae and the Shifting Sands crew, of course."

CHAPTER
SIX

"Okay," Ada-Mae said after looking thoughtful for several agonizing moments. "I think we could bind the ritual once it has started to stop it from reaching a conclusion."

This was encouraging. I mean, Ada-Mae didn't sound one hundred percent like her normal "this will be easy" confident self, but it looked like her mind was ticking it over, working on the problem. That always gave me hope.

We had felt the power that Lennon and Janis could summon when Sam's ghost had been caught in their grasp. They were likely at least two hundred years old, maybe much older. I could not imagine the experience of all those years using magic. The knowledge they must have, the second-nature familiarity with having it flowing through your body.

The idea of going up against that scared me, but Ada-Mae seemed to think that our knowledge of the coming ritual—assuming we had surmised correctly—gave us an advantage in countering it.

Zoe, Jessie, John, and I met the others at the Kelp Seafood Grill. Everyone was there: Ernie, Judd, Wendy Howie, and my mom and dad, who were sitting right next to each other. Having joined two tables together, we were all eating a late lunch. Eileen buzzed around us like she sensed something important was afoot. No one had even ordered anything, yet food kept turning up on the table until we had a feast laid out before us.

There was bread with olive oil and balsamic vinegar, plus hummus and pita to start with. Then, a tray of cornbread and cheesy grits appeared. At the same time, a great bucket of prawns in a lime and chili dressing was placed in the middle of the table, followed by crab sandwiches in a secret sauce of Eileen's own devising.

Despite the lurking presence of danger for Crystal Beach and the daunting confrontation to come, the food and the company lifted everyone's spirits. Judd was laughing at something Howie said. My mom and dad kept slipping into a private conversation, and just down the table from me, I saw Jessie's hand slip across to cover Zoe's, and the magic shop owner-slash-shifter smiled and blushed.

My own feelings in this moment were two-fold. On the one hand, I had never felt more at home in my life. These were *my* people, the ones sitting around this table. I could not have been anywhere in that moment that would have been more perfect for me. On the other hand, all of them were in terrible danger. And I knew that before the end of this day, it would fall to me to save them.

This is what I was being prepared for, perhaps the real reason I was here.

Ada-Mae's pragmatic presence was reassuring, and I was not the only one with power around this table. Every one of them could play a part. Yet before this was over, I knew it was my power that would be tested. And, in a strange way, that made me feel alone, even among all my favorite people.

For the first time, I was at peace with that. And with my responsibilities. Not because I had suddenly accepted full confidence in my abilities. Not because I knew I could beat Janis and Lennon for sure. I really didn't. But because I loved these people, and I loved this town, there was no room for doubt or questions. At some point, when love leaves you with no choice, it stops being about the weight of responsibility. It just is. Nothing in the world is more freeing than that. The knowledge that you will give your all and won't let anyone down. It will either be enough, or it won't.

"We'll need to make some preparations. The more we can anticipate and cast some early spells, the better," Ada-Mae went on. "Plus, if we have Rose and Rodney on the inside, that can make all the difference. I can instruct them to work against the ritual at the right point. They could even be a conduit into the circle for us. Also, we'll need to be close to the location. But that will be difficult if all the homes are occupied."

"Nikola Vorak's is not," John said, sounding apologetic. Yes, maybe it was in poor taste, but we were past sensitivity right now.

"That may be too close," Ada-Mae said. "We don't want them to sense us coming." She stopped and rubbed her chin. "Actually, that is a problem, now that I think about it. What if they can sense our pre-cast spells? I don't know their sensitivity, especially as old as they are. So I don't know how far away they can sense what we're up to. We do not want to give them any heads-up. This plan will only work if it has at least some element of surprise."

"Actually, I might be able to help with that one," I said, then turned to John. "Could you give me a ride in the police boat as soon we're done here?"

Before John could answer, his cell phone buzzed. "Ugh," he said, looking at it. "Coroner's here. I'll—"

Jessie put out a hand to stop him as he rose. "It's good, Chief. I've got this." She grabbed another crab sandwich. "I'll come find you when we're done."

With one last smile at Zoe, Jessie vanished with a wave to Eileen, who was returning with a bowl of mussels in garlic butter.

"Why don't you have some police activity at Mystic Dunes tonight? That would be a valid excuse to be there," Eileen suggested to John.

"It's a good point," Ada-Mae said. "Any distraction could help. After they discovered Sam's ghost earlier, they will likely be anticipating some sort of interruption. We should give them one. Just the wrong one."

"I'll help," my dad said. He looked over at John with a wry smile. "I could break in, and you could come to arrest me. That's a good reason for you to be at Mystic Dunes."

I wasn't sure whether he was joking, but either way, it was good that everyone wanted to contribute. Even Eileen, who appeared to have caught much of what was happening, oddly did not seem phased by any of it.

"Count me in, too," Eileen said.

"It will be dangerous," I warned her. "There's—"

"Magic stuff happening? Evil sorcerers, or whatever?" She rolled her eyes. "I know, Sidney. I see and hear what you all get up to. I noticed Julia-Mae and her stunning golf skills and all the other strange things and murders that go on in Crystal Beach."

She looked at John. "And I'm guessing Mr. Vorak's death this morning wasn't a suicide?"

John's reply was a shocked silence.

"You all come here and discuss what you're doing over Lobster Thermidor. *Of course,* I know what's going on in my town. So I want in."

Several of us just sort of shrugged and nodded.

"Good," she said. "Then lunch is on the house."

John and I walked pretty much directly down the street from the Kelp Seafood Grill to where the Crystal Beach Police Department's boat was kept, just behind the beach.

"It's not really the police department's boat," John said as we reached it, and he pulled a tarpaulin weighed down with concrete blocks off. "It's my boat, but seeing as I'm basically always on duty, it's kind of the police boat, too."

The boat was a white, wooden, open-topped vessel with both oars and a small outboard motor on the back. Not the kind of sleek fiberglass thing with a steering wheel at the front and a handy digital navigation screen, like most police departments by the water would have. Still, it would do the job for us.

"Does it get a lot of use?" I asked.

"I try to come out in it once a week," John answered.

"To fish?"

John shook his head. "I'm a terrible fisherman. Just to sit, really. It's quiet out there. I have a beer and listen to the sound of the water lapping against the side of the boat. It kind of... resets my mind."

I smiled. "The sound of the waves breaking on the shore does that for me. I can get lost in that for hours."

Stepping down into the boat, John turned and offered his hand to help me get safely inside. When I grasped his hand, I felt a warmth rush through me that left my hands and feet tingling. I paused, perhaps a moment too long, before I allowed myself to release his hand.

"So, you're not leaving us anytime soon?" John asked as we both took a seat in the boat.

I was a little wary of the question, even though he asked it in an innocent way.

"Of course not," I said. "I mean, everyone I care about is here right now."

"But your mom and dad probably won't stay, no?"

I didn't know the answer to that. They both had lives—separate lives—in the north and had only come down this time for Ada-Mae's birthday. Yet Crystal Beach had a way of pulling you in and, if I wasn't mistaken—or being too hopeful—it seemed to be pulling them toward each other as well.

"I'm not sure I would want to leave Ada-Mae," I said eventually. Which was true on a purely personal level but also because she was my connection to the world of magic. Then there was Zoe. Having found out about her lycanthropy and the fact that I might be able to help her live a more "normal" life with it, how could I leave and go back to Boston?

"It's funny to think," John called now over the sound of the motor he had just started up, "that you only came down here from Boston to get Ada-Mae out of jail after I arrested her on suspicion of murder."

"And she's not the only member of my family you've done that with," I chastised him with a smile.

"In fact, I arrested you the first time we met." He laughed, seeming far too proud of that fact.

We headed south, just off the coast, toward the area of Mystic Dunes at the southernmost extent of our coastal town. We were silent for a few minutes with the sense of an unfinished conversation between us. One that had faltered and didn't know whether it should continue.

"I think I belong here," I said suddenly, the words surprising me like I hadn't known they were coming. "I don't think I can leave now. The sea, the sand, and all of Crystal Beach. I belong to them. I know I'd be miserable if I went back to the city."

John didn't say anything for a long moment. A tiny smile seemed like it was playing about his lips, and he looked ahead, one hand behind him to steer the boat. He didn't even look at me when he finally spoke one word. "Good."

"Stay close to the shore," I said a few minutes later as we crossed the mouth of the small creek that ran near the northern edge of Mystic Dunes. "It would be best if no one sees us hanging around."

While a strip of golden sand fronted the rest of Crystal Beach, Mystic Dunes—as the name suggests—was mostly fronted by a large hump of sandy, grassy dunes that seemed primed to fall away into the sea in chunks. A boat as small as the one we were in, staying close to the shore, would be just about hidden from the houses by the largest dune.

John killed the engine once we were in place and took out some oars to keep us roughly in the same spot.

"So, what's this help we're looking for?" he asked.

In answer, I turned and leaned a little over the side of the boat. "Admiral," I called, "are you there?"

"Does your world ever become, like, normal to you?" John

421

asked with a wink. "It's just you never stop surprising me, Sidney Grace."

I glanced back over to him.

"Is it really as wondrous and magical and, I don't know... like a children's Christmas movie as it looks?"

I looked back down at the water. "The children's movies usually have a little less murder and apocalypse in them."

"You know what I mean."

I stared at the ripples in the water. Thousands and maybe millions of them stretched out into the endless ocean. "I've felt scared and out of my depth a lot since I've been here," I admitted. "But yeah. It's like I wasn't even seeing half of the world before I came here."

"I'm jealous and not sure I'll ever get it at the same time," John said. "My world evolves around order. On right and wrong and... certainty. I'm scared of anything beyond that."

Well, that was one for the record books—Chief John Reece admitting to being scared.

I reached out a finger and touched the coolness of the water. I turned a slow circle with it while the sun sparkled off its surface in a myriad of angled reflections, and a slight breeze tickled the hairs on the back of my neck. "Chaos is beautiful," I said. "It's connection. One day, you'll see that."

Then I saw him, a familiar old face beaming up at me from below the surface. "We need your help," I said down into the water. "Can we come down?"

We?

"Me and John. I brought the chief of police." I turned back to John.

"What do you mean by 'come down?'" he asked nervously.

"You're going to love this," I said. "It's like something out of a children's Christmas movie."

CHAPTER
SEVEN

With John's and my trip to visit Admiral Avery completed, I was now working on the next phase of our plan. I knew John was still processing his adventure, and I was sure we would be having another lengthy conversation about it in the coming days. It wasn't every day that he found himself deep underwater with no breathing apparatus.

Plus, having the admiral bring us down to his realm enabled the ghostly specter to be revealed to his guests. The expression on John's face of shock and panic that was quickly replaced by awe as Admiral Avery's ghost floated over and patted him on the back with a guffaw so big it rippled the water shell around us... was priceless.

The sun was hanging low over Crystal Beach as Zoe and I sat down on the sand behind the retirement complex. The orange glow played across the water, and the evening seemed serene— not at all like the fate of this little seaside town, which could be decided in the next few hours.

We were sitting cross legged opposite each other. Behind Zoe, the moon was already up, its glow increasing as the day's light faded. Zoe put her hands in mine. I could see they were trembling slightly, and once I took hold of them, I could feel the great tension within her. It was a terrible strain to hold herself in check with the moon where it was—just the other side of full, although that would only be noticeable to the keenest eye. Somewhere beyond it, planets and other celestial bodies were lining up unseen, creating a rare gravitational alignment that could be tapped into by those who knew how.

"Breathe," I said to her. "Just breathe and look at me. Let me take your strain. Place it within me and store it there."

As we had already connected in a similar way at her apartment—although Zoe was already a lot more wolfish then—I felt the supernatural energy that governed her change flow into me with surprising ease. Like it was keen to find another vessel to inhabit. I had already gone through a rather exhausting day, including a battle with two magic users who were hundreds of years old and using a lot of brain power in researching and planning our next moves.

Maybe my body didn't need this extra strain, but somehow it kept going. Adrenaline and the knowledge that this would all be over soon enough provided me with the fuel I needed.

"Turn around," I said. "Look at it."

Zoe's eyes looked uncertain. Through our connection, I could feel the weight of its invisible rays on her back. She turned, trembling, and looked at it for a moment, then turned back to me again. Her eyes had turned that animal yellow.

"Now," I said. "I'm going to give a little of it back to you. The point of this is not to keep the wolf at bay; it's about being in charge of it."

Zoe grinned weakly at me, then spoke in small gasps. "You're... good at this... you know."

I let a little flow back toward her while Ada-Mae and the others passed us, loading things onto John's boat down on the jetty. It was going to be a tight squeeze on that little boat.

Zoe's face changed, forming to accommodate those growing incisors and, of course, becoming a lot hairier.

"More?" I asked. "Can you take more and still stay in control?"

Zoe nodded bravely, and I let more of it flow back into her. She gasped and cried out slightly, bringing interested—and possibly nervous—glances from the rest of our party moving down the beach. The clothes on her back started to stretch, and that was when I pulled that wild energy back in toward me to save her wardrobe. Well, for now, at least. Rather than becoming more tired by the experience of our ritual together, I actually felt invigorated by the incredible power I had been holding onto.

I didn't know where the power came from that created a shifter like Zoe—I wasn't sure if Zoe even knew—but there was a raw purity to it that was both breathtaking and terrifying. I was impressed with myself, with my power to contain it, and I also understood why Zoe was so afraid of it.

"Can you keep it up while we do this spell?" Zoe asked.

Although I felt what was inside me pushing and testing the new cage that now contained it, I nodded, feeling that I could do it. Arrogant, perhaps, considering the tests that might yet lie ahead.

"When the time comes," I said, "you could be our secret weapon."

Zoe did not look so sure. "I don't want to hurt anyone. Especially not someone I love."

"You won't," I said, at least half believing it. "Not while I'm here."

We both stood up, and although we were no longer touching, I could still feel the connection between us that was helping to keep Zoe's lycanthropy in check. The others were waiting for us on the jetty. John was talking to Judd, who was sitting at the rear next to the outboard motor. "Take it easy with the motor, okay? It's a little sensitive."

"Hey!" Judd said, pretending to look offended. "I did pilot a space shuttle, you know."

My mom and dad were saying their goodbyes, as were Ernie and Ada-Mae and Howie and Wendy. I couldn't help but notice how long Jacob and Julia-Mae's fingertips lingered against each other before finally, reluctantly, sliding apart.

John and I awkwardly shook hands and reassuringly clamped shoulders for a moment before he joined Jessie, Eileen, Ernie, Wendy, and my dad. They started heading back toward Shifting Sands to begin their part of the plan to stage a fake break-in at #1 Mystic Dunes. My heart instantly rued the missed opportunity to embrace John as he moved away. Maybe it was wishful thinking, but I saw a longing in his eyes, too, as he turned to look over his shoulder at me before heading further down the beach.

That left me, Ada-Mae in her shawl of many things, Howie, Judd, Julia-Mae, and Zoe in the boat. It was crowded with all our magical paraphernalia in it as well. Sam Barlow was absent, though his ghost wouldn't have occupied any room. But barely holding onto his spectral form since being attacked when he was spying earlier in the day, he was going to have to sit this one out.

"Let's lift off then, spaceman," Ada-Mae said. Then, she added, "I think Ernie would have liked to say that."

"It's okay," Judd said. "He says something similar every time we go out in my little car together. Plus, I've promised him we can go flying if we're all alive tomorrow. I've got a buddy who owes me."

"Wait!" I cried out, spotting a small shape dashing down the beach toward us.

I was a little late, though, and the boat was already drifting away from the jetty.

Mojo reached the jetty and didn't even break stride, leaping from the end of it and straight into my waiting arms.

I'm glad you caught me, he said. *I can't believe you were off to fight evil without me.*

BELOW THE BOAT, the water opened up, the small craft bobbing about as the parted seawater passed beneath it. An area of the sea floor was revealed, although only faintly visible in the moonlight that had now almost completely replaced the light of the day.

The others would have been able to see some hints of the previous occupation if they looked closely—much-rotted bits of timber, an encrusted pewter tankard—but I could see something more like the bar that Admiral Avery's business would have been before it was wiped away by a tsunami, and him with it.

Finally, the boat slid down the face of the retreating water to land a little bumpily on the sea floor before water flowed back again above us, sealing everyone into a large rectangular open space below the waves. Just as I had done for John, I cast a spell to allow everyone in the boat to see and experience my new friend, the old seafaring specter.

"Thank you for doing this," I told Admiral Avery, who was dressed in his flashy yet regal-looking purple coat with gold embroidery and a matching tricorn hat with a brass telescope for the perfect accessory. Behind me, my poor mother was having a minor panic attack, calmed by Zoe. At the same time, Howie kept sticking his fingers in and out of the wall of water to one side, examining his fingers and saying, "Wow, man. Trippy."

John's reaction earlier in the day had been somewhere between those two extremes, and he hadn't stopped smiling for about an hour afterward.

Aye, no trouble, lass, Admiral Avery replied. *This is a reckoning that's been too long in coming. So happy to help, I am.* He looked over at my mom. *Be that lady okay?*

My mom realized the Admiral was talking to her, and she nodded, holding up Zoe's hand in hers to let us know she was okay.

"Let's get set up, then," Ada-Mae said, who was doing a good job of keeping the wonder out of her own eyes, although I knew her well enough by now.

She touched my arm as we grabbed the spell supplies from the boat. "This is perfect, dear. Well done. We can do all our preparation and casting safe from detection until it's already too late for them to stop us."

"And Rose and Rodney are ready to do their part?" I asked.

Ada-Mae's expression grew more serious. "They are. I called Rose before I left my apartment. She's terrified, the poor woman. They will be in the lion's den through all of this. We can't completely rely on them."

"We can't?"

"They will do their best," Ada-Mae explained, "but there are too many variables between us and them. We have to be prepared for the possibility that they cannot aid us in the way we hope."

I nodded my agreement. Rose and Rodney were not the only uncertain variables. Still, there was not much point in worrying about that now.

Soon, the circle was cast on the ocean floor, not more than a hundred yards from Mystic Dunes. Even Mojo sat down to take his place in the circle. I hadn't really thought before about how "magical" a cat might or might not be. I had always thought that my ability to talk with him was all about my own power, yet wasn't there just something about cats, like they always knew more than they were letting on?

My phone buzzed, and it made us all jump. It was so unexpected to hear it beneath the waves. But through some act of magic, the signal was okay here, apparently, even under the water. I looked at the text message and then at the others.

"This is it," I said. "They're starting the break-in."

CHAPTER

EIGHT

I looked at Ada-Mae. "Anything yet? Can you sense the ritual?"

She shook her head. I could see the worry there. "Nothing yet."

I glanced up at the water above our heads. Was it me, or had it gotten choppier up there?

"Can we just start our spell, anyway?"

I already knew the answer to that, but the panic inside me needed Ada-Mae to answer.

"We have to time it," she said. "If there's nothing to bind when the spell reaches its conclusion, then we miss our chance."

"But shouldn't we just be able to sense a spell this powerful? They must have started by now."

"I can only guess that they are masking it."

"But we know where they are doing it, though. It has to be at number two, right?" I posed. "Can we not just target that address?"

All of us around the circle looked at each other, the air of concern and panic growing between us as we sat quietly and motionless in our oblong cocoon under the sea. Had I been less tense, I might have let myself enjoy the extraordinary sight of the ceremonial candles burning, surrounded by water on all sides.

I looked for Admiral Avery, who was standing behind the combined remains and spectral image of his centuries-old bar as if waiting for patrons who would never come.

"Can you sense it, Admiral?" I called out to him. As a ghost, he was also an impressive spellcaster, so maybe he could feel this powerful ritual, even if Lennon and Janis were trying to hide it.

I can't, lass, he said, coming out from behind his bar. He walked around the edge of the cleared underwater space he had made for us, ghostly fingers gliding with no effect through the vertical surface of the water, like it was the wall of a prison. In some ways, maybe it was, as I had never seen the admiral on actual, proper land, only floating above the ocean.

My phone rang, and I looked down to see that John was calling me.

"Yeah?"

"They're not here," he said.

"What do you mean?"

"We followed the plan. Eileen, Ernie, and your dad broke into number one like the most unlikely bunch of burglars I've ever seen. Jessie and I turned up, making as much noise as possible. Then we knocked on number two, trying to disturb the ritual by looking for a missing septuagenarian burglar, just like you said. There was no answer, though, and it's all dark in there."

"Maybe they're hiding in there somewhere. I mean, you went inside, yes?"

"Officially, no," John answered. "But yes, of course we did. I'm telling you, no one is inside either #1 or #2 Mystic Dunes."

"Okay." My mind raced. "Can you keep looking?"

"We'll try. But the whole development looks dead, to be honest. And the weather up here... It feels like a massive storm is brewing."

"Right... thanks."

I cut the call and looked at Ada-Mae, then at everyone else around our circle, a sinking feeling pulling me down into the seabed. This was bad. Had Lennon and Janis outsmarted us somehow?

"It's already happening, isn't it?" Ada-Mae said. "And John can't find them."

I didn't reply. What could I say? Things were feeling out of control. Hopeless.

"They have to be somewhere," my mom said.

Already, I was letting myself think about what would happen when the wave hit. Would we be safe down here? Would the Admiral's magic stand up to it? Could we get the others over to us and inside to safety in time? But I could not think like that. Crystal Beach needed us—needed me—and we had to fight to try and save the town up until the very end.

"I'll go."

I looked around, and it was Zoe speaking. "Let go of your control on me. Let me shift. When I'm like that, it's like all my senses are maxed out. Including my magical ones. I might be able to find them."

I looked over at Ada-Mae, who nodded her agreement to the plan.

Zoe stood up and crossed over to me, taking my hands and placing them on her temples before she spoke an incantation. "The hexing sight, be in me. Close your eyes, Sidney Grace, and you will see the way I see." Then Zoe stood up straight again. "I don't know how it will work when I'm a wolf, but it's worth a try.

"Now, let me go, Sidney. Let me become what the moon wants me to be."

I was completely lost. "How will what work?"

"Close your eyes, Sidney."

I did as Zoe asked, closing my eyes, and was surprised to find that, rather than darkness, I could see myself. Or, more accurately, I could see what Zoe was seeing as she looked down at me. In fact, I could also feel some of what she was feeling—maybe that was a legacy of my connection to Zoe as I held onto what the moon evoked within her. In particular, I felt her fear of being set free as the wolf in Crystal Beach. But she knew she had to let herself shift. It was an act of bravery, and I felt a swell of affection for her in that moment.

"It's okay," I said. I'll still help you keep some control."

I did not know how well I could do that, especially as she got further from me.

Zoe moved to jump into the water, but Admiral Avery instead opened a path for her back to the shore. Halfway along it, I released some of that wild, shifter energy that I had been holding onto back toward Zoe. Just as the water path closed behind her, we all saw the woman morph into the creature. Then I closed my eyes.

THE WOLF COULD SMELL the magic, even though they tried to hide it. It could smell power, which was, in its way, like the magic that brought the wolf forward every time the moon called to it. Contrary to the popular idea of the shifter, the wolf did not lie dormant for almost all of every lunar cycle. Perhaps for those days when the moon was a mere sliver, when the wild call was its weakest, the wolf slept, but it was always there. Waiting. It was during the nights when the moon was at and around its fullest that the host could not resist the call of the wild. When the wolf could not be held back.

Yet, even now, even as it slipped sleek and deadly across the dunes, the wolf could feel the invisible leash around its neck. And it resented it. The same restraint that had helped to keep it at bay the previous evening until it was trapped in its cage. That hated prison.

The body that contained the power of the wolf and this other force working to keep it restricted, to try and tame it. It was a strong female presence that was linked tightly with the host. But the wolf could be patient. Until the opportunity arose when it would have no other option but to seize the moment.

For now, though, it did as asked and followed that vague scent of power as angry clouds boiled up, standing out against the darkness above them.

Soon, it turned away from the houses, the soulless structures shaped from cold iron, man-made stone, and dead wood. Turning inland from the dunes, the going became softer underfoot. Then, moments later, its paws moved through water.

The wolf recognized marshland—a small bayou it had found once before on its wanderings before the host had built the cage to keep it home when the moon was full. This was not the wolf's preferred terrain, as other predators operated here, yet this was the way to the growing source of magical power. So it continued on... like the host and interloper wanted.

At the back of its mind, however, was the idea that when it found that power, it could take a little for itself and use that to break the restraints that held it—

I can hear everything you're thinking, you know, came a voice in the wolf's head.

Bah, it was the one who helped to bind it. Sidney Grace. The one it had left behind in the unnatural space under the sea. In its wolfish ways, it mentally thumbed its nose at the intruder, and grumbling, it continued on through the brackish water and over-grown vegetation.

Even in the darkness, it could feel the presence of life every-where around it. The wolf could feel the intruder's astonishment at the sharpness of its senses and the assault of the sights, sounds, and smells. The beauty of the night. She should be impressed, it thought to itself.

Ahead now, a faint glow hung above the reeds and grasses. The wolf did not perceive colors in the same way as its human host or its erstwhile jailer. Still, a dull red glow grew brighter as the wolf got closer, the reeds finally parting enough to show the slightest rise in the middle of the bayou. A small island, currently full of people.

The wolf was distracted when a large shape moved through the water to investigate its presence. Long, ancient, and reptilian, it was the apex predator of this piece of marshland, yet it shied away upon seeing the wolf.

Wise choice, it thought. *I am no one's food. Try those slow, squishy ones up on the hill there.*

But turning back to look at the small island, the wolf under-stood that they would not be a meal for the alligator this evening, either. The red glow was a barely visible wall that surrounded the island, keeping everything else out but also keeping the telltale traces of power in, invisible to all but the keen sense of the wolf. The wolf sensed the protective barrier would stay in place until their disastrous deed was done, and it was too late to stop them.

CHAPTER
NINE

I opened my eyes. "She's found them. Zoe's found them. They are some ways south of Mystic Dunes, on a tiny island in the middle of the bayou. It looks like they've used some sort of shrouding spell to keep themselves undetected."

"How far?" Ada-Mae asked. "They can't be too far from Mystic Dunes if they hope to draw on the nexus of power."

I closed my eyes again. "Quarter mile, maybe."

Ada-Mae was slowly nodding her head when I opened them. "Impressive," she said. "If they can pull this ritual off that far from the nexus."

"Too far?" I asked, alarmed. We were at least another hundred meters further from them than that. Maybe more, as we had set up just off the shore toward the northern end of Mystic Dunes.

Ada-Mae let out a long breath as the rest of us—and Admiral Avery—watched with bated breath for her reaction to this new problem. Perhaps, a little unexpectedly, she smiled.

"I guess we'll find out," she said. "It's too late to move our setup now, anyway. Let's do this."

She quickly looked across the four of us gathered around the circle with her. In that moment, Ada-Mae looked as regal and powerful as she possibly could—and so unlike the woman who used to feed me chocolate and coconut cookies when I visited her as a little girl in Boston. Yet, she *was* still my grandmother.

Glancing across at Julia-Mae, I thought my mom, her daughter, might be having similar thoughts. An aura seemed to have grown around Ada-Mae, like she had pulled some of the available light from the candles and gathered it to her. She was part of a great magical tradition, and she was here to stand up for good and defeat the evil that threatened her family, her home, and her town.

"Everyone," she said. "Concentrate on releasing the energy stored up within your focus objects. Do it gently and release the power into the middle of the circle. We are creating a center of power that Sidney and I will focus on and send to bind the ritual.

"Once you're done, Julia-Mae, Judd, and Howie must maintain the integrity of the circle. Keep it up, keep it protecting us, and be prepared for pushback from the ritual circle in the marsh once our binding spell hits it."

I could see the faces of the other three, their feelings clearly visible across their features. All three were scared they might not be enough for this moment, especially my poor mother, who was the newest to the idea that she might have power, that she could control something unseen and previously unknown. But witch-craft ran strong and untainted through the women in our family. I knew she could do it, and when our eyes met, I let her know I had full faith in her abilities.

But I had my own job to concentrate on. The plan had been for Zoe to join Ada-Mae and me in shaping the circle's power before sending it to bind the other ritual just ahead of its completion. Now, there was only the two of us, and seeing Ada-Mae's look at the moment before the pre-cast spells on the focus objects were released, I knew that she expected me to take up the slack for Zoe. Everything I had learned until now, every attempt to shape and control my power... all of it led to this.

I closed my eyes to concentrate but found I was still connected to Zoe and the wolf. She stood hidden among the tall grass, still in control of her actions and hoping that she could help in some way. However, she could not physically enter the circle while the protective barrier stood around it. Then, as Ada-Mae and I readied to shape our own spell, I knew all we needed to do was contain the magic within that barrier.

Through the connection, I could see several dozen figures in hooded cloaks standing on the small island—most likely all the residents of Mystic Dunes, along with Rose and Rodney Gantz. And perhaps there were others.

If we were right about this ritual, all but Rose and Rodney— and Lennon and Janis—were unaware of the fact that they were among the intended victims here. All their lives would go to feeding the continued existence of those who had secretly set up the coven for this ultimate purpose. Their deaths and the end of Crystal Beach would be the price for perhaps another two hundred years of life granted to the coven's leaders.

We could not allow that.

"Let's go."

I wasn't sure if I had said it or only mouthed it, but Ada-Mae and I joined our powers to shape the great swirling mass of energy in the spell circle into a tight ball of intention. I could not see it, as I kept my eyes closed, my link to Zoe in her wolf form unexpectedly the perfect way to send the spell toward its intended target. She was like the special forces team who "painted" the target for the precision-guided missile to hit it.

Strange-colored lightning flashed horizontally across the sky above the ocean just as I felt we had gathered all the energy together as tightly as we could. In the moment before we sent it, I could feel two figures within the great circle on the island beginning to work against the dark ritual. They tried to open it up, to interfere with its rhythm, so that it might be vulnerable to our coming spell. I knew it had to be Rose and Rodney Gantz.

I didn't know how, within that circle, our allies could possibly sense us coming.

When our spell launched, physically searing its way out of the water like a rocket blasting off toward its target, I suddenly had a disturbing thought cross my mind. *If Rose and Rodney know we are coming, then do the others know it, too?*

Yes, came the voices of Lennon and Janis directly into my head at once. *Of course, we know.*

With all our power, Ada-Mae and I brought the glowing ball of our spell down on the island in the middle of the bayou. It burst against the pulsing red dome of the protection spell, glimmers of golden light sparking and then spreading out across the red shield.

That was okay, though. That was just fine. This was a binding spell, so all it had to do was contain their magic and stop their spell from coming to fruition for long enough for it to collapse in on itself.

For the first time, I considered the implications for those inside it. For Rose and Rodney, and also for the residents of Mystic Dunes who did not know what the ritual was really meant to do. The protective barrier had been unexpected, but maybe we should have thought of it because now all of them were trapped inside with the consequences of whatever happened when that spell failed to be properly cast.

And I did not know what that would be. Maybe a disappointing sputter like a failed firework. Maybe something much more terrible.

Nice of you to worry about them, came the dual voices of the two evil witches again in my head. *But that isn't going to be a problem.*

I watched through Zoe's animal eyes and saw the glowing white-golden energy of our binding spell begin to thin and fade, some of it sliding from the surface of the dim red dome of the protection spell, fizzing into the waters of the bayou.

"No!" I cried out, sending out my intention, seeing if there was anything left in me to prop up the binding spell, to keep it in place a little longer.

I was too far away, though, and could only watch helplessly as the last of our spell gave way with a blinding pulse of light, and I lost my connection to Zoe altogether.

"WHAT HAPPENED?" my mom asked. "Did we win?"

I saw Admiral Avery looking up through the water toward the bayou to the south. Lightning kept illuminating the sky above us, and the sea beyond our clear area churned. But any residual glow from the spell was no longer visible from where we were.

"They were ready for us," I mumbled. "It's over."

Ada-Mae moved from the other side of the circle and crossed over to stand above me. "I felt it," she said. "But it's not over. It can't be over. We have to try."

I shook my head. I was exhausted and had been all day, running on adrenaline and hope. Hope had fled, and now all I wanted to do was lie down and sleep. "They're too strong," I said. "And now they know we're here, too. Nothing is getting through that barrier." I stood up and looked at Ada-Mae and then down at the other three. "I'm sorry. I'm not strong enough."

Ada-Mae grabbed hold of my shoulders, shaking me. "You're the strongest witch I've ever known, Sidney Grace. There's nothing you can't do. *You* are the only one holding you back."

"So, it's my fault, is it?" I screamed back at her, trying not to burst into tears. "How dare you assume what I've been given!"

Ada-Mae stepped away and looked abashed, shaking her head. "I didn't mean that. But there's only so far I can take you, Sidney. Only so much ritual and focus I can teach you. Sometimes, you have to let go and tap into the deepest, truest, most primal thing within you. I know you can still stop this."

I shook my head. I had been shocked by my outburst and was ashamed of it, but I had nothing else left in me, and I did not even know how to create the type of ritual she spoke of. My best had been laughed away by those two leaders of the evil coven. "I don't know how," I whispered.

After a moment, I realized the others were no longer looking at me. Instead, they were looking at the surrounding water, and it took me a moment to understand what they were seeing. The water was peeling away from around us. Looking over my shoulder, I could see it was retreating quickly from the shoreline in front of Mystic Dunes. Suddenly, the landward end of our oblong sanctuary vanished. It flowed back along the side walls, and just moments later, the walls disappeared altogether, along with every drop of seawater around us.

I glanced at Admiral Avery, who gave me a "This isn't me" kind of shrug. Then, suddenly, he vanished.

Ada-Mae provided the answer. "It's coming," she said. "The water is drawing back in the path of the tsunami."

CHAPTER
TEN

"Admiral?" I cried out loud.

"He's gone, hasn't he?" Ada-Mae said. "Because the water has gone, and that was his home. His haunt. We've got to go, too."

We all ran for the shore, including Mojo, who jolted past the rest of us. It seemed a vain hope in the flat Florida landscape, but maybe if we could run far enough and climb into the highest building we could see... there might be a chance to survive. Although there was hardly a building above two stories in quaint little Crystal Beach. Indeed, the main complex at Shifting Sands, which came in at a giddying four stories in the center section, was by far the tallest I had seen in the town.

We could not get there, though. At best, maybe we could get back to the main road before the tsunami struck. Although even that might not be possible.

As we reached solid land, I noticed my cell phone ringing. It was John.

"Sidney?" He sounded out of breath. "We've found it."

"Found what?"

"The ritual. The dudes in cloaks and all that. They're on an island just south of the development."

"Listen," I said. "It's too late. We failed. You've got to get out of there, John. The tsunami's coming, and they have a protection spell up that we'll never get through now."

"Well, something did."

"Huh?"

There's a rather large dog that looks like a wolf chasing them around the island. And... oh no, that looks like an alligator crawling up there, too. Actually, make that three alligators. Yeesh."

I stopped and turned to Ada-Mae. "Sounds like their protection spell is down," I told her. "Zoe's causing a ruckus over on the island."

"Who's on the phone?" my mom asked.

"It's John."

"Are all of them there?" It was Howie. Usually laid back and calm, terror shot through his voice. "Is my Wendy there?"

"I think they all are," I answered. John had said "we," and I doubted that any of them would have given up on the hunt.

Ada-Mae snapped her fingers, a thought clearly having come to her. "They had to drop the protection to finish the ritual," she said. "They couldn't summon their soul-sucking tsunami with a protection spell up. If only we had sent our binding spell a few moments later."

"I think the coven was waiting for us," I told her. "Seemed like they were waiting for us to show our hand."

"But even though they sensed you, they obviously didn't realize our shifter Zoe was there, too," Ada-Mae said with a little wicked relish. "They don't know everything."

"Can we still stop them?" I asked.

"The ritual is done," Ada-Mae said. "The tsunami is coming. But we can go and find our loved ones and maybe stop those two evil good-for-nothings from reaping the benefit."

Even if all else was lost, I liked the sound of that, and there was no argument from anyone else. We all turned and hurried toward the far end of Mystic Dunes. Realizing that John was still on the other end of the line, I said, "We're coming, John."

He didn't reply for a moment, and I figured he was otherwise busy. I was about to hang up when he spoke again, his voice a little distant and full of awe. "Oh my gosh, Sidney," he said. "I think I see it."

WE CLEARED the end of Mystic Dunes, and I saw what John had seen. Somehow, the full moon still shone through a gap in the angry clouds, illuminating the top of the wall of water that was coming for Crystal Beach. It was still some ways away from the shore, but the mere fact we could see it at all told me just how big it must be.

I remembered the great wave that had wiped out Coral Point —Admiral Avery's settlement—in the vision he showed me before the existence of the town of Crystal Beach. I guessed that wave had not been even a quarter as tall as the one that came for us now. Janis and Lennon had perfected their ritual in the two centuries since, finding ways to make it more powerful. Then, it had only needed to wipe out a small settlement. Maybe this time, it would be enough to claim the entirety of a whole town and even some places beyond—perhaps a thousand more years of life for its evil, twisted beneficiaries.

"Can we make it?" Howie gasped.

"We have to," Ada-Mae said, moving at an impressive speed over the uneven ground for a person her age. If anyone had ever seen her ambling through the middle of town, they would never have believed she could move the way she was moving now.

It was madness, in a way, because we didn't even know what we were going to do when we got there. We were almost certainly rushing straight toward death. Yet there was a mad joy, a thrill that drove us onward, even if only to see our loved ones again before the end.

Soon, we were splashing through water and squelching through mud, the tsunami growing ever closer. The chaos around the island became visible now, and a couple of hooded figures fled past us, screaming into the night.

Zoe appeared to have retained some measure of control over her wolf, I was glad to see, as it chased the coven members, nipping at their heels or even knocking them to the ground but never genuinely attacking them as it could.

Well done, Zoe. Not sure you needed me that much, after all.

It was clear who Lennon and Janis were, as their two figures—now having shed their cloaks—were pressed back-to-back as they slowly levitated into the air in the middle of the island. They were going to avoid the tsunami by rising above the thing when it came.

A neat trick and not one that I knew myself. Even if I had, would I be able to get everyone else up and out of the way, too?

450

Belatedly, I thought of the portals that led to The Rose Garden guesthouse from numbers one and two in Mystic Dunes. Still, even that would not be far enough away to survive the tsunami that was now less than a mile from the town, growing larger and larger with every passing moment, the sound of the rushing water filling the air like an angry wind.

"Sidney!"

I turned at the sound of the familiar voice and saw John rushing toward me, splashing through the bayou. As he did so, other familiar figures came into view. My father, Wendy, the tall, loping figure of Ernie, and Eileen, who kept stumbling into the water.

Zoe's wolf, finally spent, staggered to a stop less than twenty yards in front of me, then fell to its haunches and transformed back into the shy, Goth-themed magic store owner she was the rest of the time. Jessie rushed over to her, grabbing a discarded cloak to cover her as she became human again.

We were all here together, and our adversaries were a backdrop in these last moments. A reminder of our failure, the evil witches were now suspended a hundred feet in the air above the island, watching us and waiting to see if we would do anything else.

Finally, two more figures trudged over toward us, one helping the other to walk.

"I'm sorry," Rose said, "we tried. Rodney went straight for Lennon, but..."

Rose's tall, quiet husband was bent over, clearly having suffered some wound in his battle with the dark magic users.

"It's okay," I said. "We all tried."

John reached me and, without even a pause, threw his arms around me. Unaware until then that I had been holding it in, I sobbed hard into his shoulder.

"I'm sorry," I said.

"You've nothing to be sorry about," he answered. "You're amazing, Sidney. I saw that fireworks display there. Very impressive."

I managed a small, sad laugh as his hands clasped the sides of my face.

"I'm sorry I never said it," John said, looking deep into my eyes. "I love you, Sidney Grace. I have since almost the first moment I saw you. And I think I'd like to spend the rest of my life with you if you'll let me."

I scoffed at that one. "Well, that's easy to say when we've only got about thirty seconds left. But, for what it's worth, I feel the same way." I looked up at John's face, and I saw the reflection of us happy together dancing in his eyes.

Around me, everyone I cared about was hugging and embracing one another. Even Judd got an embrace from his two best friends, Ernie and Ada-Mae, who then turned to accept a late-arriving Eileen.

"Flaming bog!" she complained like the giant wave almost at the shore was not the real problem. All of us joined hands and turned to face what was coming. Even my cat was pressed up against the back of my leg, peaking around it and staring down death.

This is so perfect. Why does it have to end?

And then the wave struck.

~

IT TOOK me a moment to realize that we weren't dead. Which was a bonus. The water was there, right next to us, yet still, our little group stood untouched.

"You're doing it, Sidney," Ada-Mae cried. "Look!"

Usually, it would be kind of redundant to tell someone to look at what they were already seeing, but in this case, Ada-Mae was spot on. The water had come right up to us—to me—and got no further. It had hit an invisible wall that was higher than I could see, the force of the wave driving the water hundreds of feet into the air.

It was my wall. I had made it, almost without even thinking about it—beyond my love for the people around me. Beyond my aching, desperate need to keep them all safe. Something primal activated itself inside me, just like Ada-Mae had predicted.

As the weight of more and more of these endless millions of gallons of water hit the wall, I felt the strain. Yet, as long my hands stayed joined with theirs, and theirs with each other, I knew that the wall, and our chain that had made it, would not break.

I glanced left and saw that the wall went all the way along the shore, protecting every part of the town from the wave that should have destroyed it.

EPILOGUE

When the water was finally gone, having subsided back into the normal ebb and flow of the ocean, we walked over to the island where the ritual had taken place. It was clear of coven members and alligators, save for just two figures lying next to each other in the middle of it.

Lennon and Janis—my nemeses—lay beside each other and looked up at us. They were barely recognizable as the people I had met once before or as the ones I had seen when Sam had spied on them. Their bodies had aged at least fifty years in only a couple of minutes, their faces now wrinkled, and the skin that poked out from beneath their out-of-date clothing was also wrinkled in a similar fashion. Only their eyes retained any glimmer of youth.

"How?" Lennon rasped. "How did you stop us?"

I thought about telling them what I knew had saved us, but it seemed clichéd.

"Love!" my mom blurted out in a sort of "hardy har har" tone.

Oh well, at least *I* hadn't said it.

Mojo glared at the evil duo and then stuck his paw in the air, his claws extended. *That's my mom you tried to destroy. She's not a witch to be messed with, foolish warlocks.*

Wow, thanks, Mojo.

Janis looked at John. "Are we under arrest?"

"You'll never take us," Lennon wheezed and stuck out his hands as if to cast some spell. Nothing happened.

"I think you're all tapped out," I said. "Used up all your mortal juice and didn't get anything back for it."

Lennon slumped backward, defeat in his eyes.

"I think I'll leave nature to take its course," John said. He turned to Ada-Mae. "What's that building no one ever leaves over at Shifting Sands? You know, except when they're—"

"The Greater Assisted Living Center," Ada-Mae answered quickly.

"That's the one. I'll speak to Administrator Jessop. No sea views for you two, though." He wagged his finger at the defeated evil coven members.

Oh, you won, then. Wow, don't they look o-o-old?

It was Sam Barlow's ghost, arriving to gloat over the two people responsible for his murder. Fair enough.

I totally didn't have my money on you, Sidney. In fact, I was going to relocate to Orlando right after my death, but it turns out my spirit couldn't leave this town until my murder was resolved. Hopefully, now I'm not stuck in this little backwater for eternity.

There are worse things, I told him. And, despite the sneer, I felt Sam agreed.

We all turned and walked back toward our town. The beach was a bit of a mess, but we had saved all the buildings. Crystal Beach was still in business.

My focus shifted towards John and the smile shining across his face. "Happy we saved the day, are you?"

"Happy I kicked you off the beach, that's for sure." His eyes twinkled.

"Yes, I can't believe I'm actually saying this...but me too. Maude and the cats asked me to pass along their appreciation for that," I said, unable to stop the flirtatious wink that danced across my cheek.

"So...is this going to be the subject of your next article?" John asked me as his hand took mine, our fingers entwining.

I smiled about that. "Time to start working for myself, instead," I said. "This one's worth a whole book, don't you think?"

IF YOU'RE ENJOYING your visit in Crystal Beach with these fun witches and you missed the first award-winning installments in the Crystal Beach Magic Mysteries, check out the series preview and start reading Familiar Troubles today.

FAMILIAR TROUBLES
CRYSTAL BEACH MAGIC MYSTERY SERIES
(BOOKS 1-5)

Meet **Sidney Grace. Quirky journalist, Hesitant witch, Professional butterfingers.** Her grand-mother believes Sidney's talent for communicating with the dead makes her the most powerful witch in the family, but she just wants to make it through the day without getting fired.

Sidney, a young writer living in Boston, is far from the small wacky town of Crystal Beach, Florida, where her spell-happy grandmother retired. She is perfectly happy with her career, her four cats, and the fact that she hasn't been on a date in... well, years. All is well until her estranged mother informs Sidney that her grandmother has been arrested for murdering a resident at her retirement community.

Sidney road-trips to Florida to discover that her grandmother has no alibi, her grandfather isn't as dead as she thought he was, and one of her cats can speak. To make matters worse, the handsome Officer Reece is tough on criminals and even tougher on witches. Who cooked up the deadly scone? And why are residents at Shifting Sands suddenly disappearing?

Now, Sidney must embrace her own magical talents to prove her grandmother's innocence and stop the killer bent on destroying anyone who gets in the way.

READ FAMILIAR TROUBLES, the Crystal Beach Magic Mystery Series, and discover what readers are calling a bewitchingly fun and heartwarming paranormal cozy mystery with charming characters that will keep you spellbound!

Available in paperback from your favorite online retailers. Audiobook is available on Audible.

SNEAK PREVIEW

CAT SCRATCH MURDER; CHAPTER 1
EXCERPT

So, I didn't know that the woman with a dead cat around her shoulders was a friend of Mr. Rask, who happens to own the magazine where I work. I mean, I hadn't even met Mr. Rask before. *I have now. He's not a fan.*

To be fair, it wasn't a dead cat, but whatever it was, it had previously been alive and was once probably cute and furry, with a significant other and maybe children. Now it was a shocked-looking shoulder warmer. And, well, the whole thing had upset me when I went to review the New Metropole Hotel in Boston and found myself waiting in line behind the woman with the fur stole. There was nothing faux about it. I couldn't stop staring at the poor creature's glass-beaded eyes that were staring back at me. Positively barbaric.

All I did was make a passing reference to it in an otherwise glittering review of this wonderful new hotel, vaguely modeled— in the way modern buildings can only ever be "vaguely" modeled —on the hotels of the late nineteenth and early twentieth centuries. It was one of my best reviews and a real opportunity to step away from the fluff pieces I had been stuck on since... well, since the last time my tendency to have strong opinions had gotten me in trouble with Marv, my direct boss. He was the editor of *Living It Large in Boston* magazine, where I worked. For now.

"Why did you do it, Sid?" Marv asked in that pained, almost pleading way of his. As "Sidney" Grace, named for my maternal grandfather, my moniker could be confusing—me being of the female persuasion. Sometimes I would tell people that I was named for the main character in the *Scream* movies, but then they would look at me and go, "Nah, you're too old for that." Well, they were right about that.

This dressing down was happening shortly after Marv had been through a noisy, ten-minute chewing out by Mr. Rask that everyone in the office had been pretending not to listen to. Well, except me, who might have taken one too many trips past the office door to the photocopier during that time, as Marv had just pointed out.

I knew it was my fault that I was the one in trouble—partly because Mr. Rask had pointed a trembling finger at me as he walked in and spat, "Is that her? Is that the one?" But also because it was always me. I was always the one doing something wrong. I was the one who fell into the cake at Marv's fiftieth birthday party. I was the one who parked in the visitor's parking space when the owner of the Boston Red Sox baseball team came in for an interview, resulting in him parking next to a tree that blew down on top of his Range Rover in a freak windstorm. *I mean, come on, how is that my fault?* Then again, I was also the one who accidentally posted the exclusive, pre-launch photos of the latest Chanel nail polish line all over social media. Me. Sidney, Sidney, Sidney.

Which, coincidentally, was what Marv was now saying. "Sidney, Sidney, Sidney, what am I going to do with you?"

"Um... get me to write a piece about the benefits of faux fur?" I tried with a sheepish smile.

Marv's eyes narrowed.

"Look, why don't I just head home?" I suggested, backing out of Marv's office. "Give you time to... you know... think through things calmly. Remember all the great pieces I've written for the magazine. Remember that poor old Sidney is twenty-nine, single, and still paying off her student loan debt. You wouldn't want to make all my cats homeless, would you?"

And with that, I closed the door and headed home, unsure whether I would have a job in the morning.

READ FAMILIAR TROUBLES, the Crystal Beach Magic Mystery Series, and discover what readers are calling a bewitchingly fun and heartwarming paranormal cozy mystery with charming characters that will keep you spellbound!

Available in paperback from your favorite online retailers.
Audiobook is available on Audible.

Would you like more Sidney Grace Adventures in Crystal Beach?

P.S. Thank you for reading the second installation of the Crystal Beach Magic Mystery Series. I hope you enjoyed **Witch In Disguise** and I look forward to *your* feedback.

Would you like to see more of these fun witches in Crystal Beach? If so, I'd like to ask for a small favor. Would you be so kind as to leave a review on Amazon? I appreciate your honest opinion because it helps me create my best work for you.

Thank you!
Karen

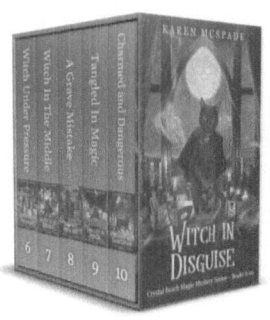

FREE GIFT

Receive your FREE exclusive copy of **Hash Browns And Homicide**, the series prequel, and get notified via email of new releases, giveaways, contests, cover reveals, and insider fun when you sign up to my VIP Mystery Book Club mailing list!

Scan the QR Code To Sign Up and Claim Your FREE Exclusive Book

FREE GIFT

Receive your FREE copy of **Dog Gone Troubles**, the Crystal Beach Magic Mystery series prequel, and get notified via email of new releases, giveaways, contests, cover reveals, and insider fun when you sign up for my Mystery Book Club mailing list!

Scan the QR Code To Sign Up and Claim Your FREE Exclusive Book

NOTE: If you're already a member of my VIP Mystery Book Club, your email will not be added again.

BOOKS BY KAREN MCSPADE

The Savory Mystery Series

Hash Browns And Homicide

Murder and Grits

Red Beans And R.I.P.

Mystery On the Half Shell

Killer Gumbo

Crab Cake Criminal

Murder at High Sea

The Deep Fried Revenge Series

Pies & Pilfering (Prequel)

Bacon, Bodyguards, and Ballistics - Book 1

Bacon, Bodyguards, and Ballistics - Book 2

Bacon, Bodyguards, and Ballistics - Book 3

Bacon, Bodyguards, and Ballistics - Book 4

Bacon, Bodyguards, and Ballistics - Book 5

Crystal Beach Magic Mystery Series

Cat Scratch Murder

Claw of Attraction

Feline Like a Suspect

A Meowing Suspicion

Paws in Space

Witch Under Pressure

Witch in the Middle

A Grave Mistake

Tangled in Magic

Charmed and Dangerous

Holiday Cozy Mysteries & Mystery Romance

Christmas Cakes and Crooks

About the Author

Raised in the Arkansas River Valley, Karen McSpade grew up with a fishing pole in one hand and her trusty .410 shotgun in the other. Exploring the creeks and woods around her hometown while hunting with her father kept her "entertained and out of jail," as her mom likes to say.

As a child, her most prized possessions were her books and her Michael Jackson album collection. These led her to a brief venture into breakdancing and poetry slamming before discovering her true passion, bringing stories and characters to life. Today, she focuses on the two things that still inspire her creativity—her love for food and dishing up mysteries with a dash of humor.

Karen's novels feature compassionate and strong-willed leading ladies determined to uncover the truth and seek justice. She loves creating stories filled with mystery, romance, magic, and adventure that allow readers to join her characters on their journey, leaving behind the real world for a few hours at a time.

When she's not writing, Karen's favorite things are spending time with family, traveling, cooking, reading, gardening, and enjoying nature. She lives in Northwest Arkansas with her family and a very spoiled Wheaten Terrier who doubles as her writing assistant.

Join Karen on Facebook for updates, fun, and prizes!

www.ingramcontent.com/pod-product-compliance
Lightning Source LLC
Chambersburg PA
CBHW030847030726
47495CB00005B/1411